Huge [obscured]
the pa[obscured]

Cows [obscured] they got, she could see long fangs coming out of their mouths, clawed hands, and red eyes, but even so, they seemed sort of human.

Cnut grabbed her hand and was dragging her back through the hallway toward the front door.

"What are they?" she yelped.

"Demon vampires," he said.

"Oh, that is just great. You say that as if it's an everyday occurrence. What'd you do at work today, honey? Nothing. Just ran into a few demon vampires."

"We have to get out of here," Cnut said. "Right away."

"No kidding. But we have to find my sister first."

Cnut pulled some kind of weapon out of a back pocket in his jeans, pressed a button, and whoosh, it became a long, thin-bladed sword. And he appeared to have grown big fangs, and his blue eyes had turned an odd silver color.

He made a low growling sound and said, "C'mon, make my day!"

By Sandra Hill

Deadly Angels Series
The Angel Wore Fangs
Even Vampires Get the Blues
Vampire in Paradise
Christmas in Transylvania
Kiss of Wrath • Kiss of Temptation
Kiss of Surrender
Kiss of Pride

Viking Series I
The Pirate Bride • The Norse King's Daughter
The Viking Takes a Knight • Viking in Love
A Tale of Two Vikings
My Fair Viking (formerly The Viking's Captive)
The Blue Viking • The Bewitched Viking
The Tarnished Lady • The Outlaw Viking
The Reluctant Viking

Cajun Series
The Love Potion (Book One)

Viking Series II
Hot & Heavy • Wet & Wild
The Very Virile Viking • Truly, Madly Viking
The Last Viking

Creole-Time Travel Series
Sweeter Savage Love
Frankly, My Dear . . .

Others
Love Me Tender • Desperado

SANDRA HILL

A DEADLY ANGELS BOOK

THE ANGEL WORE FANGS

AVONBOOKS

An Imprint of HarperCollins*Publishers*

This is a work of fiction. Names, characters, places, and incidents are products of the author's imagination or are used fictitiously and are not to be construed as real. Any resemblance to actual events, locales, organizations, or persons, living or dead, is entirely coincidental.

AVON BOOKS
An Imprint of HarperCollins*Publishers*
195 Broadway
New York, New York 10007

ISBN 978-0-06-235654-3
www.avonromance.com

First Avon Books mass market printing: June 2016

Printed in the U.S.A.

10 9 8 7 6 5 4 3 2 1

This book is dedicated to my grandsons Jefferson Hill and Max Casper Hill, who are, like me, descendants of that tenth-century Norseman Rollo (or Hrolf the Ganger), first duke of Norsemandy, which later became Normandy. What's not to love about a Viking? Especially a Viking with a sense of humor, which they both have. I can't wait to see what they'll become when they grow up and go "a-Viking."

Prologue

A VIKING FEAST MENU

Spit-roasted wild suckling boar
Sliced cold hákarl (rotten shark)
Eel in dill cream sauce
Sviâ (boiled sheep's head)
Mutton with mustard chestnut dressing
Brútspungur (pickled ram testicles in whey-pressed cakes)
Lutefisk
Reindeer (venison) steaks
Oat-crisped herring
Pigeon pie
Pickled boars' feet
Lampreys

Manchet bread, butter
Horseradish, pickles

Gammelost (stinky cheese)
Fennel sallat
Nettle soup with hard-cooked gulls' eggs
Boiled onions in venison gravy
Parsnips and cabbage porridge
Skyr (cheese)
Pea and ham hock stew

Stewed lingonberries
Dried apple-oat crumbles
Mead, ale
Imported grape wine from Francia (while supply lasts)
Honey and hazelnut oatcakes
Gingered pears with red currants

Weight Watchers, where art thou? . . .

Cnut Sigurdsson was a big man. A really big man! He was taller than the average man, of course, being a Viking, but more than that, he was . . . well . . . truth to tell . . . fat.

Obesity was a highly unusual condition for Men of the North, Cnut had to admit, because Norsemen were normally vain of appearance, sometimes to a ridiculous extent. Long hair, combed to a high sheen. Braided beards. Clean teeth. Gold and silver arm rings to show off muscles. Tight braies delineating buttocks and ballocks.

But not him.

Cnut did not care.

Even now, when three of his six brothers, who'd come (uninvited, by the by) to his Frigg's-day feast here at Hoggstead in the Norselands, were having great fun making jests about just that. They were half-brothers, actually, all with different mothers, but that was neither here nor there.

Cnut cared not one whit what the lackwits said.

Not even when Trond made oinking noises, as if Cnut's estate were named for a porcine animal when he knew good and well it was the name of the original owner decades ago, Bjorn Hoggson. Besides, Trond had no room to make mock of others when he was known to be the laziest Viking to ever ride a longship. Some said he did not even have the energy to lift his cock for pissing, that he sat like a wench on the privy hole. That was probably not true, but it made a good story.

Nor did Cnut bother to rise and clout his eldest brother, Vikar, when he asked the skald to make a rhyme of Cnut's name:

Cnut is a brute
And a glutton, of some repute.
He is so fat that, when he goes a-Viking for loot,
He can scarce lift a bow with an arrow to shoot.
But when it comes to woman-pursuit,
None can refute
That Cnut can "salute" with the best of them.
Thus and therefore, let it be known
And this is a truth absolute,
Size matters.

"Ha, ha, ha!" Cnut commented, while everyone in the great hall howled with laughter, and Vikar was bent over, gasping with mirth.

Cnut did not care, especially since Vikar was known to be such a prideful man he fair reeked of self-love. At least the skald had not told the poem about how, if Cnut spelled his name with a slight exchange of letters, he would be a vulgar woman part. That was one joke Cnut did not appreciate.

But mockery was a game to Norsemen. And, alas and alack, Cnut was often the butt of the jests.

He. Did. Not. Care.

Yea, some said he resembled a walking tree with a massive trunk, limbs like hairy battering rams, and fingers so chubby he could scarce make a fist.

Even his face was bloated, surrounded by a mass of wild, tangled hair on head and beard, which was dark blond, though its color was indiscernible most times since it was usually greasy and teeming with lice. Unlike most Vikings, he rarely bathed. In his defense, what tub would hold him? And the water chute into the steam hut was often clogged. And the water in the fjords was frigid except for summer months. What man in his right mind wanted to turn his cock into an icicle?

A disgrace to the ideal of handsome, virile Vikinghood, he overheard some fellow jarls say about him on more than one occasion.

And as for his brother Harek, who considered himself smarter than the average Viking, Cnut glared his way and spoke loud enough for all to hear, "Methinks your first wife, Dagne, has put on a bit of blubber herself in recent years. Last time I saw her in Kaupang, she was as wide as she was tall. And she farted as she walked, rather waddled. Phhhttt, phhhttt, phhhttt! Now, there is something to make mock of!"

"You got me there," Harek agreed with a smile, raising his horn of mead high in salute.

One of the good things about Vikings was that they could laugh at themselves. The sagas were great evidence of that fact.

At least Cnut was smart enough not to take on any wives of his own, despite his twenty and eight years. Concubines and the odd wench here and there served him well. Truly, as long as Cnut's voracious hunger for all bodily appetites—food, drink, sex—was being met, he cared little what others thought of him.

When his brothers were departing two days later (he thought they'd never leave), Vikar warned him, "Jesting aside, Cnut, be careful. One of these days your excesses are going to be your downfall."

"Not one of these days. Now," Cnut proclaimed jovially as he crooked a chubby forefinger at Inga, a passing chambermaid with a bosom not unlike the figurehead of his favorite longship, *Sea Nymph*. "Wait for me in the bed furs," he called out to her. "I plan to *fall down* with you for a bit of bedplay."

Vikar, Trond, and Harek just shook their heads at him, as if he were a hopeless case.

Cnut did not care.

But Vikar's words came back to haunt Cnut several months later when he was riding Hugo, one of his two war horses, across his vast estate. A normal-size palfrey could not handle his weight; he would squash it like an oatcake. Besides, his long legs dragged on the ground. So he had purchased two Percherons from Le Perche, a province north of Norsemandy in the Franklands known for breeding the huge beasts. They'd cost him a fortune.

But even with the sturdy destrier and his well-padded arse, not to mention the warm, sunny weather, Cnut was ready to return to the keep for a midday repast. Most Vikings had only two meals a day. The first, *dagmál* or "day-meal," breaking of fast, was held two hours after morning work was started, and the second, *náttmál* or "night meal." was held in the evening when the day's work was completed. But Cnut needed a midday meal, as well. And right now, a long draught of mead and an afternoon nap would not come amiss. But he could not go back yet. His steward, Finngeir the Frugal (whom he was coming to regard as Finn the Bothersome Worrier), insisted that he see the extent of the dry season on the Hoggstead cotters' lands.

Ho-hum. Cnut didn't even bother to stifle his yawn.

"Even in the best of times, the gods have not blessed the Norselands with much arable land, being too mountainous and rocky. Why else would we go a-Viking but to settle new, more fertile lands?"

"And women," Cnut muttered. "Fertile or not."

Finn ignored his sarcasm and went on. Endlessly. "One year of bad crops is crippling, but two years, and it will be a disaster, I tell you. Look at the fields. The grains are half as high as they should be by this time of year. If it does not rain soon—"

Blather, blather, blather. I should have brought a horn of ale with me. And an oatcake, or five. Cnut did not like Finn's lecturing tone, but Finn was a good and loyal subject, and Cnut would hate the thought of replacing him. So Cnut bit back a snide retort. "What would you have me do? A rain dance? I can scarce walk, let alone dance. Ha, ha, ha."

Finn did not smile.

The humorless wretch.

"Dost think I have a magic wand to open the clouds? The only wand I have is betwixt my legs. Ha, ha, ha."

No reaction, except for a continuing frown,

and a resumption of his tirade. "You must forgive the taxes for this year. Then you must open your storerooms to feed the masses. That is what you must do."

"Are you barmy? I cannot do that! I need the taxes for upkeep of my household and to maintain a fighting troop of housecarls. As for my giving away foodstuffs, forget about that, too. Last harvest did not nearly fill my oat and barley bins. Nay, 'tis impossible!"

"There is more. Look about you, my jarl. Notice how the people regard you. You will have an uprising on your own lands, if you are not careful."

"What? Where? I do not know—" Cnut's words cut off as he glanced to his right and left, passing through a narrow lane that traversed through his crofters' huts. Here and there, he saw men leaning on rakes or hauling manure to the fields. They were gaunt-faced and grimy, glaring at him through angry eyes. One man even spat on the ground, narrowly missing Hugo's hoof. And the women were no better, raising their skinny children up for him to see.

"That horse would feed a family of five for a month," one toothless old graybeard yelled.

His wife—Cnut assumed it was his wife, being equally aged and toothless—cackled and said, "Forget that. If the master skipped one meal a month, the whole village could feast."

Many of those standing about laughed.

Cnut did not.

Good thing they did not know how many mancuses it had taken to purchase Hugo and the other Percheron. It was none of their concern! Cnut had a right to spend his wealth as he chose. Leastways, that's what he told himself.

Now, instead of being softened by what he saw, Cnut hardened his heart. "If they think to threaten me, they are in for a surprise," he said to Finn once they'd left the village behind and were returning to the castle keep. "Tell the taxman to evict those who do not pay their rents this year."

By late autumn, when the last of the meager crops was harvested, Cnut had reason to reconsider. Already, he'd had to buy extra grains and vegetables from the markets in Birka and Hedeby, just for his keep. Funerals were held back to back in the village. And he was not convinced that Hugo had died of natural causes last sennight, especially when his carcass had disappeared overnight. Cnut had been forced to post guards about his stables and storage shed since then. Everywhere he turned, people were grumbling, if not outright complaining.

That night, in a *drukkinn* fit of rage, he left his great hall midway through the dinner meal. Highly unusual for him. But then, who wouldn't lose his appetite with all those sour faces silently accusing him? It wasn't Cnut who'd brought the drought; even the most sane-minded creature must know that. Blame the gods, or lazy field hands who should have worked harder, or bad seed.

As he was leaving, he declined an invitation from some of his *hersir*s who were engaged in a game of *hneftafl*. Even his favorite board game with its military strategies and rousing side bets held no interest tonight. Bodil, a chambermaid, gave him a sultry wink of invitation in passing, but he was not in the mood for bedplay tonight, either.

He decided to visit the garderobe before taking to his bed, alone, and nigh froze his balls when he sat on the privy hole. He was further annoyed to find that someone had forgotten to replenish the supply of moss and grape leaves for wiping.

When Cnut thought things could not get any worse, he opened the garderobe door and almost tripped over the threshold at what he saw. A man stood across the corridor, arms crossed over his chest. A stranger. Could it be one of his desperate, starving tenants come to seek revenge on him, as Finn had warned?

No. Despite the darkness, the only light coming from a sputtering wall torch, Cnut could see that this man was handsome in appearance, noble in bearing. Long, black hair. Tall and lean, though well-muscled, like a warrior. And oddly, he wore a long white robe with a twisted rope belt, and a gold crucifix hung from a chain about his neck. Even odder, there appeared to be wings half folded behind his back.

Was it a man or something else?

I must be more drukkinn *than I thought.* "Who are you?"

"St. Michael the Archangel."

One of those flying creatures the Christians believe in? This is some alehead madness I am imagining! A walking dream.

"'Tis no dream, fool," the stranger said, as if he'd read Cnut's thoughts.

"What do you want?" Cnut demanded.

"Not you, if I had a choice, that is for certain," the man/creature/angel said with a tone of disgust. "Thou art a dire sinner, Cnut Sigurdsson, and God is not pleased with you."

"Which god would that be? Odin? Thor?"

"For shame! There is only one God."

Ah! Of course. He referred to the Christian One-God. Vikings might follow the Old Norse religions, but they were well aware of the Christian dogma, and, in truth, many of them allowed themselves to be baptized, just for the sake of expediency.

"So, your God is not pleased with me. And I should care about that . . . why?" Cnut inquired, holding on to the doorjamb to straighten himself with authority. He was a high jarl, after all, and this person was trespassing. Cnut glanced about for help, but none of his guardsmen were about. *Surprise, surprise. They are probably still scowling and complaining about the lack of meat back in the hall. I am going to kick some arse for this neglect.*

"Attend me well, Viking; you should care because thou are about to meet your maker." He said *Viking* as if it were a foul word. "As are your brothers. Sinners, all of you!"

"Huh?"

"Seven brothers, each guilty of one of the Seven Deadly Sins. Pride. Lust. Sloth. Wrath. Gluttony. Envy. Greed." He gave Cnut a pointed look. "Wouldst care to guess which one is yours?"

Nay, he would not. "So I eat and drink overmuch. I can afford the excess. What sin is that?"

"Fool!" the angel said, and immediately a

strange fog swirled in the air. In its mist, Cnut saw flashing images:

- Starving and dead children.
- Him gnawing on a boar shank so voraciously that a greasy drool slipped down his chin. Not at all attractive.
- One of his cotters being beaten to a bloody pulp for stealing bread for his family.
- Honey being spread on slice after slice of manchet bread on his high table.
- A young Cnut, no more than eight years old, slim and sprightly, chasing his older brothers about their father's courtyard.
- A naked, adult Cnut, gross and ugly with folds of fat and swollen limbs. He could not run now, if he'd wanted to.
- A family, wearing only threadbare garb and carrying cloth bundles of its meager belongings, being evicted from its home with no place to go in the snowy weather.
- Warm hearths and roofs overhead on the Hoggstead keep.
- A big-bosomed concubine riding Cnut in the bed furs, not an easy task with his big belly.
- The same woman weeping as she unwrapped a linen cloth holding scraps of bread and meat, half-eaten oatcakes, and several shrunken apples, before her three young children.

Cnut had seen enough. "This farce has gone on long enough! You say I am going to die? Now?

And all my brothers, too? Excuse me if I find that hard to believe."

"Not all at once. Some have already passed. Others will go shortly."

Really? Three of his brothers had been here several months past, and he had not received news of any deaths in his family since, but then their estates were distant and the roads were nigh impassable this time of year. The fjords were no better, already icing over, making passage difficult for longships.

"I should toss you down the privy hole and let you die in the filth," the angel said, "but you would not fit. Better yet, I should lock you in the garderobe and let you starve to death, like your serfs do."

Ah, so that's what this was about. "You cannot blame me for lack of rain or poor harvests. In fact, your God—"

Before he could finish the thought, the angel pointed a forefinger at him, and a flash of light passed forth, hitting Cnut right in the chest, like a bolt of lightning. Cnut found himself dangling off the floor. He clutched his heart, which felt as if a giant stake had passed through his body, securing him to the wall.

"Let it be known hither and yon, the Viking race has become too arrogant and brutish, and it is God's will that it should die out. But you and your brothers are being given a second chance, though why, only God knows."

What? Wait. Did he say I won't be dying, after all?

"This is thy choice. Repent and agree to become a vangel in God's army for seven hundred years, and thou wilt have a chance to make up for your mortal sins. Otherwise, die and spend eternity at Satan's hearth."

A sudden smell of rotten eggs filled the air. Brimstone, Cnut guessed, which was said to be a characteristic of the Christian afterlife for those who had offended their god. At the same time, he could swear his toes felt a mite warm. Yea, fire and brimstone, for a certainty.

So, I am being given a choice between seven hundred years in God's army or forever roasting in Hell. Some choice! Still, he should not be too quick to agree. "Vangel? What in bloody hell is a vangel?" Cnut gasped out.

"A Viking vampire angel who will fight the forces of Satan's Lucipires, demon vampires who roam the world spreading evil."

That was clear as fjord mud. Cnut was still pinned high on the wall, and he figured he was in no position to negotiate. Besides, seven hundred years didn't sound too bad.

But he forgot to ask what exactly a vampire was.

He soon found out.

With a wave of his hand, the angel loosened Cnut's invisible ties, and he fell to the floor. If he'd thought the heart pain was bad, it was nothing compared to the excruciating feel of bones being crushed and reformed. If that wasn't bad enough, he could swear he felt fangs forming on each side of his mouth, like a wolf. And his shoulders were being ripped apart, literally, and replaced with what, Cnut could not be sure, as he writhed about the rush-covered floor.

"First things first," the angel said then, leaning over him with a menacing smile. "You are going on a diet."

Chapter 1

LA CHIC SARDINE PASTRY MENU

Salted caramel crème brûlée—Rich cream and imported toffee, chef's specialty.

Opera Cake—An elegant gâteau of mocha buttercream spread over thin layers of pound cake soaked in coffee syrup, topped with ganache.

Assorted cookies—Chocolate-dipped madeleines; almond meringue macaroons, small in size but sinfully satisfying.

Dacquoise à la Framboise—Almond meringue filled with pastry cream and fresh berries, a seasonal delight.

Napoleons—Traditional flaky pastry layered with chocolate mousse, vanilla or coffee cream, and covered with ganache; one is never enough.

Bourdaloue peach tart—Fresh peaches and almond cream in a generous-size sugar tart shell, can be shared.

Petits fours—Assorted, including LeCygne, a miniature cake filled with vanilla hazelnut cream and Hill Farm natural strawberry preserves.

Crepes filled with fresh fruit of choice, topped with thick whipped cream and dark chocolate shavings, light and decadent.

Sister, where art thou?

"ISIS? Why would any woman in her right mind join that militant group?" Andrea Stewart remarked skeptically into the cell phone she had propped between the crook of her ear and raised shoulder. Her hands were free to stir the chocolate ganache to be spread atop the Opera Cake she was preparing for tonight's dessert menu at La Chic Sardine.

The elegant gâteau was composed of mocha buttercream spread over thin layers of cake that had been soaked in coffee syrup, topped with the ganache, then sliced into bars. One of her many specialties at this Philadelphia restaurant. As far removed from ISIS as, well, the Liberty Bell.

"How do I know why your sister does the things she does?" her stepmother, Darla, whined into the phone. "All I know is, I have a picture here in front of me, and she's wearing some kind of robe that covers her from head to toe with only her eyes peeking out."

"A burqa?" That was a switch for her sister, who was more inclined toward tight jeans and skimpy shirts.

"I don't know what they call those things. They look like tents, if you ask me. I get a hot flash just thinking about how uncomfortable they must be in this heat. Thank God I'm not an A-rab."

It was summer, and the city was in the midst of an unusual heat wave—unusual for Pennsylvania—but Darla would have the AC on full blast. *Is she in menopause? At forty-five?* Andrea did a mental

Snoopy dance of glee. *There is a God!* But that was nasty. Darla didn't mean to be such an insensitive dingbat. She was just clueless.

Andrea set aside her whisk and adjusted the phone at her ear. Sitting down on a high stool at the kitchen prep table, she sighed and said, "Celie is going purdah? That's a new one. How is she going to show off all her tattoos? And her body piercings will set off airport alarms if she tries to leave the country."

"Andy! That's not funny."

Actually, it was. Celie's ink, seventeen at last count, had started with a tramp stamp when she was only thirteen. Winnie the Pooh giving the finger. As for piercings, Andrea had personally witnessed a belly button ring, as well as multiple holes in her ears, eyebrows, tongue, and God only knew where else. *Ouch!*

To her credit, Celie had let some of the piercings grow back, but still, *what was she thinking?*

She wasn't, that was the point with her sister, who was on a continual quest to find herself.

"Honestly, Andy, this is going to kill your father. How much more of this crap can he take?"

Andrea rolled her eyes. Darla had been saying the same thing ever since she, a mere thirty-year-old, married fifty-year-old widower Howard Stewart fifteen years ago, when Andrea had been fourteen years old and her sister Cecilia a mere four. *Crap* was her universal word for anything the two children did to "ruin her life." On Andrea's part, it encompassed everything from strep throat to a dirty kitchen due to one of her latest culinary experiments. When it came to her sister, it could be bedwetting, a low grade on a math test, or promiscuous behavior as a preteen.

Darla, a former Zumba instructor, did not have a maternal bone in her well-toned body. She'd no doubt thought she'd landed a sugar daddy when she met their father, a successful stockbroker, who was brilliant when it came to the market and dumb as a Dow Jones clunker when it came to women. Little had Darla known that the Wall Street gravy train also carried some irritating baggage in the form of two kids, who hadn't been as sweet and invisible as she'd probably expected.

It was only nine a.m., and the kitchen was empty except for Andrea at this early hour. The restaurant didn't begin serving until five p.m., but employees would be trailing in soon. Andrea needed to get off the phone and get back to work. "Darla, how do you know it's Celie?"

"Because it's a video. Celie sent it to us. At least, I think it came from her. Didn't I tell you that?"

"No, you didn't."

"Oh, well, I'm looking at it on my laptop right now. Celie is talking about Allah and the evil United States and that kind of crap. She has black eyebrows. What is her natural hair color, anyway? Oh, that's right. Blonde, like yours."

Andrea hadn't seen her sister for months—in fact, almost a year. Not for any particular reason. There was a ten-year difference in their ages, and that wasn't the only difference. Celie was of average height, with curves out the wazoo. Andrea was genetically thin, rarely gained an ounce, and thank God for that with her calorie-laden occupation. Celie's hair could be any color under the rainbow, from bright purple to an actual rainbow, and styled short, long, or half long/half short. Once she even shaved her head. Andrea had sported the same long, blonde ponytail since she was a teenager. It suited her and her work.

Celie was the adventurous one. Always looking for thrills (can anyone say zip line off a cliff?), while Andrea didn't even like roller coasters. As for men, forget about it! Celie drew men, like flies or bees or whatever. Boys had been chasing her since she was ten years old. Andrea didn't even want to guess how many lovers Celie had gone through in her nineteen years, while Andrea, at twenty-nine-almost-thirty, had had two real relationships. Three, if you counted Peter Townsend. Pete the Pervert. He had the weirdest fetish involving . . . never mind.

Back to Celie. Despite their clashes in personalities and interests, they were still fairly close sisters. They had to be during those early years of their mother's death, and their father's grieving. It was just the two of them against the world. Until he married Darla. And then, it was the two of them against Darla. Poor Darla!

They just never seemed to be in the same place at the same time these days. Celie was always traveling somewhere or other. Andrea was an ambitious workaholic with hopes of one day opening her own upscale pastry shop.

While Andrea's mind had been wandering, she just realized that Darla was still talking. She interrupted her by saying, "I thought Celie was spending the summer with that cult in Jamaica, where they run around half naked and sell sun catchers to tourists. Led by that whack-job swami person who believes that world peace will come with global warming, or some such nonsense."

"That was last year."

Celie was a great one for joining cults, not that she called them cults, and mostly they were harmless. Modern-day hippies looking for the light, usually via some weed. Heaven's Love Shack. Serenity. Free Birds. Pot for People.

"Remember, I told you about her boyfriend. He's an A-rab or a Mexican, or something. Maybe Egyptian. They all look alike."

That narrows it down a lot. Darla was no dummy, but sometimes she revealed a little inner Archie Bunkerism. And Edith, too.

"His name is Kahlil, you know, like that poet guy."

"Kahlil Gibran?"

"Yes! Don't you just love his poems? They're so deep."

Talking to Darla was like trying to catch popcorn from an unlidded pot. Here, there, all over the place.

"About Celie's boyfriend?"

"Oh, right. He came to a dinner party your daddy hosted last month for one of his big clients. You were at that food convention in Las Vegas. Anyhow, Kahlil Ajam . . . that was his last name, I remember now because his last name reminded me of jelly. Do you still make that honey mint jelly to serve with lamb chops? That reminds me. Maybe I should make lamb chops for your daddy and me tonight. With those fingerling potatoes and little Brussels sprouts. I wonder—"

"Aaarrgh!"

"What?"

"Stop getting sidetracked."

"Stop being so impatient." Darla sighed, as if Andrea were the one who was irritating. "Anyhow, Kahlil just frowned the whole time he was here because we served alcohol. So rude! Honestly! Who doesn't drink red wine with beef Wellington? And he had this dish towel thingee on his head. By the way, your raspberry torte was a huge success. Did I tell you that?"

Can anyone say Orville Redenbacher? "Yes, you told me." About the dessert, not the boyfriend. "Thanks."

"Anyhow, this Kahlil fella talked the silly girl into going with him to a dude ranch in Montana run by some Muslim church. Circle of Light."

"What? That's crazy!"

"You're telling me, honey. I've been saying for years that your sister is two bricks short of a wall. You must admit, Andy—"

"I didn't mean that Celie . . . never mind. What has any of this to do with ISIS?"

"The detective says that—"

"Whoa, whoa, whoa! You hired a detective?"

Just then, Sonja Fournet, owner of the restaurant, walked in through the swinging doors that separated the kitchen from the dining room. Hearing her last words, Sonja grinned and mouthed silently, "Darla?"

Andrea nodded and raised five fingers, indicating she would be off the phone shortly. Andrea was an experienced pastry chef, but even her skills were not going to save her job if she kept engaging in these personal phone conversations while on the job, almost all of them from her stepmother. Darla thought nothing of calling up to a dozen times a day, usually about the most innocuous things, like "What's the best way to cook lamb?" Or "How do I clean the gravy stain off your mother's lace tablecloth?" Or "Why does asparagus turn my pee green?" Real important stuff.

That wasn't quite true about Andrea losing her job, though. Sonja had attended the Cordon Bleu cooking school in Paris with Andrea eight years ago and was one of her closest friends.

"Listen, Darla, I can't talk right now. Why don't I come over tonight and we can discuss this, without interruption?" Fortunately, or unfortunately, her father and Darla lived in a Main Line community only a half hour from the condo Andrea had bought two years ago.

I must have been under the influence of cooking wine when I moved back to Pennsylvania. Couldn't I find a job in . . . oh, say . . . Alaska? Or, at the least, a chef opening on the other side of Philly? Like maybe New Jersey? Or London?

"Okay," Darla said. "Could you bring some of those yummy Napoleons with you? Oh, and a few of the chocolate croissants for your daddy's breakfast?"

"Sure." She clicked off the phone and looked at Sonja, who was grinning at her over a steaming cup of coffee. "Okay, spill. What has the wicked stepmother's thong in a twist now? I swear, girl, I wouldn't have a life if it weren't for you."

"She says Celie has joined a cult on a dude

ranch in Montana that has ties to ISIS, and claims she's gone all Sharia, complete with burqa, mainlining the usual extremist Muslim propaganda. Though, how she would ride a horse in a robe, I have no idea. I didn't even know Celie could ride a horse. And, yeah, before you ask, isn't it strange that a terrorist organization would recruit from a dude ranch? Better that than the mall, I suppose. Bottom line, as usual when it involves my sister, Darla probably wants me to fix things."

"Merde!"

"Exactly."

"What does she expect you to do?"

Andrea shrugged. "Lone Ranger to the rescue, I guess, though I don't ride a horse, either. Or is it Julia Child to the rescue?"

"Warrior with a whisk," Sonja concluded.

Chapter 2

BREAKFAST IN TRANSYLVANIA (PENNSYLVANIA)

Liver mush
Amish sausages
Smoked boar steaks (ham)
Pennsylvania Dutch home fries
Souse or head cheese (meat jelly)

Blood pudding
Pan Haus (scrapple)
Bacon
Buttermilk pancakes
Cornmeal mush

Eggs, scrambled with cream or fried in bacon fat

Toasted muffins or fresh-baked bread
Skyr (cheese)

Sweet butter
Apple butter

Farmer's Market fresh jams: strawberry, rhubarb, huckleberry

Coffee
Tea
Milk
Fake-O
Fresh-squeezed blood oranges
Beer

Home, Sweet Home . . . or, rather, Home, Sweet Castle . . .

In the early morning hours of July 9, Cnut was riding his Harley up the Pennsylvania Turnpike. The black and chrome Road King, a recent purchase, was a modest model, but it had so many bells and whistles, it could do everything but fly a jet plane. He loved it. In fact, he'd named it Hugo.

Most important, the motorcycle could accommodate his size, thanks to some tweaks. His height, that was, at six foot four. Cnut was no longer big in other regards, hadn't been for a long, long time. A careful diet and a rigid exercise routine kept him at a lean, mean two-twenty-five.

Funny thing, though. Cnut still felt fat. Maybe it was like those people who lost a leg but still sensed a phantom limb. Phantom fat. How cool was that? But then, that was him. Cool-hand Cnut.

He should have bought a Fat Boy, instead of a Road King, but that was cutting too close to the bone in terms of description. He could only imagine his brothers' reaction. As if he cared!

Cnut stretched and wondered if he should pull over at the next rest stop for a cup of black coffee. The sun was just coming up over the mountains, but he was only halfway there. He'd wanted to avoid the capitol traffic as he passed Harrisburg, but then this was Saturday, the legislature wouldn't be in session. Sane people would be headed north in this heat, to the Poconos or south to the Jersey shore. No, he'd rather get this over with. No stopping. The annual Reckoning was serious business.

Perhaps he should be examining his conscience in preparation for the meeting, but then he figured he would find out soon enough what transgressions he'd tallied up this past year. Michael kept meticulous records.

The three-hour trip from his Center City apartment in Philadelphia should put him at the old homestead in Transylvania before eight. *Old* being the keyword. The vangel headquarters that his brother Vikar had bought four years ago was a rundown castle built by some crazy lumber baron a century or so ago. The hokey, tourist trap of a town, once on the skids, had been renamed a few years back to profit from the vampire craze still hitting the country.

Hah! Little do folks know, being a vampire isn't all that fun. Cnut ran his tongue over his own set of fangs, which were retracted at the moment. Otherwise, they'd probably have dead bugs on them, like windshields. Fat and buggy, that's all he needed! Truly, one thousand, one hundred and sixty-six years, and he still wasn't used to the things. Like a cock, they sometimes had a mind of their own. Popping out with the least provocation. Even with his improved physical condition, Cnut wasn't a vain man, like some of his brothers—hell, like Vikings in general—but the wolfish teeth did embarrass him, on occasion. Which was probably the point, from Michael's perspective, since he'd never been particularly fond of Vikings to begin with, and his affection had failed to grow over the years due to their irksome ways, irksome to an angel leastways.

He soon climbed the first of the Seven Mountains, sped through the scenic narrows, but then had to slow down when he got behind an Amish buggy on the way to one of the numerous roadside fruit and vegetable stands. The region was dotted with the neat farms of these "plain people," an odd contrast to a town of vampire wannabes, but somehow they worked well together. Farms and fangs. Go figure.

There were quite a few Amish farms in this region, but the plain folks kept mostly to themselves.

Soon, Cnut approached the town itself where a billboard announced:

WELCOME TO TRANSYLVANIA, PENNSYLVANIA
DRACULA'S OTHER HOME
(themed restaurants, lodging, and entertainment)

The poster was illustrated with a picture of Ben Franklin sporting fangs and a black cloak, leaning against a Liberty Bell, bats flying overhead. The usual kitschy caricature of vampires.

Cnut had left his black cloak at home, but he did have an ample supply of specially treated knives, a switchblade sword, a pistol, and the like under his black leather jacket. You never knew when you might run into a demon vampire. The castle here in the Pennsylvania mountains being a vangel headquarters had remained a secret so far from the Lucipires. The townfolk thought they were vampire wannabes planning to open a castle hotel eventually once the building restoration was complete, which might be never. Vikar further played on this idea by self-proclaiming himself Lord Vikar, as if he were some friggin' royalty just slumming it in the Pennsylvania hills.

In any case, Cnut fully expected Jasper, fallen angel and king of the Lucipires, to show up with his cohorts any day. The VIK, composed of Cnut and his brothers, were prepared for that eventuality, and, in fact, were already spreading themselves out into secondary command centers in Louisiana, Key West, and a Caribbean island, taking with them the more than five hundred vangels working under them.

Cnut drove slowly through the main street of Transylvania, where most of the businesses were still asleep. They would be teeming with visitors in an hour or two, this being the summer tourist season.

He always smiled when he saw what the town had to offer in terms of vampire-abilia. Shops sold an array of black cloaks, fake fangs, vampire stakes that did double duty as tomato plant supports, bottled blood aka red Kool-Aid, and T-shirts with logos that were sometimes creative, to say the least. "Fangs for the Memories" was one of his favorites, along with "Bitten But Not Beaten."

Garlic was sold everywhere, lots of garlic, which was known in these parts as Smelly Roses. Though where anyone got the idea that garlic repelled vampires, Cnut had no idea. Probably some medieval farmer with a surplus of the crop and a vivid imagination for marketing. Cnut personally liked a good garlic pesto on his pasta. Or garlic lime chicken. Garlic mashed potatoes. Garlic marinated filet mignon. Garlic shrimp linguine. Who was he fooling? He liked food, period, and while he didn't overindulge these days (well, hardly ever), he had become a Food Network fanatic. His secret pleasure. Other men glommed porn or ESPN. He glommed *Iron Chef* and *Chopped* and *Barefoot Contessa*. It was like those priests who self-flagellate as a penance, such as the nutcase cleric in *The Da Vinci Code*. *Yes, I watch way too much TV.* Cnut tortured himself watching Bobby Flay barbecue ribs (pun intended) or Ina Garten whip up a crème brûlée (another pun intended).

Not to be outdone by the shops, the restaurants and bars in Transylvania displayed names like Good Bites, Blood and Guts, Vlad's Vittles, Fangy Foods, Suck and Suds, Drac's Hideout. He noticed a new one that must have opened since he was here last, called Whips and Cuffs, offering Fifty Shades of Blood (Cocktails).

He stopped at a red light, and his bike idled with a *va-room, va-room* that seemed overloud in the quiet street. Two young women in waitress uniforms glanced his way, then gaped. Leather did that to some women, or motorcycles. Then again, it might be the Ragnar Lothbrok hairstyle he'd adopted the last year or so, worn by that character in that History Channel show *The Vikings* during the first few seasons. Shaved on the sides, with triple dark blond braids interwoven together from his forehead to his nape, then tied off with a leather thong to hang down his back. His brothers mocked the fashion as some weird form of vanity, but it was more a case of efficiency on his part. It kept the hair out of his face, always a good thing for a fighting man, which he was, and, frankly, it suited him, dammit. No different than the war braids Viking men of old wore, framing both sides of their faces, ofttimes intertwined with crystal beads or fine jewels. Leastways, that's what he told himself.

He gave a little nod of acknowledgment to the women, no more than twenty. Practically children to this old man. One of them giggled. The other pointed a forefinger at him, then herself, then crossed that forefinger with the one of her other hand and raised her eyebrows at him in invitation. No way when he was about to be raked over the coals by Michael! He just smiled and eased off as the light changed.

He drove out of town, then up the mountain road that led to the castle. New electronic gates had been installed, and he tapped in the code on a secure app he'd downloaded onto his cell phone. Soon he was approaching the castle itself, which was, as always, a work-in-progress. It appeared as if something was being done on the fourth-floor windows, maybe reglazing of the old glass. He drove around the side of the massive structure to the back courtyard where he could have entered the underground garage, but a note had been tacked on the door, "Lot Full, Park Outside."

So everyone must be here already. Probably arrived last night. His own dozen vangels who were stationed with him in Philadelphia would be here by noon, their presence not required until after the morning session.

He glanced around the back area of the castle, which at one time had been nothing but a cobbled courtyard but now held an in-ground swimming pool, bathhouse, gazebo, patio, and other luxuries that Cnut found hard to believe Michael had approved. Vikar, at least, was living the good life, or so it seemed. Unlike Cnut, who lived in a Philadelphia row house, the first floor of which housed his company, Wings International Security; the second floor, his austere two-bedroom apartment; and the attic, dorm-style living for his vangels.

The first person he saw when he went inside was Lizzie Borden—yes, that Lizzie Borden—who gave him a fangy smile of welcome as she bustled about, beginning to prepare the morning meal for what must be a virtual army in residence at the moment. A half-dozen, sleepy-eyed young vangel women did her bidding, pulling hams, eggs, bacon, and such from the commercial-size fridge. It was going to be a banquet by the looks of the two enormous gas ranges, where various meats and potatoes sizzled, including some of the Amish or Pennsylvania Dutch specialties of this region, like scrapple and blood sausage. A feast fit for a king, or at least an archangel, right hand of *the* King.

Cnut grabbed a carton of Fake-O while the door was open. The synthetic blood invented by his brother Sigurd tasted like curdled horse piss, but it sufficed to satisfy the vangel need for the real thing in between missions. He chugged it down with a shiver of distaste, followed by long swig of bottled water, then tossed both empty containers into a trash bin. When Lizzie's back was turned, he grabbed several crisp bacon strips that were draining on a paper towel–covered platter and popped them into his mouth. *Delicious.* Before he realized what he was doing, the plate was half empty. He reached for more, then caught himself. *No, no, no. Must resist temptation.*

He made his way toward the family room, where he could hear a television playing. Cartoons. The children must be up. You'd never know vangels were sterile by the sounds of youthling chatter. Actually, most everyone was up by now, he realized, as he passed and spoke briefly to vangels in the dining room, the chapel, the front and side parlors, the computer room, and Vikar's office. Obviously, Michael was not yet here.

He was shrugging out of his leather jacket in the hallway when he noticed Regina leaning against the wall, arms crossed over the bosom of a loose, floor-length gown which failed to hide her voluptuous form. Her silver-blue eyes, same as all the vangels, gave him a quick head-to-toe survey. "Holy freakin' fangs, Cnut! I can't decide whether you look like a rock star or a lackwit vain Viking compensating for a wee wick. Just because you can now fit into leather braies does not mean you should."

"They're not leather. They're black denim."

"You may as well tattoo *BADASS* on your forehead. I could do the job for you with my trusty rusty needle," she offered.

A low growling noise escaped his throat.

She sneered with satisfaction, having annoyed him as she'd no doubt intended.

Cnut flashed his fangs at her.

Regina flashed hers back at him.

"And who do you think you're fooling in that nun garb?" he countered. "Everyone knows you're more slut than saint."

"Everyone knows nothing," she snapped back.

Cnut deliberately banked his temper. Best not to rile Regina too much. She was, or had been, a witch in her human life, and she'd been known to throw a curse out with less provocation than the foolish insult he'd just hurled at her, ofttimes at a Viking's "wee wick." With exaggerated politeness, and one hand placed discreetly over his crotch, he said, "My apologies, m'lady."

"Bullshit, m'lord," she replied succinctly.

"Witchy wench!" he muttered.

He heard laughter behind him and saw that Vikar had emerged from the office and overheard his conversation.

Regina laughed, too, his "wee wick" was relieved to note, and walked away, hips swaying.

Vikar shook his head at Cnut. "You know she just loves to bait you."

"And succeeds," Cnut agreed.

Vikar motioned him into his office, where Trond was sitting in a side chair, wearing a U.S. Navy T-shirt and jeans, his long legs extended and crossed at the ankles. He cradled a mug of what Cnut assumed was coffee in his hands. Cnut should have grabbed one himself while he'd been in the kitchen scarfing up smoked boar strips aka bacon. Trond grinned and said, "Hey, bro! Still channeling Ragnar Lothbrok, I see."

"Definitely." He was not going to rise to another bait. Even so, he remarked, "Still channeling Rambo, I see."

"Definitely," Trond said with a grin. He was a Navy SEAL.

"I noticed that Ragnar shaved his head in later seasons of *The Vikings*." Vikar arched his brows at Cnut.

"No, I am not going to shave my head." Bloody hell! Did his brothers have naught to do but discuss his hair? Cnut sat down in the other chair. "So what's new?" he asked both of them. "Any word on what Mike has on the agenda for today?" Mike was the rude name the vangels had adopted for Michael. Not to his face, of course.

"Not a clue," Trond said.

The annual Reckonings were held to keep all the vangels in line, to tally up all their good deeds and bad ones, and reevaluate their penances. Usually, that meant more years added on to their original sentences. Being Vikings, they found it hard to be good all the time. Thus, it was no surprise that the original seven hundred years was now well over a thousand for all of them. They'd probably be vangels until the Apocalypse.

But, in addition to the individual evaluations, there was usually some big announcement. It started four years ago when Michael revealed they would be staying in the present, not bouncing back and forth through time, as they had in the past. One day a gladiator, another they could be a Regency gentleman, or a Civil War soldier, even a Greek Olympian. Once Cnut had even ridden with William the Conqueror. And Mordr, guilty of the sin of wrath, had fought against Genghis Khan. Now there was a Rambo, if there ever was one!

Last year, Michael told them that more new vangels would be created and trained in light of the increasing evil in the world, aka Lucies, the vangel nickname for Lucipires. Cnut had no idea what the exact number was by now. He would have to ask Vikar, later.

"Mayhap Mike will bring Gabriel and Raphael or some of the other archangels to help, and mayhap it will be just a cursory review of our sins, and mayhap this will be an unusual Reckoning. Fun." It was Trond offering this optimistic view.

Cnut and Vikar looked at him as if he was barmy.

"Or mayhap not," Trond conceded.

Just then, there was a strange, flapping sound outside, overhead in the skies, like thousands of geese flying north for the winter. Except this was July. And there was no honking. Just an ethereal silence and an incredible—you could say heavenly—fragrance filling the air.

It was Michael and he must have brought an entourage to help with the Reckonings. He walked in, leading a procession of white-robed angels, wings closed but stray feathers fluttering in their wake. Not Gabriel and Raphael this time, but other archangels of equal stature. They were an impressive sight, but none had the presence of authority that Michael had. With a mere lift of his hand, the angels scattered in different directions to set up "confessionals," or rather private spaces where they could interview each of the vangels individually.

At least it was not being done in a communal setting, as it had been in the old days, but then their numbers had been much smaller. The brothers had learned a whole lot more about each other than they ever wanted to know when their sins were disclosed in front of one and all. In fact, that was the first time that Cnut had learned that his brother Ivak, the lustsome one, could . . . well, never mind.

Michael nodded to Cnut and the others in greeting as he passed. Suddenly, he paused and sniffed the air, "Do I smell bacon?" The archangel gave Cnut a head-to-toe survey, as if checking for extra poundage.

Cnut sucked in his stomach.

"Busted!" Trond whispered to him, under his breath.

"Bite me!" he muttered back.

Michael heard and gave Trond a full-body examination as well, checking to see if his laziness had come back and he might not be working as hard as he should. As if that were possible in SEALs training where the motto was "Pain is your friend."

Trond blushed, and his body went military straight under the saintly perusal.

Cnut felt his own face heat up, as well. Being singled out at a Reckoning was not a good thing.

With a grunt of disgust—everyone knew Michael was not overfond of Vikings—the archangel went directly to the front salon where folding chairs had been set up in a circle with a wingback chair at one side, much like a throne. Michael sat and waited for each of them to be seated. Idiots that they were, they all scrambled to be farthest away. All seven were there, the leadership of brothers known as the VIK: Vikar, Trond, Ivak, Mordr, Sigurd, Harek, and himself.

Then, Michael said, "Greetings from the Lord."

They bowed their heads at that gift.

Vikar spoke up then, "Would you like coffee or refreshments before we start? Lizzie is cooking up a storm. Even those buttermilk biscuits you favored last time you were here."

"They *were* heavenly. Manna, truth to tell. But no, thank you. We can partake at the mid-morning break." He looked at each of them, individually, and it was as if he could read their souls. Not a comfortable feeling. They all squirmed in their seats.

"Let us start with a prayer."

Seven heads bowed.

"God bless this gathering of thy loyal subjects. Help us to know Thy path in fighting the evil Lucipires and in curing our own sinful natures. Thou art truly the light in a world of darkness. Enlighten and strengthen us. Amen."

"Amen," they repeated after him.

"Now, let us start with you, Vikar. How is your family? Have you finished training those last vangels I sent you? How is the castle restoration coming?"

"My family is fine," Vikar answered. "My wife, Alex, is a writer, as you know. She wants to write a children's book about a naughty Viking angel, if you approve."

Michael raised his eyebrows at that. "I will discuss the project with her later today."

"Gunnar and Gunnora are thriving. Both of them can read now, and they have prepared a special song for you, if you have time to listen this afternoon."

"I will make time."

"Our numbers of vangels are now up to seven hundred and fifty, spread across the world, and twenty still in training. Sadly, that is not nearly enough. Jasper's minion troops are growing. According to Zeb, they are flourishing with the rise in terrorism, perhaps even causing it. And he is about to appoint several more haakai to his high command, replacing Dominique and Haroun who were sent to their final hellish rewards. Zeb says these replacements are a most evil lot." The Zeb referred to was Zebulan the Hebrew, a Lucipire double agent who had hopes of one day becoming a vangel.

Trond was next. He and his wife, Nicole, were Navy SEALs in Coronado, California. Well, Nicole was in WEALS, Women on Earth, Air, Land, and Sea, a female equivalent of SEALs. Trond spoke of the special forces' efforts to combat terrorism. In many ways, the vangels and SEALs were the same, increasing their ranks in a seemingly endless fight against tangos, or bad guys.

"And how is our Southern headquarters coming?" Michael asked Ivak.

Ivak, who was stationed as a chaplain at Angola Prison—an irony since he was guilty of the sin of lust—was married to lawyer Gabrielle Sonnier, and they had a son, named Michael. Something that was never supposed to happen since vangels were sterile. (Yes, Ivak, the world-class suck-up, had named his son after the archangel.) Vikar and Alex's children were "adopted," so to speak. Like

Vikar with the endless renovations to the Pennsylvania castle, Ivak was restoring a rundown plantation in Louisiana.

"Can anyone say 'snakes'?" Ivak said. "The snake problem halted our progress for a while, but I hired a snake catcher, and we are moving along now. Some people down there claim there are one thousand species of snakes in the world, and nine hundred and ninety-nine of them live in Louisiana," he joked.

No one laughed, having heard that exact complaint hundreds of times already.

"Anyhow, the former slave quarters are now remodeled into apartments, and I should be able to house a hundred more vangels by the end of summer," Ivak went on.

"And not soon enough," Sigurd exclaimed. Their physician brother was retrofitting a Key West island hotel into a hospital for sick children, a front for another vangel headquarters. "We are so crowded on Grand Key Island, some of the vangels are having to sleep on boats."

"Spoiled! You Vikings are spoiled." If Michael had his way, they would probably be wearing hair shirts and sleeping on thorn bushes. "Was a time, if you recall, when sleeping on the ground was good enough."

Cnut remembered. They all did. Those first years as a vangel had been rough, to say the least. When they'd been lucky enough to find a cave, they'd considered it a luxury comparable to a Hilton suite today.

Harek, the smartest of all the VIK, told them then about the Caribbean island he was converting into an electronics center that would bring vangels into the computer age. Really, to fight modern-day Lucies, they had to become modern-day vangels, or so Harek contended. Harek was the last of his brothers to be wed, and that despite Michael's initial warning that none of them were to be involved with women. He'd married Camille Dumaine, also a member of WEALS, last year.

"And when will my archangel website be ready?" Michael asked Harek.

Michael had been badgering Harek for years to set up an Internet site for archangels to help humans.

"Um," Harek said, his face red with embarrassment. It wasn't Harek's fault that he'd failed to create a cyberspace home for the archangel. In fact, with his skills, Harek could probably build a website in an hour, but Michael kept changing his mind about what he wanted.

In quick order, Michael got updates from all the VIK. He turned to Cnut then and asked, "What art thou doing about ISIS?"

"ISIS?" he said dumbly.

"Do you not know of this ISIS?"

"The Islamic State of Iraq and al-Sham. Formerly aligned with Al-Qaeda. A worldwide terrorist threat," Cnut regurgitated a Wikipedia-like definition. That's about all he knew.

Michael nodded. "Destroy it."

"Huh? What? Me?"

"Are you not our security expert?"

"I am."

"Is ISIS not the greatest threat, equal only to the Nazi Holocaust or the evil Roman Empire?"

Cnut nodded, hesitantly, not sure what this had to do with him.

"That will be your goal for this year. Destroy ISIS."

"Me? Alone? How will I do that?"

Michael shrugged. "That is not for me to say."

Aaarrgh! That is Mike-speak for "Figure it out, Viking."

"Did you say something?" Michael inquired, too sweetly.

"You do realize that armies from around the world, not just the United States, have been fighting ISIS for years, and they just keep growing," Trond pointed out to the archangel.

Thanks for intervening on my behalf, brother. Cnut gave a nod to Trond.

"Jasper's influence, no doubt," Michael agreed.

"How can I do what thousands have failed to do?" Cnut asked.

"Not just you. All of you."

His brothers sat up straighter, no longer complacent that Cnut was the only target of Michael's outrageous demand.

"Jasper's evil hordes, and ISIS because of the Lucipire evil influence on some of its members, will be the mission of all vangels this year, and possibly years to come. That is not to say that there will not be smaller operations wherever Lucipires settle in, but mainly you all must concentrate on this abomination. Mass murders. Beheadings. Rapes. All in the name of some distorted religious belief. The Lord weeps at the atrocities." For a moment, Michael's head was bowed. Then he straightened and said, "But it will all start with you, Cnut."

"Thy will be done," Cnut agreed, but he had no idea where to start.

As if reading his mind, because of course he could read minds, Michael explained, "ISIS is no more than a glorified cult, much like those started by David Koresh and Jim Jones in the past. Yea, the numbers are much larger, but the principles are much the same. Blind worship of a false ideology. Start small with one of the cults, Cnut. Then your brothers, and other military operations, will aid you from there."

"One of the cults?" he murmured.

"There is a modern expression that applies here, Cnut. Nibbling away like ducks. That is what thou must do. Start nibbling."

Under his breath, Cnut said, "Quack, quack."

"Death by a thousand paper cuts," Ivak said, agreeing with Michael.

Cnut glanced at his other brothers and saw that they came to the same communal opinion of Ivak. *Suck-up!*

"If enough people around the world begin nibbling, they can eat away at the core of ISIS," Michael contended. "And keep in mind, it is the goal of vangels to destroy Lucipires and save dreadful sinners, not to ensure world peace."

That's a relief! Not! Cnut was doubtful of his abilities for such a huge mission, and he didn't know what he was expected to do, exactly, or where to start.

"You will know when you will know," Michael told him.

You will know when you will know, Cnut mimicked in his head. *Another Mike-ism! Clear as celestial clouds on a dark Norse fjord.*

"By the by, Cnut, your hair has become a favorite topic Up Above. Angels far and wide have adopted the style. In fact, legions of them look like dim-witted Vikings."

The archangel was not pleased.

Neither was Cnut.

He was even less pleased when he got text messages from his brothers over the next few days:

> *If it walks like a duck, quacks like a duck, and looks like a duck, it must be . . . Cnut.*
>
> *You lucky duck!*
>
> *Lord love a duck!*
>
> *A duck walks into a bar . . .*
>
> *You ever were a sitting duck, bro.*
>
> *Some ducks turn to swans, don't they?*

Actually, Cnut didn't mind his brothers' lame attempts at humor. Vikings appreciated a good jest.

Still, he responded to each of them, *Shut the duck up!*

Then he prepared to get all his ducks in a row back at his office so he would be ready for Michael's mysterious moment when he "would know when he would know."

For some reason, Cnut had a sudden and fierce craving for turducken. And that night, on the Food Network, the host of *Everyday Gourmet* made a duck cassoulet. And wasn't it a sad commentary on his life that Cnut, once a fierce Viking warrior (when he had been so inclined and/or able to get off his fat arse), actually knew what a cassoulet was? But hadn't a clue how to save the world from ISIS.

Were the fates conspiring against Cnut, or just Michael?

Chapter 3

Sweet temptation!

It was Andrea's third pass by the agency door as she gathered her nerve to go in. Her lunch hour would soon be over if she dawdled around much longer. It wasn't as if she didn't have an appointment.

Still, she peered dubiously through the shaded windows of Wings International Security, located just down the street from La Chic Sardine, trying to see inside. What kind of legitimate business had shaded windows? And a single metal desk and filing cabinet with two folding chairs? But she'd looked up the firm on the Internet, and the office appeared to be a reliable agency for tracking and protecting individuals or groups, with a special emphasis on terrorists. She'd done her due diligence. So, what was the problem?

- A creepy feeling she got up the back of her neck?
- A sense that something wasn't quite right?

- Her first time seeking outside help for her sister's shenanigans?
- Her family expecting her to drop everything and clean up another of Celie's messes?

Pick any one of those. Or all of them.

Or maybe it was just plain exasperation. *Why do I have to be my sister's keeper? No, that's selfish. I don't really mean that. I love my sister. It's just . . . just . . . frustrating. And, frankly, a little bit scary this time.*

"Oh hell!" she muttered, and opened the door. Then stopped dead in her tracks. "Holy freakin' sex on a stick!" she said in an undertone, before she had a chance to curb her tongue.

Andrea was almost thirty years old, and while she wouldn't describe herself as having been around the block, she'd had several relationships, three if you counted Pete the Perv. More important, she'd never been attracted to musclemen. But son of a biscotti!

Standing beside the desk was a man, dressed in a plain blue, tapered, Oxford-collared dress shirt, untucked, over black jeans and black athletic shoes. But that was the only thing plain about him. He had to be six foot three or -four of lean muscles from wide shoulders to narrow waist and hips and mile-long legs. His lightly tanned face was a masterpiece of sculpted Nordic features, topped by a unique hairstyle, shaved on the sides and sort of French braided from his forehead to the back of his neck, where the remainder of dark blond hair was tied off with a leather shoelace, or something.

"Are you a Viking?" she asked.

At the same time, he asked, "Are you a doctor?"

He said yes, and she said no. Then they both laughed.

And, Lordy, even his laugh was sexy. Low and husky and masculinity personified.

She glanced down at her white linen chef jacket worn over white skinny jeans and comfortable Crocs. "No, I'm a chef. A pastry chef."

"Ah, that explains it."

She raised her eyebrows.

"The scent of vanilla and fresh baked bread. And coconut. Lots of coconut."

"I was making vanilla bean crème brûlées and artisan breads this morning," she said. "But nothing with coconut." She frowned, trying to recall if she'd been handling any coconut. "Nope. Not today."

She had to stop gaping at the guy, so she sank down into one of the folding chairs, without being invited. It was either that or faint or something equally objectionable, like jump his bones.

In her defense, he was staring at her, too, but it was unclear whether he found her presence objectionable or whether he was as magnetically attracted as she was. That soon became clear when he sat down, as well, behind the desk, which was oddly empty of paperwork or any kind of personal objects, except for an open laptop computer. "What do you want?" he asked rudely.

"Uh, I have an appointment."

"No, you do not have an appointment. I would know if . . . wait. You're Andy Stewart? My twelve o'clock?"

"Yes. Andrea Stewart."

"Blessed clouds!" he swore, as if that were a foul expletive. "Why would a woman like you use such an unfeminine name?"

"Like me?"

"Sex on a fucking stick," he explained, repeating her own words back at her, though more graphically.

She was embarrassed that he'd overheard her original assessment of him and that he was viewing her in the same sexist way she'd viewed him. Not that she could ever be considered sex on anything. Not even a Popsicle stick. Her sister, maybe. Not her, even on a good day. Anyhow, she was beginning to reassess him to something more like jerk on a stick.

He must have recognized the change of expression on her face because he apologized, "I'm sorry. Let's start over. I'm Cnut Sigurdsson, owner of Wings International."

Stretching a long arm across the desk, he shook her hand. At that mere touch of palm against palm, she felt the oddest shock wave pass through her body, ripples of warm heat going to all her extremities, but mostly girl central.

Cnut caught himself gaping at the woman as the oddest shock wave passed over his body, causing warm heat to slingshot to all his extremities, especially one particular extremity. Sizzle ensued along with the scent of sweet, delicious coconut, and he didn't even like coconut, or leastways he hadn't up 'til now. He didn't love coconut now; he was ambivalent about the stuff. He much preferred chocolate or fruit on his pastries. Sometimes nuts, but not pine nuts, unless they were toasted. He'd had a chicken orzo salad one time with toasted pine nuts that was delicious, except for an overload of basil.

Can anyone say food addict?

Thank God, the woman didn't smell like lemons, too. That was a sure sign of a dreadful sinner, in need of a vangel intervention or on a fast track to Hell. Lucipires were lured by that scent, catnip to a demon soul. But coconut? That was a new one.

What in bloody hell is going on here? He dropped her hand and sank back in his desk chair. *I'm. Losing. My. Fucking. Mind.*

He'd been hanging around the Wings office for several days now, waiting for clues to Michael's mysterious mission. Although he sometimes took on private clients, providing all kinds of expert security services, this Philadelphia office mostly served as a front for his vangel activities.

"What can I do for you, Miss Stewart?" He assumed she was Miss since there was no ring on her fingers. Not that it mattered. Much. Or at all.

She was wringing her hands in her lap, eyes darting around the barren room, clearly as nervous as he was, and stalling for time. "Cnut like a newt lizard?" she asked, irrelevantly.

He winced and said, "Yes, but spelled C-N-U-T." He said the letters carefully in case he mixed them up and offended her even more.

She nodded, inhaled for courage, and revealed, "I'm here because I need help finding my missing sister and bringing her home."

There is no way I am getting involved in some do-

mestic dispute. Especially with someone who smells like a sweet macaroon. But I should at least sound interested. Be polite. "Missing? How do you misplace a person? Ha, ha."

She didn't smile at his humor. So much for being polite! "Missing from where? Did she run away?"

"I don't mean missing in that way. I know where she is, I think."

"Why don't you just go and get her yourself? Or your parents? Why aren't they here, by the way?"

Her face pinkened. "They're getting ready to go on a cruise."

"Lady, you're wasting my time. I run a serious business."

"This is dead serious," she persisted. "My sister is in grave danger."

"Was she kidnapped?"

"Noooo, not exactly."

"Is she being held against her will?"

"No. Yes. Maybe."

He rolled his eyes. "How old is she?"

"Nineteen, but—"

"Oh good Lord! I mean, oh good gourd! Miss Stewart, your sister is an adult."

"That's questionable, but age has nothing to do with it. Celie needs help, no question about that. Her boyfriend—"

Uh-oh! The boyfriend crap! Parents don't like the boyfriend, daughter runs away. Parents hire detective to bring spoiled child home. He put up a halting hand. "I don't get involved in domestic disputes. I got the impression from the message left with my answering service that there was terrorism involved. Otherwise, an appointment wouldn't have been scheduled."

"There is, there is!" Quickly, she lifted a carry bag onto the desk and pulled out a thick folder, shoving it toward him.

Oh no! Not a folder. Do not open it, Cnut. She'll think there's a chance that I will take her case.

"This is the material that the private detective gathered about my sister, Cecilia Stewart. Celie, we call her." Her voice wobbled as she spoke, and she took out a tissue, dabbing at her golden-brown eyes, which were now misted over with tears.

Oh no! Not tears. That is so predictable. "A detective?"

"Frank Randolph from West Chester. Do you know him?"

He shook his head. *I think I'll have Mexican for lunch today. That new take-out place on Chestnut Street. Maybe tacos and enchiladas.*

"He's supposed to be a really good detective."

"And he located your sister?" *With a side of rice and refried beans.*

"Yes."

"Then why isn't *he* rescuing your sister?" *Might as well have some tiramisu, too. Is it too early for a margarita? Naw, I'd rather have a beer, or three, anyhow.*

"His exact words to my parents were, 'I don't get involved with terrorists. Especially ISIS. I value my head too much.'"

That got his attention. *Looks like no lunch today.* He sighed and flipped open the folder and examined some of the photographs. An attractive blonde woman, shorter and curvier than her sister. He could tell, even with the chef jacket hiding her assets, that Andrea Stewart was one of those skinny women with no breasts to speak of. Probably anorexic. Which made it doubly odd that he would be attracted to her. And he was, dammit. *That would be really ironical. Him with a love of food and her with a hatred of food, if that was the case. But how could she be a chef and hate food? Nope. Must be something else.*

In one of the photographs, Cnut saw the sister—Celie—wearing cut-off denims and a Grateful Dead T-shirt. In another, she wore a bikini, displaying an amazing number of tattoos. Then she was covered by a burqa with black eyebrows. He also skimmed over some of the detective's findings.

"Here's the deal, Miss Stewart—"

"Call me Andy."

Never. "Andrea," he conceded, "here's the deal. Your sister is legally an adult. If she wants to run off with her boyfriend, Arab or otherwise, there's nothing you can do. It's her choice."

"But it's not," she protested. "Not willingly. Not anymore. I don't think." She pulled a thin laptop out of her carry bag, set it on the desk, and opened the lid. Tapping a few keys, she apparently got to the page she wanted and turned the computer so that he could see the screen. "My father got this e-mail attachment three days ago. A video. His wife, my stepmother, forwarded it to me right away."

A young woman in a black burqa, with a netted half veil covering her lower face, was speaking. "Daddy, I need some money. Can you send me fifty thousand dollars? It's for a good cause.

Honestly." Suddenly, tears seemed to fill her eyes and she burst out, "Help! Help me, Daddy! I can't get away!"

A male voice spewed out some expletives in Arabic, about the only Arabic Cnut recognized, *bitch* being the predominant one. The woman was yanked out of the picture, and the screen went black.

"We haven't been able to contact her since then."

"I repeat, why aren't your parents here? I would think it was their responsibility."

She shook her head. "No. Celie is my responsibility. She always has been. Daddy cares about her. He really does, but . . ." She waved a hand dismissively. "A long story."

"I understand your concern, but this isn't the kind of—"

Sensing that he was going to decline the job, the woman, who still reeked disconcertingly of vanilla and coconut, went on, "I know Celie must come across as a flake. She exercises bad judgment and has screwed up her life on more than one occasion," she said, waving a hand toward the incriminating folder, "and it's not the first time she's become involved in a cult, but they were usually harmless in the past. Mostly. This . . . this ISIS connection, though, scares me to death. I mean, everyone has seen those beheading videos. Why would anyone in their right mind join them? Pfff! My sister apparently. But, really, what an anti-woman group! If anyone told me to wear a veil, I'd tell them where to stuff it, cult or not, religion or not."

One word stood out in Andrea's lengthy plea.

Cult. Hadn't Michael mentioned cults in connection with Cnut's new mission?

Oh no! Oh no, no, no! Cnut couldn't be involved, in any way, with this woman—this sweet-scented bit of tempting fluff—lest he start licking her up one side and down the other. Now that he thought about it . . . turn the woman upside down in a vat of pineapple juice with a splash or ten of rum, and she'd be a tempting piña colada. And, boy, was he getting a thirst on!

No, no, no! At the recent Reckoning, he had been as shocked as everyone else that for the first time ever, he'd had no new years added to his penance. In other words, he'd been a good boy, so to speak. And now this!

But "cult," that was the key, wasn't it?

"Did Michael send you?" he asked suddenly.

"Michael who?"

That answered that question. But not really. This was just the kind of trick the archangel was known to pull on the VIK. Give them a mission, but have it wrapped in something sorely tempting or contrary to their weaknesses. Vikar's overblown pride was tried in a run-down castle. Trond's laziness tested in grueling SEALs training. Ivak's lust restrained in a male prison. And Cnut's gluttony . . . ?

His stomach growled suddenly.

And with a sigh of resignation, he said, "Quack, quack."

Chapter 4

A CHEF'S NIGHTTIME SNACK

(and not a Philly cheesesteak in sight)

Ginger chai tea with orange blossom honey
Belgian chocolate-dipped madeleines
Crisp-skin Peking duck slices topped with pomegranate hoisin sauce, wrapped in paper-thin mandarin pancakes
Warm candy-cane-striped beet salad
Artichokes with tart mustard aioli
Saffron-scented jasmine rice
Fresh fruit in orange curd tart

Boutique honey beer (i.e., mead for the Viking)

He was a jar. No kidding! A jar! . . .

Andrea was puttering about her apartment that evening. She'd already showered and put on her PJs, a pair of leopard-print, low-riding nylon harem pants with a matching cropped tank top. She was combing through the long, wet strands of her hair as she stood, barefooted, at the bank of windows giving her a bird's-eye view of the sun setting over the Schuylkill River.

A rowing crew was making its way back to dock at one of the famous boathouses that lined the waterway. The long, narrow scull with its multiple oars extended resembled nothing more than a centipede from this distance. She had a pair of high-powered binoculars that she used on occasion to watch the rowing teams, especially during the annual regatta, but for now this long-distance view sufficed.

It was only eight-thirty, but she tried to go to bed by ten p.m. on those nights when she knew her alarm would go off at an all-too-early four a.m. Her work began in the La Chic Sardine kitchen by five, six at the latest. Usually, she had at least six new pastries ready before noon to be added to the menu. A killer schedule for any kind of social life, but essential for her career.

She doubted she'd be able to sleep tonight, though, with all that roiled in her brain. Mainly, worry over her sister. Her only hope at the moment was that Mr. Sigurdsson—the detective or security expert or whatever he was—had not given her a definite no. He'd told her that he would look into the matter and get back to her ASAP. If he couldn't help her, he might be able to recommend someone who could. As a result, Andrea jumped every time her cell phone rang, but thus far, the only calls, which she'd diverted to her answering machine, had been from Darla and her father, who were equally concerned. Not enough to postpone their annual cruise to the Bahamas, though. Their boat departed from Florida on Friday, day after tomorrow.

"We trust you to take care of this, honey," her father had told her.

Please don't.

"Besides, it's probably the same old crap from Celie," Darla had proclaimed. "Nothing dangerous."

ISIS not dangerous? Yeah, right!

"Let me know how much money you need for travel and expenses. Whatever you need!" her father offered.

Now there's an idea. Open wallet, here I come.

"But not that fifty thousand dollars, for heaven's sake!" Darla quickly amended.

Not so open, then.

"I still say you should go to the FBI about this, Daddy." Andrea had told her father this earlier, although even Mr. Sigurdsson had been skeptical about involving the "feds." Apparently, Americans sneaking off to join one terrorist group or another was becoming epidemic. Too much for Uncle Sam to handle individual cases. And many of the times the kids had second thoughts before they even got to Syria or whatever foreign country was being used as an ISIS conduit at the time.

"No, no, no! I have clients who would run at the first hint that my family has any ties to terrorists. Even if it's not true."

"Definitely not! The publicity would kill your father."

"Now, darling, you know it's not about me," her father had cooed to Darla.

"Of course it is, sugar doll. Kiss, kiss."

Gag me with a pastry brush.

Andrea sighed deeply and turned back to the

living room, tidying some gourmet cooking magazines on the Louis Seymour coffee table she'd found in a thrift shop. She loved this condo she'd purchased two years ago in the old Concorde building, and not just because of the twelfth-floor view from the floor-to-ceiling wall of arched windows on one side of the living room. She loved the open concept in which the living room, dining area, and kitchen were all one big room, with a comfortable separate bedroom and bathroom. She loved the vintage decorative elements the developers had managed to salvage, like crown molding and random plank, golden oak flooring and built-in cabinets. She loved each furnishing in the unit that she had picked out with care, usually from a flea market or used furniture store. The result was a comfortable, albeit small, living space that was all hers.

She decided to make herself a cup of decaffeinated ginger chai before calling it a day. A nook on the back side of the condo, overlooking a rather sad garden quad down below, contained a desk, her reading glasses, a laptop, and a stack of notes for *Dessert on a Dime*, a cookbook proposal Andrea should be working on, but not tonight with her lack of concentration. She couldn't stay up all evening in hopes Mr. Sigurdsson would call, either. Once the tea steeped, she poured it with a dollop of honey into a Limoges china cup decorated with tiny roses, another thrift shop purchase. She added a few chocolate-dipped madeleines to the saucer and was about to go into her bedroom and watch an episode of *Game of Thrones* on Netflix when she saw that she had company.

"Eeeek!" With a shriek of alarm, she almost dropped the tea and cookies. Just in time, she caught herself, and set the cup and saucer on the granite bar that separated the kitchen from the rest of the unit.

Cnut Sigurdsson was sitting on one of her low couches, his long legs propped on her precious coffee table, skimming one of the food mags.

"What are you doing here?" she yelled.

"Uh. You hired me."

"I did? I mean, you couldn't call?"

"When I decide to do something, I like to get it done. Right away."

"How did you get in here?" she asked, now that her racing heart had slowed down to mere jogging speed.

"I knocked, but you didn't answer. So I just came in."

"The door was locked."

"Was it?"

She knew it had been. Living single in a city, she was diligent about always locking the door after herself. In fact, glancing to the left, she saw that the dead bolt was still in place. She would definitely address this issue later. "Do you have news?"

"Mayhap."

"Mayhap? What kind of word is *mayhap*?" she grumbled, her heart still racing from the shock of finding a stranger in her apartment.

"Old Norse. I did mention I'm a Viking, didn't I?"

Definitely a Viking! He wore the same black jeans and athletic shoes as earlier today, but on top he'd changed from the dress shirt to a white, long-sleeved T-shirt with the logo "Crab Claw" down one sleeve. Despite the modern clothing, there was no downplaying his immense height, his killer body, his sharply defined Nordic features, or that disconcerting, hot-damn-I-am-a-Viking hairdo. He looked as if he'd be just as comfortable on a motorcycle, like the one that had been parked outside his agency, as he would on a longship. *As if any of that matters!* she chastised herself.

"Great view!" he said, motioning toward the windows. "I love boats."

"No kidding!" At his arched brows, she added, "I am Viking, see me row."

His brows arched even more, this time in confusion.

"Boats, Vikings, longships, rowing," she explained.

Finally, his forehead unfurrowed and he nodded. "You were making a jest."

She almost said, *No kidding!* again, but bit her tongue. She didn't know why she was being so rude to the man, especially when she needed his help. He rattled her, that's why, she decided. And she didn't often get rattled by men.

She picked up her tea and cookies once again and walked toward him. She was decently covered, but the way Cnut stared at her exposed arms and shoulders and upper chest and waist, she felt naked. When he homed in on her leopard-print harem PJs and made a rumbling, big cat sound—a deep masculine purr that acted like a tuning fork to instantly humming hormones—she lifted her chin and tried for nonchalance. Sitting down carefully on the low matching couch that faced him, she set down her cup and saucer and said, "What? You have a thing against leopards?"

"On the contrary. At the moment I have a particular fondness for big cats."

Was he flirting with her?

No, that frown back on his face clearly spelled disapproval, or disgust, or something. "Don't tell me this time that you haven't been soaking yourself in coconut and vanilla? You reek of a sweet dessert, even more than this afternoon."

"Reek?"

He blushed. The big guy actually blushed. "Well, *reek* is mayhap not the right word. You exude sweetness, m'lady."

M'lady? First mayhap, *now* m'lady. *What next?* Forsooth *and* 'tis *and* 'twas? "And you have a thing against sweetness?"

"Hah! I have a sweet fang like you would not believe."

"Did you say *fang*?"

The blush on his face deepened. "Of course not. I said sweet tooth." He pressed his lips together, but not before she noticed that his two lateral incisors, or canine teeth, were, in fact, slightly elongated. He was probably embarrassed about his dental imperfections.

"You have news?" she said then.

He nodded. "Circle of Light is a hundred-thousand-acre property outside Bozeman. The Circle Z was a working ranch in the beginning. Then, when the cattle market crashed fifty years ago, it became what is known as a dude ranch. A dude ranch is geared more toward tourism than ranch business, relying on guests who pay for such activities as horseback riding, target shooting, hiking, camping, hayrides, whatever those are, and sing-alongs, for cloud's sake! Plus whitewater rafting and—"

"I know what a dude ranch is," she snapped.

"You have been to a dude ranch?" he asked, with surprise.

"No, but I've watched the *City Slickers* movies." It was her turn to blush.

He rolled his eyes. "Anyhow, the Circle Z was sold in 2010 to a group of foreign investors who turned it into Circle of Light. Supposedly still a dude ranch experience, along with a bunch of transcendental crap, like meditation, extreme yoga, and something called nature immersion therapy. But that's just a front. In essence, the ranch lures troubled teens and young adults as a safe refuge where they can work as housekeeping staff, riding and fishing instructors, and so on, all the while being groomed and indoctrinated, first in basic Islamic religious tenets, but then into the extremist ISIS philosophy. From there, they move on to Syria or Pakistan or Afghanistan, where they get further training in the Sharia lifestyle, including weaponry and battle strategy. As a result, most of the staff is constantly changing."

"Is Celie still there?"

"I don't know. They're very secretive. Even the guests are screened heavily. The only way to infiltrate the compound is through a guest reservation or as a recruit, both of which would be difficult."

"Hmm. I'm a quick learner. I could bone up

on Islam enough to appear as if I have an interest. Should we apply for jobs or pretend to be city slickers? Which would be quicker?"

"There is no 'we.' If I take on this mission, it will be me alone, or possibly some of my vang—my employees. It's too dangerous for you to engage with these sword-happy terrorists. They would as soon lop off a head as negotiate."

"No, no, no. *If* I hire you for this mission, I'll be with you every step of the way. It's my sister whose head is in question, and—"

"Not just your sister's head. If you poke your pretty little head in the wrong place, yours will roll, too."

She gulped at that image, and didn't even bother to react to his dubious reference to her as pretty. It was probably just a throwaway cliché, anyway. Men like him were attracted to *Sports Illustrated* swimsuit model types, not skinny nerdy girls with a white thumb. "Celie is *my* responsibility. She always has been. Besides, my sister is so stubborn, she probably wouldn't leave without me there to kick her butt. Even if she's scared to death, as she appeared to be in that video. Besides, no offense, but you're a stranger and darn intimidating in appearance." When she saw his jaw clench, she went on, "I could apply for a position as a cook. Any kind of cook, really. Not just desserts. I know some basic yoga, but I'm hardly qualified to teach, unless their standards are really low. And, of course, I could clean rooms, if necessary. How about you? Can you do maintenance work, carpentry? Push a mop? Rake stalls? Can you even ride a horse, for heaven's sake?"

"I built a longship one time," he told her stiffly, "and, yes, I can ride a horse, though I much prefer a car or motorcycle. Can *you* ride?"

"A little," she said, though it had been fifteen years since she'd gone to the summer camp where there had been trail riding. She'd had blisters on her rump for a month. Not her cup of tea.

Speaking of tea, rather *thinking* of tea, she reached for the cup in front of her and sipped at the now lukewarm beverage. At the same time, Cnut reached for one of the scalloped shell cookies, popped it in his mouth, and chewed, his eyes widening in appreciation at the delicious flavor.

"Help yourself," she started to say, belatedly, but he'd already grabbed the last two madeleines and consumed them with eyes closed in delight. She did make superior madeleines, the touch of hazelnut butter and orange substitution for lemon making all the difference.

"Are you hungry?" she asked.

"I am always hungry," he replied.

Is there a double entendre there? Is he implying that . . . no, this guy is just too sizzling hot. His hotness is giving me wrong ideas. Very wrong. Look at him, licking the chocolate off his fingers. Be still my heart . . . and other places. Yikes! "I have some restaurant leftovers I can warm up," she offered, not at all surprised that her voice sounded so husky.

He shook his head.

"You don't know what you're missing. Today's special was Peking duck."

He blinked at her several times, then burst out with laughter.

"What? What's so funny?"

"I can't stop thinking about ducks, lately, and you just mentioned ducks." He shrugged.

"Well, then, you should like my leftovers. It's made with plum truffle sauce. Our sous chef's specialty."

He waved a hand dismissively. "I meant that I've been absorbed with ducks, in general. It's an inside jest with me and my brothers."

"You have brothers?" *Good Lord! What has that to do with anything? My brain is melting here. With lust overload.*

"Six of them."

"Wow!" *They must rock a room when they're all together. If they look like him.*

"That about sums them up, in their own inflated opinions."

"Do they work with you?"

"Sometimes. Uh, are you sick?"

"Huh?"

"You were fanning your face. Do you have a fever or something?"

Oh yeah, I got fever all right. No, no, no! I do not behave like this. It's demeaning. Next I'll be wolf-whistling at construction workers. Time to put the brakes on this runaway train of steaming hormones. "If you don't know if Celie is at the ranch, what's the news you referred to when I first asked?"

"Well, I can trace her exact whereabouts for the weeks leading up to May 15 when she first entered the compound with Kahlil Ajam. In fact, I can tell you a lot about Ajam, and none of it's good. I can tell you about young people, mostly American teens, who entered Circle of Light and never went home again. I can tell you that most of them are now either dead or fighting for ISIS on the other side of the world. Worse yet, maybe being planted in sites around the United States for potential missions."

"But how can they get away with this? To be so subversive in an open way in the middle of 'enemy' territory?"

"This is the land of the free. Terrorists love your country's political correctness."

"Isn't this your country, too?"

She could tell that she'd caught him in a slip of tongue. "It is now," he said.

"Where are you from?"

"Many places," he said.

Talk about evasive! She exhaled whooshily with exasperation. "Where is your home? Where did you grow up?"

"You could say my home is Transylvania," he answered hesitantly.

She tossed her hands in the air in a so-there! fashion. "You're from Romania? Holy cannoli!"

"Not that Romania. Transylvania, Pennsylvania. Can we get back to the subject of your sister and the ranch?"

She could tell he didn't like talking about himself. Big fat hairy deal! "I've heard of that town. The *Inquirer* did a Sunday feature on the loony-tunes vampire activities up there. There's even a Dracula-type castle there that . . ." At the expression of horror on his face, she realized that she'd inadvertently hit on something important. "Oh my God! Your home is that castle."

"Well . . ." His face couldn't get any redder. With nervousness, he reached for one of the Hershey's Kisses sitting in a small, cut-glass bowl, unwrapped it, and popped it in his mouth, and was already reaching for another before he'd even started chewing. The foil-wrapped chocolates were made in a factory less than two hours from here. She used lots of them in her cooking, or for just plain melt-in-your-mouth deliciousness.

"Are you royalty, or something?"

He choked on his chocolate. "What in bloody hell would give you that idea?"

"A castle. A town fixated on vampires. Count Dracula. A natural conclusion." *Or not.*

"Oh. I see. Well, hardly a royal. I am a Viking, as I already told you. A plain old Viking. Though I was a jarl in the Norselands at one time. That was comparable to a Saxon earl."

She'd only been teasing. Jeesh! A jar-earl? In the Norselands? Where the hell was that? Somewhere in Pennsylvania, near Transylvania? She'd never heard of it, and she'd grown up here. She was about to ask, then caught herself. Enough of this skirting around the issue at hand.

"Do you have a contract for me to sign?"

"No. I'll get your sister back to you, either willingly or unwillingly. Then it will be up to you to get her deprogrammed, if necessary. I can recommend some places."

She nodded. That sounded good. "But shouldn't we have a written agreement? Payment. Time limits. Terms and conditions."

He cocked his head at her. "Terms and conditions?"

"For one thing, I am going with you to Montana."

"You are not going with me."

"I've already notified my employer that I might need to take vacation time soon." Actually, she'd told Sonja nothing, but she wasn't worried. There was an assistant pastry chef who could substitute for her for a few days.

"It should only take a few days, shouldn't it?"

"I would hope so, but you're not going with me."

"When do you want to leave? Today is Wednesday. How about Friday? My parents will have left for their cruise that day. Good timing." She walked to the kitchen while she was talking to him, over her shoulder.

"Good . . . good . . ." he sputtered, getting up and following after her to sit down at a stool in front of the counter. "Your parents are going on a cruise while their daughter is mixed up with a bunch of terrorist wannabes? Never mind. It doesn't matter. You are not going with me."

She plunked the plate of Peking duck pancakes into the microwave, along with sides of candy-striped beet salad, artichokes with mustard aioli, and saffron-scented rice. Then she poured two cone-shaped beer glasses—more thrift shop bargains that she loved—with some cold boutique beers that had been sitting in her fridge since Christmas.

His eyes widened and he seemed to murmur, "Help me, Lord!" when she placed the plate in front of him, along with fresh fruit in an orange curd tart. In fact, he made the sign of the cross and said aloud, "Forgive me, Lord." He closed his eyes, as if in ecstasy as he chewed. "Delicious. Sinfully delicious."

She took that as a compliment, although the entrée wasn't one of her creations. "So, what should I pack? Casual clothes, I would think. Jeans, boots, that kind of thing. Unless we're going as city slicker guests. Even then, I think we would go casual, don't you?"

"You are not going with me," he said.

"Will you make the travel arrangements or should I? Do you need a retainer? My father will pay, but don't go overboard. My stepmother, Darla, will have a fit."

He crossed his eyes, then glared at her. "You are not going with me."

Chapter 5

A MID-FLIGHT CARRY-ON SNACK

Chopped chicken breast salad with crisp green grapes, walnuts, and apples, topped with cranberry orange relish and arugula, served on a croissant
Penn State cheddar cheese with sesame crackers and Gala apple slices
Greek pomegranate yogurt
Easy-peel baby clementines
Apricot pecan nut rolls

The Lone Viking and his sidekick, to the rescue . . .

She was going with him.

Damn, damn, damn.

Shit, shit, shit.

Coconut. Vanilla. Coconut. Vanilla.

Madness, madness, madness.

Cnut wasn't sure how it had happened. A combination of cajolery, threats, smiles, frowns, tears, swoon-worthy Peking duck, and general coconut-vanilla intoxication, he supposed. In other words, no excuse. It was a bad, bad idea to have a woman along on a vangel mission, a human woman, that was. Especially one who was so scared, she practically wet her pants every other minute, including now, as they waited for takeoff of their Delta flight to Bozeman from the Philadelphia International runway.

And it wasn't just fear of flying that had the wench alternately wringing her hands and popping Dramamine tablets. She was belatedly realizing how dangerous this little adventure into ISIS Lackwit Land would be. "Maybe all those beheadings were just photoshopped," she proffered hopefully.

Yeah, and the moon is made of white chocolate fudge and the stars are just sugar sprinkles.

Then, too, she was afraid of horses. "Do I really have to ride a horse? All that bouncing can't be good for a person's insides. Besides, I'll probably be having my period."

I wouldn't touch that one with a ten-foot longboat oar. So much for her riding experience!

She was also scared spitless by spiders: "All those hairy legs!"

Hah! She should see the legs of some Vikings I knew. Thicker than kudzu. Luckily, mine are blond and not so noticeable. Much.

Horror movies: "C'mon, even you have to admit Freddy Krueger is creepy."

Freddy who?

High diving boards: "Do I look like I have a death wish?"

Yes!

And Ouija boards: "I didn't talk to Grandma

Stewart when she was alive. Why would I want to talk to the old bat when she's dead?"

"That, I can understand. My paternal grandsire had so much lice in his beard, it moved, and he smelled like gammelost all the time. Legend said that the stinksome cheese was served to ancient Viking warriors before battle to turn them berserk."

She blinked at him as if he was rather odd. He could only imagine how she would react if she saw him in full vangel mode—elongated fangs, bloody sword, and mists of blue wings rising out of his shoulders. Or Lucipires! Holy clouds! Lucies scared him, too, when they morphed into demonoid form, all mung-oozing scales, claws, tails, red eyes, and fangs. She would probably have a heart attack or be scarred mentally for life.

He had to give her credit, though. The girl faced her fears and barreled on, teeth chattering but chin raised pugnaciously. That was real bravery. Or stupidity.

Andrea sat next to the window, and he on the aisle, of the first-class accommodations. They'd argued about that, too—"the unnecessary expense"—along with fifty other things about this trip, but there was no way his long legs would fit into economy class.

"Prepare for takeoff," the pilot said over the intercom system.

Buckled in, the passengers braced themselves. Some more than others. Cnut glanced Andrea's way, then did a double take. Her white-knuckled fists clutched the armrests, her eyes were wide and unblinking, shivers rippled over her body. A small keening whimper escaped her parted lips.

This he could understand. Flying high above the earth was unnatural to man, and the first time he'd done it (in an airplane; he'd yet to receive real angel wings), Cnut had felt as frightened as Andrea was now. In fact, he'd clutched an armrest so tightly, the wood had cracked.

Cnut did the only thing he could to distract Andrea.

He kissed her.

Well, it wasn't the only thing he could think of. But the only thing that wouldn't get him arrested.

So, he kissed her.

No big Viking deal, right?

Wrong!

Cnut felt as if he'd fallen off the highest cliff. First, there was the shock, lips touching lips, then the incredible sense of floating through the air like a feather on an erotic wind current, as she breathed into his mouth, and he breathed back.

With one of his arms behind her back, he used the other hand to cup her cheek and turn her more directly toward him. Her face rested on his shoulder, and she surrendered with a sigh. Another exchange of breath as he shaped her lips to his and deepened the kiss.

Then he surrendered, too.

He knew about surrender. Hah! All his life, his former life, had been about surrender. To hunger. To thirst. To fornication. To gluttony in all his excesses. But this was different. This was surrender "of" not "to." Of himself. Not to some temptation.

And that made as much sense to him as practically devouring a woman in a public place. His peripheral senses, which had been on temporary shutdown, heard a giggle from the seat behind them, and a snicker from across the aisle. Slowly, he eased his mouth off hers, still cradling her face in one big hand.

She stared at him, dazed, but no longer with fear. Her brown eyes glistened like gold, her kiss-swollen lips parted as she breathed heavily, wisps of her blonde hair fluttered about her face. She wasn't pretty, exactly, but she was more attractive, to him, than any woman he'd met in more than a thousand years.

"You smell like peppermint," she said breathily.

He let out a hoot of laughter and moved his hand off her face, reluctantly. He also eased his other arm from around her shoulder. "That's me. A big old Peppermint Pattie."

"Or a peppermint stick."

"And you smell like coconut. That's some combination. Cocomint. Or peppernut." He was trying for jest to lighten this amazing cloud of sensuality that seemed to cocoon them.

But she took him seriously and said, "Hey, don't knock it. I bought a scented candle one time that was just that. Coconut mints."

What a ridiculous conversation! Even more ridiculous, why am I grinning like a halfbrained youthling with his first cockstand? "Well, at least you're no longer shivering like a cat in a dog kennel."

Her shoulders slumped at his flippant words, and she glanced quickly out the windows, just now realizing that they were airborne. Her cheeks bloomed with embarrassment. She had to think he'd only kissed her to distract her from airlift jitters. Which he had. At the beginning.

The flight attendant took their drink orders—a light beer for him and cranberry juice for Andrea. "Are you sure you don't want a glass of wine?" he suggested. Anything to relax her.

She made a face of distaste. "The wine they serve on airlines might as well come in screw-top bottles."

"A wine snob?"

She seemed surprised at his question, but then shrugged. "Probably. I lived in France for a while when attending cooking school. The French claim to make the absolute best wines in the world. Even the working class there appreciates a good vintage. I'm not sure that's true anymore, about French wines being superior. There's so much competition today, including American vintages."

"The Franks always did consider themselves superior beings. No surprise then that they self-proclaim themselves the kings of grape. Personally, I am more a beer guy. All Vikings are, having been practically weaned on the sweet mead of our culture."

She blinked several times at his seemingly irrelevant comment. "Okay, yes, I am a wine snob," she conceded, "but I feel the same way about food, in general. Garbage in, garbage out. Quality ingredients, quality product."

He put up his hands in mock surrender. He'd meant to distract her, not get a lecture.

She caught the frown on his face and apologized. "I get carried away on the subject. It's a sore point with me. We're a nation of processed food addicts. Quick and cheap wins over fresh and homemade every time."

"I don't disagree with you. I love good food." All food, actually, but his taste buds had become more refined over the years.

No surprise then that when the attendant came to take their order for lunch, beef Wellington or chicken Cordon Bleu, Andrea declined both and said she'd packed her own meal. He sat eating the red meat encased in a flaky crust with small potatoes, and it wasn't half bad, but he had to admit the sandwich she'd pulled from a soft-sided freezer bag under her seat looked more tempting. Noticing his stare, she pulled out a second plastic-wrapped sandwich and handed it to him. It was delicious, and he moaned his appreciation. Chicken salad on a crisp croissant, but not just chicken and the dressing; there were other crunchy things in it besides the usual celery and onion. Grapes, walnuts, and apples. And covering it all was some kind of sweet-sour relish, a combination of cranberries and oranges, maybe. The lettuce on top was coarse-chopped and bitter, but not unpleasantly so. Arugula, he guessed, from his TV food show gleanings.

She also handed him several clear bags, one with slices of hard yellow cheese, seeded crackers, and thin slivers of crisp apples. In addition, there were tiny, easy-to-peel oranges; crunchy red grapes; yogurt with pomegranates; and apricot-filled nut rolls.

A gourmet meal, he recognized, even in its simplicity. And he ate every sumptuous bit of it.

Was that a sign of his continuing gluttony, or

just an indication of his refined taste buds? He knew which one Mike would choose.

"How do you stay so slim? Eating this kind of fare every day? All day, I assume, since you must taste what you make."

"Genes."

"I would gorge myself on this kind of food and blow up like a grotesque balloon."

"Oh, I doubt that. I'm sure you get enough exercise to burn up the calories." She sized him up in a way that made him glad he was half his former size.

"I once weighed more than four hundred pounds," he blurted out, though he had never actually weighed himself back then, of course, nor would the term *pound* have been used as a measurement. It was a guesstimate. He could have said, *I once weighed as much as a small longboat*. Or, *I once weighed as much as a large, wild boar.* That would have just raised questions he was not prepared to answer, like how much exposure had he had to longboats, and how did he know anything about wild boars?

But where his sudden disclosure had come from, he had no idea. He never discussed his past life of gluttony. The only ones who knew of his shameful former self were his brothers, who loved to needle him on occasion. Usually, he ignored their jests. Betimes, he gave them a bloody nose or blackened eye, if they persisted too long.

"Really? Well, you are tall."

"Not that tall. Six foot four."

"You were obese?"

"Fat."

She gazed at him in disbelief, giving him another of those full-body surveys that warmed him in places that should not be warm in a public setting.

He nodded. "I was a glutton." *I am a glutton.* He noticed then that he'd eaten not only his airline meal, but his Andrea-packed lunch and half of hers as well. He felt his face heat and he turned away, berating himself, *Glutton, glutton, glutton!*

Sensing his dismay, she patted his hand. "Hey, don't beat yourself up. It's okay to overindulge once in a while. Besides, we'll be getting plenty of exercise on the ranch."

That's what he was afraid of.

The attendant took away their meal debris, then asked Cnut, "Can I do anything else for you, Mr. Jackson?" The message was clear, an invitation, and did not include Mrs. Jackson, at his side. He and Andrea were pretending to be Curt and Andrea Jackson, and they had valid paperwork to document their identities, thanks to Michael's angelic network. They were on the way to a dude ranch in Montana for a vacation.

"No, thank you."

When she left, Andrea raised her brows at him, "That was a bit brazen. Does it happen to you a lot?"

He shrugged. "She probably thought you were my sister."

"Yeah, right. Must get tiresome."

She was teasing, or so he surmised. Despite centuries of having lost his repulsive fat, he still thought of himself as unattractive. He was, inside. "Very," he agreed with what he hoped was a tone of sarcasm . . . and finality. Enough on that subject. "How did you get interested in cooking?"

"Necessity. At first. I was an only child the first ten years of my life. My mother kept having miscarriages every other year until she had Celie. Then, after Celie's birth, she got cancer. For three years, between chemo and radiation, remission and reoccurrence, and finally death, I became the chief caregiver for both my mother and the baby. My dad was a basket case, burying himself in work. Oh, we had help . . . a housekeeper/nurse/cook, but somehow I became the anchor of the family. I was the one who took care of the baby, Celie cried for everyone but me. Feeding her, changing her diapers, rocking her. In the beginning my mother helped, especially during the remission periods, but she just got weaker and weaker. And she begged me, before she died, to always take care of Celie. What else could I do?" She shrugged. "Even when my school and my childhood, such as it was, suffered. I never did catch up academically. Barely graduated from high school."

He could see now why she felt such a responsibility for her sister. It was like a blood oath to her dead mother.

"Then, after Mom died when I was fourteen and Celie only four, my dad met Darla, a yoga instructor half his age, and bam, he got married again. Less than a year after he buried Mom. Not that I blame him. Mom was sick for so long, and he was lonely, and . . ." She shrugged again.

And he was a horndog, Cnut concluded, *as most men are when without sexual release. Try being a celi-*

bate vangel! For centuries! "Things were better for you then? Once you got a new mother?"

"Hah! You haven't met Darla." She rolled her eyes. "To give her credit, Darla tried, but Celie and I had been on our own too long by then, and we would have resisted any new woman in the house. We made her life miserable, and she wasn't the maternal type to begin with."

"So, you continued being the 'little mother'?"

She nodded. "To this day."

"That doesn't explain the cooking interest."

"Oh, right. Anyhow, my mother was a really good cook, and a gardener, too. She had the neatest little vegetable and herb garden out back. A raised bed that Daddy built especially for her. Darla had it plowed and paved over with flagstones for an extended patio when she moved in.

"While my mother was healthy, she grew the best heirloom tomatoes, and string beans, and beets, and a variety of lettuces, and incredible white icicle radishes. Nothing in the world will ever rival her fresh tomato sandwiches. We even ate radish sandwiches with only salt and pepper on buttered white bread. Yum!" She sighed. "The smell of basil and rosemary and dill always remind me of her. Someday I'd like to have a house where I can have my own garden." She sighed again, deeply, then continued. "Mom always seemed to have an apron on, and she was always teaching me things in the kitchen. Simple cooking but wonderful dishes, using fresh ingredients, with high-quality utensils. My memories of her will always be associated with the kitchen, not with the sickroom which became her prison later on. When I have that little house I mentioned, the kitchen is going to be fabulous, the heart of the home. Nothing fancy . . . no stainless steel, institutional look. More soft colors, butcher block, farm-like." She glanced at him and seemed to realize how much she'd revealed with her ramble. "Sorry, but you did ask."

He waved a hand to dismiss the need for apology. He was intrigued by the mind picture she painted. "Like Ree Drummond's kitchen."

"Exactly, except not so big." Her brow furrowed as she turned to look at him more directly. "You watch *The Pioneer Wife*?"

His face heated but he told her, "Hah! I watch all the cooking shows when I am between missions. My brothers much prefer war movies or shows like *The Walking Dead*, but I prefer Food Network."

"Lots of people find them soothing. Comfort food in troubled times."

Exactly, though his brothers thought they were not manly subject matter for a Viking warrior. It pleased him that she understood. Sort of.

"Do you like to cook?" she asked.

"Holy clouds, no!"

She laughed. "Typical man!"

He wished! "So, why are you not married and living in such a dream home? I mean, I assume you are not wed." He stared pointedly at her ringless fingers.

"What makes you think I need to be married to have my own home? I'll have you know, I own the condo I'm living in now."

"I forgot. Women in this ti—uh . . . country are independent of men. You are not . . . um . . . are you?" Surely his Viking radar was not so far off that he would not recognize that kind of woman. But then, women had been fooling men since the beginning of time. Take that wily Eve, for example. Got Adam in a hell of a lot of trouble.

She laughed. "No, I'm not gay. And before you ask, I am not, nor have I ever been married."

"Why not? Are you opposed to marriage?"

"Not at all. I hope to marry someday and have children, hopefully three."

That rules me out. "Should you not get started soon then before—"

She swatted him on the arm. "Don't you dare mention my age. I am not too old for children. Not for another ten years, at least."

That was a stretch, in his opinion, but dumb as men were purported to be, even he knew not to mention that fact.

"How about you?" She glanced at his fingers, which were also ringless, which meant nothing, of course. Men did not wear wedding rings in his time, and in fact many men didn't do so today, either, for obvious reasons.

"Never wed. No desire to. Same goes for children." Enough on that subject!

Of course it wasn't.

"Why not? A guy who looks like you must have to beat women off with a stick."

"I told you afore, I did not always look like this."

"How long ago was that?"

"A long time." A very long time!

"Well, how about today? No significant other?"

"No." *The only significant other in my life is an archangel with an attitude who has thrown me into the duck pond.* He took a flight magazine from the seat pocket in front of him, a silent signal to her that he was done talking.

"Sorry. I didn't mean to ruffle your feathers." She put her hand on his, which was resting on the armrest between them.

For his sins, he turned said hand so that they were palm to palm. In fact, he twined their fingers together and said, "Ruffle away."

Chapter 6

COCKTAILS & NIBBLES AT HORROR CASTLE

Deviled eggs and deviled tongue (from fertile females)

Wicked wings soaked in diablo sauce
Blood fondue with toast points
Black Mass caviar on small blinis with crème fraîche
Lucifer's Loin Chops (mini lamb lollipops)

Bite-size devil's food cupcakes
Crispy lady fingers
Designer marshmallows toasted over hellfire
Satan's Whiskers Rambutan, the hairy fruit (beware of occasional maggot)

Bloody Marys (with thanks to Lucipires-to-be Mary Higgins, Lady Mary Ethridge, and Mary Contraire)
Hooch from Hell
Beelzebub's Beard Punch (it will put hair on your chest, if not your chin)
Devil Juice (nonalcoholic but sinfully good)

Yippee-ki-yay, get along little dogies, uh, demons . . .

John Wayne was walking down the hallway of Horror Castle in the remote icy mountains of northern Scandinavia, beyond Svalband, presumably an uninhabited area too cold for humans to withstand. That was the very feature that appealed to demons. Spend a minute in Hell and you develop an appreciation for ice. A lack of neighbors was also an asset. He could only imagine what would happen if someone knocked on the door to borrow a cup of sugar and was confronted with a Lucipire. The scream would be heard 'round the world.

The spurs on his cowboy boots jingled as he strutted his long, tall *Rio Bravo* self, complete with chaps, hip holster holding a pair of Colt pistols, and the traditional Stetson Silver Belly hat. He even walked a little bowlegged, *from all that horse riding, dontcha know?* he joked to himself. *Or another kind of riding.*

Bloody hell, but it's great to be me, thought Jasper, king of all the demon vampires. Not John Wayne, of course, but a good facsimile Jasper had chosen of the Old West king for a new Lucipire mission he was contemplating. Usually, Lucipires were huge creatures with scaly skin and claws and fangs and red eyes, not to mention a long tail, but they could transform their bodies into any outward appearance they wanted, including humanoid ones. Thus, his choice of John Wayne this time.

"Are you still sulking that I didn't choose the

Lone Ranger and Tonto?" he asked Beltane, his French hordling assistant who skipped every other step to keep up with Jasper's long strides. There were many classes of Lucipires, the highest being Seraphim haakai demons, like himself, who had formerly been archangels eons ago, followed by the high haakai, then mungs, hordlings, and Satan's foot soldiers, the imps.

"I never sulk, master," Beltane replied with affront. His longtime assistant was relatively young for a Lucipire, having been taken from the 1700s Vieux Carre in New Orleans, compared to himself and some others who had been around for thousands of years.

"I know, I know," he said, patting Beltane on his scaly arm. "I was just teasing. I did try, though, I want you to know that, but the mask wouldn't fit over my bulgy eyes."

Jasper was on his way to the council chamber of his castle for a meeting with his high commanders. Important business would be negotiated this day, and not just about the new mission. He intended to surprise a few of his lieutenants, including the loyal Beltane.

Along the way of the Corridor of the Condemned, he took note of the life size killing jars that lined either side. Inside the tall, glass cylinders—his inventions modeled on butterfly killing jars—were newly captured, naked humans, the vilest of sinners—rapists, murderers, terrorists, pedophiles, and the like—in the process of being turned into demon vampires. Some were already in a state of stasis, others still fought against their fate, eyes wild with fright, banging the sides of their containers with bloody fists. Jasper's cold heart lifted with joy at the sight. So much evil! So many new bodies to torture! Life was good!

"Bring me that one later," he told Beltane, pointing to a red-haired wench with cone-shaped breasts and a bald pubic mound. No more than twenty, the girl had given a heroin overdose to a ten-year-old boy, just to amuse herself and a drug-addict lover. The lover was here somewhere, too. The boy was in a coma in a London hospital.

"Good choice. She still has some fight in her. I know you like them unwilling."

"For a certainty," Jasper agreed.

"I must warn you," Beltane said, hesitantly, as if fearful of Jasper's reaction, "Heinrich is here already, and he has a particularly gloating expression on his face."

"I know," Jasper said, gritting his teeth, not an easy task with fangs that were extended somewhat, even when retracted. "But he will not be gloating for long, if I have my way."

Heinrich Mann was a former Nazi general who, unfortunately, had a direct line to Satan's ear. He was an arrogant, anal, annoying bastard who was constantly name dropping, as in "Luce told me . . ." or "When I was sharing a fireball with Luce . . ." or "Luce and I were just thinking . . ." or "While jogging with Luce last night . . ." Luce was Heinrich's nickname for Lucifer.

The Nazi asshole was so full of it. Everyone knew demons did not jog. Tails and all that. Even in humanoid form. Jasper knew because he'd tried it one time, and all that jarring caused his fangs to keep hitting his bottom lip. There was so much blood dripping from his mouth, a passerby called 911.

On the other hand, he wasn't about to call Heinrich a liar. Not outright, leastways. 'Twas best not to offend the man too much because he reported every little thing back to the Big Guy. A snitch who carried around a rubber stamp of a swastika—*can you believe it?*—which he used on every paper he touched—*probably had it imprinted on his toilet paper.* You'd think he invented the thing.

Heinrich was a mere mung, with aspirations to be on the Lucipire High Council. No doubt, he wanted Jasper's job eventually. While Jasper usually chose his top commanders from the upper ranks of the haakai, he knew that Satan wanted Heinrich to be given a position of authority as a reward for some evil or other. Probably the Holocaust, which demons preferred to call the Holycause. Talk about evil!

Jasper had put this favor off for too long, and now Satan's wish regarding Heinrich was sounding more like a command. Jasper knew of Satan's wish because his boss sent him an e-mail last week. *Yes, an e-mail from Hell! Don't ask. Suffice it to say, if you get an e-mail from Lucifer@hades.com, you better answer.* That didn't mean Jasper couldn't do the devil's will and at the same time get some satisfaction in doing things his own way. *Surprise, surprise, Heinrich!* Jasper chortled to himself.

Beltane rushed forward to open the double doors of the conference room for him. "Ah, everyone is here," Jasper said to Beltane. "And I can see that you prepared a fine repast for our guests."

Beltane beamed. "Yes, even the Russian caviar you wanted."

"Good, good!"

There was a large U-shaped table in the room with name plates arranged at various places. At the end of the room, a buffet table had been set up in front of a windowed wall that gave a panoramic view of the bleak, icy mountains. About fifteen Lucipires stood about, conversing among themselves as they ate and drank. All of them had received personal invitations. They were in humanoid form today, these haakai, mungs, and hordlings, dressed in the finest designer clothing, out of respect for Jasper. Everyone knew he set high standards for his minions and was displeased when they appeared before him in sloppy attire. Even Zebulan the Hebrew, one of his favorite council members, wore a dark brown Hugo Boss suit over a pure white, silk T-shirt, instead of his usual denim braies and Blue Devils cap.

There were also a half-dozen newly turned Lucipires walking about to serve the needs of the visitors—young, naked, nubile men and women with studded collars on their necks and weighted rings hanging from pierced nipples and nether regions. As a special treat for his guests, Jasper had ordered that these young demon vampires be force-fed just one specific fruit for weeks, and now when his guests sampled their blood, they would get hints of pineapples, strawberries, oranges, mangos, pears, watermelon, and so on. If they took a swig of vodka or whiskey first, it would like having a fresh fruit cocktail. *Ingenious!* he complimented himself.

They all turned as one to stare at him before bowing their heads in deference. Zeb was the only one who dared speak his mind, "Planning to ride broncos at a rodeo, Jasper?"

"There's an idea," he commented. "Not for me, though. I think you would look good bouncing your arse on a randy bull."

At the expression of sudden suspicion on Zeb's face, Jasper said, "I have a new mission in mind. Not the rodeo, my friend. But we can discuss that later. Everyone, grab a drink and take your seats. Those who are not council members but invited guests can sit anywhere at the end of the table." He smiled at each of them to let them know he acknowledged their individual presence and was pleased to have them here. It was something he learned from one of his minions who'd written a book called *Secrets of a Successful Leader*. Unfortunately, that particular fellow had failed to follow his own rules and ended up bilking hundreds of people of their life savings and, worst of all, getting caught at it. Well, unfortunate for his human self. Fortunate for the Lucipires.

When Heinrich tried to take the seat next to him at the center of the U-shaped table, Jasper hip-bumped him to indicate a seat off to the right. Instead, he placed Zeb on one side of him and Hector, a former Roman soldier, on the other side. Yakov, the Russian Cossack, was on Hector's other side. "As you know," Jasper said right off, "Zeb and Hector and Yakov are the only members of my High Council left, with the passing of Haroun al Rashid and Dominique Fontaine."

He bowed his head, and the others followed

suit to mark the passing to Hell of their comrades, who had failed as Lucipires and were now doomed to Hell on a permanent basis, though Jasper couldn't think of a single soul who would mourn Dominique's absence. Never had there been a more irritating, repulsive creature, even worse than Heinrich, in Jasper's opinion.

"As a result, the Lucipire command is weakened, and we cannot have that," Jasper continued. "Therefore, we will fill Haroun and Dominique's seats on the council today by transferring current members, and add three new people to the council."

Through his side vision, he could see Heinrich preen, knowing what was coming. Hah! He thought he knew what was coming.

"Hector, you will continue with your base command at Terror." Hector's so-named compound was in the catacombs under the Vatican. "It is always a delight to see you tempt the sinners drawn to the Holy City, even the supposed holy ones. Satan is particularly pleased at the increase of sins among the priesthood. We do not like this new pope and his efforts to clean house, so to speak . . . God's house. So, beware."

Hector nodded, both an acknowledgment of the compliment and agreement to be diligent in the future. Hector had been a Roman general, once assigned to the Colosseum, where he forced Christians to become lion kibble. He liked staying in Rome, even if it was under what had once been the seat of a great empire. In fact, he still wore his military uniform: knee-high belted tunic with sheathed short sword; cross-tied sandals; gauntlets; a red, satin-lined cape; and a bronzed helmet. If Hector had his way, they would be raising man-eating lions and erecting another Colosseum, perhaps here at Horror.

Not going to happen. Not that it wasn't a great idea, but it would be too expensive, and they didn't have any lion keepers among the current batch of Lucipires.

"Moving on. Yakov, your long years of service to Satan and to me are noted and appreciated." Yakov maintained a headquarters named Desolation in Siberia. "Therefore, you are being transferred to Gloom."

That caused Zeb to sit up more alertly. Gloom was Zeb's command in the honeycombed volcanic caves of Greece. He had to wonder what Jasper had planned for him.

"I am sure you will find the climate in Greece much more to your taste," Jasper said to Yakov.

"As you wish," Yakov said with a smile.

"And you, Heinrich." He turned and looked directly at Heinrich. "Our esteemed Lord Lucifer wants to reward you for services well rendered, and I of course agree. You should be given a position on the High Council."

Someone snickered at that last remark. It could be anyone. Everyone knew how much he detested the Nazi, except for the Nazi, who was beaming like a bloody moron.

Not for long.

"And isn't it fortunate that we have the perfect opening. You will take Yakov's place in Siberia." He cast a fangy smile at the Nazi, who didn't seem to understand what he'd just said.

"Huh? What? No."

"No? You no longer wish to be on my High Council?" Jasper asked.

"Yes, of course. I mean, no, not in Siberia. Why not Haroun's old territory, or Germany. Yes, Germany would be good. I could regenerate anti-Semitic sentiments and—"

"Are you questioning my judgment? Already? Keep in mind, you are a mung, Heinrich. This is a great honor I bestow on you. Mayhap you will even rise to the level of haakai someday, if you prove yourself worthy. On the other hand, you do not have to accept."

Realizing his mistake, Heinrich bowed his head. "As you wish, master."

"Good, good," Jasper said. "Yakov can give you some tips before he leaves today."

"Invest in a good pair of long underwear," Yakov said, and everyone laughed with him.

Heinrich was not amused. Already he was pulling out his cell phone on his lap, placing what he thought was a surreptitious text. To Satan, no doubt. To complain. Little did he know that Jasper had commanded one of his geek minions to place a block, or whatever you called it, on Horror for the day so that no communications could go in or out. Jasper would inform Satan of his decisions on his own, thank you very much, Nazi asshole tattletale.

A murmur of low conversation went on around the room as folks discussed among themselves these changes.

"Good call!" Zeb murmured from his right side.

"I know. I can just picture him goose-stepping over the tundra," Jasper whispered back.

"Maybe the ink on his rubber stamp will freeze," Zeb offered.

"We can hope."

"You mentioned three new appointments," Hector reminded him from his other side.

"Ah, yes." Jasper used his anvil to hammer the room to order again. At the same time he made a conscious effort to wipe the smile of satisfaction off his face. It was hard not to smile when Heinrich was obviously miserable. "Now you, Zeb." He felt Zeb stiffen beside him. "With Dominique's passing, we have a huge hole in the United States." Dominique had run her operation from a restaurant named Anguish in the French Quarter of New Orleans. "You will take over the southern half of America, from the East to the West Coast. Virginia to California and Nevada. Lots of sinful cities in that territory. I will leave it up to you to decide where you want to settle. New Orleans would be good, or Las Vegas, but you may have a better idea."

No one questioned Zeb's suitability for that location since he worked so often in the States, in particular California where the Navy SEALs were located. SEALs were a group of elite militants that Jasper yearned to capture. Even one SEAL-turned-Lucipire would be a huge coup.

"As you wish," Zeb said.

"We need another woman on the council. Equal rights and all that," Jasper kidded. He could care less about equal rights, but he did have a good female candidate. "Red Tess will take on the northern part of the United States, from Maine to Washington State, up to and including the Canadian provinces. Stand and introduce yourself, Tess."

Up stood a tall Amazon of a woman with pale green eyes and flaming red hair so bright it hurt the eyes. She was almost six feet tall, even in human form. She wore tight leather braies covered by a belted tunic of finest brushed green wool. Large gold hoop earrings hung from her ears. Wide gold armbands graced her muscled upper arms. She was beautiful, even with the scar that ran from her left eye to her chin, causing her to look like she was smiling lopsidedly, all the time. "Tess was a notorious pirate sailing the Spanish seas three hundred years ago. In her time, she caused many an innocent to walk the plank. How many would you estimate, dear?" he asked her.

"Three hundred," Tess answered.

Everyone clapped in appreciation.

And Tess bowed.

"Zeb will introduce you to your new stomping grounds," Jasper said. "Right, Zeb ?"

"Of course."

"Next, let me introduce you all to Ganbold the Mongol, who served with Genghis Kahn as one of his top lieutenants." A short wiry man with Oriental features and an impressive mustache and goatee stood and bowed, then sat down abruptly in a no-nonsense way. He wore the long, traditional Mongol, robe-like coat of leather armor belted at the waist. Jasper envied its style. Perhaps he would have one made for himself. "We are honored to have Ganbold here with us, along with his scimitar, Blood Maker."

They all looked at the ornate weapon propped against the wall behind Ganbold.

"'Tis said that fifty million foe were killed by the khan's armies, many of them under Ganbold's command," Jasper told the others, then said to the new man, "I particularly like one of your famous tortures that involved pouring molten metal into your captive's eyes and mouth and ears. Perhaps you can teach one of my hordling tormentors how to do that?"

Ganbold just nodded.

Jasper wasn't sure he liked Ganbold's silent demeanor, as if he were too good to join their ranks. Or rather too bad.

"Ganbold will take over Haroun's territory in the Arab lands. An important post, as you all know, with the rise in terrorism. Do you accept, Ganbold?"

"As you wish, master," Ganbold replied.

Right answer, even if the Mongol said it without a smile of pleasure. He should be pleased at such a plum assignment.

"One last action before we move on to new business. I have a promotion to make. Beltane the Creole will become a member of the council, as of today."

His announcement was greeted with silence. Beltane, frozen in place where he stood near the buffet table, gaped at him in stunned disbelief. "I know what you are all thinking. Beltane is a mere hordling, and never has there been a hordling on the council. But then, there has never been a mung, either." He glanced pointedly at Heinrich, who was still futilely tapping away on his cell phone. The idiot! "And I know that Beltane has no warrior skills to speak of. But his loyalty is unquestioned, and he will serve not as a Lucipire operative in the field, but as director of operations, a coordinator of all activities. 'Tis what he does already." He paused. "Any objections?"

There were clearly many, but Heinrich was the only one who spoke up. "Outrageous, that's what it is. It demeans the office of council member."

"Some would say that a mung on the council is demeaning," Hector pointed out.

"Who really cares?" Yakov said. He was still gloating over leaving Siberia.

"As long as Beltane serves no military role, I have no objection," Zeb said.

"Tess and Ganbold?" Jasper inquired.

"As you wish, master," they both said.

"So it is agreed, then," Jasper declared, then smiled at a still-stunned Beltane. "Congratulations, my boy." There were actually tears of gratitude in Beltane's eyes. It was enough to warm a demon's cold, cold heart.

Jasper asked for reports from Zeb, Yakov, and Hector on recent dealings, and Beltane gave an update on kills and turnings during the past year. They now had a thousand full-blown Lucipires and eighty-seven in training. Business was good, despite some losses in Nigeria last year, including the passing of Haroun. Heinrich grudgingly reported that Satan was happy with the proceedings here on Earth.

As if Jasper didn't already know that! It's not as if Satan didn't communicate with him, too. Jasper cleared his throat. "I have a new mission in mind for all of you, as evidenced by my attire today."

"What are you supposed to be? Hopalong Cassidy?" Heinrich asked.

Jasper gritted his teeth and responded, "You date yourself, Heinrich. I am John Wayne. The Duke."

"Of what?" Heinrich scoffed.

"The Old West."

Jasper turned away from the moron before he asked more asinine questions intended to embarrass Jasper, and continued, "As I was saying, my attire should be a clue as to our next mission. Zeb and Tess and I will be working on this particular project in the United States. All others will be working out of your own territories. Same mission, different locales. And it all involves ISIS, that extremist Muslim group that is terrorizing the world, praise be to Satan."

There was a communal "Ah!" of understanding. At least, somewhat. He hadn't yet explained the Old West connection.

Now that he had everyone's attention, he explained. "ISIS is by far the most evil entity in the world today, thanks be to Satan. We already know that the world's population is increasingly more immoral. ISIS banks on that propensity to wickedness and hardly needs to recruit new members. They seek the terrorists out. Especially in the United States but also in Europe and South America, as well, young people are flocking to join in their terrorist groups. Cults, that's what many of them are, conduits to terrorist evil on a massive scale. The Internet makes it all so much easier. Social networking for sin."

"And our role in this?" Zeb asked.

"We are already infiltrating the ISIS ranks. Haroun was actively engaged in those endeavors before his passing. Ganbold will continue with those efforts. We need to harvest some of the worst of the ISIS members, but not so many that our presence will be noticed, or that the organization will be weakened. But in addition, we will grab some of those recruits and new members before they have a chance to repent."

"Why would they repent?" Tess asked. "Most of those foolish young ones engage in the cults willingly. Why would they change their minds and repent?"

"Vangels!" Jasper, Zeb, Hector, and Yakov said as one.

"They are like bloody shadows, those vangels are." Jasper slammed his cowboy hat down on the table in anger. "Wherever we go, they show up behind us, saving sinners before we have a chance to turn them and killing off our best demon vampires. Our numbers would be doubled if not for them."

"And the John Wayne attire?" Zeb prodded him.

"Ah, yes. One of the cults I wish to target is working out of a ranch in Montana. That is where we will start." He looked pointedly at Zeb and Tess.

With perfect timing, Beltane passed out stapled sheets of paper to each of the council members.

"On these handouts you will see a list of fifty of the most important ISIS recruiting headquarters across the world. Starting on July 15, for three days only, we will target those locations. In and out. Shock and awe, as the Navy SEALs say. Right, Zeb?"

"Right."

"We don't all have to wear cowboy gear, do we?" Heinrich asked.

"No, Heinrich," Jasper said, as if speaking to a child. "The operation in Montana is the only one located on a ranch, as far as I know." But then, he added, "there is one using a flamenco dance club in Spain as a front. Do you dance?"

Heinrich's jaw dropped open.

Jasper guessed the answer was no.

"We can discuss the details in depth this afternoon, but in the meantime . . ." He motioned to Beltane, who had the naked boys and girls rush to serve everyone a glass of champagne. When they all had glasses in hand, Jasper raised his and said, "A toast to our new council members."

"Hear, hear!" everyone said, and took a sip.

"And to sin!"

That got even more cheers.

On days like this, Jasper was glad to be on the other side.

Chapter 7

Home, home on the range . . .

Andrea was exhausted but nervously excited when they drove to the ranch the next morning. Hopefully, they would find Celie with little effort and be able to get her out of this beautiful, but scarily remote area. The farther they'd gotten from the city, other than occasional deer or antelopes seen from a distance, and of course cattle, lots of cattle, there were few homes or signs of human habitation. Montana was one of the biggest states but also one of the most sparsely populated.

Luckily, Cnut had insisted on renting some fancy SUV at the Bozeman airport and not the cheaper economy-size sedan. Even in the 4WD vehicle, the three-hour drive north was bumpy at times over the occasional dirt roads and hazardous inclines. No supermarkets. No gas stations. No small towns. Just long stretches of unpaved roads. But beautiful. Oh-my-God-beautiful! No wonder it was called Big Sky Country. With the snow-capped Rocky Mountains as a backdrop, the land stretched out forever, with blue skies visible for many miles in every direction. They even saw buttes, like in old cowboy movies, the flat-topped, steep-sided hills that sprang up seemingly out of nowhere, as if carved from rocks and soil eons ago by a giant with a huge chain saw, but more likely the result of glaciers and erosion. It was like stepping into an Albert Bierstadt landscape painting.

There was hardly any traffic, and thank God for that, because occasionally some of the free-range cattle wandered onto the road, and Cnut had to slow down until they passed.

Cnut was wearing denim jeans and an open denim shirt over a white T-shirt. Scuffed, flat-heeled boots on his feet. *Can anyone say, "Mothers, Don't Let Your Daughters Grow Up to Love Cowboys"?* Except for the absence of a cowboy hat, which he'd refused to buy at the airport, despite her prodding, he fit the ranch scene perfectly. He probably didn't want to mess up his fancy hairdo.

She'd dressed appropriately, too, in a plaid shirt over a T-shirt tucked into her favorite well-worn, True Religion skinny jeans and a pair of gorgeous Old Gringo "Razz" boots in distressed leather with a blue embroidery design she'd bought half price for $215 at Nordstrom's yesterday.

She'd justified the expense by telling herself, *They're not really an extravagance. I can wear them all winter. Yep, overpriced snow boots.*

The T-shirt carried that raunchy country music title on back, which Andrea now had misgivings about and therefore had yet to uncover: "Save a Horse, Ride a Cowboy."

What was I thinking?

And, yes, she'd also bought a white cowgirl hat. Talk about touristy!

To shade my face from the sun. Jeesh, give a girl a break!

Cnut probably thought she looked foolish. He didn't actually say so, though. In fact, she'd caught him checking out her butt this morning. She might be thin and a mite deficient in the breast department, but she had an admirable caboose, and she knew how to work it.

When they entered Spruce Sap Valley, it took another ten miles of dirt road before they approached a sign announcing, "Circle of Light Ranch." Along the way, they began to see high tensile wire fencing enclosing endless pastures and periodic warnings: "No Trespassing!" and "Caution: Electrified Fence."

"You'd think this was a prison compound and not a cattle ranch, or even a dude ranch," she commented. *What has Celie gotten herself into?*

Cnut just grunted, becoming grumpier and grumpier the closer they got to their destination. He seemed increasingly more focused on their surroundings, scanning the horizon with narrowed eyes. "Do you smell something?" he asked.

"No. Just the air freshener." A little cardboard pine tree hung from the radio knob, giving off an artificial spruce scent.

He shook his head. "This is not good," he said enigmatically.

"The smell? I can throw it away."

He shook his head again and continued to scowl.

She was afraid to ask what he was looking for. Surely not some ISIS terrorist lurking behind a tree. This wasn't the Old West where bad guys had smelled from lack of bathing. Heck, even the good guys hadn't bathed very often. Was he thinking ISIS followers had particular B.O. or something? If so, he ought to inform the Navy SEALs. They could probably use that intel to sniff them out. *Sniff. Get it? Ha, ha, ha! Maybe I won't share that thought with him. This time. But, really, his moodiness is irritating.*

Up ahead was the gatehouse to the ranch with a sign warning: "Stop. Identification required before entry."

She dug in her purse for her driver's license. "I didn't know that ranches even had gatehouses."

"They don't, usually." Mr. Tall, Blond, and Silent said nothing more.

Okay.

But then, she noticed that the gatehouse was empty. "There's no one here," she pointed out.

He gave her a no-shit! look.

Someone needs a grumpy pill. "Maybe it's one of those automatic things where a person flashes their ID and the gate opens."

"Must you talk constantly?"

Well, that was rude. "I talk when I'm nervous. I'm worried about my sister," she said. "So sue me."

"I know you're worried. You wouldn't have hired me if you weren't."

"You got that right."

"I told you to stay home."

"Bite me."

"Later."

"Ha, ha, ha! Now you're a comedian."

"I wasn't joking."

She put down her window and leaned out to get a better view. "Phew! I smell it now. Rotten eggs. Must be manure." She immediately put her window back up.

He laughed. "Cow shit doesn't smell like sulfur."

"Well, how would I know? I'm a city girl. What's that puddle of slime over there? Cow puke?"

"You do not want to know." Cnut unbuckled his seat belt and opened the driver's door. "Stay here." He was carrying a pistol in one hand, which she hadn't noticed earlier. Of course, he would carry a weapon. This was a dangerous assignment. She just hadn't thought about the need for weapons beforehand.

Walking over to the small building, he pointedly stepped around the puddle of slime. The door was open, an oddity in itself. Through the window in front, she could see him fiddling with something on the desk. Suddenly, the electric gate swung open, and he came back to the vehicle, got in, and turned on the ignition again.

"Holy freakin' Ponderosa!" she said as they drove up to the lodge a mile or so later. The massive log structure was something straight out of that old TV series *Bonanza*. If long-dead Ben Cartwright—who was a fictional character for cripes' sake!—stepped onto the front porch, she was out of here! "Uh, Cnut," she said tentatively, "have you ever watched reruns of *Bonanza* on TV?"

"A time or two. On the Western Classics Channel. Why?" he replied as he parked the vehicle in the lot on the side of the building, which was discreetly screened with tall hemlocks to preserve the historic image. There were eight or nine other vehicles parked there, mostly pickup trucks and a silver Mercedes with New York plates, but no people about.

"Doesn't this remind you of that TV show?"

"Huh? No. Holy clouds, woman! This isn't the Ponderosa."

"Of course not," she said. "Silly me!"

Realizing that he must have spoken sharply to her, Cnut softened his voice and said, "I'm fairly certain that show was filmed in Nevada. I have a brother who lives in Vegas, and he told me something to that effect one time. In fact, the TV set had been a tourist attraction for many years after the series ended, a theme park or something, until it got torn down."

Logic told her that he was right, but, even so, this giant log house stood in the clearing like a testament to another era. Of prosperous ranching. Cowboys. Big families. American values. The Old West at its best. It saddened her to think that what must have once been a family home was now turned into a dude ranch lodge. Changing economic times, she supposed.

Made of richly grained, golden logs, it appeared to be a two-story dwelling that spread out in two directions, as if it had been added on to several times over the years. And there were lots of outbuildings as well, including a massive barn. She thought she heard the sound of a horse neighing from that direction.

But no people. At all.

"Uh-oh!" she said.

"Tell me about it," Cnut said, opening his door.

"Maybe you better stay here in the car while I check things out. Lock the doors."

"Not a chance," she said, and opened her door as well.

"Stubborn woman!" Cnut muttered.

"Smart woman!" she muttered back.

They walked along the side of the building, around to the front, and onto a long porch where four rustic rocking chairs sat empty. She noticed that Cnut had his handgun out again, which was rather alarming. Also alarming was the front door, which was open.

They stepped hesitantly into a wide central hallway whose only furnishing was a receptionist desk, minus a receptionist, a half-dozen rolled-up prayer rugs, and a long console table under an antique mirror that held a Koran and stacks of touristy kinds of literature. A blackboard display listed activities for the week. Lots of yoga and meditation, indoors in the solar and outdoors, weather permitting. Riding lessons. Koran study. Fly fishing. Holy yoga. Skeet shooting. Mediating with Allah. Roping and horse shoeing. Understanding jihads. Line dancing. Internet recruitment. Campfire sing-alongs. Capitalist devils. An overnight trail ride that coincidentally took place last night into this morning. A Sharia way of life. Coming up on Saturday was a hoedown, whatever that was. Some kind of dance party, she guessed. Yippee! It didn't seem to fit in with all the propaganda-type programs, but maybe that was a way of hiding their true intents here.

Which one of those activities would Celie be involved in? She liked yoga, but for a higher purpose? Line dancing? Yeah, but in a burqa? As for fly fishing, Celie wouldn't even touch an uncooked fish. Too yucky!

All this Andrea took in while Cnut went into a side parlor. There were several parlors, actually, on both sides of the hallway, their main features being comfy low leather couches and huge stone fireplaces. All the furnishings were Old West chic.

Here and there lay puddles of slime, similar to that by the gatehouse.

"It smells like bad farts in here," Andrea said.

"Are there good farts?" Cnut asked with a raised eyebrow. "Don't touch that stuff."

She was leaning down near one gooey pile to see what it was. Her head shot up at the alarm in his voice.

"It's sulfur you smell. You know, fire and brimstone kind of sulfur."

"How do you know that?"

"I just do," he said. "For my sins, I *know*."

"What's going on here? Where is everybody?"

"I don't know for sure, but I have my suspicions."

"What?"

"Shh!" he cautioned, and walked slowly down the hallway.

She followed close behind.

There was a large dining room with an enormous pine table and benches that could seat sixteen, along with several smaller tables and chairs, equally rustic. Half-eaten meals sat on the tables—pancakes and syrup, sausages and bacon, toast, cups of black coffee. No slime here, but there were several piles of clothes, right down to boots and watches and jewelry, as if people had just disappeared right out of their clothing, top to bottom.

Was this one of those clothing-optional places, on top of its ISIS connection? No, that didn't make sense. Of course, none of this made any sense.

"What's going on here?" she asked again. "Where's my sister?"

Cnut didn't answer. Instead, he had pulled out his cell phone and was speaking to someone.

"Vikar? Big trouble on dude ranch."

Tell me about it.

The other person must have been saying something because Cnut paused.

"Who are you talking to?" she asked.

My brother, he mouthed silently to her.

"Your brother! Shouldn't you be calling the police? Or the owners of this place?"

He put a forefinger to his lips and continued his phone conversation.

"We just got here. There's nobody around. Just Lucie slime and sinner harvests."

Huh? What's a Lucy? And a sinner harvest?

"I don't know how many were here to begin with, or how many might be out and about the ranch. Based on the cars in the lot. I'm thinking at least a half-dozen guests, and several dozen employees, not to mention all the recruits. No, I haven't investigated outside yet. Barns and outbuildings. Yeah, send my team here ASAP, and some of yours as well."

More talking from the other end. *So, Cnut has a team, huh? Of what? Detectives? Security guys? Basketball players?*

Cnut was walking while he listened, peering

out the windows, leaving the dining room, taking a quick look into an office where there was slime again, then on to the massive kitchen with its commercial-size gas range and stainless fridge and freezer. It was a dream kitchen to an experienced chef like herself. All high-end appliances and tools.

She went over and turned off several knobs on the range where breakfast had cooked down to a burnt mess—oatmeal turned to concrete and pancakes hard as hubcaps. In front of the stove was another pile of clothing, what appeared to be a long robe, sandals, and an apron. Cnut came up and peered over her shoulder, then continued on his cell phone.

Andrea was beginning to freak out. Whose clothes were they? Celie's? *Oh God! Oh God!*

"Must have happened within the past hour. The leftover food hasn't drawn maggots or flies yet, and the slime hasn't evaporated."

Suddenly Cnut stiffened and said, "Holy shit!" as he looked out of a side window. Quickly, he went to another window and said, "Holy fucking shit! They're coming. Dozens. Gotta get outta here."

She looked outside now, too, and yelped. Huge animals—at least she thought they were animals—were rushing across the pasture, headed this way. And they weren't cows. Not by a bovine long shot. Unless they were the Jurassic kind. From this distance, they did look like scaly prehistoric kind of creatures. Maybe they were cattle of some kind; this was a cattle ranch, after all. Yeah, mad cow–diseased creatures. But cows that ran on two legs?

No. The closer they got, she could see long fangs coming out of their mouths, clawed hands, and red eyes, but even so, they seemed sort of human.

Cnut grabbed her hand and was dragging her back through the hallway toward the front door.

"What are they?"

"Demon vampires," he said, at a run now.

"Oh, that is just great," she said, running to keep up with his wide strides. "You say that as if it's an everyday occurrence. What'd you do at work today, honey? Nothing. Just ran into a few demon vampires. Jeesh, don't go so fast."

"We have to get out of here. Right away."

"No kidding. But we have to find my sister first."

He came to a skidding halt at the front hall. Through the open front door, she could see more of the monsters coming. This was fast becoming a bad horror movie, and she was the star.

"Forget your sister. For now. They're already in the parking lot," he pointed out, glancing toward a window in the second parlor. "Upstairs. Quick."

"I don't understand," she cried, even as she rushed upward. She was halfway up when she turned and saw that Cnut hadn't followed her. Instead, he pulled some kind of weapon out of a back pocket in his jeans, pressed a button, and whoosh, it became a long, thin-bladed sword. A switchblade sword? Holy cow! In the other hand, he had the handgun. And he appeared to have grown big fangs, and his blue eyes had turned an odd silver color. In fact, he made a low growling sound not unlike a wolf, although she'd never actually encountered a live wolf before, and said, "C'mon, make my day!" He was talking to one of the creatures who suddenly appeared on the porch, not her. It must have come from the parking lot. The large band of things was still some distance away. But getting closer.

She almost fainted and had to hold on to the stair rail for support.

Cnut wasn't looking her way. He was concentrating on the lone animal/monster/human thing that was raising its own sword. A bigger, longer one. No matter. Cnut lunged with his weapon, nicking the creature in the arm, then swiping the point across its scaly chest where two breasts burst open like melons. The thing had breasts, for heaven's sake! A female beast, then. *Oh Lord! Oh Lord!* Cnut ducked and swiveled to the side when the creature swung its sword in a wide arc intended to decapitate him. *Can anyone say ISIS?* Then Cnut went in for the kill, literally, running his long, thin spear directly through the heart of the creature.

It was all over within minutes, but felt like hours. The creature was already dissolving into a puddle of slime. Cnut, breathing heavily through fanged teeth, glanced up and saw her standing there, frozen with shock. Was he a creature/monster thing, too? He didn't have the same horrible body, but the fangs . . . yuck!

"You're still here!" He made a sound of disgust at her having disobeyed his order to go upstairs. Through the still open front door, she saw that the other creatures were even closer to the house now, only fifty yards away or so. He slammed the door shut and locked it while she turned, finally obeying his order. She needed to escape, and not just from the creatures outside.

Rushing upward, he picked her up by the waist from behind and took two steps at a time, despite her screeching and kicking. Going into the first bedroom they saw, he set her down and made sure the door was locked, even pushing a dresser in front of it. She heard the splintering of wood downstairs. And voices. The creatures could talk?

"Oh God! Oh God!"

"That's right, sweetling. Pray."

Cnut seemed to be studying the situation, going from one window to another, speaking on his cell phone again.

"A goat fuck for sure. Ha, ha. A cow fuck, then. Very funny. Get serious, Vikar. Send a *hird* of vangels. Right away, dammit."

Did he ask someone—his brother—to send a herd of angels? Cnut was the one who needs to get serious. Meanwhile she was saying an Our Father in her head, but she wasn't asking for God to send her angels, more like a battalion of police.

Cnut paused as he listened.

"You're already on the way. Good. Why didn't you say so? Quack, quack to you, too."

He pocketed his cell phone then and gave her a direct look that scared the spit out of her. His fangs were mostly gone and the eyes were blue again, but still . . .

"Who . . . what are you?"

"A vangel."

"You? An angel?"

"A vangel," he corrected. "I don't have time to explain now."

Maybe she'd gotten knocked on the head and this was some strange afterlife. "Are we dead?"

"I am. You're not. Yet."

"What? Don't come near me, you . . . you . . . thing."

"I'm not going to hurt you, Andrea. I hope to save you, God willing."

"And you have a close connection with the Big Guy, huh? That is just great. You have fangs, by the way." She backed up, hitting the wall.

He retracted the fangs the rest of the way, and now just had two pointy lateral incisors.

"Make me feel better, why don't you?"

He halfway grinned at that. "We can't get out. I could fight off one or two, maybe a half dozen of them. But there are too many."

"I could maybe shoot some if you gave me the gun." *Or maybe I will shoot you, Fang Man.*

"Do you have weapon training?"

"No, but those beasties are so big, how could I miss?" *You make a big target, too, even if you don't weigh four hundred pounds, which was probably a lie, come to think on it now.*

"Beasties?" he choked out. He came up to her then and wrapped his arms around her.

Now? He was going to hit on her now? "Oh no, no, no!" She struggled and tried to push him away, but he was bigger and stronger.

"Be still and listen. I have no choice but to teletransport us out of here," he said, drawing her tighter into his embrace. Even in the midst of all the danger, she noticed that he smelled like fresh mint, clean and alluring. Not at all scary.

"Teletransport? Like, beam me up, Scotty?" she joked, even as she heard movement outside the door, then a claw-like scratching on the wood.

"Something like," Cnut replied. "Hold tight, baby. I've never done this with a human before."

"Human?" she began to gurgle, but then lost all ability to speak or even think.

She wrapped her arms tightly around Cnut's shoulders, and his arms encased her back, and they began to twirl and twirl and twirl up into space. Or something. They were in a mist. Maybe like the eye of a tornado.

And then she lost consciousness.

Or died.

But, no, she wasn't dead.

She was still in the bedroom, but she was lying on the bed. It was the same room, and yet it was different. Coming awake slowly, she noticed the wallpaper was different. Instead of the full-bloomed roses, there were now evergreen boughs and pinecones. And instead of the two double beds with rustic print bedspreads, there was now a multicolored coverlet, something she'd heard called a hap on *Antiques Roadshow*, on just one double bed. And instead of a bedside lamp, there was an oil lantern.

Cnut was standing at the window, staring at something outside.

"Are they gone?" she asked.

He turned. "You're awake," he stated the obvious. "Yes, they're gone."

Even though his fangs were mostly gone and his eyes were back to being blue, Andrea couldn't forget what she'd seen. She felt like Alice in Wonderland having fallen down into some weird garden hole, except that the Mad Hatter's world here was a ranch with terrorist owners and inhabited by strange beasts. And Cnut was the strangest of them all.

"I think I'd like to go home," she said, sitting up on the side of the bed. And suddenly the prospect of being back in her cozy apartment and restaurant job, safe from any danger except a burnt soufflé, held much appeal.

"You can't go home. At least not right now."

"Why? Because of Celie?"

He shook his head. "I made a little mistake when I teletransported us." His face was flushed, as if he was embarrassed.

She rolled her eyes. "You're some teletransporter, Cnut. I've got news for you. We're in the same place. Is that the 'little mistake' you mean?"

"No. We're in the same place, but not the same time."

"Huh?"

"We're in the Old West now. The real Old West."

She was beginning to think Cnut was a little bit crazy, and he was rubbing off on her.

"C'mere. Look," he said.

She walked over to the window where he still stood. Looking out, she saw several horses tied to a hitching rail.

"That's where the parking lot used to be . . . I mean, will be."

"What are you trying to say?"

"We traveled back in time. I'm guessing about a hundred and fifty years."

"And this lodge?" She waved a hand at their surroundings.

"Is someone's home."

She started to laugh and couldn't stop. It was

probably hysteria. "That's some mistake. Undo it."

"I'm not sure I can."

"Are you saying we are trespassing in someone's house, and it's the Old West, and the owner will probably come at us with pistols blazing?"

"Something like that."

In fact, she heard some voices outside, a man and a woman. She and Cnut both went to the other window. The man and woman were coming from the barn and headed toward the house, chatting amiably. The woman had gray hair swept off her face in a bun or something. She wore a long-sleeved blouse tucked into an ankle-length, buckskin skirt and low-heeled boots. The man was much taller and younger, wearing a cowboy hat and cowboy boots. Andrea blinked several times. It was either Barbara Stanwyck and a young Michael Landon, or else they had doppelgängers.

She turned and smacked Cnut on the arm. "You idiot. What did you do?"

"I told you, it was a mistake. We vangels used to time-travel all the time on our missions. Back and forth through the centuries until a few years ago when we got stationed permanently in the twenty-first century."

She hadn't a clue what he just said. It didn't matter. He was the one responsible for this mess, that much was clear. She smacked him again, then latched her arms around Cnut's neck and hitched her legs up so that she straddled his hips. Surprised, he just held on to her.

"Get us out of here. Right now," she demanded.

"What?"

"You heard me, you freakin' moron," she practically shrieked. "Do that damn transport thing. Again. Take me home."

"I'm not sure if—"

Suddenly they were covered with the mist once again, and this time they were falling, falling, falling, as if off a cliff. She might have screamed. Cnut was definitely swearing.

And then she lost consciousness again.

Or maybe she was really dead this time.

She pinched herself. Nope. Alive.

But she was freezing cold.

Rising from the snowy ground where she must have fallen, she stood and saw a massive fort-like wood structure on a flat-topped hill in front of her. Sort of like the Montana buttes, but different. Possibly man-made.

Cnut was standing beside her, equally stunned. "I do not believe this. I do not believe this," he kept repeating.

"Another little mistake?" she asked.

"A big one," he replied, without looking at her.

She smacked him again on the arm.

He just ignored her.

"Where . . . are . . . we?" she gasped out, shivering. This wasn't just cold. It was Alaska cold. It was North Pole cold. It was restaurant walk-in freezer cold.

"Home." He was staring forward, still not looking at her, but she could see his breath frost in the air before him.

"Home . . . where?"

He turned toward her and said, not at all happy, "The Norselands. And it's 850 A.D."

Chapter 8

Back to the future, in reverse . . .

Cnut began to climb up the path built into the motte toward the wood castle that had been his home for more than ten years long, long ago. He had mixed feelings about returning home.

One, he didn't know if this was a teletransport mistake on his part, like the brief spurt into the Old West had been. Or was this something deliberate planned by Michael? It had to be the latter. Nothing happened without Michael knowing about it. On the other hand, Michael liked nothing better than seeing a Viking fall on his arse, so to speak.

Two, was it a punishment or a second chance for him to make amends for his sins of the past? How did he feel about that? Well, he'd been making amends for a thousand and more years already. Didn't that count for something?

Three, he had an obligation to help Andrea, who kept swatting at him every time she caught up with him, and calling him various names, like moron, idiot, and the more imaginative nincompoop, whatever that meant, something to do with shit, obviously. Probably shithead. "What about Celie?" she kept asking. Over and over and over.

At the moment, he had no idea where he would be five minutes from now, let alone where her sister was. He could handle only one problem at a time.

Four, he wasn't sure where they'd land if he tried the teletransport again, considering his first two efforts today. Possibly a cave in prehistoric times. With Andrea along as his very own Ugga. And the only food an occasional dinosaur bone to gnaw on. Michael did have a warped sense of humor betimes.

Five, Cnut had come to enjoy all the modern conveniences of the twenty-first century. How could he now live without them? Cars; restaurants; television; good, plentiful food and alcohol; indoor plumbing; doughnuts (preferably cream-filled); electricity; cheeseburgers; bottled beer; delivery pizza—the list was endless. On the other hand, there was something to be said for the simple life. He couldn't think of a thing at the moment, but there surely was.

Six, he wondered if he was even a vangel anymore. Had everything that had happened these many centuries been for naught, wiped out, and he was back where it had all begun? But no, evidence of that stood beside him reeking of iced coconut. Besides, he thought, running his tongue under his upper lip, the fangs were still there. And he would bet the wing bumps were still on his shoulders. What did it mean?

Seven, Cnut's stomach rumbled, and he felt a

voracious hunger and thirst come over him. He wanted . . . *needed* food and drink. Just like the old days. A horn of ale and a hunk of manchet bread dunked in honey would do in a pinch, until something more substantial could be found. Mayhap Andrea could whip up one of her—

"Oh my God! Bears!" Andrea squealed suddenly and grabbed on to his arm, almost toppling him over.

"I wish you wouldn't swear," he said instinctively. Then, "What bears? Oh, those bears up on the motte." He laughed.

She swatted him again. "What moat? Do you see any water or a drawbridge? There is no moat, idiot!"

"Motte, not moat," he corrected. "I'll explain the difference later." To the "bears," he yelled out a greeting, "Hail!"

Andrea repeated, "Idiot!"

They'd reached the flat-topped surface of the motte where they were confronted by three heavily armed hirdsmen holding forth swords and spears and battle-axes. They wore long bearskin cloaks and pieced–squirrel fur hats with ear flaps and gloves of reindeer hide. Their faces were heavily haired with winter beards and mustaches.

"They're not bears," he told Andrea. "They're men."

"Why don't I feel better knowing that?" she said. "They smell like bears."

"Well, yes, it's winter, and bathing—"

"Halt!" one of them said.

"Begone, you villains. There is no food for you here," the second one yelled, raising his spear.

Still another said, "Was it you who killed the master's prize horse? We could smell it roasting in yon village, all the way up to the castle."

Andrea shivered like a wet kitten, and put her hand in his. She was probably frightened. Well, of course she was. She thought she was in the presence of three bears.

He squeezed her hand in reassurance and drew her closer to his side. Despite the cold and shock, he had to smile at the sweet scent of coconut that wafted around her. Snow had begun to fall in big flakes that he imagined were coconut flakes come from the sky. Mocking gifts from Michael. He barely caught himself from sticking out his tongue to catch a few.

"Is that you, Ivar?" he asked the young fellow who'd mentioned the dead horse . . . an issue he would address later, but he could guess which horse it was. His other Percheron. For some reason, loss of a horse, albeit a very expensive one, didn't seem important right now. "Why is your father not here doing sentry duty?" Ivar Jorsson was the son of Jor Snaggle-Tooth, his chief *hersir*, head of all the Hoggstead housecarls.

"Me father passed on to Valhalla a sennight ago. Mauled by a rabid dog, he was."

"Who has taken his place?"

"No one. Yet," Ivar said as he narrowed his eyes to peer more closely at Cnut. "Is that you, master? Where you been?"

Around the world.

"Everyone searched for you, even up to the northern woods. We figgered you was dead."

I was. I am.

"You look different. Skin and bones. Was it the wasting disease?"

More like a diet to lose two hundred wasted pounds.

"Master?" Andrea questioned him.

He put a forefinger to his lips. "Later," he whispered. To Ivar, he offered his condolences, "My sympathies on your father's passing. He was a good man. Sorry I was not here for his funeral rites, but I had to, um, go away for a while. No wasting disease. Just, um, lack of food."

"Hah! Don't we know about that! The villagers raided the second storage shed, and we are nigh starving up at the keep, too." It was the second hirdsman speaking. Cnut recognized him now by his bright red facial hair. It was Red Ranulf. "Was you captured by Huns? Or them bloody Saxons? Mebbe outlaw Vikings? Did they starve you?"

No, I starved myself. 'Tis called a diet. "Something like that," Cnut replied.

"Asbol the Witch claimed a vision," the third hirdsman, Boris Bad Breath, said on a waft of bad breath, "where she saw the villagers turning you on a fiery spit and feeding their babies your entrails."

Yuck!

Ivar elbowed Boris, who had the grace to blush.

"Ivar, you mentioned that your father died a sennight ago. How long have I been gone?"

"Four sennights," Ivar answered, staring at him warily at what must have seemed a barmy question.

"A month!" Cnut exclaimed before he could catch himself.

"Is it really Jarl Sigurdsson?" Boris asked Ranulf.

"It is, it is," Ranulf declared. "I can tell by the way he frowns. Praise the gods, the jarl has returned."

"Jarl?" Andrea questioned again. "Not the jar business again!"

"Now things will be better," the third hirdsman said.

With a flurry of movement up ahead, Finngeir the Frugal, Cnut's steward, came out of the doors that led to his great hall. "What is all the commotion out here? We could hear . . . is that . . . nay, 'tis impossible. Master Sigurdsson?"

"Hello, Finn," Cnut said.

Finn fell into a dead faint.

A short time later, they were inside the keep. Andrea was parked on a bench in front of one of the great hall's hearths, thawing out, muttering every imprecation against him she could think of. Finn had been taken to his pallet to rest from the shock. And Cnut was being besieged with questions, rather complaints, from his men . . . and women.

"Did you bring food?"

No, but I brought a chef.

"We're hungry."

So am I.

"Greta stole my best gunna. You must hold court and punish her."

"I did not. It was my gunna to begin with."

"You gave it to me!"

"I lent it to you."

Forget the damn gown.

"I'm sick of gruel. Me stomach needs fresh meat."

"I could eat a boar, all by meself."

I prefer a pizza with pepperoni, sausage, mushrooms, peppers, and extra cheese. Even made on a circle of manchet bread.

"The bread is moldy and stinks of mice shit."

Forget the pizza. A boar flank will do.

"The privy is full, and someone needs to dig a new one."

Don't look at me.

"Ye can't dig a new one in frozen dirt, ye lackwit!"

"Who you calling a lackwit?"

"Finn put a lock on the mead barrel. My throat is parched."

On and on the complaints went until Cnut raised both hands and bellowed, "Enough!" Glancing around the hall, he began to take note of the conditions, "This place is a pigsty!" Grabbing the closest members of his household, a pair of twin youthlings, he ordered, "Get some rakes and remove all the rushes in this hall. They reek. Then lay down new ones."

"Huh?" The twins looked at him as if he'd ask them to piss blood.

He gave them a fierce glower, and they ran off to find rakes.

"And you, Britta," he said, pointing to an elderly servant who was sidling along the wall, probably attempting to escape his attention. "You are in charge of scrubbing down these tables. Lye will probably be needed to penetrate the grease and built-up filth."

"Me?" Britta squeaked out.

"You. Get several maids to help you." He

pointed to three women in the back of the hall. "You, and you, and you. Help Britta." When they all just stood, gaping at him, he hollered, *"Now!"*

They jumped and scuttled off like scared rabbits.

"Ivar!" he called out to the young soldier standing in the doorway. "Gather together all the housecarls. We will meet here in . . ." He glanced down at the watch that he was surprised to see was still on his wrist. He was about to say, *In two hours,* but instead said, "After the first meal of the day."

To others, he ordered the hearth ashes to be hauled and taken to the scullery for soap making, firewood to be gathered, all the platters and serving utensils to be taken to the kitchen for washing.

"Who is the head laundress?" he asked no one in particular.

"Edwina was but she has the ague and lies abed this past sennight," one blowsy-looking wench told him.

"You take over then," he told her. "I assume the bed linens and clothing are in the same condition as this hall. I want them all washed."

"But . . . but . . . it's winter, and . . ." Blowsy Wench protested.

He favored her with one of his glowers.

"If anyone wants to eat here, ever again, they better be working. The new rule, idle hands have empty stomachs."

He turned then to see Andrea standing before the hearth watching him. She arched her brows and gave him a little salute.

"You!" he said, walking toward her, almost tripping over a dog bone buried in the dirty rushes.

"Come with me to the kitchen and see what kind of mess we have there."

"Is that an order, *master*?"

"No, that's a request. With your cooking skills, perhaps you can assess just how bad things are food-wise and give me some advice for fixing things."

"Are we staying here? What about my sister? I hired you to find Celie and bring her back to Philly."

"Give me time to figure out what's happening. Trust me, Andrea. I'll help you and your sister as soon as I can. Will you give me that time?"

She nodded. What choice did she have? Something else seemed to occur to her then. "Everyone's speech is so strange here, and yet I can understand. Why is that? Some magic vangel trick?"

He laughed. "No trick. Old Norse and Saxon English were similar enough in this time period that we could understand each other, somewhat, enough to get by. On the other hand, you probably shouldn't be able to make any sense of medieval English." Shrugging, he took her hand and was about to lead her from the hall when he looked back and noticed everyone gaping at them.

Halting momentarily, he tucked Andrea in at his side and announced to the room at large, "This is Andrea of Philadelphia. She is your new mistress."

Then he gave her a kiss, a long one, before she could call him an idiot again.

Even while he was kissing her, and she was too

stunned to smack him, he heard someone in the hall ask, "What is that strange smell?"

"I don't know, but I like it," another person replied.

He did, too.

It was coconut and peppermint.

Chapter 9

A miracle worker, she was not . . .

Although it was only midday, it was dark outside. They didn't call this the Land of the Midnight Sun or Polar Nights for nothing. Andrea knew that bit of trivia because she'd checked on the Internet when Cnut had mentioned, at their first meeting, that he came from the Norselands. *How's that for hysterical irrelevance? Hey, with everything that's happened to me today, I deserve a little hysteria.*

Cnut, with a torch in hand, led her down a chilly, dark hallway toward the kitchen, which was presumably connected to this vast, sprawling building, but somewhat separate. Because of the fire hazard, she assumed. Even from here in the corridor, she could feel the heat of the kitchen cook fires up ahead. Otherwise, it would be as frigid as it was outside.

He stopped halfway and turned to her, "You're angry."

"No shit, Dick Tracy!" she said, using one of her father's favorite expressions. She rarely used crudity, but this situation seemed to warrant it. He still held one of her hands, and she jerked it loose. "Of course I'm angry, you idiot. Why wouldn't I be? Mistress? You think I'll be your mistress, just because you kiss me? And it wasn't even a good kiss." Actually, it was a very nice kiss. Excellent. But he didn't need to know that.

"That's what has your braies in a twist?" He seemed surprised.

"My bra isn't in a twist, and I'd rather you didn't mention my underwear."

"Not bra, braies. Like breeches, or long pants." Then, he paused and cocked his head to the side. "It wasn't a good kiss? Ah, I'm out of practice, I suppose. I could try again."

He placed his torch in a wall bracket. There was darkness all around them, except for the light of the kitchen at the other end. She could see him clearly, though, in the torch's circle of light that cocooned them. In fact, it gave off a bit of warmth.

"Don't you dare!" She assumed that was why he'd freed his hands. The better to kiss her.

He laughed. "The torch was burning my hand." He waggled his eyebrows at her, knowing perfectly well what she had thought. "In any case, I didn't mean that kind of mistress, unless you want the position. Nay, I was giving you a position of authority so my people would follow your orders. Rather like mistress of the household."

"Oh," she said, even though that was presumptuous of him, too.

He leaned against the wall beside her and brushed some strands of hair off her face that had come loose from her ponytail. She realized in that instant that she was still wearing the silly cowboy hat. What must the people in the hall have thought of her, a woman, in this attire?

"And the kiss," Cnut said in a husky voice as he stared at her lips, "was to show all the men in my keep that you are off limits."

"As if that's for you to decide."

"Believe you me, a comely woman in a Viking hall would result in fighting among the men to see who got first dibs."

He thinks I'm . . . comely? Skinny Andy Stewart causing a riot? That is ridiculous. And what exactly does he mean by dibs? Ooooh, the jerk is trying to divert me when I have bigger bones to pick with him. "You somehow teletransported us through time to land in some Dark Age hovel."

"A hovel? Really? My castle is a hovel?"

She waved a hand to encompass their surroundings. "A wood castle that's more like a fort than my idea of a castle. Yeah, it's hovel, a big one. And you brought me here, *without my permission*!"

"Would you rather we'd stayed at the ranch and been demon fodder?"

She hated when he was being logical. And she hated when he stood so close to her that the scent of peppermint came off him in waves, enveloping her. She barely stifled a moan. "But what about Celie? Oh my God! I knew she was in danger with the ISIS creep, but those other . . . things!"

"Your sister is in no danger from the Lucies. Demon vampires are only interested in dreadful sinners which they can take back to Horror and torture into becoming more of their kind. And vangels, more than anything, Lucies want to capture vangels. The only time they kill innocents is when they get in the way of their evil goals."

"In other words, I could have stayed."

"And been surrounded by Lucies. Would you have wanted to stay there alone?"

"Yes." *No.* "Send me back." *But I'm so frightened! I don't want to go alone. Can I go alone? I might have to. For Celie.* "Take me back." *Yeah, that's better. Don't give him a choice.* "Now!"

He shook his head. "I can't. Not right now."

"Why not?"

"We were sent here for a reason."

"What reason?"

"Um . . . I can't tell you."

"Do you know?"

"Um . . . yes."

She narrowed her eyes at him. He was lying, or keeping something from her. "Idiot," she muttered under her breath. Then aloud, "Will we go back?"

"I think so. Eventually. As for your sister, she might have already left the ranch. For Syria or Pakistan or God only knows where. If she's still there, my brothers will rescue her. I notified my brother Vikar of the conditions, just before we left. There would have been a *hird* of vangels there before that bedroom door was broken down."

"That makes me feel much better," she said in a tone of sarcasm. But it actually did. Not that she wasn't still worried about Celie, but it appeared as if her sister would be in capable hands. But that brought up another question. "If your brothers were coming, why didn't we stay?"

"Because there was that period before they arrived, even if was only ten minutes, when you and I were vastly outnumbered. We had to leave."

"I still can't believe what happened back there, not that I really know what happened."

"I'll explain it all later when there's no chance we will be interrupted." As it was, people kept peering down the hall, staying away only because they sensed their master wanted some privacy. They wouldn't be put off indefinitely.

She put her face in her hands. "Maybe I'm already dead, and this is my Purgatory, though I don't think I've done anything bad enough to merit such punishment."

"Hoggstead isn't that bad," Cnut said with affront.

She lowered her hands and saw that he was serious. "Hoggstead? How perfect! A pig farm!"

"Hoggson was the name of the original owner of this estate. It's not a pig farm, though I imagine a pig or two would come in handy in the midst of this famine."

"A famine? That is just great. Demons, vampires, tele-damn-transport, and now a famine! What else do you have planned for me?"

"I'm not planning anything. And you're not dead, and this isn't some Other World. It's the same world but a different time period," he tried to explain.

She wasn't buying it. "Maybe it's a bad dream. A nightmare. But I've never dreamed in such vivid color before. And the detail! And all the different characters! And the smell! Phew!"

"Enough! You've made it clear what you think

of my home. And, now that I see it through modern eyes, I have to admit, it is a bit of a mess."

"More like a debacle."

He looked so dejected that she almost felt sorry for him. Almost.

She was trying her best not to recall what she'd seen back at the ranch. Those horrid creatures. And Cnut was apparently some kind of creature, too. *With fangs!*

"What are you?" she asked suddenly.

"A vangel. I told you before."

"That explains everything."

He closed his lips over pointy lateral incisors. "Vangels are Viking vampire angels, created by God and commanded by St. Michael the Archangel to rid the world of Lucipires, demon vampires."

"The creatures we saw? You called them Lucies."

He nodded.

"And you're an angel?"

"Sort of. A vampire angel. Suffice to say, we are the good guys, or as good as a Viking can be."

"You realize this is impossible to believe."

"It is what it is."

"Well, at least there are none of them here."

An odd expression crossed his face.

"What?"

"There were none when I was here last, more than a thousand years ago. Leastways, none that I was aware of. But I cannot imagine that they don't exist in this time, too. After all, sin is ageless. Lucifer is older than the Creation, isn't he?"

"You're asking me?"

"Just be careful."

"You are an idiot." She smacked him on the arm, for about the tenth time.

"You might want to consider toning down the anger. Some might construe that as sinful. And Lucies are attracted by the lemon scent of sinners, like bees to a honeypot." He sniffed the air. "No lemons. Yet. Just coconut."

He was probably teasing.

She was in no mood for teasing.

Just then, a man pushed through the crowd, which was blocking the far end of the hallway, still watching them. It was the man who'd fainted earlier on first seeing Cnut.

Cnut turned and smiled at the approaching man, who was smiling as well. He was a head shorter than Cnut and two times his age, but nicely dressed in a belted tunic over slim pants. His long, gray-threaded blond hair hung in a thick braid down his back, and he had a neatly trimmed mustache and beard. More than anything, she noticed that he was clean, unlike many she'd seen here so far.

"The gods have smiled on us today. You are not dead!" The man opened his arms and hugged Cnut warmly.

That is debatable. Vangels are dead, aren't they?

"Thank the One-God," Cnut said and hugged him back.

The older man arched his brows. "A Christian now?"

Cnut ignored the question. "I take it the situation is dire here?"

"Worse than you can imagine."

"Andrea, I would have you meet Finngeir, my steward and longtime friend. Finn, this is my . . . um, companion. Andrea Stewart of Philadelphia. She is a far-famed cook and expert in kitchen matters. A magician when it comes to food."

It was a nice compliment, but a clear embellishment of her credentials. The devious lout was buttering her up for something.

"I am hoping that she will be able to help us solve our most critical issue . . . feeding the masses."

Yep. Butter, butter, butter.

"I welcome any advice you can give me, m'lady." The steward looked at her, as if he wasn't sure of her place here.

She wasn't sure, either, but she quipped, "As long as you don't expect me to turn five loaves and two fishes into a feast for thousands."

Cnut understood what she meant, and cringed, but Finn frowned in confusion.

"Like in the Bible. What Jesus did. A miracle," she explained.

"Ah, the Christian Holy Book," Finn said, though he gave Cnut another questioning look. Apparently, they weren't Christians here.

Turned out, once they entered the hellhole that purported to be a kitchen, it really would take a miracle to turn this place around.

The kitchen itself was a massive room, about half the size of a basketball court. Two hearths, each big enough for a person to stand in, blazed with fires in which cauldrons bubbled and haunches of meat roasted. Ovens were built into the stonework on either side of the hearths.

That was the best that could be said about the place. There were no rushes on the floor here, so close to the fires, but the packed dirt floor itself was greasy and squished with unmentionable spoiled foodstuff when stepped on. Here and there were bones left by the dogs, who apparently roamed the kitchen, too, as well as the great hall. The long prep tables were covered with days-old food, maybe weeks-old. The room smelled, and it was not a good kitchen smell, either.

A short, fat woman, who was yelling at a boy who apparently failed to turn the spit rapidly enough, turned on hearing them enter. She wore a blue gown, belted at the waist and covered with a full-length, white, open-sided, apron-type garment attached at the shoulder straps with crude brooches. In fact, most of the women here wore similar attire. A kerchief of some kind tied around her head failed to hold in all the curly gray hair underneath. She was relatively clean, in sharp contrast to the filthy kitchen she supervised.

"There you are!" the woman said on seeing Cnut, as if he'd just stepped out and returned moments later, not a month later. "Frigg's foot! Wherever you been musta had famine, too. Yer near a starveling now. And what happened to yer hair? Was it the lice you needed ta shave off?"

Cnut laughed and said, "'Tis good to see you, too, Girda."

"Would you just look at this mess?" She waved a chubby hand to encompass the kitchen area. "I been gone fer six days ta care fer me sister up the mountain and this is what I find when I return. Half the food stores gone, and not a pot scoured."

She pointed a long-handled soup ladle toward a wide archway into an adjoining room, the scullery, where it appeared as if every pot and wooden platter and utensil owned by this estate was out and dirty. Girda then glared at Finn as if he were to blame.

"I told Freydis to take over your duties," Finn tried to say.

"That halfbrained wench! The only thing Freydis knows how ta do is spread her thighs fer the menfolks. I swear, the fool has brush burns on her rump."

Andrea looked at Cnut, who was trying to hide a grin.

"Andrea, this is Girda, the cook and commander of the kitchens here at Hoggstead. Girda, this is my friend Andrea of Philadelphia, who will be helping you fix the food situation."

"She gonna end the famine?" Girda scoffed.

A famine. That's the second time I've heard famine mentioned. If it wouldn't attract too much attention, she'd like to smack Cnut again. Along the course of this nightmare day, she'd discovered she had a violent streak in her that could only be satisfied by swatting the fool.

"Where do you come from that ladies wear men's braies? Wanton, it is. Do women wear hats like that in yer land? Or is it jist magicians?" Girda asked. "Bet it keeps you dry when it rains."

Feeling her face heat, Andrea removed the hat and placed in on a wall peg. "Definitely. And it shades me from the sun, too."

"Whass wrong with the sun? Wish I had me some more sun."

Cnut snickered.

If they were alone, she would have hit him again.

She crossed her eyes at him.

And he winked at her.

Yep, a good smack!

"You a witch what's gonna wave yer magic broom and the famine's gone?" Girda asked Andrea.

"Well, no," Andrea said, stepping back at the assault. Why was the old lady picking on her? Did she think Andrea wanted her job? No, thank you! "Although I do wield a mean whisk. Ha, ha, ha."

The woman didn't even crack a smile. "What in bloody hell is a wiss?"

"Now, be nice, Girda. You know you need the help."

Girda made a harrumphing noise of assent.

"Show them what you showed me earlier today," Finn advised.

They followed Girda into the scullery, which smelled even worse than the kitchen and not just from food-crusted pots and wooden dishes. The scullery apparently also served as the laundry, and dirty clothing was piled almost ceiling high, some of it wet and musty. There were rushes on the floor in here, but not up close to the laundry fireplace, which would be used to heat water.

Beyond the scullery, there was a locked door. Both Girda and Cnut took torches from the wall while Finn pulled a key off the ring at his belt and opened the door into a dry storage room with many shelves, half of them empty. What they did have was stored in barrels, or pottery containers, or baskets, or was hanging from the ceiling. "You can see how depleted our supplies are," Finn said. "Only five barrels of good flour; the rest is filled with weevils because someone failed to secure the lids." He gave Girda a pointed look of condemnation, and Girda bared her surprisingly clean teeth at him. "There's some barley and some raw oats, but not much."

"We got a hundred and ten people ta feed here," Girda said defensively. "Not ta mention the village starvelings what come up to beg fer food every day. Even though some folks would refuse them even crumbs from the table." Her condemnation was clearly directed at Cnut.

Who blushed.

Odd! Did Girda blame Cnut for the starving people?

"All of the pears and dried fruits are gone, along with most of the nuts. Got a barrel of shriveled apples. Lots of cabbages, but the only root vegetables left in any amount are neeps. We got a whole bin full of neeps because nobody likes the buggers," Finn went on, and ducked his head at Andrea in apology at his rude word.

She'd heard lots worse in the kitchens where she'd worked. Lots! And what was wrong with turnips? She liked them.

"Ain't but a tun of ale left and no mead. Finn, who has become trollsome of late, if ye ask me, has kept the last of that under lock and key." Girda glared at Finn again.

He didn't even flinch.

"Your men are drinking water now, or milk from the three milch cows and four goats what are left, thanks ta guards kept at the barn night and day. We still have enough fer butter and cheese. You know what happened ta yer horse, dontcha, master?"

He nodded, a grim expression on his face.

Andrea guessed that the horse must have been killed for meat. She could understand that if the people were starving.

"We also have fish out in the smokehouse but not nearly enough to last the winter," Finn went on. "Large trout and bass and cod. Plus herrings aplenty, and even a small shark. And salt pork aplenty. But the eel barrel is empty, and not a single seabird or pigeon."

Girda said, "We do gots some chickens, though, four dozen at least in the coop, but they's mostly laying hens, and I ain't putting them in the pot, lessen I got no choice. Guards are there, too, to keep out wolves and thieves. We need the eggs. I'd like ta kill that bloody rooster, though. Meaner than a cross-eyed cat with the shits."

"Don't you need a rooster for the hens to lay eggs?" asked Andrea.

"No, the hens only need roosters if they want chicks. Jist like people. Women don't need men unless they wants babies." Girda gave Cnut and Finn direct looks, daring them to disagree with her.

Not a chance. They both remained silent, though Cnut did wink at Andrea behind Girda's back and said, "Some people say the lady chicks are more fertile just having a manly rooster around."

"Must have been a man who said that," Andrea commented.

"I'm just sayin'." Cnut grinned at Andrea.

A commotion could be heard back in the kitchen, and Girda made a sound of disgust. "Odin's eyeballs! You show 'im the rest, Finn. I gotta get these slugabeds aworking if we're ta have any dinner this eve."

And off the cook went, shouting orders here and there.

"Bjorn, build up the scullery fire.

"Bodil, get the kettles boiling fer laundry.

"Dotta, sort out the smallclothes from the braies and the tunics and don't let me hear any complaints about the smell, either.

"Tumi, bring in some firewood. What splinter? I'll give you a splinter, you lazy sod!

"Why aren't those rushes raked in the scullery yet? Loki's liver! Do I hafta do everything?"

Her voice trailed off, and Cnut and Finn exchanged looks that pretty much said, *Oh well!*

Andrea had so many questions, but Finn was unlocking another door, and Cnut held a torch as they followed him down the steps to what was a root cellar. Very, very cold. Damp and dirt-smelling.

Andrea shivered, and Cnut said, "We'll just be down here for a few minutes."

Skinless animal carcasses, covered with green mold, hung from the ceiling like trophies in a macabre serial killer's den. Several deer, a hog, a few rabbits, and various other animals she couldn't identify. It was here the turnips and cabbages and some stray carrots and onions were stored.

When they were back upstairs amid the bustle of the laundry and the kitchen, where at least a dozen servants were now working industriously,

Cnut asked Finn, "Bottom line, how bad are things?"

"A sennight, two at most, if we continue to dole out some food to the cotters, and I don't care what you say, master, I could not turn them away."

"You must think me a selfish bastard based on past behavior," Cnut said. "You were right to do so, Finn."

"Keep in mind, it's less than a month until Jól. Some yule season we will be celebrating this year!" Finn continued.

"Things will be different now." Cnut patted Finn on the shoulder.

Cnut looked at her then and added, "If it's not too late."

The despair on his face almost broke her heart. She couldn't help herself then. She took his hand in hers and promised, "We'll make sure it's not too late."

Chapter 10

A Viking's work is never done . . .

Cnut was so ashamed.

Who was that man he'd been? And he didn't just mean the obesity. He had to have been an egocentric bastard, selfish to a monumental degree, to ignore the needs of his people! Hoggstead had been in his mother's family for generations. They really were his people. But he'd let them starve.

No more! he vowed.

He ordered Finn to gather all the men into the great hall where he was about to address them. He stood at the head table while the rest of them, more than sixty in number, sat on benches or leaned against the timber walls.

At first, they seemed more concerned about the changes in his physical appearance than the plight of Hoggstead. Mostly they were burly, hardened warriors who'd as soon split an enemy's head with a battle-axe as show any softer emotions, but they were Vikings, and Viking men valued their good looks.

"Why do you wear your hair so, jarl?" asked the

bald-headed Igor, who'd been shaving his head since Cnut could remember. In fact, he claimed that women liked him to rub certain parts of their body with his shiny pate.

Cnut had noticed a lemon scent when he passed Igor earlier, further evidence that Cnut was still a vangel. But also evidence that Igor was guilty of some grievous sin, or was about to commit some evil. If there were any Lucipires about, the man would be demon fodder soon, sure as sin.

An expression of disgust had come over his steward's face, when asked about Igor. "Rumor is that Igor and Red Ranulf have been raping some of the village women, sometimes in exchange for food, sometimes with threats that they will kill their husbands if they tell."

Red Ranulf hadn't been emitting a lemon scent when they'd met that morning, but then they'd been outside in the cold, and Ranulf had been heavily clothed. Cnut would have to keep an eye on both men.

"And you are clean-shaven, too. Was it lice, or fleas?" a young squire, Atli by name, called out. By the looks of him, he probably had more than a few of both crawling over his dirty body.

Vikings valued cleanliness. And he had a steam bathhouse for winter bathing. What was going on here in his keep during the short time he'd been gone? Why was no one bathing?

On questioning Finn, he learned there was a problem with the bathing house where hot springs provided warm bathing. A clog was preventing dirty water from escaping.

Atli's friend, Tostig, jabbed Atli in the arm with

an elbow. "Lackwit. Ye don't ask the master a question like that."

"Why not?"

"No lice or fleas," Cnut answered. "I saw a Viking one time who styled his hair this way, and I liked it." As simple as that. Of course it was on a television show, which they would not understand.

"What Viking?" someone demanded to know. It was the blacksmith Ogot.

"Um . . . Ragnar Lothbrok."

"That peacock!" remarked the graybeard Vestar, who'd sold his sword for many a king in his time. "Ragnar would wear peacock feathers in his hair if he could find one of those pretty birds. I saw him one time with three gold loops in one ear. No doubt he walked with a tilt to one side."

Everyone laughed.

"Do the women like it? That is the important question," commented Thorkel Long-Limbs, who fashioned himself an expert in the sex arts, even worse than Cnut's brother Ivak. Thorkel was one of his *hersirs*, whom he'd already asked to take over Jor Snaggle-Tooth's job as chief *hersir* over all the Hoggstead housecarls.

"I have no idea," Cnut said.

But no one believed him. They probably suspected him of withholding some secret to sexual attraction. Like that would have done him any good in the past one thousand, one hundred and sixty-six years of celibacy! Or near celibacy. Not that they knew that.

"Why are your two teeth so pointy? I don't recall them being so pointy before. Oh!" Atli gasped. "Did your captors torture you by filing your teeth?"

Cnut pressed his lips together to hide the fangs, which were recessed, but still . . . yes, pointy. But then he thought, *I never said anything about being captured. Did I? Well, let them think that, rather than try to explain.*

"Why do your braies have metal over your man parts? I noticed when we went to the privy. Is it like armor?" still another man asked. "A codpiece?"

"A mighty thin codpiece, if you ask me," Ranulf hooted. "Mayhap for a man with a needle cock. Ha, ha, ha."

Zippers? How do I explain zippers? And is Ranulf implying . . . ? Hmm. Mayhap Finn is right about Ranulf and Igor.

"I like those little bone decorations on his *shert*," Ulf the Archer commented. "Methinks my Helga could make some for me from antlers."

Buttons now. Please. This is way off subject. "Listen, everyone, the situation here at Hoggstead is dire," he proclaimed, as if they didn't already know that. "Here is what we're going to do. It's too late in the season, and the fjords too frozen, to go to any of the market towns to replenish our supplies. So, Gorm, you will take one of the wagon sledges and head east on the frozen fjord. Stop at every estate or farmstead along the way until your wagon is full of foodstuff. Anything and everything that is edible, from oats to meat. And ale or mead, as well. You will use this to pay for the goods." He lifted one of the sacks of gold and silver coins that lay before him.

He saw several eyes widen at his being willing to part with his precious wealth. That was the old Cnut, they would soon learn, although he had to admit it hurt to part with so much. He'd liked collecting so much wealth. Truth be told, he still did. Once a glutton, always a glutton? He hoped not.

Gorm nodded. "Many are as bad off as we are with the famine, though. I cannot guarantee results."

"Just keep going 'til you fill the wagon, even if it's only a little here and there. Take as long as you need, but hurry, if you can."

Gorm nodded again.

"And you, Farle," Cnut said, raising another bag of coins, "you will do the same with a sledge to the west."

"I hear Jarl Rolfsson had a fair harvest," Farle informed him. "I will try there first."

"Arnstein and Ingolf, you will start ice fishing. That spot beyond the cliffs has been good in the past. And Olaf and Gudrik, travel as far as the ocean and see what fish or seabirds you can catch."

He could see that his men were pleased with his plans so far. They were good men, not the lazy oafs they'd apparently been of late. They just needed leadership.

"Andor, Gismund, Njal, and Sven, you and I will pick five men each to form hunting parties. Choose the best archers. I know, I know, it is difficult to find game this time of year, but needs must. We will go in five different directions. Two of you can take the dogs." Hoggstead had a number of prime elkhounds that were good for hunting, the ones that had been banished from the hall his first night back. "First one to kill a deer gets a silver coin. A wild boar, two silver coins. And a bear, please God, merits gold, I would think."

There was much laughter and clapping.

"And what do I get if I catch me a whale?" one man called out.

"A bucket of ale," Cnut quipped. The only way any of the Vikings were able to catch a whale in their longboats, which were often smaller than the sea mammals, was if the animal washed up on shore. They should be so lucky now!

Cnut glanced at one elderly warrior, who had seen at least fifty winters, and said, "Aslak, you ever had a talent for setting snares. Dost think it's too late to catch us some rabbits, or possum, or quail, or grouse?"

Aslak tossed his long gray beard over one shoulder and boasted, "Not for me!"

"Let us all set forth at first light on the morrow, and may God be with us," Cnut declared.

The others did not catch his reference to a single god, but Finn did, and he frowned. Cnut wasn't sure how his Vikings would react to his conversion. His conversion hardly mattered at the moment, considering the desperate circumstances, though a multitude of prayers wouldn't hurt.

You can say that again, he thought he heard a voice in his head say.

Michael? he immediately inquired of the saint who had been ominously absent of late. *What's up with this time-travel business? And why did you send Andrea back here with me?*

His head was as silent as a hollow melon.

But then Finn said, "Your lips are moving. Are you talking to yourself?"

"Would seem so. Guess I lost a bit of my mind as well as half my weight while I was gone."

Cnut went with Finn then down to the village where he attempted to assure his serfs and cotters that he planned to help them. The people were angry and bitter. No surprise there. But also hesitantly hopeful.

"Why should we believe you?" one young man asked.

"Because I give you my word. Because you have no choice."

It took him hours before he talked with all the villagers and farmers, sometimes in groups, sometimes individually. Starting tomorrow, each person who came up to the castle would be handed an allotment of food per person, only a daily amount at first because of the scarcity, and it would be plain fare, he told them, but filling.

Several women carrying babies began to weep.

Which made him feel lower than a snake's belly.

"And one cup of milk per child and breeding mother," he added.

Finn was looking at him with alarm now. Generosity was fine, according to his steward, but he was perhaps going too far.

It was very late when he and Finn arrived back at the castle. They handed their horses over to a stable boy and made their way through the back door of the keep, into the empty kitchen. Empty except for Girda, who snored loudly from her pallet by the fire, and several youthlings, girls and boys both, who slept on the stone floor, lured no doubt by the hearths where embers still threw off heat. Dinner was over long ago, of course, so he and Finn grabbed a circle of manchet bread and a hunk of meat each, to be washed down with water, though Finn offered to go unlock the private larder where he'd hidden the ale.

A tremendous hunger and thirst gnawed at his stomach and dried his throat, as fierce as the old days. Was he destined to gluttony again? Would he blow up like a fat balloon, again?

Not if I can help it, he vowed.

Cnut was cold and bone-weary by the time he made his way up the stairs to his bedchamber, where he was greeted with a warm fire, a very clean room without any rushes, and a woman under his bed furs. He didn't need to uncover her to know who it was.

The room smelled of sweet coconut.

And he was hit with yet another temptation, more powerful than that for food or drink. Blood drained from his head and heat sizzled across his skin from his scalp to the tips of his fingers and the ends of his curled toes. Between his legs, his balls shifted and his staff seemed to yawn and stretch and come to life. If cocks could smile, his was doing a happy dance of anticipation. He moaned, and, suddenly weak, sank down into a chair.

He was no longer tired. He was energized, as if he'd just mainlined Red Bull. Or testosterone. Like he needed any more of that!

What to do? What to do?

He hesitated, but only for a moment, before

standing and shucking out of his clothing. He was going to sleep in his own bed, but not before taking care of business. Taking his cock in hand, he stroked himself. Up, down. Slow, then fast. He knew just how to bring himself to completion. He'd done it more times than he could count over the centuries. Was it a sin? Yes, but not nearly as sinful as what his body really wanted. The whole time he watched Andrea. Stroke, stroke, stroke, stroke. Only her face showed above the bed furs, but he had a good imagination for what lay underneath. Soft skin, small breasts, a curvy ass, long legs. Faster, faster, faster. In all, it probably took only two minutes before he climaxed with a long groan of pleasure/pain. Was it good for him? Hell, no! But it satisfied him for the moment.

He went over to the washstand, where he splashed cold water on his face, then washed his face and genitals. Then he turned to the bed, still aroused but not voraciously so, his sexual appetite overridden by the aches and exhaustion of the long day.

He could go downstairs and seek an empty pallet, or he could lie here on the hard floor before the fire, but he was so damned weary and muscle-sore from all the riding. Besides, he didn't want to, dammit! She slept so soundly, she wouldn't even notice that he shared the bed furs, the bed being wide enough for two people, three if so inclined.

Lifting the bed fur on the far side from the hearth, he slid inside the delicious warmth of the two furs. Fur side up on the bottom, fur side down on the top. These were two large skins, soft and thick, of bears he'd killed himself many years ago, before he'd gotten too heavy to walk or ride on long hunts.

He yawned widely and let himself relax into the furs. There was a body width of space separating him from Andrea. He was safe. He might even be able to escape in the morning before she awakened, without her ever knowing they'd shared a bed.

Turning on his side, away from her, he let his mind wander. There were so many problems to be resolved here at Hoggstead. And so many questions about his role here or in the future. Still more about what to do with his reluctant travel companion. But he settled almost immediately into a deep sleep.

And came instantly awake in the middle of the night.

He was lying flat on his back, arms folded under his head, legs spread, still on his side of the bed. But Andrea had moved. Like a kitten, she was cuddled up against him, her face on his chest, one leg over his thigh, the knee nudging Neverland, or what she would consider Neverland if she were awake, and the palm of one hand resting over his chest.

Couldn't she hear the loud thumping of his heart? Couldn't she feel the rhythm of his breathing? Couldn't she tell that her coconut essence was becoming a sex trigger to him?

Oddly, he could smell mint now, too. His own unique body odor? And he liked the way it blended with the coconut. An odd combination, coconut and mint. But perhaps not so odd. In fact, it felt too right.

He lowered his arms carefully and pulled the bed fur more closely over them both. The fire had died down, and the bedchamber was cool. Then he let his arms envelop her. Just to keep her warm. It was not an embrace. It wasn't. It wasn't. The most incredible sense of peace came over him. Had he ever felt peaceful before in his entire pitiful life? He didn't think so. This was almost . . . heavenly.

He smiled at what Michael would have to say about that.

When a dim dawn light came streaming through the arrow-slit window, he awakened to a loud screeching noise and someone pummeling his arms and chest. "Idiot, idiot, idiot!" Andrea was yelling at him.

He did not care. For the first time in centuries, he had slept like a baby. So he just smiled up at her and said, "Was that as good for you as it was for me?"

As she knelt on the bed in a thin chemise she must have borrowed, her blonde hair rose in tufts of bed-mussed disarray about her face, which was red with fury. Her jaw dropped at his words. "Are you serious?"

She didn't know whether they had made love or not. Hah! She would know if they had, or Cnut was not a Viking whose sex skills were inborn. But he wasn't about to tell her that. Let her squirm.

"You didn't?" she sputtered at him. "Did you?"

Me? Why does she assume I did something? He eased off the bed and stood, bare-arsed naked, with a morning erection that should be embarrassing, but wasn't, and stretched, deliberately displaying himself, before saying, "I didn't. You did." Let her interpret that as she would!

Her jaw dropped and she just stared at him. It was always good to turn a woman speechless. You could say he'd learned that in Viking 101.

A voice in his head said, *It's a sin to tell a lie.*

"But not as big a sin as I could have committed," he countered.

Oh, you of little faith!

"I have faith. I have plenty of faith," he protested. "If I didn't have faith that there was some method to this latest antic of yours, I would just succumb to madness."

He didn't realize he'd been speaking his thoughts aloud until Andrea remarked, "There's a method to your madness, all right, and when I discover what it is, I'm going to squash you like a bug. No, not a bug. A big, old, flat-as-a-pancake Peppermint Pattie."

"Good. At least I'll be food to stave off someone's hunger." He paused. "Will you eat me?"

He really didn't mean that the way it sounded. Really.

But she didn't know that. "You are an idiot."

Chapter 11

FAMINE FARE FOR THE NON-STARVING

Beef-flavored turnip soup with rivels
Thin-sliced pork roast
Stewed turnips
Skyr cheese
Manchet bread

Cabbage soup with turnips and rivels
Shredded pork turnip hash
Manchet bread

Mashed turnips
Lutefisk
Manchet bread

Rivels in turnip butter
Salt herring
Turnip fricassee

FAMINE FARE FOR THE STARVING

Acorn flour bread
Possum pottage

Leftover smoked horsemeat

Nettle soup

Pickled wild onions, endive, and various roots

Women's work . . . it never changes . . .

Andrea was dressing in her same clothes when a maid and a young boy came in, one carrying an earthenware pitcher of water and the other an armful of firewood. She shrieked at them for entering without knocking and held her T-shirt in front of her bra. They deliberately avoided looking at her.

The boy made quick work of dumping the wood on the burning embers, causing sparks to fly.

"Lackwit!" the woman said, thwapping the boy aside the head with her palm. "Get the chamber pot and empty it in the garderobe. Then go wash it out and bring it back here. Do you hear me, Kugge?"

"They heard ye in the village," Kugge whined, rubbing his sore head. The boy couldn't be more than seven or eight.

"What did you say?" The woman put her hands on her hips and glared at the boy.

"Nothing, *móðir,*" Kugge said, kneeling to draw the lidded pot out from under the bed and carrying it, precariously, through the still open door.

The woman looked at Andrea and grimaced. "My son. Needs a bit of prodding now and then, he does." There was obvious pride in her voice.

"My name is Dyna. Master says I am to take care of you."

"Oh, did he? And where is the . . . um, master now?"

"Off with the hunters."

"When will they return?"

Dyna shrugged. "Mayhap tonight. Mayhap on the morrow." She shrugged again. "They will come when they have meat for the larder, gods willing."

That is just great. Stuck in this Outlander *time warp or whatever it is until the lord and master—in other words, the idiot—comes back. At least Jamie Fraser didn't have fangs. Cnut is probably afraid to face me again. He should be. I'm developing a real mean streak.*

"The other men have gone ice fishing, or rabbit snaring. Still others have gone to neighboring estates to purchase foodstuffs. Praise the gods for this is the first time our jarl has been willing to release coins from his treasure room to help with the famine," Dyna confided. She was moving about the room, tidying up while she talked, making a pile of Cnut's dirty clothing, wiping off the washstand, sweeping ashes off the floor near the fireplace. Andrea could have done these small chores for herself—in fact, she'd cleaned the room herself last night—but she refrained from saying so until she got the lay of the land, so to speak. She didn't want to offend or take away someone's job.

"A bit tight-fisted, was he?"

"That is not for me to say."

Yeah, right.

"Handsome as a god he is now that he has shed

half his weight. In just a month! How is that possible?"

Andrea shrugged. As far as she knew, from Cnut, he'd really been gone more than a thousand years, not just four weeks.

But Dyna must have thought she was being skeptical about Cnut's weight loss because she went over to a wall peg and took a pair of male pants which she spread out wide to an almost grotesque size. Andrea assumed it was an old pair of Cnut's.

"Wow!" was the only thing Andrea could think to say. Was "wow" even a word in this time period? "I mean, that's amazing."

"'Tis not just amazing. It's nigh impossible to believe. Mayhap our lord was taken captive by one of the gods who wielded magic powers over him to make him change in appearance. The jester god Loki would do just that kind of thing." She looked to Andrea for corroboration of her theory.

"Uh . . . I don't know anything about gods and magic."

"Do you know where the master has been for the past month?"

"No. I just met him recently."

"Really?" Dyna wasn't buying it. She, like many of the others, thought they were lovers or something close to that. Especially after last night. "I'll tell you something else, m'lady. Jarl Sigurdsson is a different man now. He cares. Perchance all that fat was making him selfish." Dyna clapped a hand over her mouth, belatedly realizing who she was speaking to. "Sorry. Betimes my tongue runs faster than my good sense."

"It's all right. I won't repeat what you've said." *But maybe Weight Watchers would be interested in a new slogan. Go on a diet and become a saint. No, not a saint. An angel. They could call it Holy Weight Watchers.*

Suddenly, she thought of her sister, who had gone to a Weight Watchers meeting one time when she was sixteen to lose five pounds. She'd come away gaining five pounds. Didn't matter. Celie had been a perfect size six, but some boy had made a snide remark about her "bootie." *Where are you, Celie? I am so worried about you, and I feel so helpless.*

"Even when the master was fat, he was a good lover, I have been told."

Andrea realized that Dyna had continued talking while her own mind had been wandering.

"But then, all Viking men are skilled in the bed arts. Many a fault do they have, the sweet louts, but bedsport is not one of them." Dyna paused in straightening some of Cnut's clothing that hung on wall pegs. "Do you not agree?"

At first, Andrea didn't understand, but then she said, "Oh, it's not like that with us. We're just companions. Travel companions." And, whoo boy, wasn't that the truth? As for *sweet* louts. Andrea wouldn't go that far, but then Cnut was the only Viking she'd ever met . . . before being slingshotted back in time.

Maybe I should hike on over to Scotland and compare notes with Claire Beauchamp Fraser. Fellow time traveler and all that. But, no, that was a different time period.

Yep, I am losing it here.

"Not for the lack of his wanting, though," Dyna assured her.

"Huh?"

"You said the master was not your lover."

"I did?" *Of course I did.*

"And I said it wasn't for his lack of wanting to be. I saw him staring at your rump when you left the hall yestereve."

Men were always staring at women's behinds, when they weren't ogling their boobs. It was an inborn testosterone trait. Didn't mean a thing. But she didn't have a chance to expound on that to Dyna, who wouldn't know testosterone from turnip juice, anyhow.

Kugge had returned with the clean chamber pot, and Dyna ruffled his hair, gave him a quick kiss, and told him to go down to their sleep nook and change his tunic. He'd spilled something on it. Andrea could guess what.

Dyna was younger than Andrea had first thought, probably no more than twenty-five, possibly not even that old. Her pale blonde, almost white hair was tucked neatly into two braids that she'd wound into a twist at the back of her head. She wore the same apparel Andrea had seen yesterday on many of the women. A long, open-sided apron over a full-length gown, both of a plain homespun material in two shades of faded green. Bronze rosebud brooches held the shoulder straps on the apron to the bodice.

"Is that a harness you wear on your bosom?"

"What? Huh?" Andrea glanced down and realized that Dyna referred to her bra. A plain white one edged in lace. "No, this is a bra, or brassiere. A type of undergarment worn where I come from."

"Is it like a chastity belt for the breasts? Bloody

hell, is that not just like a man to fashion another device to ensure his woman's purity? While he goes off, waving his dangly part like a bloody elephant. I saw one of those at Birka when I was a girling, belonged to a trader from one of the eastern lands."

Andrea laughed. "Women wear bras to support their breasts so they won't sag."

Dyna narrowed her eyes with skepticism. "Seems to me you don't have much to sag."

That was true, and she did often go braless. "It also keeps the nipples from showing through thin shirts. And women with big breasts don't jiggle so much."

"That I understand. The menfolks do go barmy over a set of teats that bounce." Dyna glanced pointedly at her own well-rounded assets and rolled her eyes. "Ulf the Archer wed his second wife, Helga, the homeliest woman in the world, just because she has a big bosom. Lest you think I am being unkind, just know that you will recognize Helga by the mole on her chin the size of a grape with stiff black hairs sprouting from it like cat whiskers. And"—she grinned conspiratorially at Andrea—"I know for a fact she shaves the mustache on her upper lip."

Andrea couldn't help but smile. She liked Dyna. "Do you have other children?" she asked as she pulled her T-shirt over her head, then put the plaid shirt over it. She'd put her jeans and boots on before Dyna and her son came in.

"No. Just Kugge. He is more than enough for me to handle."

"Do you have a husband?"

"I did, but he died two winters ago of the

lung fever." She put a hand to one of the rosebud brooches at her shoulders.

"I'm so sorry. Do you have family?"

"No."

"It must be hard raising a child alone in these times . . . I mean, in a place like this."

"No harder than anywhere else. Until the famine, of course."

"Have you considered remarrying?"

"The last time I married for necessity. I was breeding with a child that I lost in the first months anyhow. My husband, Jomar, was not a nice man, especially when under the alehead madness. Next time, if there ever is one, it will be for better reasons. Passion is nice, but more than that I want a man of worth who would accept Kugge as his own, who would be faithful to me, mayhap even loving."

"That doesn't sound too much to ask. Is there no one who meets those criteria?"

Dyna blushed. "There is one man, but he is hopeless. He swives every comely wench he sees. Has so many notches on his lance, he should fear it splintering apart during battle."

Andrea knew a few like that herself, including Pete the Perv. She should tell Dyna about Pete. Maybe her guy wouldn't seem so bad then. Maybe later.

She went over to the washstand and poured some water from the pitcher into the bowl. Cupping handfuls of water, she splashed her face and washed her hands. Looking about, she saw nothing that resembled a toothbrush; so, she just gargled and spit into a basin Dyna held out toward her and then placed on the floor. "Do you think you could get me a small container of salt later? Just a small amount that I could use to clean my teeth?"

"For a certainty. And you could use these as well." Dyna pointed to several twigs whose ends had been shredded. "They are good for teeth cleaning."

And, in fact, except for no toothpaste, they worked just fine.

Andrea noticed that Dyna had nice teeth, and come to think on it, many of the Vikings she'd seen did as well.

"I guess I should go down to the kitchen to help Girda. Has breakfast been served yet?"

"The men who left at dawn ate a cold meal, but we usually do not break fast here until mid-morning, and then again in the evening."

Dyna stayed behind to brush out the bed furs when Andrea left the room to go downstairs. Finn was supervising the further cleaning of the great hall, where three huge hearths that ran down the center of the room blazed with fires that provided much-needed warmth. The arrangement of the room was actually ingenious, for the times. Wide benches lined two walls of the room, on opposing sides. Trestle tables were pulled up to them at meals, but at night they became sleeping benches with bedding that had been hidden in niches built into the walls. There were also some sleeping closets for folks of the upper classes, in addition to two other bedchambers upstairs. Bigger than the average longhouses of the Vikings she'd seen in schoolbooks, but smaller and more primitive than any castle she'd ever heard of.

She gave a wave to Finn and continued on to the kitchen, where the heat hit her with welcome warmth. Obviously, the fires had been going for some time. A number of workers were already baking the circles of manchet bread, which had to be baked every day because they had no leavening and therefore went stone-hard stale rapidly. The flat bread circles had holes in the center, and as the bread cooled, they were stored on upright poles.

Girda wasn't about. One of the helpers said she was in the storage room. While she waited for Girda to return, Andrea checked out the huge cauldrons on swinging cranes in the two hearths. One held the porridge or gruel that would be served this morning. She tasted it with a long spoon, and it wasn't too bad. A bit of salt and honey had been added to make it more palatable, but it was still bland. If nothing else, it would be filling. The other kettle was a different case all together. It held the pottage, a stew that was added to over days with whatever vegetables or grains were available so the pot was always full. It might have originally had meat in it, but by now was just about ten gallons of grayish green sludge. God only knew how old it was. Andrea wouldn't even taste it for fear of food poisoning or stomach issues.

She decided to seek out Girda and perhaps come up with a plan where she could help her during the hopefully short time she was here. She walked through the scullery, where a half dozen women were busy doing laundry. Every peg on the wall and a length of rope across the room held wet apparel. Still more boiled in lye water or was being rinsed in another kettle of cold water. This was work far better done outside, but there was no choice in the winter, she supposed. All of the dirty pots and dishes had been washed and put in a special kitchen closet the day before under the cook's command.

"Look at this," Girda said when she saw Andrea enter the storage room. The woman reached into a barrel and brought out a handful of flour. It was dotted with little black specks. Weevils. "I'm trying to decide what ta do with this. With people starving down the village, we can't afford ta waste it."

"The insects probably won't hurt anyone, but isn't there any way to remove them? I don't suppose you have a sieve."

"A sieve?"

"Strainer."

"Not that I can think of. We use loose woven cloth ta strain the honey, but that wouldn't work with flour."

"How about we put a white cloth on one of the tables and spread the flour over it, several cups full at a time. Let some of the children with small hands pick out the insects. It wouldn't be a perfect solution, but we might get it fairly clean."

Girda shrugged. "Ye can try, gods willing."

"There's something I want to say, and please don't take offense. That pottage in the kitchen is probably rancid."

Girda bristled, but then she nodded. "The kettle probably hasn't been emptied since I went ta see my sister. And it was already cooking fer at least three days before that. We'll put it in the slop bucket fer the dogs. They won't mind."

"Can I make another suggestion?"

Girda frowned. Andrea was obviously pushing it. "Can I stop you? Could a herd of Valkyries stop you?"

"Of course. You're in charge here. I'm just a pastry chef, and I don't see much chance for making sweet desserts here at this time." She blinked her eyes with innocence, trying her best to be self-deprecating. "Will you let me try to make one of my favorite soups for the evening meal? Beef turnip soup with rivels."

"What are rivels?"

"Little dough balls. They're similar to noodles."

"Noo . . . what?" Girda asked. Then waved a hand dismissively as if it didn't matter what they were. "If you can make turnips appeal ta these Viking clods, give it a try."

"Good. And I won't even need any of the good parts of that cow over there. Just the long bones of the flank. They make good marrow bones. Even the deer bones would do."

Without hesitation, Girda took an axe off a long table and hacked off the cow's leg up to its rump, and it did the same thing with one of the deer, handing the two bloody stumps at her.

Andrea almost dropped the two limbs, they were so heavy. "I didn't mean right now," Andrea tried to say, but Girda was already off, giving orders to two young men to bring one of the barrels of weevily flour up to the kitchen and told a woman wearing a yellow apron to find a clean, white bed linen. The yellow apron was a bright spot in an otherwise dreary setting.

Andrea stared at the two limbs in her arms

then and placed them on the aged, much-cleaved butcher block where Girda had stuck the axe. There was nothing else Andrea could do but lift the axe high and chop the bones into sizes that would fit into the cauldron. It wasn't easy, and it took several tries each to sever the bones so the marrow would be exposed, but finally she had six sizable chunks, which she carried back to the kitchen.

Without asking for permission, Andrea brought a bucket of clean water over to the table and dunked each of the meat pieces thoroughly to make sure they were clean. She didn't care if they took offense at her actions. Who knew what dirty hands had touched this meat already? Then she took the bucket outside and dumped the contents in the snow. It must have stormed during the night and was still flurrying now.

She placed the bones on one of the tables until she had a clean pot to cook them in. In fact, it would be even better if she roasted them a bit first. So she placed them in the embers of the fire. It took only a few minutes for them to brown on one side. Stooping down on her haunches, she turned them with a long fork. Within ten minutes she had nicely charred meat, which she shoved to the cold side of the hearth.

Girda and several of the others were watching her intently, but said nothing. They probably expected her to burn her fingers or set herself afire.

Two boys were carrying the heavy pottage kettle outside for the slop bucket. It would probably have to be soaked in boiling water for hours to loosen the crud on the bottom. "Do you have another clean pot?" she asked Girda, who was now supervising the laying of a white sheet over the other table, where four children were anxiously awaiting the fun of putting their hands in flour.

"No, no, no!" Andrea said quickly, and saw Girda frown at her appearing to override her authority. "You children must wash your hands and dry them completely before handling the flour."

"I wuz gonna say that," Girda said, giving her a warning look. "There's another kettle in the cupboard." She motioned with her head toward the massive floor-to-ceiling closet that took up almost all of one wall. It held all the kitchen and dining utensils for the entire place.

The boys who'd taken the pot outside returned, shaking snow off their hair and stomping the frozen particles off their boots. The snow must be coming down harder now. Would snow impede their time travel back to the future? She sure hoped not.

Again, without asking for permission, Andrea took another bucket off the water bench and poured its contents into the kettle along with the meat. She would add more water later. The pot had to hold at least ten gallons, which made sense for as many servings as would be needed. At sixteen cups per gallon, that should be enough for everyone who wanted a taste. Even with only one bucket of water, she was barely able to lift the heavy pot onto a crane to get the soup started. When she was done, and more water was added, she would be unable to handle it herself. She would worry about that later.

"I'm going back to the storeroom for my other ingredients," she told Girda. "Can I get you anything?"

"Not right now. Will there be enough of that"—she pointed toward the kettle Andrea had just set on the hearth fire—"ta feed some of the villagers when they come ta the door this afternoon?"

"There should be."

"Good. Most of 'em will bring their own bowls."

"Perhaps we could put chunks of that day-old bread at the bottom of each bowl first," Andrea suggested.

"It's hard as slate."

"The hot liquid will soften it." She hoped.

On that conciliatory note, Andrea made her way back to the storage room, where she grabbed a large basket and began to fill it with turnips, which would be a good substitute for potatoes; the few onions and leeks and carrots that were left; a small cloth bag of barley; and a dozen eggs. There was also plenty of parsley and even a little wild celery.

When she returned to the kitchen, Andrea placed her basket near the hearth. Girda took note of what she'd brought up but didn't comment. Andrea tossed the barley into the pot, but she wouldn't add anything else for several hours. She wanted to give the bones a chance to infuse the water with all their goodness. She supposed she could mix the rivels, though she wouldn't add them until the very end.

She went to the cupboard again and found a large pottery bowl. Back at the table, she cracked twelve eggs into it and began to beat them with a wooden fork, the only utensil she could find for a whisk substitute.

"You know, Girda," she remarked, "the people here don't seem to be that bad off, considering the famine. They're not gaunt or starving, or anything, like I would expect."

"We only began rationing here at the keep the past sennight or two. The master had enough stored. And I'm shamed ta say, we weren't sharing with those down below until then."

Until Cnut was gone, she meant.

"You haven't seen the village folks yet. Sad it is, very sad!"

Okay, Andrea, why don't you bring up another cheery subject? Like this icky flour. Oh well! On those survivor shows, they're always talking about how much protein is in insects. "Is it all right if I use some of this flour that's been de-bugged?" Andrea asked.

Girda nodded and watched as she placed her bowl just under the edge of the table and whisked some of the flour into it with her fingers. Still standing there, she braced her bowl on the table and whisked the egg mixture some more. It was still liquidy. So she repeated the flour process until she had the dough the right consistency . . . slightly wet. She placed a piece of linen over the bowl and set it aside. After wiping off her table and taking the dirty utensil over to the tray of items to be washed, she went back to Girda and said, "What can I do to help?"

"I'm thinking about roasting a side of boar fer t'night's meal. So I'll hafta move the porridge kettle ta the other crane on yer fire. Don't wanna wait too long ta get the hog started. Boar can be tough as leather if it don't cook a long time over a fire what's not too hot. 'Course it would be better if we could bury it in hot coals and let it go fer a couple of days, but that works only in good weather. The embers would go out with all the cold and snow."

"Are you sure that serving the pork as a meal is wise, considering the shortage?" *Oh God, here I go again, offering my unsolicited opinion. What the hell! In for a penny, in for a pound.* "What if the men don't bring back sufficient game to last the winter, shouldn't those few animals down in the cold cellar be used to infuse flavor into a larger dish, rather than be the main dish?"

"Huh?"

"I'm just saying that we have to find a way to spread the meat and poultry and fish among a large group of people over a long period of time so that everyone is satisfied. Or at least their stomachs are filled."

"That's what I'm trying ta do, girl . . . I mean, mistress. I kin slice boar real thin. Gotta give grown men at least a taste of something substantial, lest their body humours get all twisted. They can't live on soup alone."

They can if they have to, body humours or not. But she didn't want to argue with Girda. "Whatever you say. Just make sure to save a little meat on the bones."

"I use'ly give 'em ta the dogs."

"Not anymore. Not until they've been through the soup pot at least once. Even rabbit bones or fish bones can serve a second purpose. For example, pork bones and sauerkraut would be good.

Do you have sauerkraut here . . . I mean, at the present time?"

"No, but I kin make some up. We got cabbages enough. But gods help us, the farting in the hall after eating sauerkraut is bad as rotten eggs."

Couldn't be any worse than that Lucipire slime! Andrea thought. Which immediately made her think of her sister, and worry. *Oh God, please let Celie be safe.*

She thought she heard a voice in her head say, *Have faith, my child.* Could it be God, answering her prayer? No, it was probably just wishful thinking. In fact, that was what Cnut had told her, pretty much, "Trust me." And he was no god. Though he looked like one. Not like the Lord, but one of the Norse gods. Yeah, Chris Hemsworth as Thor.

I am going over-the-cliff bonkers here. The sooner this food/famine crisis is taken care of here, the sooner I can return to the sanity of my own time. I hope. And Celie can escape the insanity of whatever she's involved in. I hope. With that in mind, she suggested to Girda, "How about we make a menu for the week?" It was like pulling teeth to get Girda to think that far ahead, but they did it finally, pitiful as the fare was.

At the end of the day, Andrea had what she considered a brilliant idea. She was making her own sourdough starter. Since there was no yeast or baking powder in this time period, she needed something for leavening. Wood ash might do. Years ago, when she was in cooking school, she'd taken a class on bread making, and one of the things early pioneer women did was start their own dough mix, which they carried with them, even on the wagon trains, just adding to it every time they removed some batter. There were no glass jars here, but Andrea figured an earthenware container should work just as well.

Girda just shook her head when Andrea explained what she was going to do. "Flour what ferments like ale? Sounds like rot ta me."

"You'll see. It will make delicious bread. And other things, too."

Despite the frigid cold outside, it soon became almost unbearably hot in the kitchen and Andrea removed her outer shirt, which led Dyna, who was mending a pair of her son's pants, to ask what those letters meant on the back of her shirt. At first, Andrea didn't understand, then she remembered. "Save a Horse, Ride a Cowboy," she explained.

"What's a cowboy?" Dyna wanted to know.

"A man who rides a horse and tends cattle."

Dyna paused, pondering Andrea's meaning, as did others in the room who were listening in. Bodil who was folding laundry. Helga who was churning butter. Dotta who was sweeping the dirt floor. Girda who was peeling turnips. Even the two boys who tended the fires, Tumi and Bjorn.

Dyna was the first to burst out with laughter, followed by giggles, and snickers, and outright guffaws from the others. Some of them gave Andrea a suspicious look at the same time they were enjoying the humor, perhaps wondering about the morals of a woman who was a walking invitation to sex.

But Girda got the humor. "Would that be like, Save a Longboat, Ride a Viking?"

"Exactly," Andrea said.

A week passed with her doctoring her sourdough starter twice a day, like a baby. It kept her from dwelling incessantly on the fact that there was no sign of Cnut or the other men, except for the fishermen, Arnstein and Ingolf, who brought them strings of bony trout. Girda said she could do a better job with spit and a stick. So, they went off again. And again. If nothing else, they had bread and fishes, like the Bible. The Good Book hadn't mentioned all those bones, though.

But no Cnut.

Was it an ominous sign that Cnut hadn't returned?

What if he'd returned to the future without her?

He wouldn't do that. Unless he was forced to, against his will.

And what about Celie? Ten days with no idea what was happening with her sister. Or even if she was alive.

Face it, she had to trust that Cnut would come back and help her.

He was her anchor in this time-travel madness. Without him, she would have to be strong if she was to survive this ordeal. Without him, she would have to sink or swim, on her own merits.

She decided to swim.

"Hey, Girda," she called out, "Did I tell you I make a great seafood chowder?"

"Whass chowder?"

Andrea explained.

Girda groaned, "Son of a troll! Soup again!"

Chapter 12

They ran into everything except Eskimos . . .

Cnut was gone for ten days. He'd run into a few problems. Like a bear the size of a bus that they'd tracked for three days. Then they'd had to build a sledge to pull the thing back to the castle. A good problem, right?

Wrong.

While they'd been struggling in the midst of a sudden blizzard to put together the conveyance, which he and his five men would have to pull by hand since they'd traveled on foot, they'd run into two Lucipires who'd been tracking Igor's lemon lure.

As far as Cnut knew, there had been no Lucipires in this territory when he'd lived in the Norselands before, but maybe they'd just never traveled this far below their arctic homeland, or one of them. But they were definitely here now. The question was how many, and how Cnut could let Michael or his brothers know of this presence.

For now, he had his frightened housecarls to deal with. Try to explain ten-foot-tall mungs with red eyes, six-inch fangs, scales, claws, and a tail to five Viking warriors, who wouldn't blink at the sight of a troop of Saxon soldiers, or a bear the size of a bus, but were petrified by these unexplainable beasts.

Even worse, one of the mungs got his teeth into lemon-scented Igor, which caused him to dissolve into nothing, from his bald head down to his stinksome toes, his clothes lying atop the snow. Forget Valhalla, this Viking sinner was now on a fast track to Lucipiredom.

Cnut was able to handle the two mungs with some expert swordwork and stabs through their evil hearts. Some skills you never unlearn. Thankfully, he still had his switchblade sword with him that had been treated with the symbolic blood of Christ. He could have killed them with a regular sword, but then they would have come back to "life" again as demon vampires. This way they were sent with tails between their legs, so to speak, to Hell for eternity. These two Lucies dissolved, as Igor had, but into pools of sulfurous slime.

But then Cnut turned and saw that his four remaining men were gawking at him like he was a monster.

With quick thinking, Cnut asked, "Have you ne'er seen a Lucibear before?"

"Huh?" Ulf the Archer, whose arrow had provided the final wound bringing down the real bear, stared at Cnut suspiciously. "What is a Lucky Bear?"

"Not a Lucky Bear, a Lucibear," Cnut lied. "They come from the far north. Rarely do they roam this far south of their polar home. We will have to tell our skald Brian to write a saga about this adventure."

Ulf and the others seemed satisfied with that explanation but Njal just stared at him. Njal was older than all of them and had no doubt gone a-Viking more than fifty times and traveled to more countries. He had lived too long without ever hearing of such creatures.

The five of them were left to drag the gutted thousand-pound bear on a poorly constructed, toboggan-like sled. It was like a not-so-funny re-enactment of the Three Stooges, except they were the Five Stooges.

That's when things got even worse. A pack of white wolves, attracted by the smell of bear blood, began to stalk them, then came rushing out of the woods. If they weren't so deadly, they would be a beautiful sight. The snow wolves, or arctic wolves, were rare, and traveled as extended families. In this case, there were about ten of the snarling, teeth-bared creatures headed their way. The men dropped their ropes attached to the sledge and raised their weapons. Four of the animals escaped, but there were six good-size bodies lying on the ground soon after. At least a hundred pounds each and five feet long. Wherever they'd been feeding, there must not be a famine.

The men were all panting heavily, exhilarated by the challenge well-met, more than they'd been panting with the bear, even. If they had some mead, they'd raise a toast.

"We can't take them with us," Cnut declared then. "The sledge is too heavy already."

"We bloody hell will," Thorkel declared right back at him. "Holy Thor! These white furs are worth a fortune. I'll carry them myself if I have to."

"You ain't keeping all these furs fer yerself," Ogot the Blacksmith protested.

"Too bad we can't eat the meat!" Ulf was poking one of the animals with his long sword, checking its sex. Apparently the male fur was more desirable.

"Wolf meat is too stringy fer my eating," Njal said. "And gamey! Phew! The stink is enough ta gag a maggot!"

"Tell that to the villagers whose bellies are bloating with starvation," Ogot remarked. His words were sympathetic but his tone was indifferent.

Thus it was, as a compromise, that they spent more time skinning the six wolves and building a fire to ward off any other predators that had an appetite for bear meat. They left the wolf meat behind, however, far from their campsite.

That night, around the fire, as they took turns at guard, their conversation turned to what else? Women.

"We need to invent a new sex spot," Thorkel said.

"What's wrong with the Viking S-spot?" Ulf wanted to know.

Thorkel shrugged. "The Viking S-spot is all well and good, but it is located in the women, and while men get much satisfaction from making their women scream when we touch them there, I think it is time for a male sex spot."

"Some people say there is nothing new in sex. Anything we think of now must have been thought of before," Cnut said.

"I don't believe that," Aslak said. "Once, whilst a-Viking, I met this man from the Arab lands who said his harem girls are taught to do the spiral. The man is on the bottom and the woman, straddling him, places his cock right at her opening. Then she starts rolling her hips in wide circles, starting big at the beginning and getting to smaller circles at the base of his cock. Then she does it over and over until the man peaks like a rutting pig."

Nice picture, that, Cnut thought. Not the corkscrewing maneuver, but the pig sex.

"Hah! I don't think I'd ever be able to talk my Ingrid into doing that," Ogot said.

"My Helga would," Ulf bragged.

No one said anything, the silent consensus being that who would want her to. To say that Helga was uncomely was an understatement.

"Did you ever make a woman fart during the bedsport?" Thorkel asked. "That is a sure sign the woman has lost control if she lets loose one of those."

"Helga does all the time."

Way more information than Cnut wanted, especially when Thorkel began to muse on Andrea's talents in the sex arts. "I never saw the attraction in flat-chested women," Thorkel commented.

"Yea, but Cnut's woman has a fine arse. I noticed in those braies she wears." This from Ulf. You'd think he had more than enough on his hands with two wives, one of them being the fearsome Helga, to be ogling a new woman.

"Is she a wanton, wearing such garments?" Njal asked.

Whoa, whoa, whoa! This had gone far enough. "Andrea is not my sex partner."

"Does that mean she is on the market?" Thorkel was twirling the edge of his mustache.

"No, she is not on the market."

"Do you speak for her?"

"I am her . . . uh, protector." Cnut hoped Andrea didn't hear that. He was pretty sure she wouldn't like that designation. It sounded too much like a mistress situation.

"No need to protect her from me. I am good with women," Thorkel proclaimed. "Methinks I will leave the question up to her to decide. Surely you cannot disagree with that, my jarl."

"I thought you had your sights on Dyna," Njal remarked.

"I did. I do, but she will not spread her thighs without the marriage vows. Even then, she demands fidelity."

All the men, except Cnut, clucked their tongues at the unreasonable expectation.

"I for one need to get some sleep," Cnut said with a wide yawn. "Tomorrow may prove to be even harder than today."

And it was.

Can anyone say wild boar?

Next time Cnut went on a hunt he was not going to pray for God's blessing on their mission. Or mayhap not so hard. A classic case of "Be careful what you pray for."

There are breadwinners, and then there are bearwinners . . .

Andrea was tending her sourdough starter, which was coming along nicely, when she heard a loud commotion outside in the back courtyard, if the flattened dirt area could be called that, of the castle. While the wooden fortress sat atop a motte, or flat-topped hill, from the front, leading down to the farms and villages, the back of it ran into the steep, heavily wooded mountain that began about a half mile from any of the outbuildings.

Everyone went outside to see what was going on. It was from that forest that the loud whoops and hollering could be heard.

Fortunately, it was that brief period of day where there was some light. So they could see clearly.

Cnut and some men were dragging a wooden contraption on which there was a huge mound. All of the men wore white skins of some kind—wolves, maybe—with the animal heads atop their own heads and the skins draping their shoulders. Two men carried a long pole from which hung a wild pig by its hindquarters.

Food. That's what Andrea and the others concluded with smiles and cheers of welcome.

It was too cold to remain outside without a coat or outer garment; so Andrea and some of the others returned to the kitchen. Although it was midday and the next meal wouldn't be served until this evening, the men would be cold and hungry. Without being directed to do so, Andrea moved the hearth crane so that last night's soup would reheat. It was made with the hated trout bones, as well as some cod and various other varieties of fish. Heads, tails, skin, and all had been cooked, then strained for bones, and the good meat picked out. Andrea had to be careful not to get the soup too hot or it would scorch. She still wasn't proficient in cooking over an open fire.

Girda was pulling out circles of manchet bread that had been baked that morning, a slab of butter, some applesauce, and a huge bowl of mashed turnips. Andrea broke stale bread into small pieces to be used like crackers.

Girda glanced over at Andrea, and they smiled at each other. Comrades in Food who'd proven two cooks could survive in one kitchen.

Cnut was the first to come bursting into the kitchen. "We got a bear," he announced with a huge smile. He usually didn't smile so broadly because of his pointy teeth. He shouldn't worry. He had a beautiful smile.

He was looking at Andrea when he made the announcement.

And she smiled back at him. "And some wolves, too," she said, looking pointedly at the animal on his head. "Is it some kind of hunting ritual?"

He put a hand to his head with surprise, having forgotten he was still wearing the carcass. "No," he said with a laugh. "We couldn't put any more weight on the bear sledge without it breaking, so we skinned the wolves and . . ." He let his words trail as he pulled the wolf off and threw it on a nearby bench.

She saw then that his face was bristly with

whiskers, as well as the shaved sides of his head. The braid that ran down the center of his head was half undone. But his blue eyes danced with joy, and she felt her heart leap and her skin tingle. Even from across the room, she smelled peppermint. How was that possible when he was covered with a long, heavy, wool cloak and layers of other clothing? In addition, with all the blood and gore the men had undoubtedly been handling, and lack of bathing or washing clothes, the men reeked. Thank God for peppermint!

"We got a bear," he announced again as he shrugged out of his cloak and did a little fist-pumping, hip-thrusting dance toward her unlike anything these gap-jawed, incredulous Vikings had ever seen, but would be good competition on *Dancing with the Stars*. Who knew the big guy could dance like that! If he put the wolf head back on, he could call it *Dancing with Wolves*.

She set down the ladle she'd been using to scoop flour into her sourdough mix, and he lifted her by the waist high in the air. Flour scattered from her hands, which were braced on his shoulders for support. He laughed and twirled her about, then kissed her full on the mouth. A delicious, wet, peppermint kiss.

She would have protested, or kissed him back, but he'd already set her down, and was doing the same to Girda. Well, maybe not a wet kiss and not directly on Girda's mouth. "We got a bear! We got a bear!"

"A bear fer the yule feast? What luck! Mayhap it will be a happy Jól, after all," Girda said, back on her feet.

Andrea hadn't a clue how to cook a bear. Was it even edible? Must be, or everyone wouldn't be so happy. If nothing else, she could try to make bear soup, she thought with silent humor.

"And we got a small boar, too. We'll give that to the villagers," Cnut announced. "Now we know where the boar herd is wintering, we can go back out on the morrow and get more."

On the morrow. Andrea repeated Cnut's words back to herself. The longer he was back in this century, the more he was beginning to sound just like his people.

The atmosphere in the castle, which had been grim, turned suddenly joyous. The famine wasn't over, but there was hope now.

"What about the others?" Cnut asked. "Have they returned?"

"Arnstein and Ingolf come in every other day with fish. Mostly smaller fish, but they are trying to cut the ice in a different spot today," Girda told him. "The gods may bless them with bigger fish there."

She noticed Cnut flinch slightly at the mention of multiple gods, but he didn't correct Girda. Instead, he inquired, "And the others? Those who went afar, to the ocean? Those who went to our neighbors for help?"

Girda shook her head dolefully. Andrea knew the cook was worried, just as she'd been worried about Cnut and all the game hunters.

Cnut told them about the demise of Igor and how they didn't even have a body for funeral rites. Then Thorkel, who'd come in by then, too, related some wild tale about Igor being devoured by Lucky Bears, huge, scaly beasts with fangs and tails that Cnut had then destroyed with a special sword. Andrea's eyes connected with Cnut's in question, and he nodded.

Lucipires? In the Dark Ages? What next?

"Ah, well, Igor must be in Valhalla by now with his very own Valkyrie, drinking mead with the gods," Thorkel said. "Odin be praised!"

The look in Cnut's eyes disagreed with Igor's fate. What was the name of the place Cnut had told Andrea about? Ah, yes. Horror.

Despite the death of one of their own, the people had much to be thankful for, and they celebrated in the way Vikings knew best, by breaking open one of the few remaining kegs of ale.

But first, Cnut and the returning hunters went to the bathhouse, which was fed by a steam-filled hot spring, to wash off the detritus of animal blood and remains, not to mention a week of sweat. One of the channels leading to the spring had been clogged with leaves and other debris, just like a bath pipe, and hadn't been useable until it was fixed yesterday. Since then, people had been taking turns bathing. Vikings, unlike many cultures of this time, valued bodily cleanliness.

While Cnut and his comrades were bathing, two other groups of hunters returned. They were preceded by the loud yipping and yapping of the hunting dogs. The hunters weren't quite as successful as Cnut's group, but still they brought more game for the larder. Two reindeer, another boar, and several beavers, whose fur was desirable and the meat edible if not appetizing. Aslak came back from his snaring with a brace of small animals. Rabbits, squirrels, possums, and quail.

An air of festivity swept through Hoggstead then. Even the villagers who came for their daily rations were not their usual gaunt, grim-faced selves. And when given one of the boar and a deer, the men, as well as the women, appeared teary-eyed.

Girda was practically orgasmic with delight over all the work to do. Yelling out orders like a drill sergeant, she soon had an assembly line of workers outside, skinning and gutting and defeathering the animals, and cutting up the massive bear. The dogs were equally ecstatic over the feast of stray parts, in addition to the entrails they'd eaten while in the woods. Girda would have liked to make black pudding, or blood sausage, but the hunters had drained the animals while in the field, by necessity.

Soon, everyone was crowded into the great hall, anxiously waiting for the hunters to finish their quickly prepared meal of fish chowder and venison with manchet bread. There was also a bowl of skyr, the Norse cheese product similar to yogurt and modern cottage cheese. No one seemed to mind the plain fare. In fact, they raved about Andrea's soup, and she preened. Was there any greater satisfaction for a cook than an appreciative diner?

Finally, stomachs as full as they were going to get, the men leaned back on their benches—Cnut was sitting below the dais with them—and began to regale the crowd with tales of their brave expeditions. Andrea barely listened to the details; she was more interested in Cnut, who was content to sip from his horn of ale and let others take the glory.

He looked every bit the Viking warrior in belted tunic over slim pants as he sat there with a slight smile on his face. He'd shaved his face, but he'd left his head bristly where it had been bald before, and he'd undone the braid that ran from forehead to nape and beyond. Instead, he now had a swath of hair down the middle of his head, tied with a leather thong, like a low ponytail, similar to her own long blonde French braid. She assumed he was going to let his shaved hair grow out. Too bad. She kind of liked the Ragnar look.

Andrea was wearing Viking attire, too, after bathing in the steam house last night. A long, pale blue gown, called a gunna, minus the apron, which she'd left behind in the kitchen.

Cnut noticed her looking at him and motioned with his fingertips for her to come join him. Finn had just vacated the chair on one side of him. She hesitated, then walked over.

He watched her through slitted eyes as she approached. "I want to thank you for all your help while I was gone. Girda tells me you have worked hard and given her ideas for better ways to use what we have. Though she did have some complaints about an excess of soup."

"Soup is the poor man's caviar."

"Whoever said that has never eaten caviar."

"Or maybe whoever coined that phrase knew that a good soup makes a wonderful meal."

He motioned with a forefinger in the air as if

giving her a point. "You're looking very Viking-ish today." He gave her a full-body survey before she sat down.

"So are you. Very Chris Hemsworth Thor-ish."

"I had to borrow clothing from Thorkel. My old garments are twice my size now."

Glancing downward, she said, "I'm not totally Viking-ish." She still wore cowboy boots, there being no extra Viking shoes for her.

"Actually, it's rather a nice mix of old and modern," Cnut observed. "Cowgirl Viking vintage. The only thing missing is the cowboy hat."

She smiled and sat down beside him. "Someone confiscated my hat. I think it was Girda. It might be her sun hat come next summer."

"I'd like to see that!"

That possibility filled her with alarm. "We won't be here that long, will we?"

"I don't think so," he said. "By the way, I have news for you. Good news." He pulled his cell phone out of a leather placket hanging from his belt. "While we were hunting, up high on the mountain, I noticed that I had an e-mail message."

"What? Give me that? I didn't know you had a cell phone. Let me call my father, or someone who can help us . . ." Her words petered off as she realized she didn't know anyone who could aid them in reverse time travel. In fact, all the people she knew hadn't even been born yet, and wouldn't be for hundreds and hundreds of years. *Aaarrgh!*

Cnut held the phone out of reach and said, "It would do you no good to try. Obviously, there is no reception here."

"Then how did you get an e-mail message? And who was it from?"

"It must have been sent before our time travel was completed. It's from Vikar." He noticed that they were drawing attention. She'd like to see how he explained cell phones, or even plastic, to Dark Age people. So he handed her the phone. "Look. You can read it."

Andrea could tell right off that there was little battery life left on the cell phone, but she pressed a few buttons in order to read the most recent message. It came from Vikar@hotvangels.com:

> *Lucies overrunning ranch. Out of here. For now. Cecilia Stewart rescued. Where the hell are you?*

Tears filled her eyes.

"What? I thought you'd be happy."

"I am. I mean, I'm relieved, somewhat, but I'm not sure what 'rescued' means. Does it mean she's injured but out of ISIS hands? Or she's uninjured but still in ISIS hands? Or she escaped the demon thingees, but is still at large?"

"I think you're overthinking this."

"I need to see Celie for myself, Cnut. Can we go back now that there's food for your people?"

He shook his head. "The hunts were good, but that's not nearly enough to last through the winter. I have a hundred and twenty or so people here at Hoggstead to feed, and another fifty in the village."

"It seems odd that you have more people living up here in the castle than you do in the village and farms."

"Not so odd. This is just the winter occupation. During spring and summer and early autumn, the blacksmith, weavers, and various workers move into outbuildings. It's too difficult to heat them all during deep winter."

She nodded hesitantly. He still hadn't answered her question about going back to the future.

"To answer your question, no, we do not have enough food or supplies yet. Soon we'll be snowbound until the spring thaw. There will be no opportunity then for hunting or anything else."

"That's what Girda said. A month at most is what she predicts before the food is gone, even with rationing. Is that possible?"

"Probable."

"How could this happen? Not the famine, but the shortage. Why didn't they plan ahead?"

"Not they. Me," he told her. "I could have prevented the dire circumstance Hoggstead is in now, or at least forestalled the worst by letting loose of some of my hoarded coins and treasures to buy goods where there is no famine. There was time. But I am a selfish glutton. I ate, nay, gorged myself while others starved. I cared more for my wealth than for those under my shield. My appetites rule me."

"You're different now."

"Not all that different. Not totally. I still want to devour a whole haunch of boar when no one's looking. Before we returned to the keep today, I was tempted to eat the bear's heart raw. I fear how much ale I will drink afore I fall into my bed furs this night. And you . . . ah, spare me Lord, but I want to ravish you so bad I can taste your coconut. I have fantasies about . . . you do not want to know!"

She blinked at him. Was he kidding? No, that smoldering look in his silver-blue eyes was no joke. She licked her lips, and inhaled his peppermint scent. Delicious. Intoxicating. No, no, no, she couldn't succumb to this insanity. "How long? How long before we can leave?"

He shrugged. "If we make it until spring, all should be well. I can empty my treasure room, if necessary, or sell a few longships."

A few longships? How many does he have? Never mind. That's not important now. "That could be as much as four or five months!" she wailed.

He nodded. "There's one thing you must understand. Like most deluded people, you believe you can control the path of your life. I know better than most, through a thousand and more years of living on the Earth, that only the Lord steers our destiny. We cruise along in life thinking we have done all the proper planning—education, righteous living, good jobs—therefore ensuring a certain future, but then God, or St. Michael, sticks out his big toe, and bam, we are flat on our faces, wondering how our carefully laid plans could go so awry."

She had to laugh at the image. But then she realized something. "Let's cut to the bone here. Are you trying to say you have no control over when, or if, we go back?" She felt herself panic at the prospect of being stuck here forever.

"Yes."

She swatted him on the arm. "You idiot! You led me to believe—"

"No, no, no! You assumed I could wave a magic wand, or sprout angel wings, or something, and we would suddenly be back in the future in the exact time and space I wanted. It doesn't work that way, or exactly."

"How does it work, exactly?"

"Sarcasm ill-suits you, m'lady," he said with a grin.

She swatted him again and muttered, "M'lady, my ass."

"That, too." He winked at her and tried to hold her hand in his, but she tugged it away. She wasn't going to be soft-soaped by winks or sweet touches.

"In the past, for many centuries, we vangels went back and forth through time, up to and including the twentieth century. Never at our own selection. Just a sudden relocation when one mission was completed and a new one started. We lived in caves. We lived in castles. We were knights and slaves, gladiators and lion food, Cossacks and pilgrims, wherever there were grievous sinners and Lucipires, we went. But then Michael decided at the beginning of the twenty-first century that there was enough evil there to warrant a permanent detachment of vangels staying there. So now we may move sideways, from place to place in present times, but no more back and forth through the ages."

"How do you explain our coming back then?"

"I can't," he said. "I only know that Michael had to have a hand in this. I'm assuming he wants me to correct my past mistakes. Or rid this region of Lucipires. Or punish me. Maybe all of those, or something else altogether.

"Or maybe we made a wrong turn on the time-travel highway. Maybe it was a mistake, like Ivak getting Gabrielle pregnant, even though he's sterile, was a mistake that Michael never anticipated." He shrugged. "It's hard to tell with Michael."

"Why can't he be more clear?"

"I wish! It's not the way he works."

"Why am I involved? I mean, I can see how it works for you. You're a frickin' vangel. I'm just a pastry chef."

"I'm not sure."

"That's just great. If you don't know, who does?"

"It may have something to do with that life-mate crap."

"Um, what's a lifemate?"

"You know, the sex lures we both apparently exude, just to each other, coconut and peppermint, but those aren't sent by Michael, I don't think. In fact, they interfere with his plans, usually, and that annoys him."

"At the moment, I'm not worried about annoying anyone, even a saint."

"You should be," he said. "If we're intended as lifemates, we're essentially one person in vangeldom. Where I go, you would go. If I die, you would die. So, it makes a kind of warped sense that if I teletransported myself, you would come with me."

"That makes as much sense as this whole ridiculous situation."

"It is what it is."

"I hate that expression."

"It is what it is."

She swatted him. "If we're going to have to stay

here for a while, I would appreciate it if you would stop doing that thing you do to me."

"And you say I don't make sense!"

"Tingle. Every time you come near me, I smell peppermint, and my skin gets all tingly. Look." She drew up the long sleeve on her gown to show him her forearm where the blonde hairs were standing on end. "See. Tingly."

He grinned at her, not taking her seriously at all. Or so she thought. Until he extended his own forearm to show her the dark blond hairs raised like a field of erotic antennae.

"Coconut tingles," he explained.

Chapter 13

A VIKING FEAST (just a little one)

Filet of venison, thin sliced in drippings
Slow-roasted bear flank with horseradish glaze
Poached bear brains in curdled milk sauce
Deer foot jelly
Bass in garlic butter

Turnips and mixed livers in onion butter
Turnips in bear marrow aspic
Mashed turnip custard

Honey-glazed doughnuts

Oh, the appetites of a virile Viking man! . . .

Cnut couldn't stop thinking about Andrea, ever since he'd returned. Who was he kidding? Before that, too.

He loved the way she'd stepped right up to help him with his problems here at Hoggstead. Girda said she had no airs about her and was willing to take on even the most menial tasks in the kitchen, not just her own culinary creations.

He loved the fact that she hadn't gone hysterical, like many women would, on realizing what had happened to them. Well, except for the constant swatting and calling him an idiot.

He loved her coconut smell. He wondered if she smelled that way all over. Forget that! He wondered how she tasted. All over.

He'd spent most of the day in the midst of blood and guts, cutting up all the carcasses, putting some pieces in the smokehouse, salting down others, and just hanging some parts in the root cellar to dry and age . . . unless they needed the meat before then.

The other hunters had come in this afternoon with a small amount of game, but they would all go out again tomorrow. Best they get in all the hunting they could before the big snows came.

"Give me an idea of how much we need to survive the winter," he said to Finn, who was at his side on the low dais that evening, enjoying a better meal than any of them had enjoyed for a long time. It had probably been unwise to release a whole deer and quarter section of bear for roasting, not to mention a ten-pound bass Arnstein had brought in today, but Cnut figured his people needed some reward for all their suffering. They would resume rationing after tonight. Ulf was given the bear heart, roasted but still oozing its juices, because his had been the final shot to bring the massive animal down. It was so big, he'd shared it, though. Glutton that Cnut was, or is, he probably would have gulped down the whole damn thing himself.

"Not counting the villagers and farmers, or the oats for the cows and horses, we would need at least fifteen boar; two dozen red deer, or reindeer; a hundred or so rabbits; an elk or another bear would be nice; all the fish we can catch to supplement the main dishes. Dried fruits if we can buy them somewhere. And vegetables—anything except turnips. Another milch cow or two would not be turned away. And another ten barrels of flour, or the barley or rye to grind our own. Otherwise, we will be making flour out of acorns like some of the villagers already do." Finn sighed as if it were impossible. "Of course, there are different ways of working those numbers. Less boar, more deer, that kind of thing."

Cnut put his face in his hands, but then he raised his head and assured Finn, "We'll make it." Somehow he knew they would. Even if it meant praying for manna from heaven.

Andrea had been elusive all evening, declining to sit and dine with him. Instead, she was bustling about, helping to bring full dishes in and take dirty trenchers out. He noticed some of the men, and women, too, snickering as she walked by, which caused Cnut to bristle. After all she'd done for them!

"What's that about?" he asked Finn.

Finn glanced where Cnut was staring pointedly and laughed. "Oh, 'tis just a jest of sorts. Your woman wore a *shert* with a message on it, which some women took offense to, but the men consider an invitation."

"What message? What invitation?"

"Save a Horse, Ride a Cowboy."

At first, Cnut couldn't believe what he'd heard.

"A cowboy is a man who rides a horse and tends cows," Finn explained.

"I know what a cowboy is," Cnut snapped.

"'Tis comparable to saying, 'Save a Longboat, Ride a Viking,' I am told."

Cnut choked on the ale he'd just swallowed and splattered drops of the liquid all over the front of his tunic.

"I think she meant it as a jest. A lewd jest."

When she passed by next time, Cnut said, "Stop and rest a minute. I want to talk to you."

"Not now. I have a surprise for everyone. I'll be right back." And she scurried off to the kitchen again.

"I think I've had enough surprises for one day," he murmured.

Apparently not.

Because Andrea and Girda and Dyna were carrying in trays heaped with what he could swear were doughnuts. Glazed doughnuts. "Be still my Krispy Kreme heart," he exclaimed.

"What?" Finn asked.

"Be prepared for a real treat," he said to Finn, even as he gave the beaming Andrea a little salute. Somehow, she'd managed to use her pastry chef talents in a Dark Age kitchen. Turned out she'd concocted some sourdough starter, which she'd used to raise the doughnuts in lieu of yeast or other raising agent, and instead of sugar, they were glazed with watered honey. Magic! Well, not *magic* magic. He knew about sourdough starter because he'd watched it being made on one of those Alaska homestead shows on TV.

And so he discovered another thing he loved about Andrea. Her doughnuts.

And so did more than fifty Viking men who not only envisioned their sexual appetites being met by becoming Andrea's own private horse, but her satisfying their sweet tooth appetites as well.

Cnut needed to have a talk with Andrea. Or something.

After he ate another doughnut.

Ting-a-ling-a-ling . . .

Andrea was so pleased with herself. She'd finally sat down beside Cnut, sipping at a cup of bitter ale, and she relished the exhaustion of a day well spent.

Her doughnuts were a huge success. Even if they hadn't risen as much as they should and were heavier than lead sinkers, and even though the honey glaze wasn't as sweet as she wanted, everyone claimed them to be food from the gods, which made Cnut cringe (the mention of multiple gods, that was), him being an angel of sorts. Supposedly.

At least it had shut the mouth of some of the men who'd been making sexual innuendos to her all night about her T-shirt.

"I give a good ride, m'lady. All the wenches say so."

"Wouldst care to try my saddle?"

"My longboat goes in and out, in and out, for a smooth ride in the waves."

"Forget a smooth ride. My longboat can take rough waves. Up, down, up, down."

Men! Andrea just ignored the lot of them. Most meant no harm, except one man who'd gone too far, touching her breast. She'd kneed him in his "longboat," which wouldn't be leaving its harbor anytime soon.

"Did you really wear a shirt that says 'Save a Horse, Ride a Cowboy' to the ninth century?" Cnut had asked with a shake of his head.

"Well, how was I to know I was going to the ninth century?"

"You have a point there. Was it any better carrying that message to a ranch with cowboys?"

She'd blushed but countered, "For all I knew, they were all terrorists there, not cowboys. And, as it turns out, beasts with tails, too. Believe me, I had no interest in riding them!"

That conversation had been hours ago. Now she took another sip of ale and sighed. There was a festive air in the hall tonight, unlike anything she'd seen so far. Girda and others had assured her that this was not a feast, like would be held at Jól, which was similar to the yule season for Christians, or when there was visiting royalty, or one of the Norse days of revelry. Just a minor celebration of thanksgiving for a good hunt and fishing.

It seemed pretty feast-like to her, though she wouldn't even taste the bear brains, even with the tangy mustard condiment that accompanied many of the meats. Andrea had eaten some strange foods in her culinary history, but brains was pushing it for her. She had promised Girda to make some dish with the bear and deer tripe tomorrow, as long as it wasn't soup.

When he'd first entered the hall, before he sat down at the "high table," Cnut had raised his hands and said, "Let us give thanks to God for the good hunting and fishing which has come our way. May He bless this food we are about to eat, and be with us in the future as we work to end the agony of famine. Amen." He'd raised his horn of ale then and smiled. "Cheers!"

There had been much murmuring at Cnut's words. Why weren't they thanking Odin, or the other gods? Why was their master suddenly a Christian? Next they would be having a priest sitting at a high place in the keep. Despite the grumbling, most of the people had joined in on the toast. Andrea suspected that the Vikings wouldn't be converted just because Cnut wished it so. If that was even his intent.

Now, Andrea noticed Dyna leaning against a nearby wall with that handsome rogue Thorkel, whose elbow was braced above her head, putting them almost face to face. Was he bothering her? Should Andrea intervene, or ask someone to aid the woman? No. Dyna was smiling up at Thorkel as he spoke earnestly, trying to convince her about something. Andrea could guess what. But Dyna wasn't fighting him off. In fact, she appeared to be flirting . . . oh, so this must be the man Dyna had alluded to, the one she liked but who couldn't keep his penis in his pants. Hopeless, was Andrea's guess.

After the meal, there was music. One of the men, an Irishman named Brian the Skald, played a lute type instrument and sang softly of Kristin, a maid whose lover, Erland, went a-Viking and never returned. Was the man lost at sea or did he find another love? Years went by, her hair grew white, and still she waited for her jarl to return.

Then a woman who proclaimed herself a skald as well stood up and said she knew a different version of that story. Apparently, it was unusual for a woman to be a poet, and the crowd appeared uncertain about whether she should be given the floor to speak. The skald with the lute was definitely not happy. They all looked to Cnut for direction.

"Wonderful! I have always wanted to hear a female point of view in these sagas. And there is naught wrong with having more than one skald in a keep. Go on, Luta."

Erland went a-Viking
As men are wont to do.
Kristin stayed at home
As women are wont to do.

Erland loved Kristin
But he loved other women, as well.
In fact, his dangly part
Would always swell.
At mere sight of a shapely
Arse. Oh well!

What Erland didn't know
All Viking men didn't, in fact,
Is that their lady loves
No brains do they lack.

Whilst men are out a-playing
Swiving everything in sight,
Their women are doing the same
With a much-younger knight.

So, Erland, go about your ways
Ride your silly boat
Because Kristin isn't pining,
Your absence she does not even note.
For she is busy at home doing
A-Viking of a different sort.

The moral of this saga is:
What is good for the gander
Is good for the goose.

The women hooted and cheered. The men looked a bit disgruntled, but they smiled as well. And Cnut called out, "Well done, Luta! Well done!"

Andrea loved that these Vikings had a sense of humor. There was nothing sexier than a man who was self-confident enough to laugh at himself.

Whoa! Where did that observation about sexy men come from? Andrea glanced down and saw that the fingers of her free hand were laced with one of Cnut's. When had that happened? He was always doing that, since he returned this morning. Touching her in passing. Brushing against her. Taking her hand. Caressing her with his eyes.

Now that she'd noticed their joined hands, she became intensely aware of the sensations there. The pulse at her wrist beat a counterpoint with his. His thumb unconsciously stroked her thumb.

And she tingled! Oh . . . my . . . goodness! Like ripples, the tingles started where their skin touched and went out in long, slow waves to other parts of her body. Her breasts seemed to swell and the nipples engorged. Between her legs, there was a rhythmic pulse, matching that at her wrist.

It was alarming and, at the same time, felt so good.

She glanced up and saw that Cnut was staring at her. His eyes had become so silvery, they were more gray than blue. "What are you doing to me?" he asked.

"The better question is, what are *you* doing to *me*?" She shivered as a massive wave of tingles passed over her, and she was assaulted with the scent of peppermint. She would never be able to chew gum in the future without getting turned on. Assuming there was a future for her.

"I feel such a hunger," he said.

Oh! He'd told her before that he was a glutton. "Do you want something else to eat? The doughnuts are gone, but—"

"It's not food I hunger for." He squeezed her hand.

More tingles, and now she could smell coconut mixed with the peppermint. Someday, she was going to make a three-tiered white peppermint cake, with a frothy whipped cream frosting, and coconut and peppermint sprinkles on top. She was going to name it Tingling Mint Coconut Dream Cake. It would be a hit, she just knew it would.

"What is it you hunger for then?" she asked, as if she didn't already know.

"You."

Meanwhile, back at the ranch . . .

Jasper was having a hell of a good time. The Circle of Light was overrun with Lucipires and evil terrorists. *Yay for our team!* The innocents had run for the hills, or were dead if they'd been dumb enough to get in a demon vampire's path. *Big dumb deal!* The vangels had been chased away. *Tomorrow is another day.* Lucipires had ruled the day.

The Lucipires had almost caught one of the vangels, a lackwit Viking boy who fashioned himself Michael Jackson reincarnated, moonwalking and all. The boy had escaped, but a good bite had been taken out of his leg. He wouldn't be dancing any time soon. In fact, he might very well perish. *I can only pray . . . uh, hope.*

Life was good! Or, rather, nonlife was good.

"Tell me again why we're sitting out here on our arses with a smoky fire, being bitten by flies the size of baseballs," Zeb complained, swatting at yet another of the buggers who zapped him in the neck.

"Because I always wanted to try wienies on a stick and marshmallow s'mores. You should have stayed in demonoid form, like me. The bugs can't penetrate scaly skin."

Zeb was laughing like a loon a short time later when Jasper and the others around the campfire were trying to lick gooey chocolate and marshmallow from their claws. "Next you'll be wanting to have a sing-along," Zeb gasped out.

Jasper couldn't be offended. It *was* a mess. A bad idea. Besides, he was too happy over today's results to let a little thing like sticky claws spoil his mood. They'd harvested two dozen evil humans, most of them terrorists guilty of despicable crimes, who were already in butterfly jars back at Horror, halfway to stasis.

Jasper's troops didn't take all of the ISIS folks. In fact, they'd deliberately left behind some of the worst. Based on a principle Zeb had told him about from his association with Navy SEALs, called force multiplication, Jasper hoped that those remaining terrorists would continue to convert more people to their dogma, which in turn would multiply the ranks of evil humans. The Lucipires would swoop in periodically to take more of them for their own conversion. Voilà! A win-win situation for everyone. Everyone evil, that was.

Later, when they were back at the lodge and Jasper was in humanoid form, he had his bare feet soaking in a basin of Epsom salts water. The damn cowboy boots had given him blisters. *Did John Wayne ever have this problem?* "What happened to that Cnut Sigurdsson who was here with some human woman?"

"No one knows for sure. Yet. Not even his brothers," said Zeb, who was eating one of the leftover hot dogs on a bun with mustard and onions, a can of cold beer beside him on the kitchen table. "He's probably hiding somewhere, from Michael, for failing in his mission here."

"Who was the woman?"

"No one important. An innocent human looking for her sister, who also disappeared."

"Together? I mean, all three of them?"

Zeb shrugged.

"So, tell me your plan," Jasper encouraged Zeb.

"Well," Zeb said, wiping his mouth with a paper napkin, "I believe the vangels will return. They weren't expecting so many of us Lucipires and were so greatly outnumbered, they decided to retreat. I can't help but think it was a temporary retreat."

"So we should be prepared for an attack?"

"Yes, but they'll be hovering over the wounded vangel first, trying to heal his wounds. Good luck with that!" Jasper commented gleefully. Lucipire venom was almost impossible to remove, even if a bite wasn't deadly. "Should we retreat like they did and come back another time?"

"I don't think that's necessary. We have a hundred demon vampires scattered around this ranch. If I hear that they're bringing bigger numbers, I can call on Tess to pull from her legion in New York. Or I can call in the rest of mine from other assignments."

Jasper accepted Zeb's counsel. "Have you established a new headquarters yet?"

"No. I'm using New Orleans for the time being. But I might try Los Angeles later."

"Good, good. Both sinful cities." Jasper sighed with pleasure over a day well-spent. "I bet the Sigurdsson bastards are upset over the events here today. I bet they'll come back themselves for retribution. Holy Hades! I would love to have me a vangel, especially one of the VIK. On second thought, bring in more fighters, just in case."

Zeb nodded, finished off his hot dog in one big bite, and washed it down with a long swig of the beer. He was about to rise from his chair and leave but Jasper put up a halting hand.

"Beltane," he said to his assistant, who was fussing about the kitchen, cleaning up dirty dishes left by those there before them, "leave us alone. I would have a private word with Zebulan."

Zeb's head shot up at the use of his full name, and he went immediately alert. Jasper was fond of the Hebrew demon, always had been, but Jasper was troubled by news of late.

Jasper stepped out of the water onto a towel and allowed himself to morph into his full demonoid form, which was formidable, even to other Lucipires. More than seven feet tall, sometimes eight, and massive in breadth. His tail extended all the way to the dining room, knocking over a bench.

"Why have you killed no Navy SEALs and brought them to Horror?" Jasper asked right off. That had been Zeb's mission the past few years, and while Zeb had worked hard harvesting sinners in general, not one of them had been a member of the elite special forces who valued bravery and loyalty and all those good things most hated by Satan.

Zeb also changed into demonoid form. He was large and fiercesome but not nearly as big or strong as Jasper was. "It's hard, but that's no excuse. I have failed you, master. Do you want to pull me from that assignment?"

"No. Not yet. But there have been complaints about you."

"Complaints? From whom?" Zeb hissed through elongated fangs. "Who dares to criticize me behind my back? It was probably that Nazi Heinrich."

Jasper conceded the point with a tilt of his heavy

head, and he almost burped. All that chocolate and marshmallow was upsetting his stomach. He needed a good dose of blood, preferably a virgin sinner's blood. *Good luck with that!* "Heinrich, yes, but others, too. It has been called to my attention that even though you bring in large numbers of kills, they are mostly dreadful sinners who would never repent anyway and would have ended up in Hell without any prodding from a Lucipire."

"That's not true!"

"Mayhap not! Be on alert, though. I am watching you, and so are others."

Zeb knew better than to argue with him. Instead, he bowed his head and said, "What would you have me do, my lord? How can I prove my loyalty?"

Jasper didn't hesitate. "Bring me a Sigurdsson."

He could see the alarm on Zeb's face. Was it because he feared he would not succeed, or that he did not want to succeed? Jasper hated doubting his most trusted friend . . . or a comrade he'd thought was his most trusted friend. "Go for Cnut, the one who is missing," he suggested. "Since his brothers are yet unaware of his whereabouts, you should be safe in tracking him down. The vangel will be vulnerable without his brothers' protection."

To give him credit, Zeb did not hesitate. "As you wish, master."

Chapter 14

A-Viking they did go . . .

Cnut stayed down in the hall as late as he possibly could without falling asleep, face in his beer. And, yes, he'd overimbibed. More intoxicating beverage than he'd drunk in centuries. But it wasn't the ale that was intoxicating him. It was a coconut blonde who was igniting the fire in his belly, and lower. What appeared to be the biggest temptation of his life.

He made his way through the tables, those that had not been dismantled for the night, heading toward the stairs. Along the way he noticed Thorkel snoring on one of the benches. Earlier he'd seen him kissing Dyna with the finesse he was known for, but apparently Dyna was playing for bigger stakes than a roll in the horndog's bed furs. Cnut's bet was on Dyna in this battle of the sexes.

As for himself, it wasn't even a battle. Not like Thorkel's, anyhow. To wed or not to wed. To bed or not to bed. Well, mayhap the latter. But that would be a foolish argument to have with himself when the future was so unknown.

But then, when hadn't the future been unknown for him? Even back when he was a living human being.

All these questions—should he, shouldn't he? could he, couldn't he?—were driving him barmy. Cnut couldn't put off his bed any longer. In the morning, he and a group of his housecarls would depart for more hunting. He needed his sleep. Andrea would certainly be asleep by now. Leastways, that was the excuse he gave himself for climbing the stairs. He was strong; he'd proven that with centuries of celibacy, except for a few lapses in the early years. He would be strong now, too.

All his good intentions were for naught when he entered the room and found Andrea still awake. And waiting for him. She stood before the hearth wearing a thin shift that was made near transparent by the small fire that still burned. What he couldn't see clearly of her body, he imagined, and he had a good imagination.

"You're awake," he said dumbly.

"Damn right, I'm awake. What's in the mead anyhow? An aphrodisiac?" A fire was burning in the hearth, but the room was still cool. Even so, she lifted the thin shift that barely covered her chest as if she were overheated. For added emphasis, she fanned herself.

It took less than a second for her words to sink in. She was turned on? His mind went blank, and his knees almost buckled, forcing him to hold on to the back of a chair for support. Once composed, he smiled.

"Your fangs are bigger," she observed.

So is something else. "That happens when a vangel is in a state of high emotion. Like preparing for battle," he told her, "or about to make love."

"Whoa," she said.

Was that a good "whoa" or a bad "whoa"?

But then she added, "So the booze turned you on, too?"

Definitely good. "No. *You* turned me on."

"Oh." She licked her lips as she watched him toe off his boots, then take his short sword from its sheath at his side and prop it against the chair. He undid the belt, dropping it to the floor, but still she said nothing in protest; so he lifted off his tunic and dropped it to the floor as well. He was left with stockinged feet and low-hung braies.

He raised a brow at her in question. When she just raised a brow back at him, he unlaced himself and stepped out of his pants. He was almost embarrassed by his size. He knew it was due to his long period of abstinence—of the two-person sort, that was—but what must she think?

"Why are you so suntanned?"

He glanced down at himself and realized she was right. He was bronzed all over, as if he'd been lying in a Caribbean sun, rather than out hunting, fully covered, in the frigid snow. "Vangel skin develops a healthy glow when we have either saved a dire sinner or vanquished a Lucipire."

She arched her brows at that, still not wholly believing what he was, apparently.

"In any case, you're beautiful," she said.

Cascades of pleasure swept over him at her words like unfurling ribbons. It was New Years' Eve and a Broadway tickertape parade combined.

The only thing missing was the confetti. But wait, were those flakes of coconut and peppermint floating in the air? No, just a misty aura, cocooning them in the subtle, tempting scents that were their personal downfalls. Not that he'd known he had a weakness for coconut before.

He was getting fanciful, and Vikings did not get fanciful. They clouted their enemies on the head with battle-axes, they swived their women in the bed furs. Expert. Matter-of-fact. No thinking about the pros and cons. No fanciful analysis.

Cnut closed his eyes for a moment, finding it harder and harder to concentrate and make logical decisions. No longer could he hold a rein on his runaway passion.

"Are we going to make love?" she asked.

He didn't know about love, but it appeared they were going to do something. "For a certainty," he said.

The odd thing was, he didn't feel guilty, now that the decision was made, the line crossed. Maybe this was how his brothers had felt when they met their lifemates. Resistance at first, then a resignation that what would be would be. Inevitable punishment be damned.

"If you are agreeable," he added, and prayed that she was. He almost crossed his fingers behind in back in that foolish youthling gesture.

"I have no choice." She yawned and stretched as she spoke, causing her small breasts to rise against the thin linen fabric, the nipples engorged.

His enthusiasm grew by leaps and bounds, lodging with a hot ache between his thighs. He tingled all over, for cloud's sake! He even put a hand over himself in an attempt to press himself down. It didn't work. "There is always a choice," he rasped out.

"Pfff! Not when I'm under your spell."

He was a drowning man. With each of her honestly spoken words, he sank deeper and deeper into the depths of his arousal. If he wasn't careful, he would ejaculate prematurely like an untried youthling seeing his first naked woman. Maybe that would be for the best. Embarrassing, but an end to this madness. He stepped behind the chair and waited for that to happen. No such luck . . . or misfortune. "You're no more under my spell than I'm under yours. Face it, we are both ensorcelled by . . . something."

"Should we do something to stop it?"

Oh God, will she never stop chattering? I need silence to think, to concentrate. Still, he asked, "Like what?"

"I don't know. Go outside and roll in the snow."

Is she serious? "Brrr!"

"Or go jogging."

Yeah, in the snow, in a pair of boots, or my wool socks, nude, that would do it! "I could barely climb the stairs tonight; my knees creaked so."

"Something besides stare at each other like a warm apple pie after a week of fasting."

"Or a coconut cream pie." He could almost taste the sweet pastry.

"Or peppermint bark at Christmastime. Yum."

Next she will be talking about licking my peppermint stick. Enough of this malingering banter! He made a motion with his hand and said, "Lose the shift, Andrea."

She hesitated.

Smart girl!

It was a moment of truth for her, too. A line that, once crossed, couldn't be reversed.

Then she undid the laces at her neckline and let the shift drift down over her body to puddle at her feet. She was slim, as he'd expected, and her breasts were small, but she was perfection. Her hips swelled out from a narrow waist. Her legs were long but with some muscular definition, as were her arms. She must jog, or do some exercise. And her breasts . . . they were like halved peaches with pale rose-colored nipples, a nice size for her slender frame. And her buttocks, what he could see from this angle, would be his undoing. High and round and sweetly enticing.

He walked over to her and cradled her face in his trembling hands. "I . . . want . . . you . . . so . . . much," he murmured, and between each word he whisper-kissed her forehead, her jaw, her neck, the side of her mouth. And then he took her lips in a kiss of intense aggression, a reminder that he was man, and she was woman.

Her breath caught in a soft gasp, and then she was kissing him back, as much as he would let her with his hands controlling the angle of their heads, the depth of their kiss.

She put her hands on the tense muscles of his shoulders and darted her tongue into his mouth, in challenge? For a brief second, it seemed as if she was licking his fangs.

A violent shiver swept over him. He raised his head to gaze at her, to see if she was teasing him or if it had been an innocent reflex. Hah! She knew exactly what she was doing, or leastways it was her innocent attempt at seduction.

She was succeeding.

He reclaimed her lips in a kiss even more voracious than the last.

She kissed him back just as voraciously.

Enough! He cupped her bottom in his hands, lifted her, and walked them both to the bed, lips still locked until he tossed her onto the mattress and came down over her.

"Tell me, Andrea, have you ever gone a-Viking?" he asked, nuzzling her neck before raising his head.

"No," she whispered, a glow of anticipation in her golden eyes.

"Then you are in for an interesting journey, m'lady."

It was true what they said about Vikings . . .

Andrea didn't consider herself a sexy woman. Not even close. Oh, she liked sex, except for Pete the Perv, but her experience was limited, and she had to admit to a low sex drive. Compared to her friends, anyhow, who had active sex lives, if they could be believed, and according to *Cosmo,* which implied that women got laid on a daily basis, multiple times, and loved it. Yearned for it. Did everything in their power to seek, find, and enjoy the perfect bed partner.

"99 Sexy Ways to Touch Him."

"Untamed Va-jay-jays."

"Tease Him and Please Him."

"Foreplay Men Crave."

Jeesh! Talk about one-track minds! Other women's one-track minds.

But all that changed since Andrea had met Cnut, who'd somehow tapped into her dormant sexuality. At some point in the past week or so, her libido had kicked into overdrive. And she was off to the races. Yes, she should put on the brakes right now. But she didn't want to, and probably couldn't if she tried.

So she sucked in a huge whiff of peppermint and said to the hunk of burning love leaning over her in the bed, "Has *People* magazine ever contacted you?"

She could tell her question disconcerted him, especially since he was poised over her on braced arms, his thighs spread between her spread thighs (*how had that happened?*), his erection (*and, whoo boy, what an erection!*) aimed at her lady parts like a dog on point, and he was huffing away like a locomotive in his attempt to slow down the runaway train of his arousal.

"What? No. Why?"

She shrugged. "You have to be the sexiest man alive." And that was the truth. He had a perfect body. Wide shoulders, narrow waist, six-pack abs, muscular arms, and long legs. Not overly hairy, and what was there was silky blond. His face displayed sharp Nordic features with high cheekbones and full lips, a straight blade of a nose. Except for the pointy lateral incisors, he was perfection, and even they rather added to his allure, except they were more pointy than usual now.

He let out a hoot of laughter, then collapsed on her in a continuing fit of shaking humor. She felt the shaking on her breasts where his chest hairs abraded her nipples, and between her legs where his "dog on point" was jabbing a sensitive part of her body.

"What's so funny?" she asked.

"Andrea, I'm fat. Oh, I know I no longer weigh four hundred or more pounds, but to me, I will always look that way. Far, far from anyone's vision of sexy man. Thanks for the compliment, though."

She understood what he meant. It was all in self-perception. She saw herself as the sexless, skinny kid who'd once been wounded by a neighborhood boy when he gave her the nickname Beanpole and it stuck. Hmm. Could that have something to do with her lack of interest in sex? Until now? *We are what we perceive ourselves to be. The best sex is when we feel good about ourselves. Cosmo* again!

She was feeling really good about herself at the moment and took the first step by running her fingertips over the breadth of his shoulders and down his arms to his elbows.

He shuddered in reaction, and goose bumps rose on his skin.

That made her feel even better about herself. She must have smiled in satisfaction because he murmured, "Witch!" and leaned down to nip at her lower lip. Without hesitation, he came back for more in a kiss so hungry and devouring she could hardly breathe. Then something amazing happened, he was breathing into her mouth, and she was exhaling into his mouth. Back and forth, it was as if they were breathing for each other. Breath kisses.

She felt dizzy and disoriented. A blue haze rose from his shoulders and swirled above and around them. At the same time, she smelled peppermint and coconut, an odd but wonderfully complementary combination. Nothing overpowering, just a wispy tease to the senses, coming and going.

She tore her lips away from his and gazed up at him. His eyes were pure silver now, not their usual blue. His lips were swollen from her kisses, and even though he kept his lips pressed together, she knew the fangs were extended inside his mouth. A double whammy for the male of the vangel species, she supposed. Their arousals couldn't be hidden because they got fangs as well as erections.

"I want so much to explore your body, to touch you. Here." He brushed his fingertips over one breast.

She inhaled sharply at the exquisite pleasure.

"And here." He cupped her pubic bone and brushed his middle finger over the wetness between her legs.

Her heart stopped for a moment, then started a beat/counterbeat with her clitoris.

"But I cannot wait."

And he thinks I can? She was a tingly mass of beating cells that were passing over her body in waves. She closed her eyes and arched upward. She might have moaned.

Cnut used that opportunity to lift her knees and

press them upward, opening her to the sudden plunge of him, hard and big and smooth, into her body. He filled her.

And she welcomed him with repeated clasps of her inner muscles that moved and shifted to accommodate his size. Her clitoris felt wide open and vulnerable when he drew back and thrust in again, hitting her in precisely the right spot.

A shattering mass of nerve endings exploded between her legs, causing a reverberation of spasms to pass to other parts of her body. Everywhere. Her breasts. Her toes. Her palms. Even her scalp.

That preliminary orgasm stretched her inner walls and allowed him to enter even more deeply, so far she swore her womb shifted. And it was preliminary because she felt as if this was just the beginning, and Cnut definitely hadn't got his satisfaction yet. Sweat beaded his forehead, and muscles strained in his arms as he began a rhythmic thrust/retreat, thrust/retreat, thrust/retreat, in and out of her body, accompanied by a wet, sucking sound down there that would have embarrassed her if she had the sanity to understand what was happening. The strokes started long and slow but then became short and hard, but over, and over, and over, each time hitting her overstimulated clitoris. If she got any more lightheaded she was going to faint.

"Now! Now!" she begged.

"Not yet, sweetling. Relax."

Relax? Is he crazy? But she liked the sweetling endearment, or she would if she had any particle of brain left in her head to recognize what was happening, let alone being said.

She planted her feet on the bed and tried to arch upward to hasten this maddening assault of tortuous pleasure. That only seemed to arouse him more. He made a raw sound deep in his throat and rolled his hips from side to side when embedded in her.

She screamed then. Something she'd never done before. But she couldn't help herself. The orgasm that came over her was so powerful and so long, it shook her entire body. Pulsing hotly between her legs, up through her convulsing vagina, out through all her limbs, causing her breasts to swell and her nipples to ache.

When she was able to look up, she fully expected Cnut to be laughing at her. So needy and sexually deprived that she would act like this!

But he was in the midst of his own earth-shattering climax by the look of him. His back was arched back and his teeth were bared, but he seemed to be in some distress. "I can't . . . oh bloody hell, I can't come." His eyes connected with hers then and she saw the pain in them before he whispered, "I'm sorry. Sorry, sorry, sorry . . ."

On those words of inexplicable apology, he unbraced his arms and used his fingers to comb through her hair, adjusting her face to the side. With one last "Sorry," he lowered himself and sank his fangs into her neck.

It didn't hurt, except for a pinprick sensation, and it happened so quickly she had no chance to protest. And then . . . oh my God, *then* . . . she seemed to swirl up in the air, the two of them entwined in a full-body orgasm. Twirling, twirling, twirling, like a reverse tornado funnel. She felt him ejaculate inside her, and then they seemed to melt together and fall to the earth . . . to the mattress . . . together. It was as if they'd fused into one being.

She lost consciousness.

When she awakened, Cnut was licking her neck as if to heal his mark there. "I'm sorry," he said. "I didn't mean . . ."

She pressed her fingertips to his mouth to halt his words and shook her head. "Don't apologize. It was the best sex I've ever had." She paused and added, "How soon can we do it again?"

She felt his laughter all the way down to his half-limp penis, which was still inside her. Which proved to be convenient.

Chapter 15

Piña coladas and peppermint sticks . . .

Cnut wasn't about to ignore an invitation like that.

He flipped over so that he was on his back and Andrea was on top, straddling him. And the best part was, he was still inside, even if only half ready for action.

She thought to shock him by saying she'd just experienced the best sex of her life, but he had news for her. It was the best sex he'd ever had, too, and he had a whole lot more years under his belt, so to speak.

She blinked at him. "I didn't mean right now."

"Oh. Well, then, you can rest for a while." He reached to lift her off, disappointed but not crushed that he would have to wait.

But she slapped his hands away. "I can relax where I am."

He doubted that very much, but he wasn't about to argue. He was no fool, leastways not all the time. Her eagerness excited him. A lot.

"Fine," he agreed. "Just relax and let me . . . let

me make it good for you." He stroked his fingertips over her collarbones, along the smooth skin of her shoulders, then down to the curve of her elbow and over her forearm. He was fascinated by the fine hairs he was able to raise by just that soft caress. Was she tingling? He certainly was, just watching her reaction.

"Good? Good?" She stared at him with disbelief. "Any better than the first time and I might need shock therapy to revive me."

Modern women had such a way with words. Rather jarring at first, but pleasing nonetheless. "I'm sure I can come up with something shocking."

"As long as it's not perverted."

Jarring is too small a word. "Define perversion. There are good perversions and not so good perversions." *In fact, I recall—*

"Hah!"

He was admiring her thighs and her buttocks, which rested on his own thighs . . . admiring with the palms of his hands, that was. That's probably why she was nigh speechless for the moment—*Thank you, God!*—waiting for what he would do next. He wasn't sure himself.

"You know a lot about perversions, do you?" What next? Her belly button, which was inverted in an adorable fashion, or her equally adorable breasts? he mused. Instead, he just made a quick pass over her blonde curls.

Her breath hitched, and she jolted, but still she was able to reply, "Plenty. Let's just say Pete the Perv and leave it at that."

So much for her speechlessness! He folded his

hands behind his neck to prevent any further distractions, by himself. "Now you have me intrigued."

"Golden Showers."

"Huh?" *Surely, she doesn't mean . . .*

"Didn't you ever watch *Sex and the City*?"

"Um."

"Carrie's partner wanted her to pee on him during sex."

He'd thought she was going to liken him to Mr. Big, but he hadn't been expecting anything like a reference to urine. In fact, her reference had nothing to do with him, precisely. His eyes went wide and he burst out laughing.

"Do that again."

"Do what again?"

"Laugh so your penis moves inside me."

"Ah, Andrea, you are a delight."

She smiled. "I don't think I ever delighted anyone before."

"I promise I won't ask you to relieve yourself on me. There are too many other things I want to do to you, and you to me." He thought of something then and chuckled.

"What?"

"Thorkel claims there is great pleasure in making a woman fart during sex play. A clear indication that the man has made the woman lose control."

"Don't you dare!"

"Okay. No Golden Showers and no farting."

"I can't believe I'm having this conversation, especially in the midst of you . . ." She motioned toward the place where their bodies were joined.

With his hands still folded under his head, he flexed himself to show he understood.

She gasped. "You're good."

"I know." Then, like a master puppeteer, he began to pull Andrea's strings. He took her hands and showed her where he liked to be touched.

Everywhere.

She, on the other hand, had a preference for breasts and the backs of her knees.

No problem. Then he placed his hands on her hips and showed her how to rock for the best effect on both of them. Forward, backward, fast, slow. They all worked for him.

She seemed to prefer slow and long rocking.

When her hips began to roll wildly, he put his hands on her butt cheeks to guide her in a more even rhythm. Her slickness, a combination of both their fluids, wept around him like hot honey, easing the friction of his massive erection.

"Kiss me," she said, leaning forward, her glazed eyes drifting half shut.

"Open first," he demanded, and when she complied, he thrust his tongue into her mouth, mimicking the strokes down below. At the same time, he moaned in pleasure and caressed her breasts, rubbing his palms over the turgid nipples, then rolling them between his thumb and fingers.

Her inner muscles convulsed around him.

So I can make her come just by touching her breasts. He tabled that information for future note.

She tore her mouth from his and gasped, "You taste like Christmas candy canes, and Halloween treats, and toothpaste, and everything peppermint. Clean, with a bite."

"That's me," he laughed, "and you taste like coconut cream pie and piña coladas."

"Nice combination."

"We do make a nice combination," he said, surprising even himself. He glanced down to where they were joined, pubic bone to pubic bone, a blend of her honey-blonde curls and his darker, almost brown ones, like gold and bronze. Let her think that's what he meant, not, God forbid, a life-mate kind of combination. "Lean forward a little, sweetling."

"Why?"

"So I can fondle your breasts and bring you to peak again."

She blushed. "While you lie there like a statue, unaroused?"

"I would hardly call this unaroused," he said, and thrust his hips upward several times so she could feel how hard and big he was. Hot and pulsing with life. Un-statue-like, for a certainty!

"Holy . . . moly!" She leaned forward to hold on to his shoulders for support. "How do you do that?"

"What?"

"Keep yourself from climaxing?"

He shrugged. "Long years of practice."

"This is embarrassing. I must have come five times already to your one."

"You're keeping count now?"

"Hard not to."

"There is naught to be embarrassed about. Your peaking is my pleasure. It is as it should be."

"Said the macho Viking."

"That remark deserves a punishment, m'lady,"

he said, and took one of her breasts into his mouth, areola, nipple, and all, and began to suck with a hard rhythm. He used the other hand to hold her in place by the nape of her neck. Then he did the same to her other breast.

By then she was a spasming mass of moaning, wanton want.

Not to be outdone, she took him in hand, right where they were joined, making room for her fist. Then she extended her fingers to tickle his balls. He about shot off the bed.

And the two of them shattered to a mutual climax that stunned them both. She held on tight, he held on tighter, lest they fly away, in pieces. For a long time afterward, he lay on his back, holding her in his embrace, her face on his beating chest, one of her thighs extended over one of his, the knee nudging his finally quiescent man part.

"Mine," he whispered, kissing the top of her head. He had no idea what that meant or where the thought had come from. Luckily, she hadn't heard him, or if she had, she wasn't mentioning it.

Instead, she was circling one of his nipples with a forefinger when she asked idly, "When's your birthday?"

"Huh? I have no idea. We did not mark birth dates in my time. Except for kings and those of great fame. Even then, they were guesstimates."

"Let's pick March 15 for your birthday, in modern times, several months from now. I'm assuming . . . hoping . . . that we'll return to the future by then. We'll celebrate with something special on that date."

Uh-oh. Just like a woman. One tup and she is

making plans. But he was feeling generous, so he put a hand on her rump and said, "You've already given me something special."

"Not that," she said with a laugh. "I've been concocting a special recipe in my head that would be perfect for a birthday cake. Candy Cane Coconut Cake."

"I'm lying here wondering what carnal activity I can try with you next, and all you can-*cock* in your mind is food."

"Who says food can't be sexy?" She raised her head and winked at him and then, wanton wench she was proving to be, she crawled over him, knelt between his legs, and showed him what she could do with a peppermint stick.

Blend my WHAT?

They didn't sleep at all that night.

Andrea should feel guilty about that, knowing Cnut had to be up early to go out into the frigid weather again and hunt for more food. But she didn't, especially when he told her that vangels didn't require much sleep. They stored sleep energy like some animals stored body fat and therefore could go long stretches without rest.

Besides, the little bit of blood he'd taken from her had energized him, too. Like a Raging Bull, the popular vodka Red Bull cocktail, with an Oyster Shooter for a libido lift chaser, he told her.

She had to think about that one for a while.

Cnut got up several times to put more logs on the fire to maintain some heat in the room. For a man who claimed to feel his phantom fat, he seemed at ease with his nude body, and she enjoyed watching him move. The supple pull of long muscles in his thighs and the tightness of his butt as he bent to lift more wood. The breadth of his shoulders and the strong tendons in his neck as he stretched. His narrow waist and hips. The human body—*his* human body—was a work of art.

At one point, they talked, in bed, while she combed and rebraided his hair. "Will you shave the sides again?" she asked.

"Maybe. Maybe not. Not while I'm here, anyway. Too much trouble."

"And how long do you think we'll be here?"

He sighed. "I know you want precise answers from me, but I just don't have them. Mike is being ominously silent. I can't reach my brothers. That's deliberate, of course. I'm expected to figure out the mission on my own."

"Like you being given a second chance to help your people in the famine?"

"Probably."

"You sound doubtful."

"Our missions are never that simple."

"Something related to the demon vampires, as well?"

"Possibly. I may know more after tomorrow if I run into any more Lucies, especially if I can keep one alive long enough to answer some questions. In particular, why are they showing up in this time period suddenly? It's not like the famine would affect them, unless people become more sinful during harsh times."

"I still don't understand why I'm involved."

He remained silent.

"That lifemate nonsense?"

"I can't discount it, especially after the kind of sex we just engaged in, which was beyond a physical act, you must agree."

Must she? She didn't want to admit to that, just yet.

"Or maybe you were just at the wrong place at the wrong time," Cnut went on, stretching forward so she continued the braid down his neck. "An accident."

Andrea shook her head. The things that were happening—the emotions swirling between her and Cnut—they were no accident. No way!

"Tell me about your life before. Why do you think you became a . . . a . . ."

"Glutton?"

"No! I meant to say vangel, but I find it hard to refer to you that way, to think you are anything but a human being."

"Well, the two are probably tied together, and I don't have a clear answer for either one. Hoggstead was my mother's home, and my maternal grandsire's before that, but I grew up at the Sigurdsson estate with my half brothers. I was sickly as a child—probably some kind of respiratory ailment that I eventually outgrew—but while a youthling my mother coddled me, overfed me, would not let me run and play like the others, that kind of thing. She died suddenly when I was about ten, and I became lost in the immense household. My father had many wives and concubines and children, both legitimate and not. I was a needy child, craving attention, and when I didn't get it, I filled the hole with food, and later drink and sex and other excesses. Not a new story. I understand that now, but back then I just became selfish and self-centered in my gluttony.

"Later, when I became jarl of Hoggstead, as long as I had food and drink, I ignored what was happening to my people. Even now, we here in the keep are fed sufficiently while others starve."

"So, you were a glutton, but how did you become a vangel?"

"Make no mistake, Andrea, I am still a glutton. Why else would I be swiving you 'til I wear my cock down to a nub, uncaring of whether you are sore or tired or generally uninterested."

She laughed and smacked him on the shoulder. "Idiot!" she said, but not with her usual disdain. "Do I seem uninterested? If I were tired, I would be asleep. Instead, I feel as if I've inhaled the same energy drink you have."

He turned and smiled at her. "Pleased I am to have pleased you."

More of the Viking talk! "You are so full of it. Pleased you are to have gotten your rocks off, multiple times," she accused him.

"Guilty as charged. Can we do it again?" He repeated her words back at her, then took the comb from her hand, tossed it to the floor, and rolled over on top of her. "Have I told you about the famous Viking S-spot?"

He hadn't, but he did now. And whoo boy, the Vikings could make a fortune by writing a book about that particular talent, hitting all the talk show circuits, becoming celebrity sex experts. On the other hand, they were probably better off keeping it a secret.

If that wasn't enough—*and, believe me, it was more than enough!*—toward dawn Cnut showed her he was a modern Viking, as well. He'd read somewhere—*probably* Cosmo, *though he denied it*—about something called a Blended-O, and wondered if she'd like to try it.

Of course not. Silly man! Why would I want to top off the best night of my life with a showstopper of a carnal experience? Not that the Viking S-spot wasn't phenomenal. But, jeesh, she might never get this chance again. What was it they said about a window of opportunity? Jump while the window is open, babe. So she grabbed him by the ears, yanked him down, and whispered against his gaping mouth, "Tell me." Then she bit his bottom lip and added, "Show me."

Amid bouts of laughter, and then no more laughter, Cnut showed her how a woman could have a blended orgasm of both the clitoris—*though he called it her honey spot*—and her G-spot from the inside—*he claimed only Vikings with long fingers could multitask like this.* Suffice it to say, she came like a Fourth of July fireworks. If the people below could hear her moans and screams—she hoped they couldn't—they would think Cnut was torturing her. He was. Torturing her with pleasure.

She had the wits, still—*and wasn't that amazing?*—to entertain a sudden thought. Cnut was going out tomorrow, hunting. Not just hunting wild game, but demon vampires, as well. In other words, dangerous. He'd implied earlier that a vangel was strengthened by taking blood. Did that mean that even the small amount taken from her, an innocent, so to speak—*okay, not so innocent at the moment*—would make him stronger?

Upon asking him, he nodded hesitantly.

She tilted her head to the side, in invitation.

He made a low growling sound, feral almost, and clamped his fangs, which were eerily long by now, onto her neck and sucked. She felt the suction all the way to her fingertips, her toes, her breasts, and the place where they were still joined. Cnut yanked his bloody teeth off her neck and reared back, roaring into his own inner fireworks. It was glorious to watch.

She fell immediately into a deep, sated sleep. He was gone when she awakened, but she could swear she'd heard him whisper in her ear before leaving. "Mine!"

Was that the glutton in him speaking, or something else?

Chapter 16

Then he got a devil of a shock . . .

Cnut couldn't stop smiling the next day. And his men remarked on it. More than once. They were worse than his brothers, poking their noses in each other's business.

"A companion he named her. Hah! I wish my companions could make me grin like a goat with two cocks."

"How many times did you peak?"

"Was it good bedsport or so-so bedsport? Not that sex is ever bad for a man."

"Was she an enthusiastic bed partner? Betimes my Solig lies there like a lump of whale blubber."

"I wonder if she rode him like a cow man?"

"Dost mean a cowboy?"

"Boy, man, same thing."

"Did ye make her fart?"

"Did she make you fart?"

He changed the subject by asking Thorkel about Dyna.

Thorkel sighed deeply. "I want her. Badly. But, holy Thor! None of my usual charms are working."

"What charms are they?" asked young Atli, one of the squires, who was taking Igor's place on Cnut's hunting expedition.

The others snickered, but Thorkel took the question seriously. "Well, I usually regale women with tales of the battles I have engaged in."

Ulf, Njal, and Ogot nodded at this.

"But I have not fought in any battles yet," Atli complained.

"Then I let her know how much pleasure she will get from my bedsport skills."

"By then, the women are usually drooling, ready to shed their gunnas before you can finish your horn of ale. Is that not right?" asked Ulf.

"Usually. But with Dyna . . . well, I have to admit, she just laughs."

I would, too, Cnut thought. *Was I ever this dumb about women? Honestly, Thorkel is generally a smart man, a great warrior. What is it about women that turns men into morons?*

"I am far-famed in bedsport skills, but Dyna won't give me a chance to prove myself. What do you think, Cnut?"

Me? Why me? "Have you asked her what she wants?"

"She wants marriage."

"So you have said before," Cnut pointed out. "How old are you? Why is that a problem? Mayhap it is time you took the step all men must take if they want sons. Legitimate sons."

"Twenty and five. It is not marriage itself that is the problem, but Dyna demands that I promise to take no other wives or concubines, that I promise never to beat her or her son, and any children we may have together, no matter the circumstances, and that I never, ever try to make her fart during sex. Who was it amongst you, by the by, who blabbed that fact to her?"

Ulf's already ruddy face got redder. "I might have mentioned it to Helga who might have mentioned it to Girda who might have—"

Thorkel clouted him with a leather glove. "Lackwit. Some secrets are meant to be kept amongst us men."

"I don't know, Thorkel. One woman only for life. Sounds like torture to me," said the elderly Njal, who had to have had at least three wives and God only knew how many concubines over the years. Even at his advanced age, there were two women who lived with him.

"Best you look elsewhere," Ogot the Blacksmith advised. "Women are like swords. You can always find a better one."

"On the other hand," Cnut found himself saying, "the good ones are worth more than gold."

They all looked at him for further explanation, for which he had none.

Cnut had taken three of the dogs with him today, and they soon sniffed out the herd of wild boar that was feeding in a forest near where they'd caught the one before, and within the hour, a half dozen were lying on the ground, arrows or swords or lances protruding from vital body parts. This was cause for celebration, especially since several other bands of men were out hunting, as well, in other parts of the region. Reindeer would be welcome. Too much to hope for another bear during this hibernating season. A brace of grouse. Ducks and geese were long gone. Perhaps, God willing, it would be a happy yule at Hoggstead this year, after all.

It was especially propitious that they'd killed so many boar on this first day out because the air was growing colder and the wind more blustery. Njal confirmed Cnut's premonition by rubbing his sore knees and saying, "A storm is coming."

After gutting the animals and draining the blood, with the dogs gorging themselves on the innards, they built a fire and camped for the night. Before that, some of them worked on sledges to carry the game back to the keep. The next morning, though, Cnut noticed something . . . or someone . . . in the trees beyond their camp and announced, "You men go back. Take the dogs with you. I'm going to do a little exploring farther north. See if there's evidence of any more Lucibears."

They all protested that it would be dangerous to go on alone, especially with the storm brewing, but he was adamant, assuring them, "I will be fine. I won't take any chances." Each of the men in turn offered to accompany him, but he needed to be alone.

The presence he'd seen in the woods had been none other than Zebulan the demon vampire, who might or might not be a double agent for the vangels. No one was sure if he could be trusted. Cnut couldn't ignore Zeb's sudden appearance, though. It had to be deliberate that he'd shown himself to Cnut.

But it was mid-morning, after hours trudging along on the snowshoes he'd finally donned, before he found any sign of Lucipires. The pungent smell of rotten eggs . . . sulfur . . . came to him on a rising breeze. He unsheathed his sword and moved carefully toward a clearing where three Lucipires had surrounded a man. He recognized the man. Ivan Long Beard, a fur trapper. A meaner Viking there never was. He'd seen him cut off a woman's hand one time for failing to cure one of his beaver skins properly. And the slaves he kept to help with his trapping business often had haunted looks in their eyes.

Well, under normal circumstances, it would be Cnut's job as a vangel to try to save the sinner before the Lucipires could take him to an early grave, and therefore to be transformed into a demon vampire. But it was too late for Ivan. He already had several bite marks on his skin; in fact, hunks of his fur cloak, wool tunic, and skin came away in the massive Lucie jaws. Ivan fell onto his back and the three Lucies began feeding on him, in such a frenzy that they didn't notice Cnut at first.

Cnut was able to pull a treated knife from a scabbard on his belt and throw it directly into one mung's back. With a roar, the beast rose and began to melt into noxious sulfur slime. Ivan himself was dissolving just as fast, leaving only his clothing and weapon behind.

One of the other Lucies, a female hordling, had been wounded by Ivan—a bloody gash across her neck—but she would recover in time. It was not a mortal wound. But she had been weakened and thus was easy pickings for Cnut's broadsword, which he wielded in a wide arc, decapitating the creature and nicking the heart. (*And one might ask,* Cnut mused, *how I knew it was a female? Ah. Think breasts. Scaly breasts with red nipples the size of cherries. Can anyone say, "Honey, I have a headache."*)

Okay, two down and on their way to Hell. They would no longer be Lucipires but mere demons. Satan would not be pleased. Which left only one Lucipire—a haakai, but a young one. Still, haakai were not to be dismissed easily. He bellowed his outrage on viewing the diminishing remains of his cohorts and lunged at Cnut, sword raised ahigh.

Cnut was able to dance away at the last moment. Which infuriated the haakai, who hissed and gnashed his fangy teeth, drool dripping down his scaly chest. He came at Cnut with more deliberation now, thrusting and parrying his sword, playing with Cnut, confident of his superior skills.

But Cnut was more skillful, and a more devious fighter. He lured the haakai to a certain position so that when he lunged this time, the evil creature slipped on the puddles of slime. Cnut immediately stood over him, sword poised over his dead heart. Before Cnut sank in the blade, he said, "Give Satan my regards."

He was breathing heavily then, realizing belatedly that he hadn't kept one of the Lucies alive long enough to interrogate. Oh well. Maybe there were others. Of course there were. Lucipires were like cockroaches. Kill one and two others pop up.

At first, he didn't recognize the sound off to his left. But then he realized it was clapping.

It was Zebulan, of course, sitting on a boulder, clapping his huge clawed hands. Zeb was a high haakai, a member of Jasper's command council. As such, he was a huge mother of a creature, at least seven feet tall, fangs the size of walrus tusks, a tail that could whiplash an elephant. And he stunk like rotten eggs. If Cnut didn't already know him, he would be scared. Hell, he was still scared.

"What are you doing here, Zeb?" Cnut asked, sitting down on a fallen log a short distance away. He was cleaning the blood and slime off his sword with clumps of snow as he spoke.

"The better question is: What are you doing here?"

"I have no idea."

"I had a hell of a time finding you."

Now that sounded ominous. Why would Zeb be looking for him? "Why are there Lucies here in the ninth century in the middle of nowhere?"

"We go wherever there are dreadful sinners, and you Vikings do it so well. Plus famine brings out the worst in some folks." Zeb morphed into his humanoid form, wearing blue jeans, athletic shoes, a sheepskin jacket, and his signature Blue Devils ball cap.

"Why aren't you back at that ranch in Montana in 2016 doing your demon vampire thing?"

"Jasper has another 'demon vampire thing' for me to do." He was staring pointedly at Cnut as he spoke.

Uh-oh. "Spit it out, Zeb. What's up?"

"People . . . demons . . . are complaining about me. They think I'm slacking off. Jasper has given me orders. Bring back a Sigurdsson, or else."

Nothing new there. Jasper has been salivating over a VIK coup for centuries. And he almost accomplished it when he captured Vikar a few years back. "Define 'or else.'"

Zeb looked scared suddenly, an expression Cnut

had never seen on his face before. Face it, demons, especially demon vampires, had seen it all when it came to evil, but what Jasper could deliver when angry defied imagination. Zeb shook his head, finally. "You do not want to know. There was a demon vampire one time, two centuries ago, who betrayed Jasper in some manner. Argon was . . . is his name. Argon is still in the torture room at Horror, being brutalized daily. Sometimes he is skinned. Other times, disgusting objects are stuck in every orifice of his sad body. Once he was burned at the stake. He lived in a snake pit for a year. He hung upside down on a cross another year. On and on. And Argon was not as close to Jasper as I am. Ah, well, no need to worry about that."

"Why is that?"

"Because you, my friend, are a Sigurdsson, and you are lost, temporarily. Your brothers will not come to your aid until it is too late."

Zeb is thinking about turning me in. To save himself! This is news Michael would like to hear. "But then, my friend," Cnut replied, "you will never get to be a vangel. I thought that was your greatest wish."

"It is. It is. I sicken at the thought of what I am forced to do as a Lucipire. But there are no promises from Michael that he will ever add me to his team. In truth, forgiving a demon has never happened before, let alone turning one into a vangel."

That was true.

Also, Zeb wasn't even a Viking or of some Norse descent, as all vangels were. The vangels could no longer call themselves Viking vampire angels if Zeb joined them. It would have to be Viking vampire angels, plus a Hebrew. Or would that be a Jew? No matter. It would probably never happen, and Zeb knew it.

At most, Michael had only hinted that he might consider Zeb's request to become a vangel if he played double agent for fifty years or more. No promises. No guarantees.

Cnut saw Zeb's dilemma. Give Cnut up, or give himself up. Cnut couldn't deny he felt fearful himself. He wasn't sure he could withstand the type of torture Jasper would employ to persuade a vangel to become a Lucipire.

"So, what are you going to do?" Cnut asked. He was prepared to fight, but he wasn't sure he would win with Zeb, who was much older and more experienced and stronger than he was.

"I don't know," Zeb said. "You might consider praying."

"For myself?"

"For both of us."

"One last thing, Zeb. Contact one of my brothers. You and Trond are close. Tell him where I am and that he needs to get Andrea out of here."

Cnut expected Zeb who ask who Andrea was, but he didn't. He was already gone.

It wasn't Santa, but the Abominable Snowman who arrived . . .

Andrea was happy as she went about her work all day following Cnut's departure. In fact, she found herself singing bits of that Pharrell Williams

"Happy" song and occasionally breaking into a little improv happy dance, which caused the folks at Hoggstead to gawk at her. They probably thought she was going crazy.

In fact, one kitchen maid whispered loud enough for everyone to hear, "Lady Andrea has gone barmy."

But Girda had smacked the girl with a long-handled wooden spoon and replied, "Hush yer-self, Freydis. The lady has just got herself swived silly."

That about summed it up.

Hard to believe she could feel so contented with all that had happened to her, and so much that was unsettled. Amazing what a good bout of sex—who was she kidding, a phenomenal bout of sex—could do for a woman. But it was more than that, and she knew it. She was probably falling in love. And there lay disappointment. But she wasn't going to think about that now.

There was much work to be done even with a reduced population in the castle. Preserving the meat and fish brought in the day before by smoking, salting, pickling, drying, or just hanging to age in the cold cellar. Cooking and cleaning. Endless laundry. Feeding and milking the cows. Spreading feed for the chickens and gathering eggs. Making butter and cheese. Making flour by grinding oats or barley in handheld stone querns. Weaving cloth. Making clothing. Mending clothing. Tending fires. On and on.

Andrea was beginning to realize that the people who lived up here on the castle motte spoke of famine, but they hadn't really suffered like the people down below. Apparently, they'd been able to live reasonably well with stored meat and goods. It was only during the recent weeks that they'd begun to feel the pinch of rationing, lack of variety in diet, and fear of what would happen when all the food ran out.

But, oh, the village people who came to the door every day tore at her heart. They were starving, and they looked it. Andrea and Girda, and Finn, too, did their best to give them enough to subsist, for the time being, but would it be enough? How could anyone see a starving child with bulging eyes and sunken cheeks and stick-like arms and legs and not hand over everything you had? How could you eat when little ones could not? Apparently, Cnut had done just that.

She was having trouble reconciling that Cnut with the one she'd lain with all night. They weren't the same person; that was the only conclusion she could come to. Otherwise, how could she care for such a monster?

At least twenty-five of the men had gone out, hunting, fishing, or trapping. Normally an estate, or whatever you called it in these days, wouldn't be left so ill-manned against possible siege from enemies, Girda told her at one point when Andrea was showing her how to care for the sourdough batter, in the event Andrea was no longer there someday. *From my lips to God's ears.* But apparently attacks rarely happened during the harsh winter months, and, besides, the famine was weakening everyone's defenses.

Girda listened patiently to her explanation, then patted her on the shoulder, as if she were a small child, homing in on the part of what Andrea had told her about going away. "Best ye settle yerself in fer the winter, m'lady. Ye ain't going anywhere 'til the spring thaw when the fjords open up."

Wanna bet? "You could be right."

Dyna confided in her that afternoon that Thorkel was pressuring her to be with him.

"To marry him?" Andrea asked.

"Well, not exactly, though I imagine if I hold him off long enough, he would offer wedlock."

"But that's not what you want?" Andrea guessed.

Dyna shook her head miserably. "I wed Kugge's father when I was breeding, as I told ye afore. I let my wanton passions rule, and ended up with child and having no choices. I will not take that risk again."

"Why is it a risk? I mean, Thorkel would marry you, wouldn't he? And now that Cnut named him chief *hersir*, he has prospects for the future, I would think."

"Yea, Thorkel would offer wedlock. Under pressure. With no protections for me. I do not come from a highborn family that could secure a dowry on me and all the restrictions that go with it. All I have is me and Kugge."

"What exactly is it that you fear, Dyna?"

"I fear having sex with the lout and becoming pregnant, giving over all control to my man, like I did last time. I fear being a first wife. The *more danico*, multiple wives, is accepted practice amongst our people."

"How about multiple husbands? Is that accepted?"

"No. But who would want more than one? Not me!"

Andrea laughed.

"Too many times I have seen what happens to first wives when their husbands take on second or third wives, or numerous concubines. She becomes little more than a servant to those who follow her into the bed furs. I fear Kugge having no birthright when other sons may come. I fear so many things, and yet . . . and yet . . ."

"And yet you want Thorkel?"

"Desperately."

"Well, there is one thing I can help you with."

"There is?" Dyna questioned dubiously.

"Where I come from there are methods of birth control, ways of having sex without conception."

"Oh, you mean the man pulling out before peaking?" Dyna asked. "Pfff! The man always promises he will, but in the heat of passion, he rarely does, and then the woman is, once again, waddling around with a big stomach."

Andrea laughed. "Actually, that's not what I meant. Where I live, there are ways women can control their own destinies. There are devices they can use, or insist that their partners use, to prevent conception. I have none of those here, but there is a rhythm method of birth control that some people use. It's not perfect, but it works most of the time if it's followed scrupulously."

"Rhythm method. Like having sex in a certain rhythm? Pfff! That sounds like something a man would say when in high enthusiasm." Once again, Dyna was regarding her with skepticism.

Once again, Andrea laughed. "No. Rhythm

based on a woman's menstrual cycle. It's called natural family planning. A way in which couples can avoid pregnancy by abstaining from sex on the days of a woman's ovulation cycle when she's most likely to conceive."

"Huh? I thought a woman could catch a man's seed any day of the month, even if she is bleeding."

"Not really."

"What is oh-view . . . oh-view, whatever you said?"

"Ovulation," Andrea said and explained it in basic terms. "Like I said, the method isn't perfect, but it is at least something that can be tried. And, really, there are only eight days or so of the month when the woman is fertile. Five or so days before ovulation, the day of ovulation, and up to two days afterward. Keep in mind that the male sperm . . . um, seed . . . can live for a couple days inside a woman's body and connect with a woman's egg before it dies off."

Dyna was frowning with puzzlement. "Explain this to me. In detail. Slowly."

Andrea did, or as much as she was able to remember from her high school health class where teenagers were given a belated introduction to sex education.

"Explain it again."

Andrea did.

"And again."

Andrea did.

Then Dyna smiled. "I could see this working for me, as an unmarried woman. I can rebuff a man's advances . . . Thorkel's advances . . . whenever I want, but a married woman would have more trouble doing that."

That wasn't so, but Andrea wasn't about to get involved in a discussion of female liberation and the right to choose if and when to have sex, even when married.

Besides, wasn't it ironic that Andrea, who was trying to teach others about contraception, was depending on a man's word that he was sterile as a birth control precaution? It was all about trust, and she was placing her trust in a Viking vampire angel who'd managed to land them in a time-travel debacle. Oh boy! When she said it like that, it didn't sound so good.

By the end of the day, six other women came to Andrea, asking her to explain the method to them. And Girda laughed. "M'lady, you are going to have more than a few men raging at you for interfering with their bed rights."

"Bed rights, be damned," Andrea muttered under her breath.

But Girda heard her and laughed some more. "So ye can say when ye've been bedded right and good already."

"Hmpfh!" was the best Andrea could come up with.

That night, the female skald, Luta, amused the women in the great hall after dinner—though only a few of the men appreciated her work, especially her male counterpart Brian—when she told a particularly funny saga. She called it, "A Woman's Woe."

Didst ever know a man
Who named his manly part?

Like pets they are to the lackwits,
With names like Sword or Blade or Dart,
Avenger, Rooster, Bull, and Lance,
Or how about Randy, Lusty, or Love Mart?

Women, on the other hand, are not so vain
About the luscious field betwixt their legs.
Not even when the man so wicked
For her compliance he begs and begs.

Let me touch yer velvet folds,
Let me lick yer sweet honey,
Let me tickle yer pert teats
Betimes men are so funny!

If only men knew
What women really think
When first they drop their braies,
And we can only blink.
Is this the beauteous object
They cannot for even a day neglect?
Why it looks like nothing fierce or pretty
As they led you to believe.
In fact, 'tis just a wobbly stick.

Andrea slept alone that night and found herself missing Cnut's warm body. And other things. But the next morning she awakened with anticipation. It was possible Cnut and his men would return today.

The men did return that night, along with the three dogs they'd taken with them, but not Cnut. The fool had stayed behind to look for Lucibears, they told Andrea. Hah! She knew what that meant. Cnut was looking for demon vampires out there, all alone, and with a winter storm brewing, according to Girda, Njal, and all the old ones in the keep.

Well, at least there were six more boars to add to the larder, along with some fish, three reindeer, an elk, a bunch of grouse, and rabbits brought in by the other men. How they were able to catch so much game in the midst of a famine was a miracle brought by the gods, many of the people proclaimed. Andrea tended to think it was one particular God, and his sidekick, St. Michael.

"You're the commander in charge here. Shouldn't you go back out and look for Cnut?" she asked Thorkel later that evening when Cnut still hadn't returned.

He shrugged. "The jarl told us he would find his way back himself."

"Fool!" Andrea said.

Thorkel was taken aback because he wasn't sure if she referred to him or Cnut. Actually, both. But then Thorkel's attention was diverted by Dyna, who'd suddenly taken to flirting with him. When Andrea caught her attention one time in passing with a tray of bread, Dyna winked at her. Several men gave Andrea dirty looks, though. Apparently, their women were in fertile periods, and they'd declined their advances.

The next day the snows started. Oh, there was already snow on the ground, but this was a full-blown, steady downpour of flakes the size of golf balls. Beautiful, but potentially deadly for someone stranded in it. Andrea was tempted to go out herself to hunt for Cnut, but recognized immediately how futile that would be. She barely knew her way to the steam bathhouse.

She was distracted for a while when one of the two wagon sledges returned, finally, from attempting to purchase goods from other estates. It was only half full, and apparently Gorm had been required to go much farther afield than he'd expected to get even that much. The famine had affected a wide area, even those who had planned for the harsh winter better than Cnut had.

At least now there were oats and barley to feed the horses and make more flour, plus some root vegetables, mead, spices, and such. Andrea got the idea then to begin preparing for Christmas, or the Jól season, as the Vikings called it, which was only a few days off, less than a week. It would lift everyone's spirits in the midst of this famine depression and give them something to look forward to. In her case, perhaps she could stop thinking about Cnut and whether he was in danger somewhere by himself.

Turned out many of the Christian rituals for Christmas originated with the Norse pagan ones coinciding with the winter solstice. They celebrated for more than a week to commemorate the return of the sun. From then on the days would be longer, and the darkest days of winter would be over. Oh, the cold and dark wouldn't be over by any means, but it was an annual promise that brighter days were coming. Sort of the Christmas coming of Christ with a promise of new days.

Andrea bundled up in her old jeans, T-shirt, outer shirt, Old Gringo distressed leather boots with blue embroidery (which had been intended for good looks, not wet snow or ice; oh well!), fur-lined gloves, and a heavy wool, hooded cloak. Her cowboy hat was still missing. Dyna, Kugge, and the other children who accompanied her did likewise, except for the vanity boots. They all wore the big, awkward snowshoes laced to their boots, which felt like badminton rackets, but were actually very helpful for plowing through the deepening snow once she got used to them.

It was fun. Andrea taught them some Christmas songs, "Deck the Halls," "Over the River and Through the Wood," "Jingle Bells," and "Here Comes Santa Claus." Of course she then had to explain the concept of Santa Claus and the North Pole, which intrigued the children, and Dyna, too.

"I wish we had Santy here," Kugge said wistfully as he gathered yet another holly branch with bright red berries. "He would bring me new ice skates."

"I would get a new carved wooden kitten to play with," a little girl, Elsa, said. "The tail broke off my old one."

"And it only has one eye," Kugge pointed out with boyish insensitivity.

"Kitty is still beautiful," Elsa insisted.

Kugge rolled his eyes and was about to say something more when Dyna swatted him on the head.

Another boy, Oslik, who was a little older than the others at about ten, said, "I would get my very own pony. A real one."

The others didn't disagree, but their consensus

was that the chances of that were as likely as a pony falling from the sky.

"I like the way Santy—I mean, Santa—has reindeer. We have reindeer here. And he lives in the North Pole which we have here, even if it is a distance away. And he gives gifts. We Vikings like to give gifts, when we have the coin to buy them or the goods to make them. Once my father gave me a set of colored ribands. It was the best gift ever." All this from Dyna.

Once they had enough holly branches, which they piled onto a sled, they began searching for mistletoe that grew on oak trees. Dyna then told her the legend of the mistletoe and why it was considered so important to Vikings. Apparently, the god Balder was killed by a mistletoe arrow but came back to life when his mother, the goddess Frigga, wept tears over him, turning the red mistletoe berries to white.

One of the more skeptical of the children, a snot-nosed little urchin by the name of Dorf, said, "Ain't no Santy. Ain't no magic god or goddesses, either. Ain't no healin' powers in the mistletoe. If they was, wouldn't be no famine. If they was, me mother would still be alive." He wiped the green snot on his sleeve.

That put a damper on the festivities. For the moment.

By the time they got back to the castle, the sled was piled high, and they each carried huge bundles of holly and mistletoe and evergreen boughs, and they were back to being in a jolly mood. When Girda opened the back door, she was serenaded with a rowdy rendition of "Jingle Bells."

"Frigg's foot!" she exclaimed. "You folks been eating berries from the barmy bush?"

They all laughed and shook snow from their clothing onto Girda and anyone who came near them. By evening, the great hall and all the doorways were decorated with the fragrant greens, and Andrea had even talked Finn into opening Cnut's treasure room to her, where she found some red silk fabric that, much to Finn's consternation, she cut into strips and made bows to adorn her creations. She'd also taken a few coins that she used to commission the woodworker, Hastein, to make carved animals as secret Christmas gifts for each of the children under the age of ten.

With each item Andrea took, Finn kept clutching his heart and muttering something about the lord going to have a fit. She was pretty sure he wasn't talking about the Lord above.

By the next morning, Cnut still hadn't returned, and the snow continued to fall. What if he didn't come back at all? What if she was trapped in this time period forever, or until she died? What if Celie wasn't safe, as Cnut had assured her? What if Celie was about to have her head lopped off by terrorists? What if Cnut had been captured by the demons and was being tortured at this very moment? What if . . . What if . . .

To keep herself from going insane with all these speculations, Andrea tried to talk some of the men into bringing an evergreen tree into the hall. More than one of them declared her "barmy," others said she was "demented." It wasn't that Vikings didn't bring a tree indoors for the yule season. In fact, their traditional yule log was actually an immense evergreen—she was guessing twenty feet tall or more—that they dragged into the hall on the evening of the winter solstice. They propped it trunk first into the largest of the hearth fires and continued to feed it forward during the following days.

Now, *that* was demented, if you asked Andrea. Which no one did, of course.

She cornered Thorkel, though, and had better luck. "If you get me a tree, I could put in a good word for you with Dyna," she coaxed.

"You already have." He waggled his eyebrows at her.

"Then you owe me."

"Thor's hammer! You are a persistent wench." Belatedly, he realized how rude he sounded, and added, "Sorry I am, m'lady if I offended you, but—"

"It doesn't have to be a huge tree," she said. "Halfway to the ceiling would be fine."

"Halfway to the ceiling!" he exclaimed, looking upward. It was probably a twenty-foot ceiling. "And what will you do with the tree? You do know that a dead evergreen will begin to shed almost immediately?"

"We'll put it in a bucket of water and decorate it with candles and ribbons and gold braiding."

Finn overheard them as he was walking by and slapped a hand against his heart. "More decorations!" he moaned. "Lord spare me!" He was, of course, referring to his worldly master, not the celestial one.

Later that day, the tree held a place of honor near the dais, with unlit candles (They wouldn't be lit until solstice), more red bows, and garlands of gold braid that would normally be used to trim fine garments. Everybody oohed and aahed over it.

Except for Finn. She was pretty sure he was hitting the locked barrels of ale, what was left of it.

By the next morning, she was frantic over Cnut. The snow had stopped falling, but it was waist-deep. "You have to go find him," she begged Thorkel. He was the only one who would even listen to her.

By noon, he agreed, but only after Dyna added her pleas to Andrea's and made him a few promises of a nature Andrea could only guess. He took three men with him.

Four hours later they returned carrying something. Or someone. Whatever it was, it resembled the Abominable Snowman. Covered with snow and crusted over with ice. Eyes frozen shut. Icicles hanging from its nose. Its lips cracked with frozen blood.

With a cry of horror, Andrea realized that it was Cnut.

"He's still alive," Thorkel assured her, but one of the men added, "But barely."

They carried him into the great hall and laid him near one of the hearths on a trestle table, where Andrea helped them remove his garments. Not an easy task with their being so frozen. But the heat of the fire soon began to melt the ice.

"Be careful how you handle him," Andrea warned. "He might have frostbite."

"That's the least of his troubles," Girda said, clucking and rattling out orders for warm water, clean cloths, dry clothing. "And warm up some of that ale, Finn, and don't ye be saying there is none or I'll personally give ye a heart attack."

It didn't seem to matter to any of them that they were exposing Cnut's nude body to the scrutiny of one and all, although Girda at one point ordered everyone to step back and give them room for breathing. Cnut didn't have frostbite, which was a miracle, but he *was* blue in spots, especially his toes and fingertips and the edge of his nose.

She breathed a sigh of relief when his body began to shiver, and once she removed the warm cloths from his eyes, he turned his head to the side and said, "There's a tree in my hall."

"Andrea insisted," Thorkel said defensively.

Cnut turned toward her then.

"What happened?" she asked, taking one of his hands gently in hers.

"I got lost. Again." He tried to smile, which caused his cracked lips to start bleeding.

Which prompted Andrea to start crying. She wasn't sure if she was crying with joy over Cnut's return, or crying with dismay over the pathetic Viking who kept getting lost.

He squeezed her hand and said, first licking the blood off his lips, "I missed you."

And then Andrea cried for love of her Viking.

Chapter 17

Your coop or mine, Ms. Hen?

It took several days for Cnut to recover. He wasn't sure he'd ever be warm again. In fact, at one point, when he feared being frozen into a living statue out in the forest, he'd pleaded with Mike to help him.

But Mike remained absent. He was punishing Cnut for something. Cnut had a fair idea what that something was. And it wasn't gluttony.

On the other hand, maybe Mike was the one who'd sent Thorkel to find him. Although Thorkel claimed it was Andrea who had beleaguered him into going out to search. Okay, so, maybe Mike sent Andrea to prod Thorkel into searching for him. Same thing.

His head hurt from all that thinking.

But another thing. Cnut wasn't convinced that he'd gotten lost all on his own, despite all the jests about him at Hoggstead, implying he couldn't find his way around a privy anymore. No, it was Zeb who'd somehow muddled his mind so he lost his way. That was his theory, and he was sticking to it until proven otherwise.

Anyhow, after a day in bed under three bed furs and another day of a hacking cough and a third day of Andrea force-feeding him so much chicken noodle soup he was growing feathers (how she'd bullied Girda into giving up one of her hens was another story, and there were some black specks in the noodles that were suspicious!), he made his way to the bathhouse, which was thankfully empty. And why not? It was the middle of the night.

Andrea had declined to share his bed while he was sick, and instead slept in the spare bedchamber. Well, he was sick of being sick.

The bathhouse was an ingenious facility put together by his great-grandsire Bjorn Hoggson, taking advantage of a natural underground hot spring. The circular bathing pool was about fifteen feet in diameter, with stone steps leading down each side to a maximum depth of three feet. The neat thing was that water came in and ran out in a continuous slow current, rather like a self-cleaning tub. The warm waste water from the bathing house was often used for laundry, although there was a deep well closer to the keep.

He lit several wall torches and used a sharp knife, some soft soap, and piece of shiny bronze to shave his itchy beard and then the sides of his head as well. Not as good a shave as provided by modern razors in front of illuminated mirrors, but it sufficed. Then he sank his stinksome body into the steamy water, scrubbed himself clean, and half reclined along the steps so he was covered up to the waist. He felt human at least now, or as human as he would ever be again.

He heard the door creak and cracked an eye open, half expecting Thorkel or one of the men to have come out after a night of bedsport. But it was Andrea instead, coming in on a waft of coconut.

"What are you doing here? I hope you aren't planning on pouring more of that soup down my gullet."

"What? You don't like my soup?"

"I like your soup fine. But after five bowls, I'm beginning to cluck."

She didn't even smile. "I was worried about you," she said, sitting down primly on one of the benches, tucking her long wool cloak around her tightly and crossing her booted ankles. Her blonde hair was pulled off her face in a ponytail tied with a red silk ribbon. Finn had told him what Andrea had done with several ells of priceless samite silk fabric, not that he particularly cared, though there was a time when he would have. "I went in to check on you in the middle of the night and you weren't there," she continued.

"Do you always check on me?"

"I have been since you got sick. You shaved."

He nodded and rubbed his chin. "I was getting itchy."

"You look good, though you've lost some weight, I think."

"It will come back, believe you me."

"What happened out there? Did you run into some of those . . . things?"

"I did."

"And?"

"I killed them."

"Them? More than one?"

"Three."

"Getting information from you is like pulling teeth. What aren't you telling me?"

He hesitated to tell her, but what if Zeb should follow through on his mission from Jasper? Shouldn't she be forewarned that she might be left here alone? "I met someone else. Something else. Zebulan the demon."

"Whaaat? The demons have names?"

"Of course they do. Why wouldn't they? Anyhow, Zeb is sort of a double agent for the vangels. He hopes to join our ranks one day, or so he says, and therefore feeds us information on occasion."

"And why does your meeting with this guy . . . thing . . . Zebulan have you worried?"

"How do you know I'm worried?"

"I can tell."

"Am I oozing even more peppermint eau de cologne?"

"You don't have to be so sarcastic."

"Sorry. But how do you know I'm worried? Do you think you know me so well?"

"I hardly know you at all. But if we're lifemates, I can probably sense your feelings."

Whoa, whoa, whoa, whoa, whoa! What leap of faith or logic or insanity made her suddenly believe we're lifemates?

"Not that I think we're lifemates."

Whew!

"You should see the expression on your face. I should be offended."

"Very funny." He made a face at her. "Here's the deal. Zeb has been given orders to bring back one of the VIK, meaning one of us seven Sigurdsson brothers. And it appears I'm it."

She stiffened and went silent before asking in a small voice, "Can he do that?"

"He can try."

"What will happen if he succeeds?"

"He'll take me to Jasper's castle of horrors which is aptly named Horror."

"And?"

"And try to convert me into a Lucipire."

"How?"

"Torture. Endless torture. Possibly for years. Once Vikar was taken, but only for a few days. We could scarce recognize him when he returned. Among other things, he'd been crucified." Cnut realized immediately that he shouldn't have been so candid with Andrea.

She had both hands to her mouth. Her eyes were wide with shock. "Can't you fight him off . . . Zeb, I mean . . . like you did the other Lucipires?"

"I can try, but he's older and stronger than me. It would be an even match. Fifty-fifty."

"Cnut! We have to get out of here!" She stood as if it was that simple. Decide to leave and poof, you leave.

"*You* have to leave. I obviously can't. But if I should suddenly disappear, this is what—"

"Don't you dare! Don't you dare say that!" She dropped her cloak, and she was nude underneath.

"Oh my God!" he said, and, for his sins, it was not a prayer. Leastways, not a holy one.

Wearing nothing but her blue leather boots, she

stepped into the steam pool, stomped down the steps and over to him. Standing above him, she wagged a forefinger at him. "You are not going anywhere without me, is that understood?"

Did she actually expect him to answer when she was standing before him looking like a *Playboy* Cowgirl of the Month centerfold? The only thing missing was the cowgirl hat. Bloody hell! The boots were enough!

"What are you looking at?" she demanded, putting her hands on her hips.

"Are you kidding? What do you think I'm looking at? I'm looking for staples."

"Huh?"

He snaked a hand out and grabbed her by the wrist, tugging her forward. She almost fell, but he caught her, and somehow, talented fellow that he was, he managed to settle her on his thighs, astride.

"Ride 'em, cowgirl?" he asked with a laugh.

"This is serious," she said, pushing against his chest.

He wouldn't release her, not even when he noticed the tears welling in her eyes. "Hey, I was just teasing. What's wrong?"

"You," she said on a sob, swatting him on the shoulder. "You're an idiot."

"I know," he agreed. "Why am I an idiot?"

"You got lost, and I was afraid you were dead, or something, and I was stressed out worrying about you, and about myself, I admit. I didn't know what I was going to do. And then you showed up, and you looked half dead, and you finally got better, but now you say you have plans to get yourself captured, and maybe crucified, and I'm definitely going to be lost in the past. And what am I going to do without you?" She took a deep breath after her long diatribe, and added, "And I think I've fallen in love with you, idiot that I am."

"Maybe we're both becoming idiots. Ah, sweetling, I wouldn't deliberately leave you here."

"And that's supposed to make me feel better?"

"What I meant was, I've been making plans. I think Thorkel is planning to wed Dyna. I'm going to have a private talk with him. If I should suddenly disappear, I want him to take over as jarl at Hoggstead. I've already made him military commander. Even if the famine continues, he'll have the authority to use whatever money or goods I have left to survive."

"And that's supposed to make me feel better?" she repeated.

"My next priority is to get you home. Since I seem to have lost telepathic communication with other vangels, I told Zeb to contact one of my brothers and tell them what has happened. You need to be removed from this situation."

"Seriously? You expect me to leave while you stay here and just wait for the demons to come?"

"Well, yes. This is my problem. Not yours."

"Idiot! Idiot! Idiot!" she said, smacking him on the shoulder with each word. "Didn't you hear me say I've fallen in love with you?"

"Of course I did, and I thank you for the compliment."

She smacked him again.

"I was waiting for the right moment to say that I love you, too."

"Oh, really? And when did you decide that?" Her words were waspish, but he could tell she was pleased.

He was, too. Amazingly, Cnut didn't recall ever having said those words before. To anyone. "When I was sitting on a stump in the middle of nowhere, lost, and turning into an icicle, I realized that the most important thing I would miss is you. Are you going to cry again?"

"Of course I'm going to cry."

He thought about putting his arms around her, but she was still in a mood and would no doubt swat him again. "Uh, one question, dearling? Why were you naked under that cloak?"

She wiped her nose on her forearm, then sloshed it clean in the water. "I was going to join you in your bed tonight. I figured you were well enough by now to have a bed partner."

"You could be right about that," he said, glancing downward where his favorite body part was standing at attention. And no wonder. He was nude. She was nude, except for the boots. And it had been four whole days since last it got any attention. Then he looked at her and smiled. "Cock-a-doodle-do?"

She was a bloody fool . . .

"I missed you," she told him with all the heartfelt feelings she'd bottled up the past few days as she'd worried over his absence and then worried over his sickness. "I know, I know," she added before he could speak, "I'm putting pressure on you right now that you don't need. You shouldn't have to think about me when you have all these other problems to face. The famine. The demon thingees. Our time-travel dilemma. The Zeb threat."

He put his fingertips to her lips and shook his head. "You don't put pressure on me. I put it on myself. I think about you all the time. Night and day. And that is not a bad thing. Despite my sins, I have been blessed with you in my life."

"What a nice thing to say!"

He shrugged. "It is what it is."

"I'll tell you how far gone I am. If you are destined to stay here in the past, that's where I want to be, too."

He nodded his understanding. "Then it is agreed. We are lifemates?"

"What else could it be?"

"Well," he said, and grinned at her. "Lifemates are all well and good, but I prefer lust mates. At least some of the time." He spread his knees wider, which caused her legs to spread and open her up to his erection, which was already prodding at her center, as if to remind her of their positions.

As if she could forget! With the warm water under her butt and the warmth of arousal beginning to course through her body, she had to agree. "Lust and love. I'll take that."

"Will you?" he asked, and lifted her by the waist up and onto him.

"Oh," was the best she could come up with, a reaction to both what he asked and what he did.

He smiled and said, "We are going to be so good together."

His pointy teeth had elongated into fangs, and she didn't even mind, so far gone in love was she. "Going to be good? Hah!" she disagreed. "We are already good." She wiggled her hips from side to side to show just what she meant.

"Whatever you say, dearling." He groaned and rolled his eyes up in his head.

Her eyes were probably rolling in her head, too, like cherries on a slot machine. She already felt like she'd won the jackpot.

A hazy blue fog rose from his shoulder blades then and swirled around them, cocooning them in a scented bubble of peppermint/coconut bliss. They were in this world, but not part of it.

As Cnut leaned farther back and brought her with him, mouth to mouth, it caused his lower body to arch up, and his erection reached higher and wider inside her body's sheath. When she thought she could take no more, her inner muscles shifted to accommodate whatever he wanted.

Their deep kisses and his deep strokes became a giving and taking of remarkable intensity. The lines became blurred between where he began and she ended, and vice versa. Truly, they became one.

If this was what lifemate loving was like, it was the world's best-kept secret.

"I love you, heartling," he said against her open mouth.

"Love you, sweetheart," she said back.

Their rise to orgasm was a gentle evolution this time, unlike the fierce, tumultuous, previous ones, but no less powerful in intensity. Each time she became further aroused, he halted whatever he was doing. Then she reciprocated with soft caresses and rocking undulations until he made her halt. They kissed 'til they couldn't breathe for their racing hearts. They tingled. All over.

When they'd reached and backtracked several times from the precipice, she whispered, "Bite me."

"I thought you'd never ask," he whispered back, and when he sank his fangs into her neck, her own blood felt as if it was rushing, warmly, in waves through her body, heating her, making her skin simmer with sensation. They held each other tightly while they melted together, then reformed into one joined being. It was an illusion, of course, but no less real to both of them.

As she lay in his arms later, back under the bed furs in his bedchamber, she yawned and stretched lazily before snuggling closer. He was on his back and she lay on her side, half on and half off him. "How come you get to do all the biting? Do I ever get to taste your blood?"

Cnut's callused palm had been caressing her back, from nape to buttocks. He stopped suddenly, and she could swear she heard his heart thump faster. "You could if you wanted to, I suppose," he said. "Wouldn't you consider it kind of . . . I don't know . . . gross?"

"Maybe," she replied and yawned widely. "It's just that it feels amazing when you do it to me, and I just thought . . . never mind. Forget I said anything."

He rolled over, so fast she almost fell off the bed. With a speed only a vangel could manage, he had her pinned beneath his body and growled, he actually growled. "Forget? Forget? M'lady, there are some invitations that can't be taken back."

Chapter 18

A HOMECOMING CELEBRATION

Reindeer steaks au jus
Whole roasted boar
Pickled lampreys, sucking mouths and all! (also known as vampire fish)
Bass stuffed with stale manchet crumbs, chopped venison heart, walnuts, and various other vegetables, including, yes, even turnips
Carrot, onion, and turnip medley
Salted herring
Buttered lutefisk or lye-fish (beaten and broken into fibrous pieces)
Mashed turnips with pork gravy

Manchet bread
Sourdough rolls with butter

Honey oatcakes

And then a Christmas visitor arrived . . .

Cnut kept Andrea by his side most of the next day. Every time she wandered off to the kitchen to help Girda with some task, or to feed her precious sourdough starter, he sought her out. For some reason, he needed her within touching distance. It probably had something to do with the lifemate business, which he could no longer fight. What would be would be.

Andrea asked at one point what Michael would say about their making love, and told her, "You don't want to know."

"Why?"

"Vangels are supposed to be celibate."

"Vikings celibate?"

"Exactly."

"But you said that your brothers are married."

"It wasn't supposed to happen. The only way a male and a human can wed is if the woman agrees to live only as long as her partner does. Vice versa for female vangels."

That had puzzled her, but only for a moment. "But that could be five hundred years."

"Or five days."

"Wow! What will Michael do to you for breaking your vows of celibacy?"

"Oh, probably add another couple hundred years on to my sentence."

"What?"

"Don't worry about it." He wasn't.

Throughout the day, even as he held her hand or stole the occasional kiss, and more, he made precautions for Hoggstead to survive if he did not. First, he sat down with Finn and Girda at the far end of his great hall to make an inventory. Andrea was given scrap sheets of parchment, quills, and thick oak gall ink to make their lists. It took several splotchy failed attempts and some modern swearwords that Finn and Girda did not understand before she was able to get legible words down. Her list read:

¾ brown bear
12 boars
14 deer (red and reindeer)
22 grouse (Andrea jokingly asked if the plural of *grouse* was *greese*, but Finn and Girda just exchanged raised eyebrows, not getting the joke. He got it, though, and kissed her on the top of her head to show how much he appreciated her humor. She was busy glaring at her inky fingers. He was not about to tell her that it would take days to wash it off.)
6 seabirds
50 rabbits
12 squirrels
3 large bass
2 extra large cod
10 lampreys
62 trout
Dozens of assorted fishes—roach, bream, pike, perch, herring
2 large sacks of onions
1 small sack of carrots
1 small sack of wild celery
1 small sack of endive
1 small sack of mushrooms
1 small sack of dried peas
2 big sacks of turnips (Would they ever escape the dreaded neep?)
25 heads of cabbage

1 basket of dried apples
3 barrels of oats for bread and animal feed
1 barrel of barley
2 tuns of ale
1 small barrel of mead
Assorted spices, small quantities of dill, coriander, cloves, pepper, cardamom, nutmeg
12 honeycombs and 3 jugs of honey
Mustard seed
Vinegar
Plenty of salt

"That seems like plenty to last until spring, even with tonight's homecoming meal for Cnut, and the yuletide feasts," Andrea said to Finn and Girda.

Cnut heard the hope in her voice. She was thinking that, if there was enough food, they could make a concerted effort to go home. He hated to disappoint her, but then he didn't have to. Finn and Girda did it for him.

"There are one hundred and twenty people to feed here in the castle and more than fifty down below. Closer to two hundred, all totaled," Finn said. "'Twill be a least four months 'til the longboats can manage the fjords. This will never last that long. And, besides, we are assuming the spring planting will be successful or, truth to tell, whether there is seed enough for planting."

Finn painted a bleak but honest picture.

Then Girda added to it. "I once worked in the royal kitchen of King Hakon. I was only a girling, and my mother was one of the cooks, but I remember like it was yestermorn. For one of his feasts alone were prepared twenty boar, twenty deer, fifty ducks, and a thousand boiled eggs."

They all gaped at Girda, but then Cnut said, "Well, we are no royal household, and we are in the midst of famine where we must ration food, not spread it about in a wasteful manner."

"Hmpfh!" Girda said. "Does that mean soup for the yule feast?"

Cnut saw Andrea bristle and he jumped right in before a war of the cooks started, "Andrea makes wonderful soups, Girda. Did I not eat six bowls of her chicken soup yesterday? But we do not need to serve only soup at the yule feast. It is your decision, after all."

Girda's response was another "Hmpfh!"

Andrea's was an elbow jab at him; she knew how he felt about the vast amount of soup he'd eaten, but luckily she remained silent.

When they were alone again, Cnut said, "Don't be disappointed. I know you thought there would be enough for us to leave." *Assuming we can leave.* "Look how much progress we've made so far. Have faith, sweetling."

"Says the Viking or the vangel?"

"Both," he said, giving her a quick kiss, and then a not-so-quick kiss.

"If you were given the choice, would you want to stay here in the past? I mean, you seem so contented today."

"I'm contented today because of you, not my surroundings," he said, giving her another quick kiss. He couldn't help himself, even if his men were starting to gaze at him as if he'd lost his mind as well as the pounds. "Seriously, though, I guess it would depend on whether I were a vangel or human in either place. But, no, that isn't true. Give me a choice between a good French baguette with soft Brie cheese, or a hunk of manchet bread with a smear of skyr, and you know which one I'd take. Or sliced boar with a side of turnips, compared to a rare T-bone steak with a baked potato dripping with butter and sour cream? Then there are the different beers to choose from. And desserts." He smiled at her.

"So it's food and drink that would make the difference for you?"

"Not just that. I like travel by longship, but I love my motorcycle. And television has its merits. And so many modern conveniences. What do you miss?"

"Warm showers and bubble baths. Gas stoves and my professional kitchen tools. Norah Jones music. The *Game of Thrones* series on HBO. Gourmet food stores and farmers' markets. Thrift shops and yard sales."

"It didn't take you long to come up with a list."

"And that's only a start."

Thorkel came into the hall then, and Cnut motioned him over. "Have you told the men I've scheduled military exercises for this afternoon?"

"I have," Thorkel said, accepting a horn of ale offered by a passing maid. "They whined and complained about the cold, but they . . . all of us recognize that we have been lax of late. The most exercise we've had is dragging that big tree inside for Lady Andrea." Thorkel winked at Andrea as he said the latter.

Cnut didn't like Thorkel winking at Andrea. And he didn't like her smiling in return.

"By the way, are we going to have a yule log tomorrow night, Cnut, or a yule tree like Dyna tells me you've had in the past?" Andrea asked.

Thorkel perked up at the mention of Dyna.

And Cnut said, "Whatever you want, dearling."

She beamed.

And he added, "You can thank me later."

"Whatever you want, dearling," she countered.

Which caused Thorkel to choke on his ale.

"Moving right along," Cnut said, nudging Andrea's knees under the table, "there is something important I want to discuss with you, Thorkel."

"Good. There is something I need to discuss with you, too," Thorkel said.

"Should I leave?" Andrea asked.

"Stay," Cnut and Thorkel both told her.

"You first," Cnut said.

"Dyna and I have decided to wed, and we were wondering if we could do it during the Jól festivities."

"Congratulations, Thorkel. I know you and Dyna will be happy together." Andrea reached across the table and squeezed Thorkel's hand.

Cnut didn't like her squeezing Thorkel's hand, even if he was betrothed.

"The Christmas . . . I mean, yule celebration will be a perfect time for a wedding, don't you think, Cnut?" Andrea asked him.

"Certainly," he said. "Thorkel, I agree with Andrea. Best wishes.

"What did you want to discuss with me?" Thorkel asked then.

"Right. Here's the situation, Thorkel. If I should disappear suddenly, I want you to take over as jarl of Hoggstead."

Andrea bristled, thinking he meant *disappear,* as in being taken by Zeb. Thorkel bristled at the suggestion that Cnut might be taken captive again, or whatever had happened to him last time.

Cnut put up both hands for them to halt before they protested. "You know that I left without warning before," he pointed out to Thorkel. At the same time, he noticed Andrea relax, getting his direction now. "I can't predict that it will ever happen again, but if it should, I need to know steps are in place to safeguard Hoggstead."

"I am not qualified to be jarl," Thorkel said.

"You are as qualified as anyone else here, and I will instruct you over the coming days. Do you agree?"

Thorkel nodded hesitantly. "Gods willing, it won't be necessary."

Any further discussion on the subject was curtailed by several children, including Kugge, running into the hall, shouting, "Visitors coming! Visitors coming!"

When they went outdoors, wearing heavy cloaks and mittens against the ice and snow—not just them, but practically everyone in the keep—they saw Farle and the missing sledge that had gone west more than three sennights past in hopes of purchasing food products from any estates or markets with excess. Farle's wagon sledge was piled high with goods.

But that wasn't all.

There were three more sledges behind him,

piled equally high, and behind them a drover leading two cows and several goats.

"Bless the gods!" Girda was heard to remark.

"Who is that woman?" Thorkel asked, peering through the snow. "Frigg's foot! I think it's Princess Reynilda."

"Who is Princess Reynilda?" Andrea asked.

"The horniest maid in all of Hordaland," Cnut remarked.

"Who used to be betrothed to Cnut," Thorkel noted with a chuckle.

Cnut gave Thorkel a dirty look and said, "I thought she married Jarl Esgar."

"She did, but he died recently. Some say from too much bedsport," Girda contributed. "She better not be havin' sex in me scullery like she did last time."

"Who was she having sex with in the scullery?" Andrea asked with narrowed eyes.

"Yea, who?" asked Dyna, who'd just come up beside them.

"Not me!" Cnut and Thorkel both said at the same time.

"I suspect this is going to be a very interesting yule season," Cnut said, putting his arm around Andrea's shoulders.

"Hmm," Andrea said, shrugging away as she tried to get a better look at Reynilda, who was being helped down from her seat on the wagon sledge. Then Andrea muttered, "Oh shit!"

Reynilda was stunning, no doubt about it. She wore a red cloak lined with white ermine. Her black curls emerged from the hood, which was also trimmed with the precious fur, framing a perfect heart-shaped face. She was beautiful, no doubt about it. Red Riding Hood in a bustier, so to speak. And devious as the Big Bad Wolf.

"Cnut! Beloved!" the woman said, opening her arms as she rushed toward him.

Beloved? What a load of you-know-what! He was the one who said, "Oh shit!" then. And he had no choice but to open his arms, too, for a welcome embrace.

When he glanced back, he saw that Andrea was gone.

That night, during his homecoming feast, Reynilda sat on his left side at the high table, chattering away inanely, as if they were still betrothed, touching his sleeve, batting her eyelashes as if in a sudden dust storm. And Andrea was missing. Cnut couldn't help but notice that there were no honey-glazed doughnuts. And he didn't tingle. Not one bit.

Later, he slept alone in the guest bedchamber from which Andrea was also missing. When it became clear she was not joining him, and he wasn't about to embarrass himself by hunting for her, he put a bar across the door.

Women! Would he ever figure them out?

Not even in a thousand years, a voice in his head said. He was probably talking to himself.

There are red-eyed Lucipire monsters,
and then there are green-eyed monsters.
Both formidable creatures . . .

Andrea was so angry, she could spit, and so jealous, she could spit green. From the get-go, the lovely Reynilda drove her, and everyone else, bonkers.

On the surface, she was all sweetness and innocence, but a cunning brain worked behind those baby blue eyes. Andrea would bet her favorite frosting spatula on that.

"You don't mind if I take your bedchamber, do you, Cnut? It's the biggest, and I have so many garments."

Cnut hadn't said anything, so Andrea had proceeded up the stairs and removed her own belongings, scant as they were.

The designing Reynilda's sly eyes had taken note of the fact that Andrea had been sharing Cnut's bed and she said, all honeyed innocence, "Andrea . . . that is your name isn't it? How quaint? Would you please unpack my bags, and be careful of the gold-threaded robe? The threads have a tendency to break. Oh, you're not a servant? So sorry. Tee hee hee! What are you, exactly?"

Cnut (suddenly deaf and dumb) hadn't uttered a word, so Andrea had said, "A cook."

"Good. Make sure there are no turnips or anything made with turnips at the high table for the yule feast tomorrow night. You are having a feast, I hope, since this is the first night of winter solstice. Neeps give me a rash."

Once again, Cnut the Mute hadn't said anything, even though Andrea had rolled her eyes at him.

Girda had spoken up, though, "Rash my arse."

"Be nice, Girda," Cnut had warned.

Now the idiot chooses to talk!

Andrea, Dyna, and Girda all exchanged looks.

You could be sure there would be turnips buried in something on the Jól table, maybe in everything.

Needless to say, Andrea found a sleep closet to lay her head down that night. She didn't sleep much, though. Instead of counting sheep, she was counting fifty ways to kill a lover.

The next morning, the entire castle was in a flurry of activity preparing for the evening's festivities, which were going to include a wedding between Thorkel and Dyna. Andrea decided to raid Cnut's treasure room once again to get some fabric to make Dyna a wedding gown. She took Dyna with her. They found some lovely pale blue wool that was so soft it almost felt like silk. There was also some white linen for the apron, with gold braiding for trim. Several of the servants proficient with needle and thread were going to do a rush job for the garment. Dyna was so overcome with gratitude that tears welled in her eyes. "Thank you, m'lady. Thank you. Thank you. Ever since you have come to Hoggstead, things have been better. You must be our good luck token."

I don't know about that, Andrea thought. She didn't feel very lucky herself, not after a sleepless night and a vivid imagination about what Cnut might have been doing above stairs. He certainly hadn't come looking for her.

She sent Dyna on her way and was about to lock the door and return the key to Finn, who was no doubt having a heart attack somewhere or predicting that Cnut would, when she noticed an emerald-green, already made gown. It was not in the Norse style, more tapered on top, with long sleeves and a rounded neck. Very plain but very Christmasy in color. It was much too big for her, but maybe with a belt . . . She threw it over her arm and emerged from the treasure room and was locking up when she saw Cnut and Reynilda come out of the two bedchambers. Separately.

No time to feel elated over that. Reynilda hadn't noticed her yet, but Cnut had.

"Good morn, Jarl Sigurdsson. Didst sleep well?" Reynilda cooed.

"Very well. And you?"

"Like a newborn babe. But I am famished now. Dost think your cook Andrea could make me some porridge with butter and sweet cream?"

"I don't know. What do you say, Andrea?" Cnut looked directly at her and winked.

Reynilda swiveled around to see Andrea standing a short distance away, leaning against the closed treasure room door. Her eyes took in both the large key in Andrea's hand and the gown over her arm. Though her eyebrows arched with surprise, she didn't remark on the items.

"I'm sure I could whip up some gruel for you, Princess Reynilda."

Reynilda nodded and turned her back on Andrea, as if she were of no importance. Instead, she spoke to Cnut, "How handsome you look today! Your housecarl Farle told us at Storm's Lair what a change there was in your appearance, and I just had to come and see. Not that you weren't handsome before."

Should I gag now or later?

"I was sooo distraught when my father forced me to marry Esgar." She batted her eyelashes at Cnut.

Oh Lord! The batting eyelash gimmick. And men fall for it every time! I never did master the art. Celie, on the other hand, could flutter her lashes like butterflies. Celie! Oh my God! I haven't thought about Celie all day, or last night. What if . . . no, not now!

Reynilda, after whispering to one of the maids who'd just come out of the bedchamber carrying a huge pile of laundry, swanned off like queen of the castle, making her way to the garderobe. Andrea hoped it smelled particularly bad today.

Once Reynilda left, Cnut turned to Andrea, grabbed her by the wrist of her free hand, and yanked her into the spare bedchamber, and had her backed up against the wall before she could even blink. The key and the gown dropped to the rush-covered floor. "I waited for you last night, Andrea love," he murmured against her neck, licking the sensitive skin there, causing her to shiver.

I waited for you, too. But you never came looking for me. She kept her lips pressed tightly together to keep from speaking those words aloud. He wasn't getting off so easily.

"Are you cold?" he asked, leaning his head back but keeping her pinned with his hands and body.

"Of course I'm cold," she said. "It's freezing in here."

It *was* cold, the small hearth fire having burned out, but that wasn't what caused her goose bumps. It was the Tinglemaster himself, and he knew it, too.

He grinned and gave her a quick kiss, probably sensing that she would bite him if he stayed too close or too long. And not a sexy biting, either.

"I know a way to warm you quick." He glanced pointedly at the unmade bed.

"Not a chance!" But she was tempted.

"I don't understand why you're so angry, Andrea." The coaxing tone of his voice was belied by the firm hold he had on her buttocks.

"Reynilda." That one word said it all, or should. She tried to shove his hands away, but they just landed on other forbidden spots. Her breasts. And traitorous critters that they were, they rose and purled like needy kittens up for a petting.

"What about her?"

At first, she wasn't sure what he was talking about, so distracted was she by the massaging of his hands. Then she shoved his hands off her and held them away from her body, staring at him with disbelief. "A fiancée? You failed to mention that you were engaged."

"Past tense," he emphasized. "'Twas of no importance."

Not important! How like a man! But I can't let him think it matters. Instead, she homed in on something else. "'Twas? 'Twas? You're turning into a bloody Viking."

"I was always a bloody Viking, sweetling."

Don't I know it? Don't I love it? No, I don't. Vikings are vain and arrogant and vicious and, damn, he's playing the sweetling card. He knows it makes me tingle. "Aaarrgh!"

"You're jealous," he said, and grinned.

"Idiot!" She smacked him.

"I love when you call me an idiot. 'Tis like an endearment."

She didn't smile.

"Listen, my love, Reynilda has a selective memory. She fails to recall the details of our short betrothal. It wasn't her father who rejected me. She herself did. In fact, she'd called me a 'fat toad,' and swore she would share her bed furs with me when pond scum turned to gold."

"I agree. You are a toad," she said huffily, though her lips twitched with humor. "How does she get to be a princess?"

"Her father, Agmundr of Lade, was a minor king here in the Norselands. Truth to tell, any chieftain, or jarl of some standing, can call himself king in these times. Technically, she was no longer a princess once she married Jarl Esgar of Storm's Lair, which is west of Hoggstead, but many miles north of Lade. But I for one don't intend to challenge her right to do so. It matters not to me if she wants to name herself Queen of the North."

Andrea felt a little better knowing Reynilda's background. In other words, she was a pretentious, self-serving bitch.

"Reynilda is up to something and it isn't my superior appearance that draws her here in the middle of winter," Cnut continued.

"At least you're smart enough to realize that," Andrea said, then added immediately, "not that your appearance isn't enough to make a saint drop her drawers."

"You do have a way with words," Cnut said, not for the first time. "The only drawers I'm interested in seeing are yours." He pinched her butt for emphasis.

"So you say!" she said with a sniff, but she was pleased.

"We have to be careful, though," Cnut warned. "Reynilda brought a pigload of food and supplies with her. Enough that our worries over Hoggstead's immediate woes may very well be ended now that our larder is nearly full. We . . . I . . . owe her."

Uh-oh! "Ah, but what is her price?"

"Precisely. And more important, why does she smell like a rank lemon?"

"She does?" That was the characteristic of a really evil person, according to what Cnut had told her previously. *Good Lord, I'm starting to believe all this stuff.*

He nodded. "And so do the half dozen men and women in the entourage she brought with her."

"You need to talk with Farle. Find out what he saw or heard at Storm's Lair."

"I will, but there are more important things we need to do first."

"Such as?" *If he suggests that I go make breakfast for the woman, he has another think coming.*

"Wouldst care to explore yon pond with me, m'lady?" he asked, making a motion with his head toward the bed. "Methinks it needs some scum."

"You being the toad, I presume."

"Ribbit, ribbit."

She laughed.

"I give good wart," he promised.

And he did.

There was a whole lot of tingling going on in the pond for the next half hour until there was a pounding on the door with a harried Finn calling out, "You must come quickly, master. Girda and Princess Reynilda are going at each other like cats in heat."

Chapter 19

A YULETIDE FEAST

3 wild boars, 2 spit roasted, 1 ember-baked
10 venison rumps
Bear shanks slow-cooked in beer (with turnips)
Pig ribs in sauerkraut-onion broth
Eels in skyr sauce
Pickled pigs' feet
Oat-stuffed pike (with turnip)
Trout in garlic butter
Herring pies
Heart and gizzard medley (deer, rabbit, grouse, squirrel)
Shredded cabbage in gelled marrow (with turnip)
Herbed beets
Creamed turnips
Peas with leeks (and turnip)
Boiled onions served in bear gravy
Lentil pottage (with turnip)
Vinegar and smoked pork over endive

Mustard
Pickles
Raspberry-flavored frumenty
Horseradish

Manchet bread
Sourdough rolls

Honey-egg custard
Apple and currant nutmeg tarts
Honey oatcakes
Cream-filled doughnuts (just a few)
Assorted nuts, glazed and salted

Ale and mead (for all)
Wine (for high table only)

Here comes the bride . . . and the devil in disguise . . .

Cnut could almost be happy living here in the past, considering his present mood. Of course, it was the Jól spirit that pervaded his keep as everyone worked to make tonight's feast and Thorkel and Dyna's wedding a success. Cnut had even invited all the farmers and villagers to attend.

Of course, first he had to break up the fight between his cook and the lovely Reynilda. Apparently, Reynilda had returned her porridge to the kitchen, complaining that milk and not cream had been used in the making, and the butter had not been freshly churned. When no new bowl had been sent to the hall, Reynilda had gone storming in, demanding her due.

Cnut separated the two of them and motioned for Reynilda to speak first. "All I wanted was my usual morning meal. Cooked oats with honey and cream. Is that too much to ask?" Reynilda's blue eyes filled with huge crocodile tears as she glanced up at him.

"Hah! I served her majesty the usual porridge what we all eat here. I even put in some milk and butter."

"The butter was rancid."

"Was not!" Girda countered. "Methinks ye wouldn't know bad butter from pig lard."

"Oh, oh, oh! Didst hear that rudeness, Cnut? You should whip the woman."

Girda put her hands on her hips, daring him to raise a hand at her.

Not in this lifetime, or any other!

"Where is that other cook? The skinny one who was stealing cloth from your treasure room."

Unfortunately, Andrea chose that moment to enter the kitchen. While she might refer to herself as skinny, being described thus by a woman she did not admire clearly did not sit well with her. Before she could speak her mind, Cnut interjected, "Wouldst care to take a walk, Reynilda? The snow has stopped, and it's beautiful outside. Mayhap the fresh air will heighten your appetite, and by the time we return, porridge to your satisfaction will be prepared."

"Oh, that would be nice," she cooed, and went off to gather her cloak.

Meanwhile, he glared at both Girda and Andrea. "Is it asking too much for you to prepare a special bowl for her?"

"I have too much ta do preparing fer tonight's feast," Girda said stubbornly.

"I'll do it," Andrea offered.

Really? He hoped she wouldn't spit in it. But then, he really didn't care.

At that moment, Thorkel came in, encouraging him to go out for the yule log, or yule tree, or whatever you wanted to call it. So he and six men, including Thorkel, went out with axes. And took Reynilda with them for the walk, and what a mistake that was! She did nothing but complain. Or offer him false compliments.

"My boots are getting wet."

"Cnut, I can't get over how handsome you look."

"It's so cold."

"Cnut, you are so good at picking out yule logs. I never would have chosen those."

"How far are we going? My legs are getting tired. Can I lean on you?"

"How strong you are in wielding an axe, Cnut. I warrant you are just as capable at lopping off enemy heads."

"Do you think I can break fast when we return to the keep? My stomach is rumbling with hunger."

"You could pick any wife you wanted now, Cnut. Best you get rid of that Andrea woman first, though. Her lack of comeliness makes you look as if you have no choice."

"Why do we not ride horses? Isn't there a sleigh we could hook up to the horses? Oh. Do we have to go into the forest where the horses cannot go? Why not go down in the village and take some of their logs? Cotters have no need of yule celebrations, especially during a famine. You have invited them to tonight's feast? Why?"

"What a generous man you are, Cnut! How admirable!"

Twice, she'd picked mistletoe off an oak tree and held it over her head for Cnut to kiss her. He did, once on the cheek, and once on her mouth when she turned quickly. The overpowering scent of lemon almost made him gag.

Cnut's men just rolled their eyes at all Reynilda's chatter. Personally, he'd like to stick a plug in her mouth.

They came back to the keep, not with a yule tree, but with three huge logs, cut from an enormous dead oak tree that must have been felled by lightning some time ago. Each of the logs was six feet long and two feet in diameter. They would burn long and hot this evening and into tomorrow.

Reynilda went off to eat her newly prepared porridge, after which, she announced, she and her maids would take over the bathhouse for an hour or two.

Andrea talked Cnut and the woodworker, Hastein, into building a simple trellis for Thorkel and Dyna's wedding ceremony. Cnut was impressed to see the array of wood animals that Hastein had carved as yule gifts for the children, at Andrea's request. Horses, cows, deer, dogs, cats, bears, and so on. Cnut should have thought of gifts himself, but hadn't. He would have to find something for Andrea . . . and for Reynilda, he supposed. After they brought the trellis into the great hall and placed it by the fragrant Christmas tree, Andrea and Dyna decorated it with trailing pine and holly boughs. He had to admit, it looked lovely. The whole hall did.

Succulent odors of cooking food permeated the

keep, along with the evergreen. Roasting meat, sweet cakes, and the like. Festive smells. Stomachs rumbled with anticipation for the special treats that would be on all the tables tonight, his included. In the old days, he would have been unable to stop himself from gorging on a five-pound slab of pork before it ever left the kitchen. He was still tempted. Best he think of other things, he chided himself. Like his other appetites. How soon could they tap the barrel of ale? How soon could he tup Andrea again?

Speaking—rather thinking—of Andrea, the witch must have invaded his treasure room again, he realized, scanning the large room and seeing all the small candles on the tree, and the dozens of thick candles sitting here and there along the trestle tables surrounded by Christmas greenery, and, yes, red silk bows. They would be lit ceremoniously before the evening meal.

He had some plans for all those red silk ribbons. Later tonight.

Some of the youthlings were practicing songs, accompanied by the lute player. Younger children were singing anachronistic "Jingle Bells" and "Here Comes Santa Claus," thanks to Andrea, no doubt.

Finally, he had a chance to talk with Farle in private. They were out in the bathing house, about to change into their yule finery—his borrowed once again from Thorkel. He'd given all his old garments to the sewing women to remake into more normal-size apparel. Some for himself, assuming he would be here long enough to avail himself of their use, and others to be dispersed among men in need of such.

"So, tell me everything you learned at Storm's Lair." Cnut was sitting in the pool up to his chest, and Farle was doing the same on the other side.

"Ah, a snake pit of intrigue it is there, master. Ye wouldn't want to spend any more time there than necessary. Rumor is that Princess Reynilda poisoned Jarl Esgar when he refused to take her to the Althing last summer and then declined King Halfdan's invitation to celebrate the yule season at his southern palace, claiming diminished funds due to the famine. There is no proof, but Esgar's eldest son by his first marriage, Bjorg, holds the odel rights of inheritance and is said to be coming from the Scottish isles to take over the jarldom. Needless to say, there is no love lost betwixt the princess and Bjorg."

"And so she comes here . . . why?"

Farle shrugged, but the answer was obvious. "I am to be her latest victim?" Cnut guessed.

"That is not for me to say."

Yeah, right.

"The group that come with her are jist as bad," Farle said. "A brother and sister what are swiving each other. A maid with loose fingers that steals anything she can lay her hands on. A man who rapes young girls, sometimes fer his mistress's enjoyment. And a cobbler who's been makin' more than shoes with the princess, if ye get my meaning."

Cnut put his face in his hands and sighed. He looked up then. "I don't understand. She seemed to come out of generosity. She brought plenty of goods with her."

Farle nodded. "As much as she could carry off before Bjorg gets there and cuts off her supply. Every bit of jewelry and clothing she owns, even some of Esgar's. A chest so heavy with coins it took two men to carry it. In truth, anything of value that wasn't nailed down or locked up. She would have taken Esgar's longships if she could have pushed them down the fjord."

"You mean she has no intention of returning to Storm's Lair? No! She can't stay here," Cnut said with dismay. "Mayhap she'll go back to her father's home in Lade."

"Mayhap." Farle sounded skeptical. "Be careful she don't poison yer lady friend."

"My lady friend? What? Who? Andrea? Why would you even suggest such a thing?"

"Anything or anyone who gets in her way dies or disappears, so they say at Storm's Lair."

"But Andrea?"

Farle shrugged.

"She wouldn't!"

"If ye say so, m'lord."

On that happy note, Cnut dried off, put on clean clothing, then stomped into the keep, where he sought out Andrea, who was on a wooden ladder hanging holly from one of the rafters. He yelled up to her, "Andrea!"

The ladder wobbled and she almost fell.

"What?" she asked, irritably.

"Don't eat or drink anything unless I've tasted it first."

"Are you crazy?"

"Maybe."

"Who's that handsome guy who just came in?"

"What handsome guy?" he asked. This time it was his voice carrying a note of irritability. He was the only handsome guy he wanted her noticing.

"Over there. By the door. The one who looks like one of the Three Wise Men. Betcha he parked his camel outside. Ha, ha, ha."

Cnut looked, and then did a double take. True, the guy wore sumptuous, bejeweled garments in the Eastern style, with a turban, of all things, on his lackwit head.

It was Zeb, the most unlikely, and least welcome, Christmas visitor. Cnut could just imagine the conversation among his brothers:

What did Cnut get for Christmas?

Laid?

Besides that?

A partridge in a pear tree?

What would Cnut do with a pear tree?

I know. Six geese a-laying . . . so he could eat the world's biggest omelette?

No, Cnut's Christmas surprise wasn't food. It was a person. Of sorts. Guess which yule visitor came knock, knock, knocking on our brother's door?

A jolly old fellow wearing a red hat?

No, a demon wearing a turban. Yuck, yuck!

On the other hand, Cnut mused, maybe there really had been a fourth Wise Man, as many historians claimed. A demon vampire. Cnut would know he was right if Zeb was carrying gold, or frankincense, or myrrh. What in bloody hell was myrrh anyhow? And who needed that kind of stuff? Better he bring a fatted calf, or some sheep. There were sheep at the Nativity, weren't there?

"Who are you talking to?" Andrea asked as she climbed down the ladder.

Oops! He hadn't realized he was speaking his thoughts aloud. As she stepped off the ladder, Cnut noticed that Andrea hadn't yet dressed for the upcoming festivities. Instead, she wore what you could call her work clothes: scruffy boots (*she's going to lose her designer creds*), tight jeans (*oh yeah!*), and the "Save a Horse, Ride a Cowboy" T-shirt (*yee-haw!*).

"Um," he replied. His brain was melting from whiffing too much holly, or something. Probably coconut overload.

"Greetings!" Zeb the King yelled out, waving his beringed hand, when no one went to give him a personal welcome.

"Oh holy night!" Cnut muttered.

Reynilda perked up from where she'd been sitting by the hearth, bored out of her gourd, while everyone else was working. Seeing the new arrival, she dusted off her gown, a concoction of rose-colored silk and ivory lace, (*as out of place in this dark, smoky hall, even with all its greenery, as a butterfly on a pile of dung . . . well, maybe not so bad as that . . . a butterfly in a flock of moths . . . or . . . oh, never mind*!), and straightened the silver fillet on her black waves. Then, like a homing pigeon on a wave of lemon scent, she made her way toward the door to welcome the new visitor.

This was not good. Not good at all.

The bride wore blue, the groom wore a grin . . .

Andrea was having the best time of her life. And the worst time of her life.

Cnut had insisted that she sit on his right side at the high table that night, and not be acting the servant. She wore the emerald-green gown, and, actually, she felt rather royalty-like with her blonde hair intricately braided and twisted into a coronet atop her head, thanks to Dyna's expertise. Of course, any pretensions she might have put on were quickly dashed when Reynilda sat down on Cnut's left, looking like the Princess in Pink, with her breasts pushed up so high in the rounded neckline that she could just as well be called Princess of Boobland.

That was mean, Andrea's conscience prodded.

So what! the other side of her brain said.

Andrea's only jewelry was Cnut's Christmas gift to her, a thin gold chain holding a gold-filigreed pendant that surrounded a piece of amber, inside of which was the fossil of a long-dead, tiny bumblebee. Cnut told her that many people carried amber as protection on long travels. Her travel back to the past, and hopefully her return to the future someday, definitely qualified as a long travel.

Regardless of its symbolism or its ick factor (wearing a dead bug), she loved it, and couldn't stop touching the stone, imagining she felt heat emanating from it against the base of her neck.

Cnut had given Reynilda an etched silver arm ring, but Andrea didn't mind. She'd much rather have the amber necklace.

Dyna and Thorkel sat on Andrea's right. Their wedding would be held soon, before the evening meal. The hall looked fabulous with all the fragrant greenery and candles lit on all the tables, as well as the tree. A bucket of water sat nearby in case of fire.

The pale blue fabric Andrea had given Dyna had been turned into a gorgeous Viking-style wedding gown with gold braiding on the neckline, wrists, and hem, but also edging the long, open-sided apron. Her platinum-blonde hair hung loose over her shoulders. Pretty silver brooches in the Norse writhing wolf design, gifts from Thorkel, adorned Dyna's shoulder straps.

Thorkel, too, looked roguishly spectacular in a dark blue wool tunic, belted over black breeches. Kugge was wearing a smaller version of Thorkel's outfit, which had touched Dyna deeply, more than any other gesture her bridegroom could have made.

The handsome new visitor sat on Reynilda's other side. And that was where the stress came in . . . in other words, bad times.

On being introduced to Zebulan the Hebrew, Reynilda had cooed, "Oooh, is it true what they say about Jewish men?"

Andrea had interjected . . . okay, she sniped, "Is it similar to what they say about Viking men?"

Reynilda had blushed at Andrea's mockery, but Cnut had grinned. And Zeb had said, with a straight face, "Yes."

Cnut had yet to explain exactly who Zeb was, but Andrea had a faint memory of him mentioning a demon vampire named Zebulan who wanted to capture him on orders from his evil master. Surely, this wasn't the same person . . . thing.

"Cnut," she whispered. "Who *is* Zebulan?"

"Do you mean *what*? You recall the name, don't you?"

"A demon? No way! You wouldn't be sitting here so calmly if he was a demon."

"What else can I do?"

"Tell him to go home?"

"As in, go to hell?"

"That's not funny." Actually, it was. "I don't believe you. You must be teasing. This guy is so handsome, he doesn't resemble those beastie things I saw at the ranch."

"I don't know about handsome. As for beasties, whoo boy! You ought to see Zeb when he's in demonoid form."

Just then, Zeb leaned forward and smiled her way.

"He has the longest eyelashes I've ever seen on a man," she observed to Cnut. "And his eyes, so big and brown and sad . . . what woman wouldn't be drawn to him?"

"Eyelashes are overrated, in my opinion. Now, if you were talking about the longest—"

She put her fingers to Cnut's lips to halt his next words and he nipped at the tips.

Just then, Njal came to stand at the head of the hall, near the trellis where the wedding ceremony was to be held. Njal, his white beard and mustache having been neatly trimmed, and what hair he had left lying in a single braid down his back, was the oldest of the Vikings here at Hoggstead, and therefore would be acting as "lawspeaker," performing the marriage rites. He wore a special ceremonial robe of dyed animal pelts in various shades of black and red.

Thorkel and Dyna rose from their seats to go stand before him. Cnut and Andrea, the witnesses, followed after them. The person who had been playing a lute stopped when it became apparent that the ceremony was about to begin. Normally, the lawspeaker would enumerate the oral history of all the Viking laws before certain events, such as an Althing, Andrea had been informed earlier, but they would forgo that lengthy diatribe tonight to save time.

"Come ye, family and friends. Come ye, gods and goddesses on this Frigg's-day, first night of the winter solstice," Njal invited in a surprisingly booming voice. "Let us all bear witness to the marriage of Thorkel Long-Limbs to Dyna of the Silver Hair."

"Hear, hear!" the crowd yelled out, raising high their horns of ale.

Njal implored Odin to give this couple wisdom as they melded their lives together and Thor to protect them from all enemies.

"Are vangels allowed to participate in pagan rites?" Andrea whispered to Cnut.

"Shh," Cnut whispered back. "Some say Odin and God are the same entity."

That is a stretch. But Andrea kept silent.

Taking a hammer off the table that had been set before them, Thorkel said, "Thor, god of thunder, I lift your mighty hammer, Mjollnir, pledging to protect my wife from all peril.

With the fighting skills learned at your feet, I will crush her enemies. Her foe are my foe. My shield is now her shield." On those words, he crushed a stone on the table with a sharp tap of the hammer.

Andrea was the only one to jump, not having known what was coming.

Njal then dipped his hand into a bowl of wheat seeds and sprinkled them over Dyna's head. As Njal exhorted Frey, god of fertility, to bless her with many children of Thorkel's loins, Thorkel grinned. Dyna, on the other hand, glanced up at Andrea and winked, a sign that she would be the one to control that particular issue.

After that, Njal asked, "Who stands witness to the *handsal* that binds this bride and groom?"

"We do," Cnut and Andrea said, stepping forward. Cnut laced his fingers with hers, and the moment felt even more poignant. No matter what happened in the future, Andrea would always remember this time with fondness.

Cnut picked up a ewer and poured red bridal wine into a two-handled cup. Dyna took the cup and handed it to Thorkel for the first sip as she recited some age-old words:

Ale I bring thee, thou oak-of-battle,
With strength blended and greatest honor:
'Tis mixed with magic and mighty songs,
With goodly spells, wish-speeding runs.

Thorkel made the sign of Thor's hammer over the cup and turned it for Dyna to drink, reciting at the same time:

Bring the Hammer the bride to bless:
On the maiden's lap lay ye Mjollnir;
In Frigg's name then our wedlock hallow.

The crowd yelled, "Skål!" and raised their horns of ale again.

Njal asked Thorkel and Dyna to extend their wrists, which he slit lightly with a sharp blade that had also been placed previously on the table. Then he pressed Dyna's wrist over Thorkel's and the two of them proclaimed together, "Blood of my blood, I pledge thee my troth."

"With the blending of their blood, I declare Thorkel and Dyna are one," Njal said.

Everyone stood and cheered, clapping their hands as Thorkel and Dyna smiled at each other, kissed, then linked their hands and made their way through the hall accepting well wishes from the attendees, many of whom were already half buzzed. Good thing the meal was about to start.

With great aplomb, three whole roasted pigs, their skin glistening with golden crispness, were carried in on huge boards lifted high by four men each and circulated around the hall for all to see before being returned to the kitchen for carving. Ten deer were likewise brought in. The oohs and aahs of the crowd brought tears to Girda's eyes. She'd worked hard, probably hadn't slept at all last night to pull this feast off. Of course, she'd had lots of help, Andrea included, but still . . . kudos to the cook!

Almost immediately, servants began carrying in the trenchers of sliced meat and joints, along with an enormous stuffed fish—a pike that had to be three feet long. There were also herring pies, spareribs and sauerkraut, and various side dishes that included cabbage, beets, peas, leeks, onions, lentils, and endive. For dessert, honey egg custard, apple currant nutmeg tarts, and honey oatcakes completed the meal. The menu wouldn't have been near so varied if not for Reynilda's food contributions, Andrea had to admit.

"I need to go get your gift," Andrea told Cnut.

He arched his brows at her, but released her hand that he had been holding almost nonstop, as if he feared she would run away, or slap him for one of his many indecent touches under the table. She returned shortly with a wooden platter holding her latest creation. "Ta-da! Cream-filled doughnuts!" she said, placing the sweet treat in front of Cnut.

He grinned. "How did you manage this without sugar?"

"Honey cream on the inside, honey glaze on the outside. And a tube made by Hastein by peeling the bark off a fat twig and removing the pith. It took me three tries to get them right."

"Hastein has been a busy fellow," Cnut remarked. "And so have you, sweetling." He was about to pick up one of his edible gifts when Reynilda reached across, grabbed one, and said, "What are these?" She took a huge bite, and sweet cream squirted out onto her face and the front of her gown.

Cnut and Andrea and Zeb just gaped at her. The crowd below the dais started laughing.

Reynilda rose with a shriek and turned with clawed hands toward Andrea. "You did that on purpose, you filthy trollop."

"Whoa, whoa, whoa!" Andrea said, holding up her hands. "Those were intended for Cnut, not you."

"Did you hear that, Cnut? Did you? She intended to make the fool of you."

"I know how to eat the things, Reynilda. Come, let me take you to your chamber where you can change your gown."

Andrea arched her brows. *And will you be watching?*

"I can take her," Zeb offered.

Yes, let him.

"No, thank you," Cnut said, and he and the demon vampire Wise Man person exchanged meaningful looks.

What is that all about? "Why can't she go herself?" Andrea hissed at Cnut.

"Trust me," Cnut whispered. "I have my reasons."

I bet you do.

Just before he left, Cnut grabbed one of the doughnuts, took a huge bite, and closed his eyes in delight. Then, he licked his lips and mouthed to her, *Thank you*. Then, to Zeb, he said, "Don't touch my doughnuts."

Zeb had already been reaching.

Once Cnut and Reynilda left, Zeb slid over onto Cnut's seat and said, "So, Andrea, how would you like to go home to Philadelphia?"

Chapter 20

Road trip with a demon . . .

Cnut had no designs on Reynilda. In fact, he was doing his best to avoid her blatant attempts at seduction. But he had a job to do, as a vangel, and it required his getting her alone, in private.

"Where is your maid?" he asked when they reached his bedchamber, which she'd taken over, as evidenced by numerous gowns and other feminine items strewn about. "I'll wait out here while she helps you undress."

"I have no idea. Hedvig disappeared right after I came to the hall late this afternoon. Likewise, her brother Kormak. I sent for them numerous times, but they are nowhere to be found. Some skin is going to be flayed on the morrow, that I promise you. If they are off . . ." She let her words trail off, probably realizing how harsh she sounded, but Cnut understood. The brother and sister who allegedly shook the sheets together were suddenly gone.

Which reminded Cnut of something else. Finn had told him a short time ago that Red Ranulf went off in a huff that afternoon when chastised for bothering one of the laundresses, and he hadn't been seen since. Ranulf and the late departed Igor were the ones who'd supposedly raped some village women.

The dominos were falling in place. Ping, ping, ping. Ranulf disappeared. Two of Reynilda's entourage, who clearly smelled to high heaven of lemons, disappeared. And he would bet others who'd accompanied Reynilda would be found missing, too. Then Zeb the demon vampire arrived. What a coincidence! Cnut had a pretty good idea what was going on. Lucipires were having a grand old feast, and not the one inside his hall. Outside, the main entrée was evil humans.

Luckily there weren't that many truly evil people left at Hoggstead for the Lucies to hang around. Except . . .

Which led Cnut to his reason for accompanying Reynilda upstairs. If he didn't move quickly, the immoral princess was going to find herself in a palace named Horror. "Reynilda, I have something to say to you, and it is important that you listen carefully."

"Will I be naked when you are telling me this important thing?" she asked coyly.

"It matters not to Him who created you."

"Huh?"

"There is no way to lead up to this. I am a Viking vampire angel sent by God to kill demon vampires, and save evil humans before it is too late."

Reynilda's blue eyes went wide, then she burst out with a fit of giggles. "Oh, Cnut! You are so funny. Really. I have no idea what a vim-pyre is, but an angelic Viking man? I do not think so."

"'Tis the truth."

"And which god did you say it was who sent you?"

"The One-God. There is no other."

"A Christian now?" Reynilda rolled her eyes. Then she turned serious. And bluntly aggressive. "Are we going to have a quick swive in yon bed, or not, before returning to the hall? Hopefully, your cock did not shrink like the rest of you has. No matter. It will be big when I am done with you. Come now, best you help me out of this gown. It laces up the back and—"

"No swiving, m'lady." *And my cock is just fine, thank you very much.*

"Because of that harlot down in the hall?"

That and other things. "Because I have work to do if I am to save you."

"Save me then," she said, and tugged the neckline of her gown downward so that her breasts were fully exposed.

They were very nice breasts, Cnut noted. Large and dark-nippled. He shook his head to clear it and with a whooshy sound, elongated his fangs.

Reynilda didn't even notice. She was too busy feeling him up.

And a traitorous part of his body noticed.

Reynilda smiled like a cat who suddenly discovers its bowl of milk is actually cream.

Pushing her hands aside, he held her arms firmly at her sides and said sternly, "Reynilda, you have committed grave sins. Repent and I can save you."

"By fucking?"

Nice talk for a princess! "By taking a bit of your tainted blood with my fangs and injecting a bit of my blood into you. Do you repent?"

She finally noticed his fangs and said, "Eeew, Cnut! What happened to your teeth?"

"Never mind that. Are you sorry for your sins? Do you promise to sin no more?"

"Bloody hell, no!" An expression came over Reynilda's face that was no longer a pretense of innocence. It was pure evil. But then her attention was diverted to something behind Cnut, and the expression changed to one of terror.

Cnut could tell by the scent of sulfur, even before he turned, that it was Zeb, and he was in full demonoid form. Swatting Cnut aside, Zeb launched himself at Reynilda, who'd backed up against the bed. "Hello sinner," he said, and bit her neck with fangs the size of pitchfork tines. Within seconds, Reynilda was dissolving until all that was left was a pile of pink fabric and a silver arm ring.

"Did you have to do that?" Cnut asked.

"I did." Swiping the back of his scaly hand across his mouth, he burped and said, "Tastes like lemon meringue pie. Yum." At Cnut's glare, he added, "She was never going to change, my friend."

Just then Cnut thought of something more important, and he turned toward the door. "Andrea!"

"She's already gone."

Cnut turned slowly, his hands fisted. He would kill the demon bastard, with his bare hands, if need be. "If you hurt her . . ."

"Oh please! She is fine. Already back in her Philadelphia apartment."

A wave of relief, and utter grief, overcame Cnut. He would never see Andrea again, he just knew it. And his premonition came true when Zeb grabbed him in a tight bear hug—or you could say, a Lucipire hug—catching him off guard, and they began a swirling ascent up up up through space, spinning and spinning until Cnut was so dizzy he could only hold on. Zeb was a more powerful Lucipire than Cnut had thought, and he'd known him to be strong before. No way could Cnut fight him off!

Cnut prayed, "Please, God, take me now. Or save me. Michael, intercede on my behalf."

Zeb laughed when there was no celestial response.

So Cnut was on his way to Horror and an eternity of torture, or a new life as a Lucipire, if he proved to be weak. Each equally horrifying.

But Cnut was wrong. Boy, was he wrong!

Home, Sweet Home . . .

Forget the Polar Nights. When Andrea came to her senses, there was bright sunlight. And she was lying on the sofa in her Philadelphia apartment.

Her first thought was that it must have all been a dream, which should have made her happy. None of those horrific things had happened. But oddly that prospect filled her with sadness because that would mean Cnut was not her life-mate. In fact, everything that had happened to them was a fantasy.

But then she put her hand to her throat and felt the amber necklace lying there, a warm reminder of Cnut's love. Tears of relief filled her eyes as she glanced downward. Yep, she was still wearing the emerald-green gown.

None of it made any sense. Maybe she was losing her mind.

Think, Andrea, think. Backtrack a bit.

She had been sitting in Cnut's great hall talking to a demon vampire named Zeb—and wasn't that a sure sign of loose screws in the brain, that she would even accept that there were such things. Cnut had gone off with Reynilda because she had whipped cream on her gown (even now, she had to smile), and Zeb had asked her if she wanted to go home. She didn't recall saying yes or no, but before she knew it, she was slingshotting through space and time until she landed here.

But where was Cnut? Still back at Hoggstead (Nobody could make up a name like that!) in the year 850? Or . . . oh my God! Had Zeb captured Cnut and taken him to that northern (way northern!) castle of horrors for an eternity of torture?

Cnut was in dire danger.

She had to do something to help him.

But what? Should she go to the police? Oh, that would be fun! She could imagine the conversation now. "You see, Officer, I was sitting at the banquet in an 850 Norse castle. Yes, a castle, a wood castle, but a castle nonetheless. Anyhow, this demon vampire captured my Viking, and I think . . ."

It all sounded bizarre and unbelievable.

So no police.

First things first. She had to find out what day it was. Sitting up, she grabbed the TV remote, turned it on, and saw by the date/timeline on the right bottom corner of the screen that it was Friday, July 22, one p.m. So only a week had passed since she'd been here last. How was that possible? So much had happened—the trip to the Montana ranch, the teletransport back to the past, the weeks at Hoggstead, the famine, the hunting, the yule celebrations, making love with Cnut, so many things—and only five days had passed by here in present times?

Just then, she noticed a news bulletin coming on the TV screen. The channel had last been on CNN; so a grim-faced Wolf Blitzer was detailing the latest atrocities by ISIS. A massacre taking out an entire village in Pakistan, the beheading of three American journalists in the capital of Nigeria, and a suicide bombing at a Florida mall, resulting in five dead and forty wounded shoppers. All this, despite the good news that had been announced three days ago by the FBI, which had broken up a massive ISIS recruiting ring on a ranch in Montana.

Andrea perked up at that news.

An update was given on the story, accompanied by pictures of the Circle of Light Ranch, a seemingly peaceful setting that had housed more than fifty of the terrorists and dozens of new recruits. A number of the militants were shown being led off in handcuffs. Some of them were Arab-looking but a number of them were other nationalities, including Americans. Then there were deliberately blurred images of a few recruits who had been rescued, although some were protesting that they were there willingly, not victims.

None of them was Celie.

The field reporter also said there were sightings of an odd slime in various places around the ranch that was yet to be identified. Samples had been sent off to the FBI crime labs.

Cnut had said Celie was safe, but . . .

Andrea wasn't sure where to start. Celie or Cnut?

She could call her parents' home to see if they'd heard from Celie, but they would be on their cruise. Maybe they had cell phone coverage. Otherwise Andrea would have to look for the paper her father had given her with the ship's contact information.

To other people, her father's carefree attitude, going on a vacation when he had a daughter in peril, might seem unsympathetic, but Andrea knew better. This latest ISIS debacle was just one in a long series of Celie mishaps. Most of them proved to be harmless. Unfortunately, like the boy who cried, "Wolf!" too often, this time Celie really was in trouble and no one was listening. Except Andrea.

Just then, she heard the shower turn off in the bathroom connected to her bedroom. Cnut? Was it possible he had come through, too? *That Zeb! What a teaser!*

But it wasn't Cnut, Andrea soon found out.

She rushed into the bedroom, just as Celie was coming out of the bathroom. Totally nude and drying her hair with a towel. "Andy," she exclaimed, rushing forward and hugging her tightly. "Oh my God! Where have you been?"

"Me? Where have *you* been, Celie?" she asked, handing her a short robe hanging on the back of the door.

"Oh, you wouldn't believe it! That Kahlil turned into a total dirtbag." She pulled on the robe and tied it at the waist. Then she took a comb off the dresser and began combing through her long hair, which was its usual blonde color now.

"C'mon, let's have a cup of tea. You can tell me about it."

They walked toward the kitchen—Andrea in her emerald gown and Celie padding barefooted over the hardwood floors.

"What's with the gown, Andy? You been to a Renaissance fair, or something?"

"Something like that."

While Celie sat on a high stool at the counter and Andrea began brewing some ginger chai (last time she'd made it had been right here, for Cnut, a lifetime ago), Andrea asked, "What happened to the black hair? You had dark eyebrows on that picture you sent to Dad."

"Yes, and it was so ugly. Kahlil insisted that I dye it, and he wouldn't even let me shave my legs or underarms. What a chauvinist!"

"I would think chauvinism is the least of his faults."

"Tell me about it. Do you know what he . . . well, he and some of his pals . . . did to a woman who refused to cover her hair when we went to the grocery store? They stoned her." Tears filled Celie's eyes.

Andrea was appalled that people did that kind of thing today, and that Celie had witnessed it. "Did she die?"

"No. They didn't use big rocks. Just gravel from the driveway, but everyone was forced to throw a handful of stones at her. Even me," she admitted. "Even so, some of the men threw really hard, and she was bleeding, and no one was allowed to help her."

At least Celie hadn't been forced to lop off any heads, Andrea thought with macabre humor. That might have come later.

"Anyhow," Celie went on, running her fingers through her wet hair, "first thing back here, I made an appointment at Mimi's Salon and had the works. Hair and eyebrows dyed back to my natural color, waxing, mani and pedi, massage."

That had to have cost at least three hundred dollars, and Celie was usually short of cash. Andrea assumed Celie had billed it to their father. "Have you talked to Dad?"

"Uh-huh," Celie said as she sipped at her tea. "They're on a cruise, y'know?"

"I know."

"Darla said you went to the ranch in Montana to rescue me," Celie said, dubiously.

Andrea could understand Celie's skepticism. The old Andrea would have been afraid to enter such a fray. Not that she'd had any clue what kind of fray there would actually be, as in, vampires of both the angelic and demonic persuasions. "I did."

"Oh my God! Is that where you've been all this time?"

She pondered how much to tell her sister and

decided, as little as possible. "You could say that."

"Good heavens! You weren't arrested or anything, were you? I mean, the news is loaded with pictures of people there being led off to jail."

"No, I wasn't arrested." *Nice of you to be so worried, though.*

"How did you get here?"

"Some really cool guys rescued me. Weird, though. They wore long capes and carried swords. I think they might have been special forces in disguise."

Sigurdssons, Andrea guessed. *Cnut's vangel brothers.*

Andrea wasn't sure if she'd ever find out exactly what happened at the ranch, due to government secrecy. Unless she found Cnut.

"How long have you been here, Celie? In my apartment?"

"Since Wednesday. Your super let me in. You don't mind, do you?"

Andrea shook her head. "You can stay as long as you like."

"I'll be gone by tonight."

Uh-oh! "Why is that?"

"I'm off to the Côte d'Azur. My friend Jilly has a friend who owns a yacht, Pierre Gaston, the magazine mogul. We're gonna cruise the Caribbean for a few weeks."

That is just great. My life is falling apart, all because of her, and she just scoots off to the South of France. But this is nothing new. This is Celie, and God knows, I love her. She walked over and hugged her sister. "Have a good time."

"Here's the best part. I'm going to be paid. It's a job."

The red flags went up again. "Um, what are going to be doing for pay, honey?"

"Cooking. I'm going to be an assistant cook." Celie beamed at her, and Andrea didn't have the heart to say that Celie burned toast and once got spaghetti sauce on the ceiling of Darla's newly painted kitchen. Probably it wouldn't matter to Pierre and his gang.

After Celie went back into the bedroom to get dressed, Andrea addressed her most important issue. Cnut. She called his business number, and all she got was his answering machine, which noted that he had twenty-five other messages. Then she called his cell phone. It had survived the travel back in time, so maybe it had made it forward. No luck there. She tried to think where else to try. Transylvania, Pennsylvania, he had said. Andrea went over to her desk where her cookbook notes lay, untouched, just as they had been a week ago. Somehow, a cookbook was the last thing in the world she was interested in now. Logging on to her laptop, she did a Google of "Transylvania, Pennsylvania castle."

She got a hit. A castle that had been built more than a hundred years ago by a lumber baron. Long neglected, it was being restored by Lord Vikar Sigurdsson—*Cnut's brother?*—and might eventually be turned into a hotel. *Yeah, right!* Unfortunately, it had an unlisted phone number. The picture next to the short article showed a really creepy-looking castle, the kind vampires would live in, for sure. The small map showing its location indicated to Andrea that it would be about a three-hour drive from Philly.

Which brought Andrea to her next problem. Her purse with all her credit cards was still back at the ranch in Montana. Probably in FBI hands by now. She had no money, or way to access it without a debit card. She would need to buy gas. But then she remembered the check her Dad had given to her for her birthday, which she'd yet to cash. Two hundred dollars. *Thank you, Daddy!* Of course, she had no ID to cash the check at the bank, but she could do that at La Chic Sardine. Sonja wouldn't mind.

So it was that two hours later, after showering and changing her clothes and stopping off at the restaurant, Andrea was cruising up the turnpike toward Transylvania. She prayed that Cnut would be there when she arrived. If he wasn't, only God could help him now.

Chapter 21

A LITTLE ISLAND MEAL

Grilled red snapper with lemon and onion slices
Remoulade sauce
Green salad with lettuce, tomatoes, onions, radishes, and balsamic vinaigrette dressing
Rice parboiled in fish stock
French baguette bread
Strawberry cheesecake
Beer

Tears of a Viking . . .

"I am going to kill you. I swear I am going to kill you," Cnut said when he finally recovered from the worst teletransport of his life. He could swear Zeb had hit every sky turbulence, rain storm, tornado, and flock of geese in creation.

Zeb was picking goose feathers off his Wise Man clothes when he reminded, "I'm already dead."

"I'll find a way to kill you again." Cnut looked around then, fully expecting to see dungeon walls with chains and whips and racks and the like. Instead, he was sitting in a buttery yellow leather recliner, which matched the recliner that Zeb lounged in with his legs fully extended. He was sipping from a can of Bud Light.

"Care for a beer?" Zeb asked.

"No, I do not want a beer. Where the fuck am I? I thought you were taking me to Horror. If this is Horror, man, have we vangels been misled!"

"No, this isn't Horror. It's my secret Caribbean hidey-hole."

He looked around, and sure enough, he could see through the windows on the one side onto a deck that overlooked the turquoise blue of a Caribbean sea. The dwelling appeared to be a banana leaf–roofed bungalow. On one wall of the large room was a flat-screen TV, and on the other, paintings that looked like they belonged in a museum. Behind them, through a wide archway, was a kitchen with red granite countertops and high-end stainless steel appliances.

"Hidey-hole?" was the only thing Cnut could think of to say, so gobsmacked was he by this side of Zeb. "What are you, like, ten years old?"

"No, more like two thousand plus years, a lot older than you, my friend. As evidenced by my being able to overpower you so easily." He snapped his fingers and pinged Cnut on the back of the head as he rose lithely from his recliner and walked behind Cnut, heading toward a back door. "There are fishing rods in the hall closet. Why don't you see if you can catch us something to eat for dinner, and I'll go get some stuff from the garden?"

Cnut got up and followed him, stunned to see the demon pick up a basket and hoe and head up a small incline toward a fenced-in garden. The island appeared to be small, but all of it was lush with tropical plants, and the garden itself thrived with all kinds of healthy plants. Among items he put in the basket were tomatoes, peppers, green beans, peas, carrots, radishes, several varieties of lettuce. There were also some lemon and orange trees.

"A gardener? You? I thought you were a Roman soldier at one time," Cnut said, leaning against a fence post, eating a small tomato right off the vine. It was delicious.

Zeb shrugged. "For my sins, I was. But I also owned a small vineyard. Being a vintner is like a glorified farmer. You should see my grapes." He pointed to some trellises where there were, indeed, huge purple and green grapes, not yet ripe. "Most of the stuff I grow just rots. I can't eat it all, and it's not like I can be carrying it back to Jasper as a gift. He would want to know where I got it. Besides, he's not much for vegetables and fruit."

More like blood and guts. "Do you always garden in Wise Man clothing? You must be hot."

Zeb glanced down, surprised. Instantly, he changed. Bare-chested, with Hawaiian print board shorts and flip-flops. "You should change, too."

Cnut *was* hot, still wearing the Viking garments intended for a Norse winter feast, not a tropical temperature.

"I think there's a Speedo in my bedroom closet."

"Not a chance. I'd rather go naked."

"Please don't."

A short time later, wearing a pair of cargo shorts and athletic shoes he'd found in the spare bedroom, Cnut made his way down the mountain path with a fishing pole to the narrow strip of beach. He returned an hour later carrying a good-size red snapper that he'd already cleaned by the water.

By early evening, he was sitting at the counter enjoying a meal with Zeb. The fish had been grilled outside on a charcoal barbecue with sliced lemons and onions inserted in the artistic slashes of its flesh. Along with it, they had a fresh salad tossed with olive oil and balsamic vinegar, some parboiled rice, a thawed baguette, and a cheesecake for dessert. And beer, of course.

"You know, Cnut, the first thing Jasper would do when he has you in his clutches is ascertain your weaknesses and fears. In your case, gluttony would be a biggie. Homing in on that, he would fatten you up, but lots worse than last time you were alive. I'm thinking he wouldn't stop until you were, say, eight hundred pounds. Then he would diet you down 'til you were skeletal. Meanwhile, homing in on your other gluttonous appetites, he would probably have you injected with super sex hormones so that you were inclined to fuck day and night. Then would begin the actual physical torture, like, oh, skinning you alive, or plucking out your eyeballs, or—"

"Enough! I get the picture," Cnut said. And he

did. Too well! "So, Zeb, what's this all about? Are you turning me over to Jasper, or not?"

"I don't know."

Well, that was promising. "What's the problem?"

"It's a tough decision. I really had my heart set on becoming a vangel someday. I've even been taking lessons on how to be a Viking." He smiled at Cnut. A rather sad smile that didn't reach his brown eyes that had, yes, incredibly long lashes.

Cnut had to admit that Zeb was a good-looking guy, just as Andrea had said, long eyelashes and all.

"Well, if you give me to Jasper, you'll never become a vangel."

"I know. Here's the deal, buddy. I could give up the idea of being a vangel if I could just stop being a Lucipire. I'd ask you to kill me, in return for saving you, but then I'd just be sent to Hell to be Satan's minion. I don't suppose, if I saved you, Michael would come save me. You know, a reward for my good deed? I wouldn't even care if he made me a vangel as long as I didn't play on the other team anymore."

"I don't know, Zeb. Mike is hard to predict. You saw that in how he hasn't made you any firm promises for being a double agent. I could try to intercede for you, but, honestly, he's never shown any particular favor toward me."

"I hear he's fond of Ivak's little one."

"He dotes on the kid." Cnut thought a moment. "How about if you come back with me to the castle and ask Vikar for protection?"

"Could he do that without Michael's permission?"

"Well, no, but—"

Zeb put up both hands. "So we are back to step one. Michael."

They finished eating and watched the nightly news while they both cleaned up. All the stations were reporting on the latest ISIS atrocities. "Satan and Jasper must be eating this stuff up," Cnut remarked.

"Yep. Like shooting fish in a barrel, all these homegrown evil terrorists just waiting to be picked off."

"Fighting them reminds me that modern carnival game. Whack-a-Mole. Ever heard of it? No. It pretty much amounts to trying to hit moles with a hammer as they randomly pop in and out of holes. Almost impossible to win. It also refers to repetitious and futile efforts to combat something."

"Like terrorists," Zeb guessed.

Cnut nodded. "And Lucies."

Zeb bowed, as if he'd given him a compliment.

After watching a couple of shows on TV—the reception was spotty and often went in and out—Zeb said he was going to bed. He had a lot of thinking to do. Before he left, Cnut asked, "Andrea? Are you sure she's safe?"

"Is she your lifemate?"

Cnut didn't hesitate. "She is."

"Then know that she's safe . . . no matter where you end up."

"Thank you for that."

"Don't thank me yet."

Cnut had a lot to think about, too. He honestly didn't know what to do about Zeb. He sensed his sincerity, and frankly, he liked the guy, even if he was a demon. But Cnut didn't feel in a position to help him.

On the other hand, holy shit! Cnut was facing the prospect of unimaginable horror at what Jasper would do in torturing him. Did any man, even a vangel, know for sure that he would withstand that kind of torture? What if Cnut turned?

Cnut got down on his knees then and prayed. "Help me, Lord. Help me to be strong."

He awakened the next morning in the spare bedroom to the scent of fresh coffee brewing in the kitchen. When he came out of the bathroom after a quick shower, he saw that Zeb was nowhere to be found. But there was a note:

Cnut:

I've placed a force field around the island. It will last twenty-four hours, after which you can teletransport out of here. Pray for me, friend. I am so frightened.

Zebulan the Hebrew

Cnut kicked the walls and swore a bloody streak. He should have known what Zeb would do. He should have tried harder to come up with a compromise they could both live with. After that, Cnut wept.

Are you there, God? It's me, Andrea . . .

Andrea arrived in the town of Transylvania at about five p.m. and got stuck in the downtown traffic for a half hour, which gave her time to look around. And, oh my goodness, what a hokey tourist trap devoted to everything vampire.

She used her GPS to find the turn-off for the castle. Soon, she came to a closed electronic gate. A sign read: "No Trespassing. Private Property!" She was so stressed out and pumped up that she probably would have tried to ram right through the thing, but luckily a man stepped out of a small gatehouse. He appeared to have been reading a book, which he still carried in one hand. A graphic novel of *The Walking Dead*. In the other hand, he carried a pistol. Although he wore modern attire, jeans and a Grateful Dead T-shirt, he was Viking to the core, with a tall, lean physique, blond buzz cut, and sharp Nordic features.

"Can't you read, lady?"

And arrogant, another Viking attitude.

"I can read, Einstein. I'm here to see Cnut Sigurdsson."

"Is that so? He's not here."

Andrea's shoulders slumped. "Well, then, I need to talk to his brother Vikar." Or someone.

"And why is that? The man was leaning down closer to her open window now, and she could see that he had slightly elongated lateral incisors and silver-blue eyes, just like Cnut.

"Because Cnut is in danger, and I need help to save him."

The man gave Andrea a pointed survey, or as much as he could with her sitting inside the car. The look pretty much said, *A skinny girl like you going to save a big ol' Viking? It is to laugh!* In fact, he did laugh. "And who might you be?"

"Cnut's lifemate," she snapped. "He's probably in Jasper's hands right now as you delay. Now, will you let me through?"

He did, and got immediately on his cell phone, she could see through her rearview mirror. By the time she drove up the winding drive to the front of the castle, she had no time to be frightened by the creepy castle that rose up many stories before her. There was a gang of Vikings waiting for her on the steps. And they didn't look happy.

No sooner did Andrea step out of her car than they started asking questions, all at the same time.

"Where's Cnut?"

"What danger?"

"How do you know about lifemates?"

"Jasper has Cnut? Where?"

And finally, one voice said, "Welcome." It was a female voice that belonged to a strawberry-blonde woman who reached out to shake Andrea's hand. "I'm Alex Sigurdsson. And these are Cnut's brain-dead brothers. You must be terrified. Come inside where we can talk."

Andrea began to weep with relief as Alex took her hand and led her through the double front doors, past parlors and dens, a dining room, and a chapel. Everywhere, Andrea saw what could only be vangels with silver-blue eyes and pointy teeth, working or standing about, watching her. Finally, they came to a large office, and everyone crowded in. Some of them, including herself, sat down, while others stood about. In a blur of introductions, Alex named Cnut's brothers, who were all present, Vikar, Trond, Ivak, Mordr, Sigurd, and Harek, and explained that they were all there because one of their vangels, Armod, had been hurt in the Circle of Light battle and they'd all come to help him recover.

Then there was silence as they waited for Andrea to speak.

She started at the beginning, back when Celie had gone missing, and told them everything—well, not the details of her relationship with Cnut, but it was implied—up until her return to her Philadelphia apartment earlier today. In the course of her lengthy discussion, someone had handed her a glass of ice water, which she'd needed to quench her parched throat. Time traveling took a lot out of a person.

"So, you have to help me save Cnut," she concluded.

They all stared at her, then they began talking among themselves.

"Backward time travel? I thought we were done with that."

"Can you imagine what they must have thought back at Hoggstead when they saw a new and improved Cnut?"

"It would be funny if it weren't so sad."

"Sad? Sad doesn't begin to describe what Cnut must be going through if Jasper has him."

"I really thought Zeb was changed. A devil doesn't change his ways, I guess."

"He had no choice, apparently. It was him or Cnut."

"He had a choice."

"Well, there's nothing we can do without Michael's say-so."

"Yeah, but you know what Mike said when he rescued you that time, Vikar? He said never again would he enter Jasper's unholy domain."

Vikar looked sick, actually physically sick, at that reminder of his onetime captivity. Which meant that Cnut was in for more horrendous torture than Andrea could even imagine. Or was he sick knowing there would be no celestial intervention for his brother.

Finally, the one named Vikar said, "Are you certain that Zeb took him back to Jasper?"

"Yes. I mean, not exactly." She took a deep breath and reiterated, "Zeb told Cnut about his orders from Jasper. Zeb showed up at the yule feast. Zeb sent me home, or took me home, or teletransported me, or whatever the hell you all do. What else can I conclude?"

"He's at Horror," one of the brothers—the grim one . . . Mordr, she thought he was called—said with finality.

"We have to contact Mike. ASAP," another brother said.

"But first, let us pray for our brother," Vikar suggested, and everyone in the room bowed their heads in silent prayer.

That scared Andrea more than anything. That they were relying on prayer to save the man she loved. What was that old saying, "Pray to God, but pass the ammunition"? She wanted ammunition, lots of it. Still, she found herself praying, "Are you there, God? It's me, Andrea."

Just then, the door swung open, and someone said, "What's going on?"

It was Cnut.

Andrea fell into a faint. Right off her chair. Kerplop onto the floor.

It was a blessing, really.

Chapter 22

Interview with an archangel . . .

Cnut sat next to the guest room bed where Andrea slept soundly after being given a sedative by Sigurd. Poor girl . . . woman! She'd been through hell, for him. He kissed her forehead, which was creased with worry, even in slumber.

But now he needed to go down and face the music. Michael would be here shortly, and there was going to be hell to pay. Mostly by him, he was sure.

At least he wasn't in Horror.

Oh, Zeb! he thought for about the hundredth time since he'd found the note yesterday morning. Over the past twenty-four hours, he'd pondered and discarded a dozen plots to save the demon. None of them would work, not without the help of his brothers. Or Michael.

When he got downstairs, everyone was waiting in the formal parlor for Michael. Soon after, he arrived in a fury, in full archangelic regalia. Long white robe, rope belt, wooden crucifix hanging from his neck, eyes blazing, long dark hair flying, his wings fully extended. He carried a sword in one hand. Heads were going to roll, figuratively speaking.

Cnut and his brothers had been sitting in chairs arranged in a half circle before a throne-like Queen Anne chair. They all stood with reverence on his entrance. Michael waved them to sit back down and turned directly to Cnut. "What. Have. You. Done?"

What is he referring to? The time travel? Andrea? Zeb? Cnut held his ground, without giving anything away. Or so he thought. "Nothing."

"Dost thou think that excuses you, sinner?"

Best to give a blanket mea culpa. "I do not."

"You plan to go off half-cocked, offering yourself to Jasper in exchange for Zebulan, don't you?"

Cnut paused. *Since when do angels use the word cock?* "Yes."

"At least you are honest. Why bother saving the demon? And why you?"

"Because he's a better man than I am."

Michael didn't concur, but he didn't disagree, either. "What would you have me do?"

"Save him."

"Pfff! Just like that, you expect me to wipe up your mistakes? And Zebulan's, too?"

"Zeb did nothing wrong, in this case. Nor did I. Not really," Cnut protested.

"Is that so?" Michael asked, raising his eyes heavenward, or at least up to the third-floor bedroom where Andrea still slept. "Mayhap if you'd been paying more attention to your life work as a vangel, this would not have happened." In other words, he'd been fucking around when he should have kept his eyes on the target.

"That's not fair!"

"Fair? Fair?" Michael roared, and they all quaked. "Who promised you fair? Where in the Holy Book does it mention life is fair?"

"In Cnut's defense," Vikar interjected, "Zeb was given orders by Jasper to bring back a Sigurdsson before he ever met his lifemate . . . um, Andrea."

Michael turned on Cnut again. "Lifemate, is it now?"

Cnut raised his chin and nodded.

"Have you considered this, Viking? If you marry this so-called lifemate and then trade yourself for Zeb, she would be sentenced to either an instant death, if you die, which probably would not be the case. More likely, Jasper would want to torture you for centuries, thus forcing your female to live all those years, perhaps eternity, without you, knowing that you are in endless pain."

Cnut cringed. "I hadn't thought that far."

"Obviously."

Michael threw up his hands in disgust.

"What should we do? What can we do? For Zeb, I mean?" Cnut asked. "Surely he's earned salvation."

"Dost think so, Viking? And who made you judge of mankind? I never promised Zebulan anything."

"Even so," Cnut argued.

"How much do you want this favor?" Michael asked suddenly.

"Desperately. With all my heart."

"Really? Would you trade places with him? Knowing what I have just told you?"

"I would not marry. That is the solution. No

lifemate to be threatened by my actions." Cnut's heart sank at his own words. But then, he had been overpowered by guilt these past twenty-four hours. It was the only solution. He gulped, but then he raised his chin. "God's will be done."

Michael stared at him in silence for a long time, then said, "Stay here. All of you. I will investigate and see what I can find." As he walked off, then disappeared from sight, the archangel was heard to mutter, "Vikings! The plague of my life!"

When love is not enough . . .

Andrea awakened in a strange bedroom. Very spare. A single bed with an Amish quilt. A dresser with a mirror. And a chair by the diamond-paned, leaded glass window. Beside it was a floor lamp. The walls were plain white, the only adornment a picture of the Last Supper. She went into the small en-suite bathroom and bathed her face in water and rinsed out her mouth.

She was still in shock over the events of the day—over the past week, actually. But she needed to do something. Starting with finding Cnut.

She made her way down a hallway toward the back of the castle, then down an enclosed staircase. She assumed it was the onetime servants' access to the upper floors. Finally, she emerged on the first floor into the most spectacular kitchen. For a person trained as a chef, this was paradise.

It was a large room with a commercial-size

refrigerator and freezer. The center island with stools had to be twenty feet long. There were multiple gas ranges and ovens. Windows and French doors looked out over a patio, pool, and gazebo.

Working about the kitchen were several people washing dishes, beating some batter in a huge bowl, entering and leaving a pantry the size of her apartment. Their companionable chatter stopped on her entrance. They watched silently as she made her way over to the older woman in a Victorian-looking gown and apron, her hair in a bun, who was chopping up several chickens with a kitchen cleaver on a cutting board and putting them into an iron cauldron.

"What are you making?"

The woman looked up. Andrea noticed right away that she had the silver-blue eyes and pointy teeth, even though she wasn't smiling. "Chicken pot pie. Amish style."

"Yum. With dumplings?"

"Rivels," the cook said.

And Andrea thought, *Is that synchronicity or what?*

"Who are you?" the woman asked bluntly.

"Andrea Stewart. I'm a trained chef, and I'm in love with your kitchen."

"I'm Lizzie Borden . . ."

Okaaay! The axe murderer. Andrea glanced at the cleaver with new interest.

". . . and you can have my kitchen any time you want. I'm sick of cooking for hungry Vikings who don't know . . . rivels from dumplings. If it was up to them, they'd have pizza and beer all the time." She grinned at that and her fangs showed more prominently. Andrea could tell she was self-conscious about them because she immediately pressed her lips together.

"I'm looking for Cnut," Andrea said then.

Lizzie motioned with her head toward the French doors.

Andrea went outside and found Cnut up by the gazebo. She waved as she passed Alex, who was in the pool teaching two small children how to swim. There were other people—or vangels—about, some lounging by the pool, others working on the landscaping or other projects, like repointing the stonework on the crumbling castle. It appeared to be a never-ending work in progress.

Cnut had been sitting with his elbows on his knees, his chin resting on his palms, when she entered the gazebo. He stood when he saw her and opened his arms. She walked into his embrace and held on tight. In fact, they held each other for a long time.

Finally, they both sat down on a cushioned wicker sofa, and he told her what had happened after she left Hoggstead. "I assume that your ancestral home will survive without you, but what about poor Zeb?" she asked.

"It's in Mike's hands now . . . or rather God's," he answered. "But I feel so guilty."

"It's not your fault, Cnut," she said, taking one of his big hands in both of hers and kissing the knuckles. "I have to believe that this was all predestined."

"But we have choices."

"Still, as hard as it is to accept, just like death is, some things are going to happen."

"Like bad things happening to good people?"

"Exactly. Or good things happening to good people. Like us. Which brings us to the question, what's going to happen to you and me?"

His eyes turned bleak.

Which scared her.

"What do you want to happen?" he asked.

"Everything," she said. "And you?"

"More than everything, but it appears that may be impossible."

Now she was really scared.

Sensing her fears, he kissed her lightly on the mouth, then not so lightly. "Would you marry me if we could? Would you link your life to mine, even if it meant living forever, or dying whenever I do? Would you be able to accept never having children?"

"Yes, and yes, and yes. Because the alternative would be an empty life, full of sorrow, feeling more dead than alive. Besides," she told him, "Lizzie has already offered me her position as cook."

"She's been trying to pass that job off for years." He laughed. "Does that mean we would have real cream-filled doughnuts and, oh my clouds! Coconut cake."

She nodded. "With peppermint filling."

"I love you, heartling," he said.

"I love you, too."

He turned more serious again. "But, can't you see, if I go after Zeb, if Michael gives his approval, I would already be sealing your fate? Instant death for you, or centuries of living alone knowing I am living in an exile of torture. An impossible situation!"

Andrea gasped. "And those are the only choices?"

He hesitated, then nodded. "Nothing has been decided yet. We can always pray." He was half kidding.

"For Zeb?"

"Well, yes, but for us, too."

They got the news a short time later when Andrea got her first view of a real live (or dead, depending on your perspective) archangel. And he *was* spectacular. There seemed to be a glow about him. A full body halo? His face was grim as he told the vangels, along with Andrea and Alex, "Zebulan the Hebrew is gone."

"Gone? What does that mean?" Cnut demanded to know.

The archangel gave Cnut a steely glare. "His fate is in another's hands. Satan's. Thy efforts would be in vain."

Cries of horror went around the room and not a little weeping. In fact, there were tears in the archangel's eyes.

"I still think I should try to—" Cnut started to say.

"Enough!" Michael made a chopping motion with his hand. "You are to stop making this a personal vendetta, Cnut. Jasper would have taken any one of you brothers. The fact that you happened to be in Zebulan's vicinity at a certain moment has no particular significance. Are you suggesting that all seven of you are equally responsible for Zeb's fate?"

"No, but . . ."

"You are not to mention his name again."

And that was final. Andrea could see that on the faces of everyone in the room.

This was the best and worst day of Andrea's life. She presumably could have Cnut now, but Zeb was gone.

"Let us pray for Zebulan, wherever he may be," Michael said then, mirroring Cnut's earlier suggestion.

And they all said, "Amen!"

Epilogue

A happy ending, somewhat . . .

Despite the dark cloud of Zeb hanging over them, Andrea and Cnut were married two weeks later before a priest at a small chapel in Philadelphia. The only people present were Cecilia Stewart, the maid of honor, and Vikar Sigurdsson, the best man. Also present were Andrea's parents and her boss/friend Sonja, along with Vikar and his wife, Alex, and their two children, Gunnar and Gunnora. The bridal couple had decided that they could take no chances of Andrea's family being at the Transylvania castle among all the vangels, and keeping the secret.

But later that day, they were married again in true Viking style in the gazebo, which was adorned with roses and officiated by a priest who strongly resembled—in fact, was—Michael the Archangel, who was heard to mutter, "Thank God there are no more VIKs to plague me with this lifemate nonsense." But at the same time, he smiled adoringly at the little boy being held by the firm hand of Gabrielle, Ivak's wife. The boy was Mikey, named after none other!

At the earlier ceremony, Andrea had worn a white dress with a gold belt and white high heels, and Cnut a dark suit with a pretty blue tie that matched his eyes, but now she wore the emerald gown and the amber pendant with a circlet of flowers on her head, and Cnut, at her request, was in Viking attire. Which amused the huge crowd at the castle who considered themselves modern Vikings, and were dressed accordingly. As in black tie and cocktail dresses.

Andrea was surprised to see so many children about but they were Dr. Sig's adopted daughter, Izzie, and Mordr's adopted family of five children. Not to mention Gunnar, Gunnora, and Mikey.

At the end of the marriage ceremony, they all said a silent prayer in remembrance of the demon who almost became a vangel. Michael left soon after, warning the vangels that their mission for the foreseeable future was to destroy ISIS. Then he was heard murmuring something about the Pearly Gates falling down, again, as he disappeared into the skies.

After that it was a wild Viking party. Rock music provided by a vangel band. The newly recovered Armod showing that he could still do a credible moonwalk. The seven VIK doing an amazing Michael dance to "Chains, Chains, Chains."

The food was plentiful and the beer flowed. Holding center place was a five-tiered cake that Andrea had baked herself in the Transylvania kitchen with Lizzie's help. It was a white cake, covered with coconut and peppermint sprinkles. Everyone said it was fabulous.

Andrea and Cnut weren't sure where they would be living. She'd quit her job, figuring she could work on her cookbook, or not. She had all the time in the world to decide. Literally.

They'd decided not to go anywhere for their honeymoon, but would be staying in her Philly apartment. They'd both had enough of travel for the moment. Besides, there was nothing he could do in the Bahamas that he couldn't do in the City of Brotherly Love, Cnut told her with a wicked Viking gleam in his eyes.

They'd already made love once at a rest stop between the city and Transylvania, between their two weddings. They could barely make it back to her apartment later that night. In fact, Cnut took her against the closed door with her gown hiked up around her waist.

"Have I told about a new sex spot I heard about? It's called an Angel's Kiss."

"That's nothing," she said (although she really didn't mean it, it was definitely *something*!). "I read somewhere that if a woman eats enough peppermint sticks, she will taste like peppermint . . . you know . . . down there."

Sometimes life was good for a vangel, Cnut decided later.

And for his mate, Andrea agreed.

And the story continues . . .

In a place, far, far way, deep inside a hidden cave, Zebulan the Hebrew lay stretched out on a rack, hunks of his flesh hanging here and there from the metal flails of the whips. He had no toenails or fingernails. One eye was swollen shut.

And Jasper gloated with glee. "Suffer, Zeb. See how I repay those who betray me. And no one cares about your fate. Except for Satan, the master, who is taking a special interest in you. Do you hear me? No one in your human or vangel world is going to rescue you. You are mine for all eternity."

Reader Letter

Dear Readers:

Whew! Seven Deadly Angels books! Never thought that would happen. And now that all seven Sigurdsson brothers have had their stories told, what next? Well, if you've read to end of The Angel Wore Fangs, *you'll know that there has to be a story for Zebulan the Hebrew. And there will be. It's titled* Good Vampires Go to Heaven. *And that one's got to be the best of all. A tortured hero with a sense of humor deserves no less. And after that, who knows? Maybe there will be some others.*

On the other hand, there are still more Viking historicals to be written. Tykir's two other sons. Alrek the Clumsy Viking. Jamie the Scots Viking. And then there are those Viking Navy SEALs Jam and Slick and Geek. And don't forget Tante Lulu, who can't keep her busybody Cajun mouth shut for long. So many choices!

I have a long backlist of books available now in both print and e-book, and even audio, formats. Sometimes there are huge bargains for them, especially in bundles. Check the online bookstores and my website occasionally for details. Or sign up for my newsletter, which only goes out a few times a year, I promise. I can be reached from my website at www.sandrahill.net or my Facebook page at SandraHillAuthor.

As a side note, The Angel Wore Fangs *is the first of my Deadly Angels books that turned into a time travel, which prompts the question: How could a modern person understand the language spoken more than a thousand years ago? We all know from* Canterbury Tales *and such literature that medieval English is almost incomprehensible to the contemporary reader. Add to that the fact that Andrea, in my story, would be in a country that spoke Old Norse, not to be confused with modern Norwegian. In fact, the closest we have today to Old Norse is Icelandic.*

Well, here's one explanation. Old Norse and Saxon English were similar. They shared many of the same words. Thus, they were able to communicate with each other, at least on a basic level. For example, these are some words that could be equally understood: anger (angr), cake (kaka), club (klubba), fog (fok), give (gefa), and outlaw (utlag). In fact, many of the concepts and terms in today's English and American legal systems came from the Vikings. No kidding! But that's another story.

As always, I love to hear from you readers. Wishing you smiles in your reading, and in your life. Until the next book . . .

Sandra Hill

Glossary

A-Viking—A Norse practice of sailing away to other countries for the purpose of looting, settlement, or mere adventure; could be for a period of several months or years at a time.

Aioli—A Provençal sauce made with garlic, olive oil, egg yolks, and seasoning, similar to mayonnaise.

Birka—Viking era market town located where Sweden is today.

Braies—Slim pants worn by men.

Burqa—Enveloping outer garment worn by women in some Islamic traditions to cover their bodies when in public.

Cassoulet—A rich, slow-cooked casserole containing meat and white beans.

Ceorl—Free peasant, person of the lowest classes.

Concubine—Mistress.

Cotter—Peasant farmer.

Crofter—Person who occupies and works a small landholding known as a croft for which he pays rent to a landlord, or lord.

Drukkinn (various spellings)—Drunk.

Ell—Unit of measurement approximating the length of a man's arm from elbow to tip of the middle finger, usually about eighteen inches.

Fake-O—Synthetic blood drunk by vangels when other blood is not available.

Fireball—Cinnamon whiskey.

Fjord—Narrow arm of the seas, often between high cliffs.

Frey/Freyr—Norse god of peace and fertility, rain and sunshine.

Frigg/Frigga—Wife of Odin, Norse goddess of beauty, love, and marriage.

Frigg's-day—Friday.

Frumenty—Thick wheat porridge cooked in milk, traditionally served with venison.

Gammelost—Stinky cheese, rumored to be so bad it turned men berserk.

Garderobe—Indoor privy.

Gunna—Long-sleeved, ankle-length gown for women, often worn under a tunic or surcoat, or under a long, open-sided apron.

Haakai—High-level demon.

Hákarl—Also known as rotten shark; fermented and dried shark meat that has an ammoniac taste and putrid scent; a Viking delicacy.

Handsal—The witnessed wedding contract.

Hap—A coarse coverlet.

Hedeby—Viking age market town where Germany now stands.

Hersir—Viking military commander.

Hird/hirdsman—A permanent troop that a chieftain or nobleman might have.

Hneftafl—Norse board game in which a king tries to escape from a besieging army.

Hoedown—Social gathering at which lively folk dancing takes place, a barn dance.

Hordlings—Lower-level demons.

Housecarls—Troops assigned to a king's or lord's household on a longtime, sometimes permanent basis.

Imps—Lowest-level demons, foot soldiers so to speak.

ISIS—Islamic State of Iraq and al-Sham, extremist Muslim group.

Jarl—High-ranking Norseman, similar to an English earl or wealthy landowner, could also be a chieftain or minor king.

Jorvik—Viking-age York, known to the Saxons as Eoforwic.

Kaupang—A Viking-age market town, one of the first towns in Norway.

Knarr—A Viking merchant vessel, wider and deeper than a regular longship.

Lamprey—Jawless fish resembling an eel with an odd, toothed, funnel-like sucking mouth, called the vampire fish.

Land of the Midnight Sun/Polar Nights—A natural phenomenon that occurs in northern regions, including Norway, in which it stays light almost all day in the summer and stays dark almost all the time in the winter.

Lingonberry—The fruit of a short evergreen shrub.

Longships—Narrow, open water-going vessels with oars and square sails, perfected by Viking shipbuilders, noted for their speed and ability to ride in both shallow waters and deep oceans.

Lucifer/Satan—The fallen angel Lucifer who became known as the demon Satan.

Lucipires—Demon vampires led by the fallen angel Jasper.

Lutefisk/lutfisk—A traditional dish made from dried and salted, whitefish preserved with lye.

Manchet bread—Flat unleavened circles of bread.

Mancus—A unit of measurement or coin equal roughly to 4.5 grams of gold or thirty silver pence, also equal of one month's wages for a skilled worker in medieval times.

Mead—Fermented honey and water.

Merde!—Shit!

Mjollnir (various spellings)—Thor's hammer.

Motte—A high, flat-topped mound; a motte and bailey castle would be a wood or stone keep on a raised earthwork, surrounded by protective ditches and palisades.

Mung—Type of demon, below the haakai in status, often very large and oozing slime and mung.

Muslim—A religion based on the Koran, with the belief that the word of God was revealed through the prophet Mohammed.

Neeps—Turnips.

Nettles—Stinging nettles can be used as an herb as well as a nutritious and delicious food; once cooked they have a spinach or cabbage flavor.

Norselands—Early term referring not just to Norway but all the Scandinavian countries as a whole.

Norsemandy—Normandy.

Odel rights—Rules regarding inheritance.

Odin—King of all the Viking gods.

Oyster Shooters—Raw oyster in shot glass, topped with bourbon (or vodka), Tabasco sauce, and squeezed lemon, then down the hatch in one swallow.

Percherons—Breed of draft or war horse, first seen in the former Perche province of France.

Pottage—Thick soup or stew made by boiling vegetables, grains, and whatever meat or fish is available, sometimes added to over days so that the content became questionable.

Privy—Outdoor toilet.

Purdah—Practice in some Muslim countries of women living in separate rooms or behind curtains, or dressing in all-enveloping clothes when out in public.

Sagas—Oral history of the Norse people, passed on from ancient times.

Sallat—Medieval salad.

Samite—Luxurious and heavy silk fabric, often including gold or silk thread.

Sennight—One week.

Serf—An agricultural laborer under the feudal system, working under a lord's estate.

Sharia—Interpretation of Islamic law requiring strict adherence to traditional precepts, very strict particularly involving women.

Skål!—Cheers!

Skald—Poet.

Skyr—An ancient Norse cheese product, still made today, thicker than yogurt but not as grainy as cottage cheese.

Stasis—State of inactivity or numbness, condition in which the person cannot move.

Tangos—Terrorists, bad guys.

Teletransport—Transfer of matter from one point to another without traversing physical space.

Thor—God of war.

Thralls—Slaves.

Tramp stamp—A tattoo on a woman's lower back.

Tripe—Rubbery stomach lining of an animal that is cleaned and cooked for human consumption.

Tun—Measure of liquid capacity equivalent to 252 gallons.

Turducken—A dish consisting of a deboned chicken stuffed into a deboned duck, which is in turn stuffed into a deboned turkey; also called the Three Bird Roast.

Valhalla—Hall of the slain, Odin's magnificent hall in Asgard (like Viking heaven).

Valkyries—Odin's handmaidens who conduct slain warriors from the battlefield to Valhalla.

Vangels—Viking vampire angels.

Vieux Carre—French Quarter of New Orleans.

VIK—The seven Sigurdsson brothers who head the vangels.

Don't miss the next

DEADLY ANGELS

novel!

Good Vampires Go to Heaven

by *New York Times* bestselling author

SANDRA HILL

Coming December 2016

Prologue

What is your secret fear?

Satan came to visit me today.

Me! Zebulan, a mere Hebrew of no great fame, in the presence of the Boogie Man of Sin! And not a welcome mat in sight. Hah! If I had one, I'd try to hide under it. And I am not easily frightened.

You probably think that I mean Satan's visit as a metaphor for some bad deed I've committed. God knows . . . rather, Satan knows . . . I've committed plenty. No, I mean the real deal, scary-as-hell (pun intended . . . can you tell I'm losing it here?), evil personified, primo devil.

Really.

Can't you see him? He is standing right there before me.

In person.

Well, not "in person" precisely because, as everyone knows, the biggest, baddest of all demons isn't a person. Never was. Lucifer, as Satan was known in the beginning, existed as an archangel for eons, if not forever, before his fall from grace, never having started as a human, or so it is said.

People do not realize that angels were *created* by God, and that humans do not *become* angels after death, no matter how good they might have been. Blame the misconception on movies like *A Wonderful Life* with the line about angels getting wings every time a bell rings. Hah!

I am rambling, mentally, as you can tell. A defense mechanism, I suppose. It's either that, or scream with fright. You'd think there was nothing worse than the torture I have undergone this past year. I've grown at least two inches, thanks to the rack. (And I was already more than six feet tall.) Flaps of skin hang here and there from the floggings. (Needles and thread would come in handy, not to mention a nurse. I would do it myself if I could. But I am tied up at the moment. Ha, ha, ha!) No toenails or fingernails. (Ah, well. Saves money on manicures and pedicures, not that I've ever had either.) Barbed wire around my cock and round the clock porn shown on a ceiling screen. (Ouch! Gives new meaning to Ring Around the Rosie.)

The only reason I still have eyes or a tongue is because Jasper, another fallen angel, wants me alive for centuries to prolong my agony. He thinks I betrayed him.

I did.

But back to Satan. Believe me, a visit from the Essence of Evil does not bode well for me, especially when he deigns to visit me in The Pit, this hidden cave deep in the bowels of Horror, Jasper's castle headquarters.

Jasper is king of all the Lucipires, or demon vampires (in case you didn't know), of which I have been one for the past two thousand or so years. Leastways, I had been until the Big Transgression. That's what Jasper calls my attempt to join the other team, as in vangels (Viking vampire angels). And, no, I am not a Viking. But I would try my damnedest to become one if it meant release from this demonic obligation. I'd even wear a ridiculous horned helmet, and learn to ride a longship, and eat that stinky gammelost, and . . .

"You find humor in my presence, Zebulan?" Satan's voice is so soft and beguiling one might be fooled into thinking his feelings are hurt. Does the Chief Devil even have feelings?

"No. I was grimacing, not smi . . ." My words trail off as I turn to look directly at Satan for the first time.

He is beautiful.

Holy hellfire! I'm not sure what I was expecting. Demonoid form, for sure. Scaly green skin and tail and drooling mung. Claws with razor sharp nails. Blazing red eyes and fangs. A darting, snake-like tongue. Maybe even horns.

But, no, he is in humanoid form, and his appearance is so attractive it startles. Even Jasper, who stands in the background, still in demonoid persona, gazes at his master with awe.

Satan has long, silk-like red hair. Who would have ever guessed a demon redhead? But then, redheads do have a reputation for fiery personalities. His skin is the creamy color of aged ivory. A perfectly muscled, tall body is shown off in black leather tunic and tight pants tucked inside tooled, ebony snakeskin boots. The chain belt around his waist is pure gold. About his neck is another gold chain from which hangs a crucifix, of all things, meant to be a sacrilege, I assume.

Satan carries not the caricature pitchfork portrayed in Christian images, but a long-handled whip with dozens of hair-thin, silver flails with weighted tails. The calm expression on his face is belied by the way he keeps tapping the whip against his knee, causing the metal to shimmer in the dim candlelight of the cave and make a metallic shushing sound.

Shush, shush, shush!

It is Satan's eyes that are the giveaway, though. Clear green orbs against a blood red background that almost seem to pulse with fury. They are mesmerizing in their attempt to draw a person into their cyclonic swirls of sin.

Shush, shush, shush.

The eyes and the repetitive rhythm of the whip hypnotize.

Shush, shush, shush.

I look away, afraid of what I might say or do if I fall under the devil's spell.

"Thou hast wasted enough time, Zebulon. 'Tis time to admit thy betrayal, beg for forgiveness, and promise to remain a Lucipire, never to stray again."

Shush, shush, shush.

Do a demon vampire's work for eternity? Continue to fight the vangels. Prey on human sinners. Kill, kill, kill. My body count is well over a thousand by now. The prospect of continuing that dark work is more horrific to me than anything Satan might do to my body. "No. Kill me and get it over with."

"You are already dead."

Shush, shush, shush.

"Just send me to Hell then. You can torture me there all you want." Brave words when I am shaking in my shackles!

Shush, shush, shush.

"Ah, that is the rub," Satan says.

Shush, shush, shush.

"Alas, I cannot take you home . . . yet."

Huh? I turn my head to look at Satan and, whoa! I understand immediately. This puts a whole new light on my situation. It almost makes the past year of torture worthwhile. Apparently, my eternal fate is in question. My good acts for the vangels must have gained me points Up Above. Oh, it wouldn't be enough to get me through the Pearly Gates, but maybe Purgatory's more tarnished portals. "My pal Michael must have put in a good word for me." I start to smile and stop when my dry lips crack and begin to seep blood again, my fangs cutting deeper. It's a wonder I have any blood left.

Satan hisses and lashes his whip across my chest. The metallic threads cause an excruciating pain, more like a searing burn. Thin welts immediately rise on my skin.

"You will not mention that name again!" Satan's red-rimmed, green eyes are now totally red. He is still beautiful, though, dammit

Satan refers to Michael, of course, the archangel warrior responsible for kicking the fallen angels out of Heaven, including Lucifer aka Satan.

"Michael, Michael, Michael," I taunt, foolishly, but with great delight.

The whip shoots out again, criss-crossing the chest welts. I probably look like a blank crossword puzzle. Give me a five-letter word for person who taunts the devil. IDIOT. My warped sense of humor is the only thing keeping me from crying out with pain.

"Shall I send for Craven?" Jasper asks Satan. "My chief tortureologist has developed new methods of persuasion that are very effective."

Tortureologist? More like one sick bastard with more muscle than brain!

"Not so effective if this sinner can stubbornly refuse to surrender," Satan remarks.

Shush, shush, shush.

"Ah, but Hebrews ever were a stubborn race," Jasper points out.

Not a wise move! Even Zeb in his pain-riddled haze knows that one does not argue with Satan.

Satan scowls at Jasper. Believe me, a Satan scowl is nothing to be encouraged. Better Jasper than me.

"I mean, of course Craven has not been so effective in Zebulan's case, but . . . ," Jasper attempts to backpedal.

"Watch and learn, Jasper," Satan snarls. "The best torture works on the victim's deepest despair. Their hidden fears. Their agonizing regrets. Their guilt. What might have beens. Their wish for do-overs."

Satan gives his full attention to me now, and I try to make my mind blank, to reveal nothing. At the same time, I brace myself, ignorant of exactly what he plans, but knowing I am in for something bad.

It proves to be worse than I can imagine.

"Do you remember Masada?" Satan asks me with well-honed cruelty.

How can I forget? That ancient rock fortress overlooking the Dead Sea, the scene of one of Israel's greatest massacres. It is the place where I lost my beloved wife Sarah, and my twins, Mikah and Rachel.

"Would you like to see how your wife and children died?"

No! No, no, no, no, no, I cry silently. It is enough that I feel guilty over their deaths. That I mourned their loss every day of my human existence, which was not that long since I took my own life, but every day of my pitiful two-thousand-year-old Lucipire existence.

My eyes are forced shut and behind the lids I see Sarah, but she hardly resembles my wife with smooth, sun-kissed skin and dancing brown eyes. No longer is she the beautiful woman who strolled through the neat rows of our small Shomron vineyard, laughing up at me, teasing. No, this creature more resembles those pictures I have seen of Holocaust victims during World War II. Gaunt, skeletal, walking like an elderly crone, rather than her twenty-five years. I know then that I am seeing Sarah as she was during the year-long siege of Masada, before the final assault, before the fires set by Roman soldiers. Of which, for my sins, I had been one.

I arch my back on the rack, attempting escape. I scream, the first time in my captivity. A long wail of heartbreaking anguish.

"Or perhaps you would like to see how your children fared?"

When I do not respond, Satan says, "Everyone has a tipping point. Everyone."

What I see then pushes me closer and closer to the point of madness. And I know, deep down, that he will force me to view this scene over and over, flails to my very soul.

It is too much!

Chapter 1

The Norselands, 1250 A.D.

There's a little bit of witch in every woman . . .

Regina Dorasdottir loved being a witch, but that had not always been the case.

Witchiness was in her blood, her mother and grandmother before her having practiced the black arts. For years, she'd fought her gifts, especially when she was teased and bullied by the village children and even the youthlings up at Winterstorm castle, but then when she was fourteen, the ignorant village folks burned her mother, Dora Sigrunsdottir, whilst still alive and inside her forest hut, blaming her for a year-long famine. This, despite the fact, that her sweet mother had been a good witch, providing healing potions to the sick, birthing babies, giving, giving, giving.

Regina could not claim the same goodness. After witnessing her mother's brutal death, a bitterness and rage grew in her like a festering boil.

She had to embrace her magical gifts, or explode. After a time, she rebuilt her mother's home in the forest . . . a hovel, actually, but she did not care. It was only temporary. Eventually, she came to excel and enjoy all that she could do, uncaring if anyone got hurt, sometimes deliberately inflicting pain on those for whom she carried a grudge. And later, over the next eleven years, she did not even discriminate in that way. Yes, she helped a great many people with her healing potions, but that became incidental. If people paid, they got her services.

She loved the power. In a time when women were rarely given authority, she had a shadowy influence over many people.

She loved making money. Forget about being paid in chickens, or barley, or mead, as many healers and midwives were. She accepted only coins, thank you very much, preferably gold, but silver would do, and occasionally copper.

She loved pretending to be an aged, skinny crone with a huge wart on her hairy chin, skin splotches painted on her skin, similar to liver spots, which village cotters referred to as devil's spittle, and a not-so-lovely, ashy gray hair. Best for a woman living alone in a remote area to appear as loathsome as possible. In fact, she had seen only twenty-five winters, her hair was an unfortunate flame red, also considered a sign of the devil. A raggedy gunna hid an embarrassingly voluptuous figure. Those folks who'd known her as a child were long gone, or unable to recognize this scary creature of the woods. They were suspicious, of course, but accepted her explanation that Regina was gone and she was a member of the coven (with the same name, would you believe it?) who'd come to take her place. The fools shivered at the word "coven" and asked no more questions.

She did not worry overmuch about suffering the same fate as her mother. She was harder than her mother and more careful. Plus, she'd honed a talent with knife throwing over the years, and her knives were razor sharp. She could pierce a running rabbit at twenty paces and gut a randy Viking bent on rape. Never openly. Best not to raise suspicions to another level.

Regina had no friends or family. She was alone, and that was how she liked it.

She enjoyed making jest of others, without their knowing. Especially fun were her threats of ridiculously impossible curses tossed at lackwit Vikings, like "Do as I command, or I'll make your cock the size of a thimble." Of late, she took great delight in being creative with her spells. "Have you ever seen a candle melt into a limp wick, Bjorn?" Or "Svein, Svein, Svein! May the winds blow so hard your braies fall off, and your cock gets twisted into a triple knot." Or "The gods are displeased at your misdeeds, Ivan, and they can turn your favorite body part black as night with running boils, stinksome as old lutefisk."

Men were so obsessed with their manparts, many of them coming to her with pleas for a magic potion to make theirs bigger, or thicker, or less ruddy. And they would try anything! Horse dung mixed with goat urine. Standing on their heads and chanting. Dipping their wicks in wax. Never once did she have a man ask to make his smaller, not even Boris the Horse who was said to resemble his namesake.

Of course, women were just as bad. Always wanting love potions. Or ways to make their breasts bigger, or smaller, their buttocks less flabby, their hips wider. Half of them wanted concoctions to help them get pregnant, the other half wanted rid of the bairns already growing in their bellies.

None of that mattered in her longtime scheme of amassing enough wealth to buy an estate in the Saxon lands and become a grand lady. Well, mayhap not so grand, but at least respectable, in a class above the cotter class. She even had a particular property in mind, a small sheepstead with a barn and fields and a lovely stone manor house. But eleven long years of skimping and saving and still she didn't have enough. She needed a bigger influx of wealth to finally fulfill her dreams, and it would come soon with the arrival of the young Jarl Efram of nearby Winterstorm.

Ah, there he was now, just in time, leading his horse into the clearing.

"Come, come, my jarl," she said with an exaggerated cackle, motioning the fur-clad lording to follow her into her woodland hovel. Efram, new to the jarldom on the recent death of his father, was little more than a youthling at sixteen years. "You can tie your beast to yon tree, next to the boulder."

She could see that he was hesitant to go near the red-coated boulder, probably thinking the stains were blood. They were, but not human blood. She butchered her chickens and squirrels for the stew pot there. She cackled again, this time to show she noticed his squeamishness. Embarrassed, he looped the reins around the post, wiping his gloved hands on his braies.

With a sniff of distaste, Efram stooped to enter the low door of her home. He might be young, but he was tall. The ceiling, from which hung numerous bunches of herbs, almost touched Efram's blond hair, which he wore in a long, single braid. Her black cat Thor hissed and lunged for Efram's pant leg, and the boyling jumped, causing dried rosemary and lavender and dill to shower his head and shoulders with aromatic dried particles.

She chuckled, rather cackled, again when he shook himself of the chaff.

He was not amused and tried to kick at Thor who was already bored and scooting away to his woven pallet by the hearth, where he stretched out and proceeded to lick his private parts. Men, even feline ones, had no manners.

Inside the thatched-roof cottage was not much better than its wattle-and-daub exterior. The hard-packed dirt floor was uncovered by rushes, but she kept it swept clean and bug free. Not that the spoiled bratling, accustomed to finer fare, would notice such details.

"Where is it?" Efram demanded. "Did you make the potion?"

"I did," she said and sat down at the lone chair beside a small table that she used both for eating and preparing herbal remedies. That left only her bed if he chose to sit down, which he did not. Probably feared fleas or lice, little knowing he had more of such up at his keep than she did here. In fact, his servants were always coming to her for remedies to rid hair and beards and bedding of the varmints.

"Well, where is it? Give it to me! I came alone, as you insisted. I have to get back to the castle before my guests arrive," he said impatiently.

Guests, as in his uncle and entourage, who considered Efram too young and inexperienced for such a large holding. An uncle who would find out just how far his nephew would go to maintain an iron grip on his inheritance . . . if Regina helped him, that was.

"Where is my payment?" Regina asked with equal impatience. "Fifty mancuses of gold." Since one mancus was equal to a month's wages for a skilled worker, she figured this amount, on top of her savings equal to about two hundred mancuses, should carry her over until her sheepstead started producing income.

"You'll get your coin after I see if your potion works."

Hah! She'd known Efram would pull something like this. "You'll get no potion until I have my sack of gold. And don't be thinking of coming back and stealing back my treasure. I have friends in these woods with swords sharper than any blade of yours." Which was a lie, of course. She had no friends. "Besides, my cousin's cousin who works at Winterstorm has orders to poison your own drink if you even try to betray me."

"Why, you . . . you . . . ," Efram sputtered, and his hairless cheeks blossomed with color. "How dare you insult me so?"

She shrugged. "'Tis just business, my jarl. Now, do you have the gold or not?"

Grudgingly, he parted his fur cloak and pulled out a leather sack tied to his belt. He tossed it on the table in front of her. "Do you want to count it?" he snarled.

"For a certainty," she replied with exaggerated sweetness. And she did in fact count out the fifty lovely coins.

While she was counting, his eyes darted about her small house, and his lips curled with distaste. "What is that horrible smell?" he asked, glanced toward the boiling cauldron over the fire.

It was cabbage soup, which was indeed smelly, but delicious. "Oh, just a porridge of rat tails, lizard hearts, pig snouts, sour milk, and oats," she told him. "Wouldst care for a taste?"

He gagged.

"Here is the potion then," she said, taking a stoppered pottery vial the size of a fist from a nearby shelf. "Be very careful. One drop would kill a war horse," let alone a full-grown man. 'Twas a mixture of deadly nightshade and water hemlock. "Because it is sweet, it will mix well, undetected, in any fermented beverage, like ale."

He nodded and reached for it, but she held it away from his grasp. "If you intend it for more than one person . . . ," and she knew that he did. Not just his uncle, but everyone in his party. ". . . then you must be especially careful. This vial in a tun of ale could be accidentally tasted by innocent parties, even women and children filling the horns of ale. Just one drop on the finger dipped on the tongue would be fatal."

Efram waved a hand airily and grabbed for the vial.

And Regina knew that he cared not who died in the process of his evil plot. She also knew that her own life was in danger once this was over because she was the only person who could disclose his plans. Ah well, she would be long gone by then.

Before nightfall, she had packed all her belonging, including her hoard of coins, onto the back of Edgar, her donkey. She'd bathed in a forest pool, tucked her bush of wild red hair into a thick braid, and donned one of the used lady's gowns she'd purchased in the market town of Kaupang. She would ride all night until she reached the harbor at Evenstead where she would sell Edgar. From there, she would take one of the merchant ships to the Saxon town of Jorvik.

She set her hovel afire before she left. Let the village folks think another witch had gone to her Satanic grave. She'd tried to leave the cat behind because he would draw attention, but the lackwit creature refused. Instead of rubbing himself up against her and purring with entreaty, Thor had pissed on her new boots and spit up three hair clumps to emphasize his disdain for that idea. Cats were like that betimes.

She'd traveled half the night when her plans hit a snag. Thor, who had wrapped himself around her neck, his head and tail resting on her bosom, hissed an alert. Mayhap a cat companion was not such a bad idea after all.

Standing directly in her path, an apparition appeared, a full-body glow of light against the blackness of the dense forest. It looked like an angel Regina had seen one time painted on the walls of a Christian church in Northumbria.

"Have you no shame, witch?" the angel roared.

Double, double, toil, and lots of trouble . . .

Michael was sick to his archangel ears of Vikings.

He'd never been fond of the vain, arrogant, brutal Vikings. But then, five years ago, God assigned him to put together a band of Viking vampire angels (vangels) to fight Satan's evil Lucipires (demon vampires). His appreciation hadn't increased with close proximity to the bothersome creatures. Especially those seven Sigurdsson brothers who'd been guilty of the Seven Deadly Sins in a most heinous way. 'Twas like trying to herd cats.

And for his sins, Michael had to admit, he was not overfond of cats. His pal, St. Francis of Assisi, patron saint of animals, would be disappointed in him. But ever since that Noah and the Ark debacle, Michael just couldn't seem to abide felines. Truth to tell, two cats had entered the ark and seventy-five emerged when the floods receded. What did that say about cats?

And Vikings were no better.

Randy, crude beings, all of them!

Now, his boss (that would be God) expected him to recruit a witch to the vangel ranks. A witch! A cauldron-boiling, potion-brewing, spell-tossing, broom-riding (well, maybe no brooms), cackling crone! Bad enough he had to deal with male Vikings, but now Norsewomen, as well, and a witch, on top of it all! It was enough to sour a saint's stomach.

Michael was in the dense forest of the frigid Norselands, freezing his holy skin under his white robes, more suited to a warm heavenly climate, when he saw his target approaching, astride a heavily-laden donkey. Not a cauldron in sight, and she wasn't as cronely as he'd expected, but that was neither here nor there. On her shoulders was . . . *(What else! It was that kind of day!)* . . . a large, black, hissing cat.

Michael barely restrained himself from hissing back, but instead roared at the woman, "Have you no shame, witch? What wickedness thou dost brew!"

"Huh?" The cat bolted off for cover, the donkey balked, and the witch jerked on the reins and flew head over heels to land on the pine-needle-laden ground.

"Regina Dorasdottir! Many men, women, and children died today at thy hands!"

"My hands are clean. I didn't poison anyone," she proclaimed, standing and dusting off her bottom. At least she wasn't denying that poison was involved. She knew exactly what he was talking about. The witch!

"Thou made the bane drink. Thou sold it for coin. It was used carelessly, not that careful murder is any less offensive. Many innocent people suffered painful deaths."

Immediately, he flashed a cloud picture in front of her so that she could see all the bodies in the rushes of the Winterstorm great hall, many of them lying in pools of vomit, others with blood emerging from their mouths and noses and even ears. Men, women, children, even the castle dogs. All of them dead.

Regina stepped back in fear, not at the sight of the dead bodies, apparently, but because she was seeing a picture in the air of an event that had already happened. "How did you do that? Are you a wizard performing some magic sorcery?"

"No sorcery. That is your business, witch, not mine. I am St. Michael the Archangel, and God is very angry with you."

"God? Which god would that be? Odin, Thor? Balder?" She was taking careful steps backward as she spoke.

"There is only one God, lackwit!" He raised a hand, and a bolt of lightning shot from his fingers, hitting the woman in her heart. She clutched her chest and fell to her knees.

"Am I to be condemned for one . . . um, mistake?" She batted her long eyelashes at him in innocence. For a brief moment, he noticed that she was not unattractive, for a witch, that was. Her neatly braided red hair acted as a frame for a sharply sculpted Nordic face and green eyes, which would turn blue before this day was done, if he had his way.

But her appearance mattered not a whit, he reminded himself. Women were ever the devious ones, using their feminine wiles to persuade men to their designs. Hah! He was immune. "Mistake?

Mistake? Woman, thou hast committed many sins. Thy transgressions are so innumerable I can scarce list them. Dozens of babes killed in the womb, the addictive poppy used to make slobbering slaves of some men, and women, too, death potions for the elderly, murder . . . and, yea, killing men who came courting—"

"What? Those were potential rapists!"

"Not all of them," he contended. "Thou art also guilty of the sin of greed." He glanced pointedly at the leather sack attached to the donkey's saddle.

"Just compensation for services," she countered.

He arched his brows at that and showed her a cloud picture of her withholding a medicinal remedy for a starving family's baby with lung fever.

"Well, that is the exception," she lied.

"Then, too, there was fornication," Michael told her.

"One time. One stinking, unsatisfying time," she argued.

"Where in the Holy Book does it say that coupling has to be satisfying?" he asked.

"What about all the good I've done? There are many people I've helped with healing herbs."

"Not for a long time," he told her, then sighed. "On the celestial scales of good and evil, canst hear the thunk of weight on the one side?"

She ignored what he said and continued to argue, "And I never practiced any Satanic rites, like some witches do."

"Satan comes in many forms. Some would say that practicing evil is the same as worshiping Satan."

"I still think—"

"Thou dost not think, that is thy trouble. Thou art a dreadful sinner, Regina Dorasdottir. Thou hast no morals. There is naught thou would reject doing if paid enough. If it were up to me, thou would burn in the fires of Hell."

She pulled a long-bladed knife from a belt-sheath and glanced briefly at him, assessing the chances of escape. But then, her shoulders slumped as she took note of the full-body halo that enveloped him, and she dropped the weapon. "So, that's it then. I'm to die for my sins."

"Not quite."

Her head shot up at that.

"In his mercy, God is willing to give you a second chance for repentance."

She narrowed her green eyes at him. "What would I have to do?"

"Thou wouldst join the ranks of vangels, fighting in the Lord's army against evil forces."

"Me? An angel?" she scoffed.

"Not an angel. A vangel. A Viking vampire angel. Put on earth to destroy Lucifer's demon vampires, wicked creatures who prey on sinful humans, killing them before their fated time of death, giving them no chance to repent."

"Huh?"

"Explanations can come later. Dost thou choose Hell or Vangeldom?"

"That's some choice! For how long?"

Michael was growing impatient. "As long as it takes. Centuries. Mayhap even until the Final Judgment Day."

"And I will live all that time, growing older and older, more feeble?"

"Dost deliberately misspeak, witch? Thou wouldst stay the same age."

"Oh. Really? Well, yes, then. Of course I agree." She paused. "But what exactly is a vam-pyre? Does it have anything to do with fire, or is—"

The time for questions had passed. She'd agreed. That was enough for Michael.

Raising both arms, he levitated her high in the air so that she twirled about, screaming as her upper jaw broke and restructured itself to accommodate newly formed fangs and her shoulder blades cracked open and grew bumps that might one day become wings. Her green eyes turned the clear blue of all vangels. *Now, do you understand what a vampire is?* At the same time, for his own pleasure, Michael sent the bristling, hissing familiar with her. *Take that, cat!*

"I changed my mind," Regina screeched.

Too late! The witch was flying through the air to parts unknown to take on her new role. And Michael was off to see what the Sigurdsson brothers were up to now. An archangel's work was never done!

Next month, don't miss these exciting new love stories only from Avon Books

Chasing Lady Amelia by Maya Rodale

Lady Amelia is fed up with being a proper lady and wishes to explore London, so one night she escapes . . . and finds herself in the company of wickedly tempting rake Alistair Finlay-Jones. Inevitably they end up falling in love and making love. When Amelia finds out that Alistair has been ordered to marry her, he must woo her and win back the now-angry American girl.

Under the Wire by HelenKay Dimon

When Reid Armstrong learns that his former fiancée has disappeared on a top-secret science expedition, he rushes to her rescue. Second chances don't come often and he needs to prove his worth to Cara Layne or die trying. Cara can't trust anyone, least of all Reid. Even if his skills get them out alive, he's a heartache waiting to strike twice. Yet being in close proximity proves their connection burns hotter than ever.

Drive You Wild by Jennifer Bernard

With his good looks, hitting records, and played-for-the-fans arrogance, Kilby Catfish left-fielder Trevor Stark makes women lose their minds and men lose their cool. But every time the major league team comes calling, Trevor keeps himself in the tiny Texas town. *Why* is heart-tuggingly top secret. Until the team owner's daughter comes to Kilby . . . trying everything up her sexy sleeve to make Trevor talk.

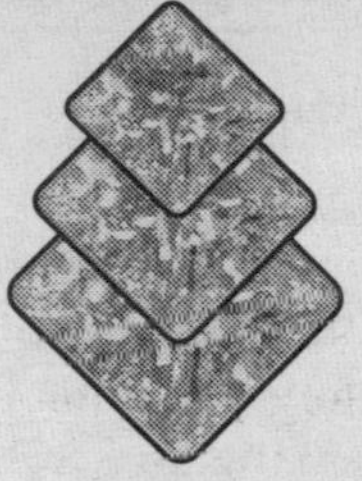